Quilly Hall

Quilly Hall

An Ode to the Holston Hills
a novel

BENJAMIN W. FARLEY

RESOURCE *Publications* • Eugene, Oregon

To

All my family

PREFACE

NOT EVERY NOVEL REQUIRES a "Preface," but somehow *Quilly Hall* mandates one. My grandmother, Catherine Foran White, a child of Virginia's Holston Valley, never wearied of telling stories. Born in 1877, she was reared in a rural time in a rural world that modernity has since forgotten. I cannot return to Abingdon's Holston Knobs without remembering her, or her cabin, or her rocker, or her smile, or her farm. She filled me with a wonder for life and a love for adventure and dreams. Of all my family, this book is dedicated in memory to her, and to my Uncle Clark, her middle son.

I am indebted to Dr. James R. Metts, Sheriff of Lexington County, SC, who shared with me his experiences and wisdom concerning the office of sheriff and its numerous demands, aspects of which I have dramatized in one of my character's career. Any mistakes in fact or judgment, however, are entirely my own. So also in the case of Major Richard Daeger, US Army (Retired), Vietnam Infantry Company Commander. Major Daeger served as a line officer during the Vietnam War. It is his memories of that conflict that innerve Thomas Edmonds' own reflections. Words cannot express the full measure of my gratitude to Major Daeger and to all who served with him.

I am beholden to many historical resources, especially to Lewis Preston Summers' *History of Southwest Virginia, 1746–1786, Washington County, 1777–1870*, whose sketches of the County's soul are preserved in his work.

CHAPTER ONE

ACTUALLY, HER NAME WAS "Quelle." Tall and enchanting, she still gazes down from her marble-top pedestal to savor the silence that hovers in the shadows of the hallway. I use the present tense, because I inherited the statue from my grandmother. Quilly's serene countenance effuses an immeasurable calm. Time after time, it has buoyed me from childhood to this very day. Quilly's braids are drawn back in a golden bun against the back of her neck, each braid interlaced with a delicate thread of green ribbon. Strands of dark honey streak her hair. On her right hip, she cradles a wide-mouth–cinnamon-faded jug, and in her left hand she tilts a second, filling a birdbath with imaginary water. Two scruffy pigeons balance themselves on the lip of the fountain; one is drinking, while the other stares up at Quelle. A brown apron covers Quilly's gossamer dress and modest curves. The statue's inner material is of plaster of Paris that sometimes leaks through, leaving white deposits that flake off. An ivory cast defines her slender face; all else is glazed in bronze and green. Her precise age remains a mystery, although my grandmother insisted that my grandfather purchased it for her at the Chicago World Fair. But that would have been in 1897. And why would my grandfather have gone to Chicago? To our family's knowledge, he never left Virginia and rarely spent more than two nights away from home. So there has always existed this mystery about "Quilly," or "Quelle," which is her name in German and which means "source," or "fountain."

The name "Quilly Hall" derived from my grandfather Edmonds. In a rare moment of uncharacteristic frustration, he reportedly blurted out: "O Hell! Why does everything have to take place in Quilly's hall? Why can't we just serve them on the porch?" He was referring to the icy mint juleps that were being prepared for a cadre of his in-town friends. The name stuck, and after that everyone began calling the place, "Quilly Hall." Before that, the home place was simply known as "the Edmonds House." Built in the late 1790s, it stands today, with its gray-and-white slab limestone

1

exterior gleaming in the sunlight, where from its grassy knoll it overlooks the road that leads from the mountains westward into nearby Abingdon.

My grandmother—Virginia Katherine Edmonds—relished our family's history, and as a small boy of six, I would rock beside her in the living room and listen. "It was a wilderness, Tommy, without roads, or inns. The Indians were gone. Only occasional raiding parties made it into Virginia. The Nations of the Iroquois had driven out the Cherokee and Shawnee. Then came Daniel Boone and those valiant men, like your great-great grandfather. Here they came, journeying into this vast domain of forests and saltlicks! Of game and a soil blessed with the rich silicates that still raise our crops taller than we are! Oh, Tommy! Think of it! How it must have blazed in their eyes and set their hearts to palpitating just to see it!" She loved hyperbole, extravagant and exaggerated expressions, and words like "palpitating" and "silicates," exact assignations when describing objects or events.

Grandmother's father had fought with units assigned to defend Chattanooga and Tennessee. According to her, he received wounds both at Chickamauga and "in the field in front of Atlanta," as the last extant roll call describes it. I have never been able to trace all of his company's movements, although my grandmother and her sister-in-law, my Aunt Viola, provided many first-hand details from tidbits the old veteran dropped from time to time. His name was Howard Campbell Lorran, a private of Company A 63rd Regiment, CSA. Unlike my paternal grandfather and his father, my great-grandfather Lorran's grave lies along the Middle Fork of the Holston River, and not in town. I must have been four or five, when one cold January day my grandmother, mother, Uncle Everett, Pearl, and I rode in a wagon to visit his grave. We had to take the wagon, as the road was impassable by car. The journey also had to be undertaken when the road's clay ruts were frozen, or had turned an iron-hard red.

My grandmother had packed a large picnic basket of fried chicken, pinto beans, biscuits, a cake of butter, and a jar of strawberry jelly. She wanted to visit her brother, Jim Lorran, and his wife, Viola, since the graveyard was on their property. "They're very poor," she explained. "I always take food when I visit them. Our whole family was poor, and I would be too, if it weren't for your grandfather."

"Mama, we've heard all this before," Uncle Everett interrupted. Uncle Everett was driving the wagon. His tall lean figure bent forward as he held the reins. His face and hands were tanned by nature's elements, his eyebrows thick and black like his hair, and with eyes "that could pierce right through a board," as Grandmother put it.

"I know, but I want Tommy to hear it as often as possible.

"Tommy, your ancestors, the Edmonds were very wealthy. And Holman, your grandfather, would come over the mountains to visit us, since we lived on one of his farms. We were poor, Tommy. Your grandfather felt sorry for us. He loved Howard, my father. Your grandfather was only a child when the War broke out. His father had fought in many skirmishes, too, but never with General Lee, or Stonewall Jackson. He commanded a home guard when the Yankees burned Abingdon. He never forgave them for setting fire to the courthouse, or for throwing a torch into his father's house in town. If it hadn't been for his mother, who picked it up and threw it back out, the house would have burned to the ground. He took a gunshot wound to his breast, defending a barricade on Main Street. He died in 1894 but managed to hold on to most of his father's farms and businesses. He did lose a mine in Saltville, a sawmill around Damascus, and one in the mountains, near Whitetop.

"Your grandfather Holman was thirty-one when I first met him. I must have been fifteen. There he came, riding up on his big sorrel mare, as handsome as could be. His black wavy hair flopped in his face. His saddle was of the finest leather, his boots dark brown. He was wearing his father's Confederate jacket, complete with the bullet hole, with gold braid on the sleeves, adorned with bright shiny brass buttons. He carried a holstered revolver and a rifle in a sling, where he could wrest it out at a moment's notice."

"Did he shoot people with it?" I asked.

"He should have," Uncle Everett offered. "The banks in town foreclosed on one of his farms. And he knew the bas . . . ," he glanced toward me and smiled, "the man that did it."

"Everett, please! Don't teach the boy bad words. I want at least one Edmonds to grow up with dignity."

"Like you, Mama?" he smiled.

"Everett!" objected my mother. "Mama Edmond's right. Tommy has a chance to become somebody. Can't you leave it at that?" My mother had long red curly hair, and strands of it poked out around her scarf. Petite in size and stature, she looked like a panda, wrapped in her white scarf and black coat. Her rosy cheeks appeared enflamed from the cold.

Uncle Everett turned about and stared hard at my mother; then he turned back, and, with a flick of the reins, slapped the hindquarters of the big horse that was pulling the wagon. Sally immediately picked up her gait.

I don't remember the drift of the remainder of the conversation, just my mother's look when Uncle Everett stared at her. I was seated between her and my grandmother. Pearl rode on the front seat with Uncle Everett. Pearl was tall, big-boned, with black hair plaited in a single long pigtail. It flopped along the back of her neck, on the outside of her denim jacket. Uncle Everett began to reach over and rub Pearl's thigh. As I reflect on the event, I think he was only teasing her, but it resulted in a swift comment from my grandmother.

"The family flaw!" she grumbled, as she put her right arm around me and squeezed me against her black woolen coat. Its stiff collar cut into my lips.

The ride to Uncle Jim's farm and my great-grandfather's grave seemed to take forever. The road climbed for a long while up and up through the Knobs. It wound its way from cove to cove, through stands of pine, poplar, and hickories, and past huge black oaks, yellow birches, and milk-gray beech trees. Suddenly, Uncle Everett slowed the wagon and reached for a shotgun under the seat. He guided the wagon to one side and pulled back lightly on the reins. "Whoa, Sally," he whispered. The wagon came to a stop, to the sound of a slight jangle of harness.

"Shhh!" Pearl added. "A turkey in the road."

I leapt like a cork popping out of a bottle when the gun discharged. Everyone laughed. But he bagged the turkey. Pearl retrieved the big bird and flung it up in the rear of the wagon. It was a plump hen, with shiny black feathers and gray warts about its comb.

Uncle Jim's place, or my grandmother's home place, finally came into view as the wagon descended the road. You could see a glint of the Holston in the distance and hear its rolling murmur from the hill. As a child, I recall no memorable reaction to the cabin, but it was a log structure, with an up-stairs room under a tin roof. I just remember the old couple coming to the door, Pearl carrying in the turkey, the warmth of the fireplace, and quilts stacked everywhere. We ate the lunch we had brought; then, while my grandmother and mother sat about the fire with the gaunt couple, Uncle Everett, Pearl, and I climbed a hill through bramble and broom sedge to an overgrown gravesite. Wooden slabs marked each grave, save for one in the middle that was of stone. I must have played around in the cold, while

Chapter One

Uncle Everett and Pearl cleared brush and thorns from the graves. My grandmother and everyone else finally came up the hill and stood about the markers for a while. There were tears in my grandmother's eyes. With quiet solemnity, she bent down and touched her father's headstone.

Moments after that, it began to snow. Tiny frozen flakes whirled in the raw wind. Light and small, they made a faint, crackling sound as they swirled about us and settled in the tufts of the broom sedge.

"Lord, we'd best get out of here!" grunted Pearl, wrapping her arms about herself and clapping her hands to keep warm.

It flurried all the way home, and we arrived in a hovering dark. I remained on the wagon with Uncle Everett and stayed with him until we had driven the wagon into its shed, unhitched Sally, led her to the barn, and brushed her down. Uncle Everett guided her toward her stall. I fetched four large ears of corn and fed them to her—one ear at a time. Before we left, Uncle Everett pitched several forkfuls of hay into her stall and patted her rump. "Never neglect your horse, Tommy. She's a good one, if I say so myself." He rumpled my hair with his hard hands and held my right hand as we walked back to the house.

CHAPTER TWO

QUILLY HALL CONSISTED OF four rooms in the main section, plus a large dining room and kitchen, which my great-grandfather Edmonds had added as time went by. A stairwell in the kitchen led up to two large bedrooms: one over the kitchen and one over the dining room. Both additions were constructed of a dull red brick, mixed and fired on the farm, with lattice interior walls, covered with plaster and left white. The rock stone part of the house had two large rooms downstairs, plus Quilly's hall, and two sprawling bedrooms upstairs. These were separated by a wide landing, crowded with a massive armoire, as there were no closets in either bedroom. My mother and I slept in the room whose back window overlooked the springhouse, apple shed, and the tarred road that led into Abingdon. My grandmother was sole occupant of the finer of the two bedrooms. All four rooms—upstairs and down—in the rock section were heated by immense fireplaces. Large wooden mantles stretched across them, crowded with clocks, pictures, and vases, adorned with dried flowers in the winter and fresh ones in the summer to match the hue of the vases. In my grandmother's bedroom, and in the living room downstairs, lacy, embroidered doilies ran the full length of the mantles.

My favorite haven in the house was the living room. Next, came Quilly's hallway, and lastly the dining room. Deep recessed windowsills guarded the three muslin-curtained windows in the living room. The side window provided a view of the back driveway; the other two looked out over the front lawn. I could climb up and sit in either of the two front windows and gaze out across the porch and into the yard. On cold wintry days, great fires blazed in its hearth. One of Pearl's many chores consisted in seeing that adequate kindling and logs were always provided in the wood boxes and that the cinders were raked out every morning and carried outside before my grandmother came down to take her coffee in front of the main fireplace. My mother prepared the coffee and would bring it in to my grandmother in a fine, china cup, half-buried in a deep saucer. Then my mother and grandmother would rock in front of the crackling logs and sip their coffee out of the saucers. They loved cream—rich, yellow, fresh cream—and plenty of it. Pearl made certain that their cups were refilled as long as they chatted there and that the cream pitcher never ran dry.

I generally had breakfast in the kitchen, in front of the cook stove, with Pearl. She'd fry me an egg and a sausage patty, or serve oatmeal, or, frequently, white milk gravy, amply ladled over a hot biscuit. After that, I would join my mother and grandmother in the living room. Sometimes my grandmother would turn her coffee cup over and place it in the saucer and wait for the grounds to dry. She'd have my mother do the same. After several moments had passed, she'd turn the cups back up and read their fortunes. For someone as sophisticated as my grandmother, I was enchanted by these "gypsy episodes," as Uncle Everett referred to them. Although my grandmother had graduated from the Martha Washington Seminary for Girls, this facet of her Holston heritage remained with her till death.

"Ah, Shaula!" she'd say to my mother. "Here's this tall handsome man again. See!" she would point in the cup. "And his beard. He has raised his hand to stroke it. And he's looking right at you. And this door! He's going to come to our very door."

"Mom! One man in my life was enough. You've got to get a new line. I'm thirty-two years old now. Who would be interested in me?"

"Well, don't laugh it off so quickly, my dear. You're still young and beautiful. Hamilton's dead. He'll never return, God rest his soul," she would stare remorsefully at me. "It's time you thought about remarrying. Besides, Tommy needs a father, someone to look up to, not just a dead hero," she'd glance at my father's photograph on the mantle.

I would look up, too. There was my father, Captain Edmonds, in his uniform, but I scarcely knew him. He left for the war after Pearl Harbor, when I was barely four. His squad was blown to bits in August of 1942, somewhere in the jungles of Guadalcanal. A purple heart dangled from one corner of his picture frame. He was my grandmother's oldest son. His loss deeply grieved her, but she rarely spoke of him. Sometimes at night, she would take his picture off the mantle, carry it upstairs to the landing, and place it on a mahogany stand between our two bedrooms. Nothing else was permitted to rest on that stand. Above it on the wall was a photograph of him in faded overalls, taken in front of the springhouse when he must have been a boy of my age. Sometimes my mother would leave our door open and slip out of bed at night and stare at his photo.

An uncomfortable maroon loveseat, a large, green silk-covered couch, stacked with green felt pillows with streaming gold braids, a deep black leather armchair, and a tall cherry chest of drawers (pushed against the wall opposite the front windows), constituted the living room's main furniture. Small tables of walnut and oak, and end tables with inlaid silver filigree bands, completed the furnishings, except for the semi-circle of rockers that faced the hearth. A painting of my grandmother dominated the wall between the front windows. She is sitting in the loveseat. Her neck and back are very erect. A large diamond pendant glitters on her chest, just above a strikingly low-cut, silver gown. Her black hair is gently fluffed. The exquisite lines of her thin face, nose, and lips catch your eyes immediately. A genteel air commands her entire presence. Her hands rest on one another in her lap. Beneath her portrait for many years hung a deteriorating pink photograph of my grandfather Holman. Long strands of gray hair encircled his face and ears. A high white collar, wide cravat, and stylish unbuttoned black coat complemented his attire. His eyes were deep set, almost coal black, and stared out in defiance. Several links of a gold chain and watch poked visibly from a pocket. Someone stole his picture, but we never knew who the culprit was. My grandmother's portrait still hangs in the living room, along with my father's photo on the mantle. I have added a photograph of my mother, as well.

Other family members' portraits and pictures were relegated to the hallway. After entering from the porch through the large, glass-paneled front door, one passed a dusty painting of my great-great grandfather on the left. It hung just passed a huge portmanteau. He sports a powdered wig, a lacy tie, and a black, smoking jacket. He holds, what appears to be, a deed in his clenched left fist. A brass nameplate heralds his title: Col. James Holman Edmonds. His chest is Atlas in size, his gaze: regal. Beside where the Colonel's picture used to hang, still looms a life-size painting of my great-grandfather, Capt. Nathan Edmonds. He is decked out in a gray Confederate long coat, with a gold sash about his waist, and a polished sword at his side. A long white beard rests curled on his chest. In spite of his military bearing, there is a roguish gentleness about his face, a soft sophistication of aristocratic noblesse. Opposite their paintings were small portraits of their wives. The women wear white bonnets drawn about their chins, their faces pale and smileless. Except for the Captain's portrait, the others hang today in my great-aunt's house in town, which became a museum after her death. As I child, I would stare at these awesome and austere people, almost afraid of them, yet captivated by their determined countenances. Plus, there was Quilly, on her marble-top pedestal, to humble and charm them into submission. Beside her, stretched a crimson Napoleon couch that provided an enchanting anomaly to the petrifying demeanor of the old women. How I loved sitting on that couch, infatuated by Quilly's beauty, while I swung my legs back-and-forth and made faces at those ponderous ancestors of old. I did have to admit, though, that my Uncle Everett had that identical look in his eye that Capt. Edmonds' portrait made transparent. I wanted to be like both of them, especially like my Uncle Everett.

One entered the parlor through French doors, opposite the living room, at the base of the stairwell. The doors were constructed of heavy oak, stained a dark mahogany and sticky from years of sweaty fingerprints. One could roll up a finish of grimy goo with practically no difficulty. Once inside the room, its spacious depth and stacked rock fireplace, which was fitted with an iron stove, appealed immensely to visitors' curiosities. The room contained wall-to-wall shelves of rare and coveted books, some reaching to the ceiling. A rickety ladder on metal rails offered access to the higher shelves, but anyone could reach the lower treasure of crumbly, leather-covered books. A magnificent new set of *The Encyclopedia of Knowledge*, consisting of forty volumes published in 1935, was wonderfully within my reach. How I enjoyed perusing each book on rainy days and soggy nights! The set was replete with pictures and photos of such far away places as India, China, Africa, the Eiffel Tower, walled German villages, and the mountains of Italy. I first learned to read from its pages, even before the first grade, thanks to the pictures and to my mother and grandmother's patience—along with the captions beneath the glossy photographs. There was even a chapter on farming and a section on Abingdon, its Knobs, the Barter Theatre, tobacco auction barns, and Daniel Boone. The chapter opened with our own Col. James Holman Edmonds' portrait and his exploits as one of the town's founding giants.

Many tomes of jurisprudence, geology, state history, the Lost Cause, horticulture, plant diseases, medicine, and literature stared down at me. I would pull out books and run my hands over them and pretend I was reading these myriad works. No daydreamer had a better backdrop for flights of chrestomathic adventure.

It was on one of those rainy mornings that I heard a knock at the front door and ran to see who it was. We were expecting Uncle Everett, and I wanted him to tell me about the various cannons that were pictured in one of the military books. But as I looked through the glass, it wasn't Uncle Everett at all, but a tall, ruddy-faced, elegant man, with a goatee and a gentleman's bearing. "Mama!" I shouted. "Grandmother! It's that man in the coffee cup! Hurry! Come quick!"

I could hear the swish of their skirts behind me, along with Pearl's. My mother arrived first. "Oh, my goodness!" she clutched her throat. "It's Marion Chappels." She opened the door with excitement. "Mr. Chappels! What a pleasant surprise! Please, come in!"

"Thank you, Shaula, if I may, I shall," he removed his hat before stepping in.

"Heavens!" exclaimed Grandmother. "I hope it's good news."

"I'm afraid it's not. Is Everett about? I need his help."

"No, but we expect him soon. At least, come on in by the fire, and have a glass of sherry, and tell us what's happened."

"That I'll do," he smiled, as Pearl took his hat and hung it on the portmanteau.

We hurried in the living room behind him, while grandmother poured him a glass of sherry.

"Well, what is it?" she asked as we sat crowded around him.

"It's Olan Crawford. He's ordered a foreclosure on your brother's place and has gone there himself to deliver it. Today!"

"Is that legal?"

"Yes ma'am and no. When Preston, Crawford, and I took over the Highlands County Bank, we agreed it'd take all three of us to issue a foreclosure. Your brother's had to borrow a lot of funds, Miz. Edmonds, especially the past five years, and he's yet to pay a penny back."

"Oh, I begged him not to do that," Grandmother lamented. "Jim's so poor. Have you ever seen where they live?"

"Yes, I have. My father and I used to hunt back there when I was a boy. Preston agreed with him and signed the documents, pending my approval. But Olan has wanted that land for years. It's got potential that Mr. Lorran's been unable to develop. What's worse, Olan obtained an eviction warrant and plans to threaten them with it. He's armed, too. The warrant he obtained falsely, since I haven't given my consent. Nor will." He looked solemnly at my mother and grandmother and gulped his sherry down with a single swallow. Slowly, he let out a long sigh.

He had no more than released his anxiety, when Uncle Everett came in.

"Well, well! What a pleasure! What's the honor, Marion?"

"Bad news. Crawford's on his way to your Uncle Jim's place, with eviction papers and a foreclosure order in hand. Can you go with me to stall him?"

"Go with you? Hell! I'll lead the way."

"Everett! Oh, Everett!" my grandmother implored. "There'll be violence. You've been spoiling for a fight with that man for years. Can't you leave it to the sheriff's office? That's his duty. Not yours!"

"Mama, Crawford is a deputy. He's been deputized since I don't know when. And that's your brother up there! His land and our land, too! I'll be damned if we need to give it to him. No sir. Come on, Marion. We'll take Mama's horses. How's Olan traveling?"

"By car. He'll never make it up the lane, will he?"

"Not this time of year."

Everett leaned down and kissed Grandmother on the cheek. "Don't worry, Mama. Marion and I know what to do. Do you have a pistol?" he asked the banker.

"I'd rather not answer. We just need to talk to him."

"Not without a pistol," Uncle Everett replied. "I've got one in the truck. Let's head on."

We followed them to the front door and watched them walk toward the barn. While my mother and grandmother returned to the living room, I waited in the hallway. I was afraid and excited, both at the same time. Just then I happened to glance up at the old Captain. He seemed to be staring at me with disapprobation and profound disgust. At that, I slipped on my coat and cap, scooted out the door and down the front steps, and hurried toward the barn. Any fear had dissipated, totally.

Uncle Everett and Mr. Chappels had already saddled the horses and were about to mount.

"Please, Uncle Everett. Let me go!"

The men swung into the saddles and goaded the horses forward.

"Close the barn door, Tommy," Uncle Everett directed. "Run on back in the house. Your mama will skin you alive, if she catches you out here. Now run on."

The horses trotted past the door and down the road. They were headed toward the lane that led back to the Knobs. I closed the big door and began running behind them. I climbed the gate that fenced off a stubble-littered cornfield and raced across it. They could see me running and trying to catch up with them. At the end of the field, another gate would open almost where they would turn. Suddenly, Uncle Everett stopped his horse and waited for me.

"Hell, boy! Get on!" he grinned, as I climbed that last gate and hopped down. He rode toward me, put his arm out for me to grab, and swung me up behind his saddle. "Hang on!" Then, off we galloped.

A light drizzle fell about us, but my uncle and Mr. Chappels paid it no attention and spurred their horses on at a quick trot. Soon we were climbing the muddy road toward my great-uncle's farm. We had scarcely begun the ascent when we passed Crawford's Packard. It had slid into a ditch. Thick brush and undergrowth were all that had prevented it from toppling down the slope. The men paused their horses; then pressed on. We could see Crawford's footprints in the clay.

"Damn, but he's determined," grunted Mr. Chappels. "He'll reach there before we do."

Uncle Everett remained silent, as he leaned forward in the saddle. "It won't matter, 'cause he'll not get out of here without facing us. Hold tight, boy!" he glanced back at me, "It's going to be slippery climbing for a while. OK?"

"Yes, sir!"

It took well over an hour to reach the hilltop that looked down across the Holston's Middle Fork and Uncle Jim and Aunt Viola's place. We could see the couple sitting on their porch, bundled in coats and shawls. They were in their rockers and stood up as we approached. Uncle Jim clutched a sheath of papers in his hands. His fingers shook badly. His eyes—almost obscured by his long white hair and day-old beard—glowed pale blue. Aunt Viola was crying.

"This ain't right," the old man whimpered. His hands were trembling and his lips quivered as he spoke. "Just one more tobacco crop. That's all I needed, Everett," he coughed, unable to suppress his disparagement, as he held the papers aloft.

"Nothin's gonna happen to you!" assured Uncle Everett. "Where's Crawford? Where's the son-of-a-bitch hiding?"

Mr. Chappels inhaled a deep breath and drew his horse closer to ours. "Don't' be hasty, Everett. We're not authorized to cause trouble."

"Where is he?" my uncle repeated, as he fidgeted in the saddle, turning the horse this way and that.

Uncle Jim nodded toward the cabin. "Inside," he motioned with his head.

"Marion, watch the boy," Uncle Everett stated in a low but calm voice. He swung quietly out of the saddle and walked toward the steps.

Just then a large man in a dark suit, with red clay splattered on his trouser bottoms, appeared at the door. He pointed a rifle barrel at my uncle's chest. "One step, Everett Edmonds, and you'll regret it the rest of your life." His voice was thin and quavering. The barrel waved unsteadily in his hands. "I'm warning you. This is legal and proper. Just back off and get on out of here. You aren't the big important man you think you are."

"Olan! Cut the rot!" Mr. Chappels interrupted. "Deputized or not, there's nothing binding about that foreclosure. You're nothing but a greedy ass. I denounce you. Once we're back in town, I'll have you arrested."

"Well, well, Mr. High and Mighty, aren't you one to talk! And just how did you accumulate *your* wealth?" Crawford sneered.

"Not your way. That's for sure."

Uncle Everett lunged for the gun barrel and yanked the rifle forcefully out of Crawford's hands. He pulled Crawford out of the cabin and hit him hard with his right fist. Blood oozed from the man's nose, as he reeled backward against the cabin.

Suddenly Crawford sprang for my uncle and, butting him with his head, knocked the wind out of his chest. He retrieved his rifle and aimed it, this time, in Uncle Everett's face.

All the while, Mr. Chappels had been reaching quietly across Uncle Everett's horse. He glanced secretly at me and secured its reins. Then, as stealthily as possible, he produced a small pistol from his coat pocket, and, without flinching an eyelash, shot the big man, squarely in the chest. Crawford sank to the floor, looked up in shock, collapsed, rolled to one side and stared off into space. A rattling sound escaped from his throat. Blood poured out of his mouth. He groaned and stretched out his legs; then grew silent. He was dead.

My lips parted in surprise. How wide my eyes were, I can only imagine. I began trembling. Suddenly I stopped and broke out in a nervous laughter.

"Quiet, Tommy," Uncle Everett said. He rose to his feet and wiped the mud off his pants. He slipped the papers out of Uncle Jim's hand, hugged the old man, and tore up the eviction. He kissed Aunt Viola on her neck and hugged her, too.

"Uncle Jim, find me a rope," said Uncle Everett.

The old man shuffled around the side of his house to his barn. He soon returned with a heavy length of hemp twine and ten feet or so of rope. Uncle Everett tied the twine about Crawford's body and secured him to a tobacco pallet, which we dragged behind Mr. Chappels' horse, all the way down the road and back to the barn.

Upon our arrival at the house, my mother vented her frustration on all three of us. You could see the exasperation on her face. "You simpleton!" she wagged her head in disbelief at Uncle Everett. "You could have gotten the boy killed! As well as yourself and Marion!"

He turned away with rebuffed sadness, but not before rubbing my head with his hand.

"Your son's a fine lad, a man," he said to my mother. "My God, woman! Time will bear me out."

She began to cry. He glanced toward Mr. Chappels, shrugged his shoulders; then he bent forward and kissed her.

Neither man was ever charged with a crime. Crawford's death was ruled: "an accidental firing of a gun in self-defense." My grandmother, mother, Mr. Chappels, Uncle Everett, and I attended his funeral, along with many of Abingdon's leading citizens. Nothing else was ever said, except by way of gossip.

CHAPTER THREE

OVER THE NEXT FEW weeks, we saw very little of Uncle Everett. I missed him greatly, for in every way he was my surrogate father. We did enjoy Mr. Chappels' visits, especially my mother. He began showing up in the late afternoons. Frequently, he brought her flowers and, occasionally, boxes of candy for my grandmother, Pearl, and me.

My grandmother effused for hours after he left. "Ah! Shaula! I told you there was another man for you. You like him. Don't deny it. That's quite all right, dear. Hamilton is dead. Tommy's daddy is never coming back. I don't mean to sound maudlin. But we have to face reality. He needs a daddy, and you're too young to waste away as a widow." It would grieve her to have to say this. Nonetheless, she would fold her hands in her lap and stare at my mother with that certain look, with that dreadful truth in her eye: that both knew that this was best.

They would rock together. Sometimes my mother would cry. Although, I was quite a large and strong child for age six, my mother would reach for my hand and have me sit in her lap. She would hold my head against her shoulder and neck, and rock and rock and rock.

Sometimes my grandmother would turn with a twinkle in her eye, and, standing with her back to the fireplace, lift the edges of her dress— ever so coquettishly—shuffle her feet in a pretend dance, and sing:

Over there, over there, send the word, send the word, over there.
That the Yanks are coming, the Yanks are coming,
The drum's rum-tumming everywhere.
So prepare, say a prayer, send the word, send the word to beware.
The Yanks are coming, the Yanks are coming,
And they won't be back till its over over there.

If she were in a more melancholic mood, however, she would remain seated and hum: "Oh, Danny Boy." Sometimes she would substitute my name for "Danny's."

After awhile, I would fall asleep in my mother's lap.

As for my mother, she possessed a spirit of grit that wonderfully compensated for any diminution in size. She could not have been more than five-one in those days. Later, she would shrink even more. Long red curls defined her, if anything. Her coiffeur set her apart from other women. Plus, her eyes: a pale shade of green behind warm eyelashes. There was a softness about her touch and her fair skin. It would freckle at the slightest exposure to sun. For this reason, she never left the house without wearing a hat that protected her face, even in the winter. Farm odors annoyed her. She would sprinkle a dainty pink handkerchief, no larger than a postcard, with her favorite perfume: *Enchanté de Paris*. How Parisian it was, I never knew, nor still know. That she could buy it in the drugstore in Abingdon during the war, says it all. It came in a tiny square bottle, which she kept on her dresser. A delicate fragrance filled the room, whenever she uncapped it.

At that time, Mr. Chappels lived in town. My mother took me to visit him one warm March afternoon. He met us at the door. "Come in young fellow, Master Edmonds," he addressed me. "I've been expecting you," he winked toward my mother. I realized something pre-planned, no doubt, was astir, but my curiosity overruled any sense of adult management. He escorted me into a large library, where he had set up an electric train near a fireplace. A circular track, with a black engine, coal car, one brown and two yellow boxcars, and a red caboose immediately caught my eye. "Oh, boy!" I must have shouted, for both he and my mother laughed. "It's all yours," he beamed.

"Marion! Please! It's too much," my mother protested.

"On the contrary! Here, Tommy, let's sit down and see if it works."

I followed his lead and sat on the floor with him, with my feet tucked under my legs. He turned on the transformer, and the train began to crawl. He increased its speed. It whistled, and smoke puffed out of its chimney. He ran it around the track a dozen times.

"There are lots of books you can look at," he pointed toward the shelves. He turned off the train's switch and rose to his feet. "Your mother and I need a few moments together," he said.

I thought nothing of his comment and, stooping forward to examine the boxcars, lifted them off the track, turned them upside down to spin the wheels, before placing them back. I did that with all the cars; then I began to explore his library. My eyes struggled to take in his holdings. They equaled anything we had on the farm. His books seemed more neatly organized than ours, and many of them still had their bright, glossy dust jackets in place. Stacks of *Life* magazines enjoyed a shelf of their own. Their covers had to do with the war, with wounded soldiers and shot-up military matériel. I stared at the soldiers' bloody bandages and dirty hands, their hollow eyes, and mess kits and canteens. I wanted to be a soldier. To carry guns and throw grenades! To kill Japs and Nazis.

It had grown very quiet in the house. I placed the magazines back on the shelf and crept across the hallway and peeked into living room. Mr. Chappels was kissing my mother. And she was letting him! My face felt hot, my heart numb. I wanted my grandmother; I wanted to run home. I slipped back into the library, closed its glass doors, and curled up in a corner by the *Life* magazines. How long we stayed, I have no idea.

More and more, my mother drove into town alone. More and more Mr. Chappels came out to the farm and stayed with us for supper.

My grandmother delighted in these arrangements. "Tommy, your mother and Mr. Chappels are going to get married. Do you know what that means?"

"I think so. It means Mama's gonna move away."

"No! It means you're going to have a new daddy, Mr. Chappels. He's incredibly fond of you and will love you as much as your father. Your mother will be very happy, and we'll all have a new life."

That there was anything wrong with our present one escaped me.

"The wedding will be here on the farm. Won't that be exciting?"

I didn't know. But as I thought about Mr. Chappels, I drew comfort from the fact that he had steadied Uncle Everett's horse that afternoon, when I was perched behind the saddle, and had then pulled out his pistol and shot Mr. Crawford, dead! I liked that. That's what Uncle Everett would have done, if he could have gotten to his pistol.

About that time my mother's sister, my Aunt Rachel, came to visit us. She generally came once a year and stayed a month or more. Though unpredictable, she could be entertaining. She paid me dimes to run errands and do special chores for her. Her arrival caused the wedding to be postponed, but that didn't anger my mother. "I need more time," I overheard her say to Aunt Rachel. "Marion frequently has to be in Richmond, when the legislature is in session. I've asked him to wait till late summer."

Aunt Rachel lived in Roanoke. She and my mother were originally from Wytheville. The two loved to reminisce about their childhood and first years of marriage. Aunt Rachel had a dark side, but if it had emerged in previous visits, it passed unremembered by me.

One afternoon, after my mother had been tutoring me in reading and simple addition, I happened to pass through the kitchen, on my way to play outside. Aunt Rachel was seated in a swing on the back screened-in porch. She was talking to herself and cussing under her breath. I stopped to listen.

"The son-of-a-bitch. I told him not to see her. By God, I taught him. Bastard!" she chuckled to herself. "Got him right in the arm! Swish! Take that!" She held her left hand up, as if gripping a knife. "Shit!" Her eyebrows arched. An ugly smile marred her thin lips. Her complexion was dark to start with, and her forehead wide and sallow. One could not call her beautiful, though perhaps she had been in her youth. Strands of uncombed brown hair hung limp about her ears. She kept tapping the floor with one foot, to keep the swing in motion. In her right hand, she clasped a pint bottle. Suddenly, she stopped, turned, and glared at me, as if through a dense haze. "Tommy! Is that you? It's not nice to spy on Aunt Rachel. Come here," she beckoned with her right hand, causing the alcohol in the bottle to slosh loudly. "I need to kiss you. Come, darling. Aunt Rachel's not going to hurt you. No sir-ree!"

I approached her with apprehension and stopped by the swing. "Kiss me!" she mumbled, with slurred speech. I leaned forward to hug her. A stagnant odor rose from her breath. I kissed her neck and stared at her bare feet.

"Run along now," she said, as she pushed off to swing more.

I ran outside, to one of the outbuildings, climbed the wooden steps to its loft, and peered out its front window toward the porch. Aunt Rachel had fallen out of the swing and was struggling to get up. Just then, my mother came to the porch. "Rachel!" she blurted. "Are you hurt?" She must have seen the bottle and surmised Aunt Rachel's state. "Oh, Rachel," she moaned. "He wasn't worth it. You've got to get over this." She bent down and helped her to her feet. Aunt Rachel staggered inside, with my mother's arm about her waist. I could hear Aunt Rachel laughing, but it was one of those cheerless, inebriated laughs.

That weekend, Uncle Everett came to take me to his place. Aunt Rachel watched him from her bedroom, upstairs, but never came down. I could see her pull back the curtains, before she withdrew from the window.

Uncle Everett drove a rusty-red pickup truck that always had handfuls of hay or straw and farm equipment in its bed. He chuckled as I climbed in beside him and my mother closed the door. She had to swing it hard to make it shut. He motioned for her to come to his window. "How much longer does she plan to stay?" he nodded toward the house.

"She'll be all right. She's sobered up now, but you never can tell," my mother replied.

She put her hand up to his door. He had rolled his window down. He placed his hand over hers. "You sure you want to do this?" he asked.

"Yes. Marion's a good man."

"I wish I could believe you," he stared at her. "Marriages are supposed to be forever, you know. That's a long time." He turned the ignition switch on and continued to study her face.

"Go on, now!" she said, lowering her eyes. "Tommy! Behave," she uttered as an afterthought.

"We'll have a great time," Uncle Everett pressed her hand once more. He turned toward me and smiled. "How 'bout it, boy? What do you say?"

"Yes sir!"

"You do what he says, now," my mother commanded me. "He'll bring you home Sunday."

"Yes, ma'am."

She backed away from the truck, as Uncle Everett turned it about in the dirt drive, and we headed for his farm.

We drove into Abingdon near the Sinking Springs Presbyterian Church; then crossed over Main and turned left on Whites Mill Road.

"Will we get to see the mill?" I asked.

"That's where we're heading. Then we'll come back to the farm."

It took about twenty minutes to drive to the mill. I had visited it once before. I had been with my mother and grandmother, and they had driven all the way across town and past the Laurel Springs Bottom, just to have a bushel of corn ground to a fine powder. It was white corn, which my grandmother preferred to yellow corn for her spoonbread and cornpone cakes.

Soon after passing the Laurel Springs, the creek began descending swiftly through a deep grassy gorge, bounded by steep hills and thorn bushes. A few cattle grazed in one of the higher meadows. I could see them nudging and tugging at the short grass between the rocky outcroppings. A long wooden trough came into view. It angled gently away from the creek but parallel with it. Streams of water poured through the seams of the wooden canal, as it fed the rushing current toward the mill. A huge paddle wheel turned ever so cumbersomely, as the water spilled from section to section. The mill, itself, rose three-stories tall. Its wooden planks had long ago transmuted into sodden, weathered boards. A copula graced the wood-shingled roof. Pigeons flew away as we stopped the truck and got out.

We entered the dusty building, redolent of milled wheat, ground corn, and stripped cobs. Stacks of powdery, swollen flour bags formed passageways through the mill. Below we could hear the wheel humming and watch particles of swirling dust sift up through the cracks in the wide floorboards. Since no one had met us upstairs, Uncle Everett led the way down a narrow flight of wooden steps to the grindstone below.

Tiny powdery clouds of sparkling chaff churned in the air. An old man with a red bandana about his mouth and nose turned toward us. "Well, well! Everett! Be with you in just a minute. Who's the boy?" He slipped the bandana off his face and brought the big grindstone to a halt.

"Hamilton's and Shaula's. Name's Tommy. Tommy, say hello to Mr. Archy."

I held out my hand to shake his. He eyed me thoughtfully, hesitated a moment, and shook my hand, "He's shore got the Edmonds brow and build. And eyes, too. Handsome boy. Your nephew, huh?" White dust covered his face and hands. Even my right hand turned white with powder.

"That's right!" Uncle Everett replied. He rubbed his hand across my head. "Got any good cornmeal? Need to fix me and the boy some cornbread tonight. He likes it with strawberry preserves. Isn't that right?"

I nodded as much.

The miller filled a small cloth bag with cornmeal from a large bin. "Ten cents," he said. He filled a second one. "This one's free for the boy." He turned his head sideways and spat a string of tobacco juice through a crack in the floor. I could hear the rushing creek below. "He shore looks like you," he glanced back at Uncle Everett.

"It's the Edmonds genes," Uncle Everett replied. "He gets them from his great-grandfather, just as I do." There was a curt edge in his voice. He seemed moody, withdrawn. "Let's just say his mother's a beautiful woman, and Hamilton won her in a way I couldn't."

"Sorry if I upset you. You Edmonds are a strange lot!"

Uncle Everett paid Mr. Archy, and we left.

The drive to Uncle Everett's farmhouse required returning toward town, crossing a rocky creek at a shallow ford, and proceeding a half-mile or so on a dirt lane. The latter followed a smaller creek that fed into one at a ford. Pastured hills rose to our left. Across the creek, three-to-four hundred acres of prime bottomland stretched halfway back to the Laurel

Springs. The land lay dark, damp and fallow, save for a wheatfield of young green sheathes. Corn shocks and trampled fodder littered a field beside the creek.

"That'll all be plowed up soon," said Uncle Everett. "We're going to fish that creek in the morning," he pointed. "And tomorrow afternoon, we're going horseback riding up on the ridge, just to see what's back there. Think that'll keep us busy?"

"Yes, sir! Will we see any wolves?"

"Not on this trip. But you never know," he smiled.

"Will you carry a gun? Can I shoot it?"

"Your mother would kill me if I did."

"I won't tell. Not even Pearl."

"You and Pearl are great buddies, aren't you?"

"When she's not busy. Uncle Everett, why won't Grandmother let me call her 'Granny?' I always have to call her 'Grandmother.' Why?"

"Tell you what I'll do. We'll talk about that tonight. Right now we're almost home, and you and me, Mr. Bigshot, have chores to do."

Uncle Everett's house came into view. It was a two-story red brick structure, with a wooden front porch, its rails painted white and floor gray. Wide brick steps led up to it. Gray shingles hung out over the porch's deep eaves. All the windows had screens. Two chimneys, one at each end, flanked the house, though a coal furnace provided its principal heat. Uncle Everett had been married but now lived alone.

After supper, Uncle Everett lit a fire in the living room's fireplace. Spring nights continued to be cold, long into May around Abingdon. Uncle Everett's house was sparsely furnished with only a few pieces in each room. Many were handmade, crafted by one of his tenant farmer's father. The old carpenter worked out of one of Uncle Everett's sheds. He was crippled and wore a large three-inch sole on his right foot. He hobbled from bench to bench but produced elegant furniture. I still have most of it, my favorite piece being a large cherry chest of drawers and a gun cabinet, stocked with Uncle Everett's shotguns, rifles, and numerous pistols, along with two of Marion's shotguns and the pistol with which he shot Olan Crawford.

I pulled up a child's rocker and sat beside Uncle Everett. The orange flames glowed softly against the blackened back wall of the fireplace. Uncle Everett took down a dark green book and turned to a picture of Daniel Boone.

"The man was a pioneer. See his coonskin cap and deerskin clothes? He lived off the land and explored this region, and over into Kentucky. You asked about wolves. When he came through here years ago, he and his party spent several nights in caves, right on the Main Street of town. The caves ran under the whole hill, where the big monument stands today. You know the one? The one of the Confederate soldier. The wolves attacked their horses and dogs. After several nights, they had to travel on."

"Did the wolves eat anybody?"

"Not that I know of. Boone's men probably skinned the few they killed. In fact, the wolves lived there a long time and weren't driven off until years later. That's why the town was called 'Wolf Hill.' But I think they were gone by the time the Colonel settled in town. But that was after he built the house where you and Mama live."

Uncle Everett closed the book and replaced it in a knotty pine bookshelf near the mantle. "Got another surprise," he said. He opened a drawer beneath the bookcase and produced a small walnut box that sported silver hinges and a silver latch. He placed it in my lap.

"Be careful. Don't jiggle it or let it fall off."

I unlatched the box and raised the lid. A collection of hand-struck flint arrowheads lay stacked neatly in rows on a green pad.

"I found everyone of them, right here on the farm. They're very old and go back a long time."

I picked up the largest arrowhead with care. Its sharp tip almost pricked my thumb. Its serrated edges were equally sharp. Many smaller but similar ones lay beneath it.

"One day, this will be yours. The whole kit and caboodle! Let's put it back now, OK?"

As he reopened the drawer, I saw another box: a shiny, cherry box, shoved in the back. "What's in that?"

"Secret! Big secret! Don't ever let me catch you in there, unless I tell you! Maybe one day I will." He forced a smile and patted me on my shoulder.

Early the next morning, we walked through the wet grass to go fishing. All Uncle Everett carried was a short cane stick. He had tied a filament of line on the narrower end and had attached a small hook to that. Along the way, we picked up a few night crawlers and dropped them in a can. We paused in a marshy meadow several yards from the stream. "Shhh! Walk softly. The fish will feel our vibrations. They spook easily," Uncle Everett said.

Uncle Everett held up the hook. "You put the worm on it," he whispered. "It's time you learned how."

I reached in the can for one of the worms, flinched as I picked up its slimy body, and struggled to spear it on the hook. Its warm digestive track gushed out all over my fingers. I tried not to frown or show fear. I wanted Uncles Everett to be proud of me.

"Good job!" he whispered. "Now watch!" He swung the line out over a deep, but swift, narrow section of the creek. Within seconds, the cane reed wobbled and bent slightly. In a matter of an hour, he caught ten pan-size rainbow trout. To my great horror, he released each. Seeing the disappointment on my face, he simply stated: "We've got ham for lunch and apples. The fish can wait another time."

My spirit sank with incredulity.

That afternoon, he saddled up one of his horses, and we rode up high into the woods that overlooked his farm. Far off in the distance, I could see the town's spires. Acres and acres of pastureland, hills, and bottomland stretched westward and to the north. Sheep and cattle grazed on the higher hills; milk cows, pigs, and chickens milled about the barnyards below. Several tenants were beginning to plow the land along the creek. Only three other farms were visible. I could see numerous sheds, Uncle Everett's tin-roofed barns, his pear and apple orchards, and two tobacco beds, protected under long white sheets of cheesecloth.

We rode around a ridge, entangled with thistles, and stopped near a large swath of granite outcroppings. "See that!" Uncle Everett pointed. "That's where your mother and Pearl will soon be picking strawberries. There's a wonderful patch just below there."

He slid off the horse and helped me down. Near a cedar-protected ledge, we sat on a lichen-covered outcropping and ate our picnic of biscuits and apples. "One day this will all be yours," he gestured toward the silent hills with a sweep of his hand. An estranged and sad countenance filled his eyes. We sat there awhile longer, then remounted and rode back down to the farm.

CHAPTER FOUR

THAT SUNDAY AFTERNOON, UNCLE Everett drove me home. As we approached the house, a yellow taxi pulled out of the drive. I could see my mother and Aunt Rachel in the back seat. Aunt Rachel's face appeared distorted. My mother was attempting to restrain her. Aunt Rachel clutched a paper bag in both hands; my mother was wiping her face with a blue washcloth. At the same time, Aunt Rachel was fending her off. Her face defied recognition. The cab driver slowed the vehicle and rolled his window down. My mother had a desperate look in her eyes. "Taking her to Marion, to the hospital," she called from the backseat.

Uncle Everett had rolled his window down. "When will you return?"

"Tonight. Mama will take care of Tommy. Behave, Tommy! Help your grandmother and Pearl. Be a good boy!"

I sat up tall in the seat to get a better look at the cab driver and Aunt Rachel. Aunt Rachel stared at Uncle Everett. A stream of profanity tumbled out of her mouth.

The cab driver winced from under his cap. "Well, Everett, at least I know the way."

"Yeah!" Uncle Everett replied.

The cab pulled forward and headed into town. We drove on in toward the back of the house. Uncle Everett turned off the truck's ignition switch and slumped in silence. "Hate for you to see that, Tommy. Your Aunt Rachel's sick. Come on. We had our fun, didn't we?"

"Yes, sir. Can we do it again?"

"We'll see!"

I squirmed out of the truck, but only after Uncle Everett had wrestled open the door.

Both Pearl and my grandmother had come to the screened-in porch. Pearl opened the door as Uncle Everett brought in my valise. It was an old brown-colored cloth piece with leather straps.

"Get in here, boy!" joked Pearl. "You missed all the fun!"

"Hush! What a dreadful thing to say!" my grandmother scolded her. "Oh, Everett, it was horrible! She drank, cursed, and wretched in the commode the entire time. Poor Shaula! I couldn't bear it any longer. 'She must go!' I ordered. 'Sister or not! Family or not. I will not tolerate her here!' I am so distraught!"

"Now, Mama, I'm not so perfect myself."

"Yes! But you've reformed. Rachel's incapable of anything but drunkenness and rage. Just an inveterate alcoholic! Disgusting! Unsettling! Look at me. I'm a nervous wreck!"

"Come on, Mama. Pearl, pour me a cup of coffee and fix this boy somethin' to eat. We can talk later."

I don't remember when my mother returned. Pearl put me to bed shortly after Uncle Everett left. Night came quickly to the farm, as darkness crept out of the Knobs, wrapping the night in its black bituminous shroud.

Aunt Rachel did not return from the sanitarium in Marion for several weeks. Her arrival by taxi created considerable commotion. Aunt Viola happened to be visiting. Uncle Jim had gone into town and had left her at the house. They had come by wagon, and Uncle Jim had gone on to purchase the usual staples of salt, spices, sugar, cloth, and kerosene. He had also packed the wagon with burlap bags of corn and wheat to drop off at the mill. In addition to the Whites Mill near Uncle Everett's, a smaller mill, about a mile from our place, bordered the route into Abingdon. Its big water wheel dripped all the time. We frequently carried bushels of corn, wheat, and oats to it for processing into flour and meal. My grandmother let Pearl have the sacks to make into aprons and dresses. In fact, our own dishtowels were made of flour sacks.

When Aunt Rachel arrived, we were rocking on the front porch. She had ordered Ralph, the taxi driver, to blow the horn. My mother accepted her joviality as a good sign, an omen announcing her cure, but my grandmother's face betrayed a darker assessment. Her cheeks had turned red and her mouth hung open with disbelief. "Would you ever!" she gasped. "The likes of it!" she placed her hands to her lips.

Aunt Rachel hung partially out of the cab's right back seat window. Two balloons—one blue, the other yellow—bounced against the vehicle's doors. When she stepped out of the cab, her purse fell off her lap, and its contents spilled across the drive. Ralph hurried to her rescue, while she reached back inside for her valise and a hatbox. She was wearing a stunning pink dress, cut rather low about the breasts, though she had so little to display. Even as a child of six, I knew a flat-chested woman from one with a fuller bosom. And poor Aunt Rachel had nothing to reveal, or conceal. She and my mother often laughed about it. But, there Aunt Rachel stood, her purse and hatbox in hand, with the balloons' strings tied about her wrist, her face aglow with renewed self-confidence and the rosy blush of sobriety. I immediately scooted from my rocker and hurried down the steps to hug her. "Tommy, Tommy!" she whispered, as she bent down to kiss my cheek. Tears filled her eyes. My mother quickly followed. Aunt Viola walked stiffly behind her. My grandmother rose from her rocker, swallowed the lump in her throat, no doubt, and made her way with a bruised pride into the circle about Aunt Rachel.

"Rachel! You break my heart, but you're what you are." My grandmother placed her arms about Aunt Rachel's neck and kissed her. "Who am I to condemn you? Forgive me, dear. Holman wouldn't have it any other way."

"Mama Edmonds, there's nothing to forgive," she kissed her in return. "I'm sorry for all the pain I've caused you, and always seem to cause. I'll be going home soon."

"Now, now! What family doesn't have its delitescent sorrows? We will survive. That's the Edmonds motto. *Sic jurat transcendere montes.* You must dare to cross life's mountains! Come dear. You must be hungry as well as tired. And you, too, Ralph. Come on in and have a bite with us."

"Thank you, ma'am, but I've got to get on. The bus from Bluefield will be arriving soon. But I'm much obliged."

Aunt Rachel reached in her purse and handed him a five-dollar bill. "Thank you, Ralph. You've been wonderful."

"It's always my pleasure, ma'am. Well, I'd best be off!" he tipped his hat and returned to his cab.

It was late afternoon before Uncle Jim's wagon came trundling into view. Grandmother tried to persuade him and her sister-in-law to spend the night, but Uncle Jim preferred to drive on. "Thanks, Kate," he called her by her middle name, "but we can be home before dark."

"I don't believe it," she said. "You and Viola need to think about boarding that place up and coming down here. I've got two empty tenant houses you can choose between. Anything could happen to you, and you know it."

"Well, we'll give it some thought."

My mother assisted Viola into the wagon, and we waved as the couple rode off.

Aunt Rachel left the following week. Her original intention had been to remain for most of the summer, attend the wedding, and then go home. But after her stay at the sanitarium, she resolved that it was time for her to return to Roanoke.

After she departed, the house seemed empty. Mr. Chappels returned from Richmond and continued to court my mother. In the meanwhile, Uncle Everett came by periodically to check on the farm and us.

With the coming of April, plowing and seedtime resumed, and great activity broke out across the land. Since I was not in school, and wouldn't be enrolled until the fall, I had a child's run of the fields and barnyards, allowed to participate in whatever caught my fancy, or my mother and grandmother consented to let me do. I got to ride on the backs of the big draft horses, cling to the drag when it came time to break up the plowed clods, take the horses down to the creek for water, and, once their harnesses were removed, feed them huge ears of hard yellow corn, or a half-pail of oats each. I also enjoyed gathering eggs, feeding the chickens, slopping the hogs, and playing with the tenant farmer's children, whenever they didn't have chores of their own.

Two of the children were close to my age, a five-year old boy named Russell, and his four-year old sister, Cruella. They hailed from sturdy mountain stock, to say the least. Russell was a tough little kid and always wanted to fight. We frequently wrestled each other and would hit each other hard on the arms. His sister liked to play with dogs, especially when the dogs were in heat. This was all new to me, and even I came away shocked one afternoon when I stumbled upon Russell and Cruella having sex with a dog. Russell was holding it by its hindquarters, while Cruella had taken off her panties and the dog was humping her back. My curiosity overrode any sense of buggery or morbid wrong. Later, the three of us played "doctor-nurse," Russell and I practicing on Cruella what the dog had more successfully performed. That continued for most of the summer until Pearl caught us doing it in the apple house and threatened to tell my mother. "You leave those thrash alone!" she reprimanded. "Good Lord, boy! Your mother would skin you alive!" I doubted that, but I had no desire to anger or hurt my mother. I avoided the two children, but occasionally I would play "husband-wife" with Cruella in the barn. She would pull down her panties and I would slip out my "winky," as my grandmother called it, and press it against Cruella's tight, little crevice. It was only in my teen years that I realized what we were supposed to have been doing. But by then Cruella and her family had moved on.

Summer ushered in many exciting activities. Earl, Pearl's father and one of the older farmhands, hitched up the wagon one noon and took me with him into the Knobs to cut a load of firewood for the kitchen's cookstove. We stopped near the top of the ridge, overlooking Uncle Jim's farm, before turning off into an old growth of hickories and oaks. Earl carried a long, wobbling steel saw over his shoulder and cut up a number of logs from fallen trees. He watched me carefully, but allowed me to assist with the sawing. Since I was a tall, stout boy, I was able to pull the saw in unison with him, but he had to do the heavier, muscular work and load the logs onto the wagon. Later, he split them into stovewood-size pieces and let me whack away with a hatchet to create kindling. He oversaw everything I did and taught me how to swing the hatchet with clean smooth strokes, creating slender sticks that would ignite quickly. He rarely called me "Tommy." Instead, he addressed me as "Son." I thought that strange at the time, but his calling me "Son" made me feel special. He had lost his only son in a mowing accident. Pearl would often retell how "his horse done reared up when he come upon this rattlesnake, and Felston fell right off, face fo-m'st in the blades. It ripped him up like a hog." It was Earl who let me sit on the drag, ride the horses down to the creek for water, and perform other chores within my range. He never once raised his voice in anger, swore, or grew impatient over anything around me. He sometimes ate with us in the kitchen, since his wife, or Pearl's mother, was dead, but he always walked back to his cabin at night. Two brothers and their wives and children lived there, as well. It was his brothers who did the larger portion of the plowing, planting, harvesting, suckering of tobacco, hay bailing, thrashing of the wheat, cutting and shocking the corn, and, at Thanksgiving time, slaughtering the hogs. The latter, however, constituted a colossal undertaking, requiring every farmhand's effort for an entire week. Not even the women were exempt. They worked harder than the men, cutting off the fat for lard and grinding up scraps for sausage, which they peppered and stored in long, greasy, cloth sacks.

During berry picking time, we descended on the hills like locusts. First, came the strawberries and later blackberries, mulberries, and cherries. Like primitive food-gatherers from some wandering ice-age tribe, my mother, Pearl and I joined the women and other children on the farm in these group forays. We scoured the hills and hedgerows, fields and by-ways, picking and filling our baskets with nature's delectable bounty. Uncle Everett came for us to pick strawberries on his farm, where we gathered the sweetest berries of all. Later, at home, my grandmother oversaw the converting of our juice-stained pails of berries into pint and quart jars of luscious preserves.

This latter bout with nature led to a discourse on Providence and the goodness of the Creator, in which my grandmother insisted Mr. Chappels participate. His presence, that particular evening, rested solely on the basis of his love for my mother. But seeing he had stayed for dinner, there was no escaping her theological confrontation.

"Now don't you find that convincing?" she began. "That the grandeur and opulence of nature, the very abundance and extravagance of creation, should reflect something of the grandeur and goodness of its Designer? Isn't that so?"

"Yes," he moaned, not wishing to contest her.

"What is your own theory? You must have one. Please share it. We're all family now, or soon will be," she smiled. Then she folded her hands in that aristocratic style she must have acquired at the Martha Washington Seminary for Girls. She waited patiently for him to commence.

"Mama, the poor man and I have a ton of things to discuss and plan. Can't we do this later?"

"Oh, Shaula! Later never comes, my dear. Occasions like this are gifts of the season. Tomorrow will sweep them all away and introduce an order of fresh new duties."

"You do have a point, Miz. Edmonds. But I see it all as nature's boundless way of hurling thousands of seeds and berries to the winds of chance, knowing that only a few will ever survive the harsh conditions of reality. She's a profligate spender, if you ask me. Whether God exists or not, or guides the process or not, or foreordained its mechanics, I fear to say. Our beliefs should match the facts, and not the facts our beliefs. That's what every successful banker knows, and God pity the ones who don't."

"Oh, so definitive! Do tell! We mustn't misguide Tommy. Not a sparrow falls, but that our heavenly Father knows it. I might be old fashioned, and out of my league when it comes to banking, but I can never doubt His guiding hand."

A silence ensued. Her brow lifted and sagged and her face grew taut. Her wrinkles swelled into grooves. Then she smiled. "We need you, Mr.

Chappels. Yes, dear man! And God knows it. Don't disdain an old woman's belief in the mercy of Providence. I know it when I see it."

"And coffee cups, too, Grandmother!" I piped up. "Remember, you saw him first in the coffee cup."

Pearl and my mother hooted with laughter. Mr. Chappels blushed with mirth. My grandmother's face turned ashen.

"Oh, goodness!" she feigned. Her cheeks burned red, even under her rouge.

"So much for dissembling, Mama," my mother said.

"'Opulence,' 'dissembling,' 'Providence'!" repeated Mr. Chappels. Does anybody ever explain these words for Tommy?"

"Or for me?" added Pearl.

"He'll learn them in time," said my grandmother. "That's far better than paltering around the boy. Once Holman redeemed me from the Knobs, I vowed I'd never allow my speech to deteriorate again."

"Nor have you!" confirmed my mother. "Marion, she knits with a dictionary at her elbow."

"I believe it!" he smiled. "Well, Mama Edmonds, if I may call you that, I look forward to being part of the family. And being your stepfather, Master Thomas," he grinned as he addressed me across the table. He enfolded my mother's left hand in his and kissed her fingers. "And to you, Tommy," he raised his voice. "May your childhood be filled with unending joy."

I don't remember if I smiled, or thanked him, or looked away. Numb is not the word. Puzzled would have been more like it. Or nonplused. I could still feel his presence beside the horse, when he slipped his hand about its reins and shot Olan Crawford in the chest. Whatever I thought about this man, or however I felt about him, I liked his quiet mannerisms and manly, genteel qualities.

June did not end happily. Late one misty evening, Earl showed up at the back screened-in door with a lantern. "Little Ouida's missing. Ain't nobody seen her a'fore supper. Please pray for her, Miz. Edmonds. Somethin's happened to her, bad. I just know it."

Ouida was Earl's niece, his oldest brother, Jessie's, baby girl. She couldn't have been more than three.

"Won't you come in?" my grandmother offered.

"No'm, thank ye. I was hoping you could spare Pearl. We're mountin' a search party for her right now. Leavin' from the barn and up through the orchard, where her mama last seen her. She didn't come in for supper."

"Oh, Earl! Let me call the sheriff. Or Everett. He's got tracking hounds. He could be here in less than an hour."

"We done got some of our own, Miz. Ginny. Ask Pearl to bring a lantern and follow us up through the woods."

By now, Pearl had come down from her room over the kitchen. "Wait, Pa, and I'll go with you."

Earl waited on the steps while Pearl tossed a shawl about her shoulders. She laced up her brogans and lit a kerosene lantern, which she had retrieved from a table in the pantry.

"Can I go?" I begged.

"Most definitely not!" my grandmother retorted. "One lost child is enough. Get on up to bed," she remonstrated. "Earl, I'll make some coffee and send it up by Shaula to the barn."

"Thank you, ma'am, we'd be much obliged."

As he and Pearl disappeared in the night, I ran to the front hall windows and peered out into the dark. The orchard lay just across the road in front of the house, and I could make out a dozen or so glowing lanterns in the mellow night, as searchers wove their way up the hill in the mist. They gathered briefly under some apple limbs, on the edge of the woods; then formed a single file of fading light that grew fainter and fainter until they were swallowed by darkness.

I pretended to mount the stairs, stomping my feet and muttering pouting sounds as I climbed. But instead I was standing by Quelle and staring up at the indomitable Capt. Edmonds, with his balderdash eyes and gigantic sword. With that, I tugged quietly on the front door and slipped out into the night. I all but stumbled off the porch, as my eyes adjusted to the dark. It had been drizzling but had stopped. A white fog enveloped the yard. I ran toward the barn and hid in one of the empty horse stalls. Soon enough, my mother arrived with a large, enameled-covered pot of coffee, a tray of cups, and a pitcher of cream.

I could hear voices on the road. It was more of Earl's kin people and a moil of dogs. The big, chained hounds were whining and baying and pulling the men behind them. They were coon dogs.

"Miss Shaula, how kind!" The men helped themselves liberally to the coffee and trudged back onto the road.

"I'll have biscuits for you in awhile, as soon as Mama bakes them," she called. "You'll need something nourishing before long."

They waved to her and slipped out of sight in the mist. I watched as my mother retuned to the house. Once she disappeared around the corncrib, I hurried after the men.

They passed through the orchard, stopped where I had seen the others pause, and stared down at the ground.

"Damn!" one of the men groaned. "That's blood."

"That's a track," another said. "A cat's track. Some panther's done drug her off."

My grandmother had often told stories of how panthers stalked the Knobs, but when she'd see how much that frightened me, she'd change her story to, "Oh, that was long ago, when I was a little girl, and Holman first came over the Knobs to visit us. They'd scream like wild women in the night. And they would drag off an occasional lamb or ewe."

This time it was no ewe, but a lamb—a lamb of a child. The dogs pulled the men onward, while I shrank back, uncertain what to do. Soon, caution gave way to fear, and fear, abetted by darkness, to panic; and, racing through the wet grass under the apple trees, I ran as fast as my legs would carry me down to the road. I climbed the rail fence, tore a hole in my overalls, cut my hands on the lone strand of barbwire on the top rail, and hurried toward the house. My grandmother was waiting for me at the door.

"You imp! You little ingrate! How dare you frighten us so! Look at you! And look at those hands! March that little butt of yours up those steps, right now! And don't stop until you get to the bathroom. Oh, the likes of it! I should flail you with a switch!"

I scampered up the stairs and fled to the bathroom. "Wash yourself!" she commanded from below. "And go straight to bed!"

In the morning, I rushed down the stairs to learn of the night's search results.

"Gone! The little thing's gone!" Pearl muttered. "They never found a thing. Just a little shoe. I got it upstairs, in my room."

"He dragged her up in some tree," my grandmother hypothesized. "Or some cave. There's a thousand caves back in there. Old mica mines, iron mines, salt mines. The Lord alone knows where she is."

"Mama, Earl asked you to pray, not prophesy her funeral," my mother commented.

"Oh, she's dead all right, Shaula. You can mark my words on that. Many a night my father would have to sleep out in the cold during the lambing season, for, if weren't dogs, a panther would kill a ewe, or carry off a lamb. They bite their little throats, cutting off the air to their windpipes; then drag them deep into the woods. And what they don't eat, they bury under leaves. Those dogs of Earl's brothers are coon dogs. Not bloodhounds, or real hounds. They probably got distracted and ran off after coons. Earl claimed as much. That's why they came back."

The entire morning past, and still no one found the child, or any sign of the child, or the predator that had stalked and killed her, no doubt. I was playing in the front yard, near the purple lilac bushes, when Uncle Everett drove up in his pickup truck. Two portable dog cages wobbled back and forth in its bed. As soon as he stopped, you could hear the hounds clawing to get out. I ran to his truck and climbed up on the bed.

"Careful," he said. "These rascals are big and hungry and the first thing I want them to smell is something of that little girl's."

"Pearl's got a shoe inside. I saw it yesterday. It's just a rag, covered with blood."

"Run get Pearl and tell her to bring the shoe."

While I scampered toward the back porch, my mother and grandmother came around from the front of the house to greet Uncle Everett. Pearl had already overheard Uncle Everett and was halfway out the screen door. "Where's the dogs?" she asked. "I heard what he said."

We hurried together to the truck.

"Don't let them smell it yet," warned Uncle Everett. "I want to saddle up Sally, or old Fred, then turn them loose on her trail. Mama, Shaula, what happened?"

"They found the cat's tracks up in the orchard," my mother pointed. "The men either lost the trail, or the dogs never got the scent."

"I couldn't tell them a thing," my grandmother protested. "Just hardheaded tenants," she shook her head with sadness. "The poor little darling! Probably never had a chance."

I weaseled in as close to Uncle Everett as I could. "Not this time, boy," he smiled. "But you can hop in and ride up to the barn."

"Don't you let him go!" my grandmother pointed her finger at her son. "Don't you dare let him on your horse."

"I won't, Mama! I've got more sense than that. But the boy loves adventure, and he needs to be free of your skirts far more than you let him."

"Well, not this time! One missing child is enough. Anything could happen. Tommy, you hear that, don't you? You come back as soon as Everett saddles up and releases those dogs. I'll not permit a second of perfidy!"

"Yes, ma'am! I'll come right back."

"Pearl, you go with him and drag him back if you have to, but he's not, I repeat, 'not going.' And that's final."

"Mama, nothing's ever final, except death," said Uncle Everett. I climbed up in the bed and peered in at his huge hounds. They whined and wanted to lick my fingers, but I knew I couldn't let them, without spoiling their scent for Ouida.

At the barn, I remained in the truck until Uncle Everett had saddled up Fred—an old but sure-footed horse. Pearl handed him Ouida's little shoe, as he led the horse by its bridle around the truck. He held the little shoe in front of the caged dogs. They yelped and bayed with excitement. "OK," he said. "Go find her!" With that, he released their kennel doors and out they burst.

Off they lunged, sniffing the air and weaving in circles. Suddenly, Roy, the larger of the two, stopped, sniffed something ominous in the wind, and, letting out a loud bark, began whining and running toward the orchard. Dixie, his sister, picked up the scent, and off she raced, yelping and whining to keep up.

"Adios, amigos!" Uncle Everett called. He swung into his saddle, and Fred trotted down the road.

"Wait!" I shouted. I ran behind him. "The gate! Let me get the gate!" I ran ahead of the horse, as Uncle Everett slowed its pace. I opened the orchard gate and looked up at him.

He smiled as he passed through. "Now get on back! A promise is a promise. I promised your mother and grandmother. There'll be other times for us. Now run on. If I find her, I'll take you there someday and show you myself."

"Yes, sir!" I groaned, as I stepped up and closed the gate and watched him gallop off, after the dogs.

He did not return until late that evening. Across the saddle, a tiny body lay draped against his waist and legs. He had covered it with a burlap sack. The dogs panted beside him, their tongues long and distended. They all but jumped into the horses' trough for water. Froth and lather dripped from old Fred. Uncle Everett handed the body to Pearl. A fetid stench accompanied the transfer. She clutched the sack in both hands and wept. Once Earl's brother and sister-in law came down, they wept, too. Leena, Ouida's mother, moaned and pulled at her hair. Jessie just stood there, looking down at his feet. His overalls were stained with mud and chaff;

his beard was black and grizzly. He took the bundle in his arms. As he cradled the child, he too let out a whimper, like the sound of a sob under a pillow. He and Leena walked off together toward their cabin. I helped Uncle Everett re-kennel his dogs. Without smiling, or saying anything, he climbed in his truck and drove away.

No one ever found the cat, or the panther. "It probably ran off across the Holston," Uncle Everett surmised. "One day we'll get it, Tommy. By jingles, next year, I'm taking you with me—promise or no promise—and will get the so and so! Whatta you say?"

"Yes, sir! We'll get the son-of-a bitch!"

"Whoa, Lord! Watch that tongue, or we'll both be in trouble!" he feigned a frightful grimace.

I understood what he meant.

CHAPTER FIVE

ONE AFTERNOON IN EARLY May, while I was playing in the loft of the old slave quarters, I thought I saw a movement near the apple house. I peered out the side window of the log building for a better view. The apple house was constructed of the same stone as Quilly Hall. It had a deep basement, walled with wooden racks for storing apples and pears. Shelves lined its walls, each laden with heavy blue gallon-sized jars, stuffed with sausages, pork loin, corn, beans, tomatoes, squash, and whole berries, including cherries, blackberries and strawberries. As late as the 1940s, my grandmother's farm was still a subsistence operation, although it turned a profit in terms of wheat, corn, hams, wool, and tobacco. No farmhands went hungry, but all bordered on poverty.

As I peered out the window, a man appeared briefly at its door. A cigarette glowed in his hands. Suddenly, he slipped away and disappeared under the limbs of a weeping willow, near the creek that flowed from the cold spring that gushed from under our springhouse. Later he crossed a fence, before dropping out of sight. Just then, Pearl emerged from the building. Disheveled hair hung in her face. She brushed off the front of her dress and wrapped her apron about her waist. She adjusted her hair, in an effort to restore her pigtail, and headed back for the house. My curiosity drifted toward other attractions in the loft.

A large, cast iron safe rested against the cabin's wall, near the loft's rock chimney. Neither a fireplace, nor a hearth, existed in the loft, although a mantle ran part way across the chimney. The absence of a fireplace made it frigid in the winter, but cool and damp in the spring and oppressively hot in the summer. The safe set on four, squat, rusting claw feet, with its heavy door open and two shelves visible. Its only content consisted of a broken cigar box, loose at one end, with its lid missing.

"Money, sweetheart. Money! It used to be lined with money. Big bills. Wads of them. All Confederate," Grandmother said. "Your great-grandfather," she'd nod toward the hallway, "the venerable Capt. Nathan, never got over the loss. He converted close to a half million dollars of silver certificates into Confederate currency. We would be millionaires, if that War hadn't occurred."

"Where's all that money now?" I asked.

"In a box at your Uncle Everett's. Your grandfather willed it to him before he died."

But now the safe belonged to me. I used it to store my secret valuables: a shiny rock from under the bridge near the springhouse, a flattened dime I had picked up beside the railroad tracks in town, and a rusted nail I found near the horse barn. The nail had oxidized to the point that it had turned into a long, flaky, dark red spine. I had heard tales of De Soto's expedition into Tennessee, and I visualized the nail as a relic of his armor. I was De Soto, Senior Hernando! Conquistador extraordinaire! I spotted some cattail plumes in a clay urn, pulled one out, and brandished it, as I marched in the loft. I stole to the window to make certain no one was spying. I pretended to be Great-Grandfather Howard, then Samson straining against the pillars, next Daniel Boone, and lastly the stern, commanding figure of Capt. Nathan Edmonds, boots and all. "Where's the son-of-a bitch hiding?" I demanded of the walls. I strutted around like Uncle Everett.

When not in the loft, I would sneak down to the creek and pretend I was my father. I would rush into the cold water, clutching a tobacco stick, firing at the hidden enemy, only to fall riddled by bullets and shrapnel. If I survived that initial assault, I'd crawl up the opposite bank and search for my father among the reeds. When I came in, wet and muddy, my overalls clogged with clay and tiny granules of grit, my mother would bend down and hug me, for she knew what I had been doing. My "wounds" were nothing in comparison with hers. "Tommy! O God, Tommy! Let's get you cleaned up, before supper."

As spring blended into summer, one seasonal demand followed another: from the setting out of the young tobacco plants, to the first hay mowings, to the building of haystacks, to the harvesting of wheat, with its throngs of tenant farmers from our own and Uncle Everett's farm, joining in with their muscle and toil to thresh and bag sack after sack. And the meals that accompanied those hot sweaty days! Plates heaped with fried chicken, mounds of mashed potatoes, bowls of gravy, beans, corn, sliced tomatoes, deviled eggs, biscuits, fresh pies, and endless rounds of tea. It required all the labor force of the two farms to sponsor these events.

Then a second and, if lucky, a third hay mowing followed, with days spent suckering and pulling fat green worms off the tall tobacco crop. Finally, came the cutting and spearing of the long tobacco stalks to haul and hang them in their respective sheds, where the crop would season until late fall to mellow and transform into aromatic shafts of fine, golden leaves.

These hot days of summer permitted little respite for the men who labored from before the rising of the sun until long after its setting. Earl alone would take breaks and come down to the house for a nap in the old slave cabin. While he slept on a pile of burlap sacks on the ground floor, I'd engage in my escapades and imaginary sorties in the loft. My grandmother, however, coveted my afternoon playtime for designs of her own.

"Tommy, get in here! An idle mind is the devil's workshop. You'll be going to school this fall. There's reading and writing to do. Now take your nap, and then we'll work a little, after it grows cooler."

Actually, I welcomed these reprieves, because the afternoon heat often climbed into the nineties, and the fields provided no recess from the sun. After a brief nap, she would wake me and bring me a glass of watered-down tea. Sometimes I would have sweated so much I could smell my own sour body. Her remedy for that was a cold wet washcloth that often reeked as badly as my body odor.

"Now, go into the parlor, and I'll be there in a few minutes."

I'd obey and pull from one of the shelves a favorite storybook or a volume of *The Encyclopedia of Knowledge*. By now, with her help, and sometimes unassisted, I could pick my way through a paragraph and read it aloud to her satisfaction. She had to help with all of the long words, but she exulted in doing so.

Afterwards, she'd play records from her collection of classical music. The huge player would only accommodate one record at a time, but she was intent on my acquiring a taste for refined music, as well as deriving pleasure from it herself. Those were arduous times for a six-year old, especially if the recordings were one of Rossini's Concertos for flutes and violins, or something equally effete and sissified. Not that I disliked her selections, but I preferred the French horns of a Wagner or Beethoven symphony, or even a sad Mozart piece, or lively Brahm's medley of folk dances, to the lethargic or bouncy melodies that brought her peace.

Then came release! And out into the hallway I would run, passed the ever-so elegant Quelle and her quiescent pigeons, passed the scornful gaze of the Captain and his father in turn, and out the door and across the porch and into the cool lush grass under the enormous elms that shaded the front yard. Time to play again, or race toward the barn in hopes of riding the weary draft horses down to the creek.

And so passed the summer. Until mid-August. And Aunt Rachel's return, in time for my mother's wedding to Mr. Chappels. Only something equally momentous occurred, simultaneous with her arrival.

Pearl came out to the cab to greet her, along with my mother and grandmother and Uncle Everett, who had dropped by. Before Pearl could say a word, she suddenly grew greenish-pale, turned away toward the house, and vomited in a ditch along its dank foundation. Everyone stared in disbelief.

"Are you all right?" my mother asked.

Pearl hugged her sides. She couldn't stop the retching. A pasty gray cast slipped across her face. Her lips turned blue. She wiped her mouth and hurried toward the back porch.

"Pearl!" my grandmother called in a loud voice. "Is that what I think it is? Tell me! Don't you dare run off like that!" Grandmother's face burned with splotches of red; her dark eyes had hardened, and sweat beads glistened on her forehead and about her thin eyebrows.

"Mama, for heaven's sake!" exclaimed my mother. "What's gotten in to you? Can't you see, Pearl's sick."

"Sick? Or pregnant? I've been watching her. I say she's heavy with child!"

A frightened Pearl covered her face with her hands and began to weep.

"Oh, Pearl!" my mother said. "Mama, don't scold her like that! Can't you see she's frightened?"

Aunt Rachel paid Ralph, who glanced uneasily toward Uncle Everett and drove away.

"Who's the one?" my grandmother demanded. "Don't you lie to me, you . . . sneaking . . . little . . . hussy!"

"Mama!" objected Uncle Everett. "My God, leave her alone. She needs our help. Pearl, go on to your room. We'll talk about this later."

"No! We'll talk about it now!" huffed my grandmother. "Look at her stomach! It's already beginning to show. I've kept my lips tight long enough. Oh, the ruin of it! Answer me! Who did it? I want to know right now!"

"It was Jessie's friend, from Meadowview. It happened the night they come over here to help search for Ouida," sobbed Pearl.

"'Happened?' And how many more times after that?"

"Only onced more. I've been afraid to say anything."

"And where is this *friend* now? Huh? Tell me that! Or can you?"

"Mama, stop it! Stop acting like a shrew. Control yourself," Uncle Everett contested. "Pearl, we'll see a doctor first thing in the morning. Don't worry. You can stay at my place, if you have to. And that's a promise!"

"Yes, sir!" she snuffled back her tears with gratitude.

"Mama, you should be ashamed of yourself! Ashamed!" he reiterated.

He glanced toward my mother and then down at his feet. "Come on, Rachel. Let's help these people in their house, before they start wallowing in more pity and blame." All that he said with an angry glare toward his mother and with embarrassment toward my own. With a heaviness of spirit, all six of us entered the house by way of the front porch. Even Pearl. Aunt Rachel held her arm, while Uncle Everett carried Aunt Rachel's two suitcases in and set them down in the hallway. As we entered, I looked up toward the old Captain. Even his countenance seemed a bit downcast. He was a man for all seasons. I sometimes felt that he actually watched over us at night and guarded the perimeter of the farm. Quelle stood stately beside her fountain, demur and quiet, watering the pigeons. At least we were home. We were all home. And that was something to regale, however dysfunctional the family might be.

In spite of my grandmother's outbursts, she had no intentions of relinquishing Pearl. She personally rode into town with Pearl and Uncle Everett to see the doctor. When they returned, she evinced a calmness that betrayed her earlier invective and churlish remarks. "Yes, we will do it!" she chirped. "We will raise the child as one of our own, or at least until Pearl can marry and settle down. It's all settled. There'll be no more dissent, no discussion or debate! I've made up my mind. Yes. As the Bible says: 'You meant it for evil, but the Lord meant it for good.' Who knows what this child might become? But God pity it! Poor little darling! What a start in life!"

Uncle Everett just looked at his mother and shook his head. "Jesus!" he hissed under his breath. He tussled my hair with his left hand, hugged his mother, Pearl, Aunt Rachel, and, lastly, my mother. "Try getting along, huh! You women will be the death of me yet!" He smiled and retuned to his car—a black Buick with rusting running boards—and prepared to drive off. "Call me, if you need me," he said to my mother. We stood back and watched him drive away.

"You know, Mr. Biggety?" my mother addressed me with a smile. "I think he was serious about taking Pearl home with him. He gets awfully lonely, you know."

"Didn't he ever get married?" I queried. "Didn't he want a wife?"

"Oh, yes-siree! You bet your bottom dollar! He was married, honey. Married to a beautiful town girl, from Johnson City. But they quarreled all the time, and your uncle was different then. Moody, a hothead, drank a lot, always had to have his way. She left him after two years. You were just a little boy."

I stared down the road after him, where he had turned passed the springhouse, before heading back to town. I waved, but the big willow tree and the roof of the apple house blocked his view.

Preparations for the wedding began almost the following day. Dresses were brought from town by taxi, tried on, rejected, returned, and new ones delivered, all within the same day. Mr. Chappels would come in the evenings, dine with us, steal off for an hour or so with my mother; then he would drive back to his house in town. Menus were discussed, cakes baked, cured hams sliced and placed in the refrigerator and some even stored in an old icebox on the porch. Still, the day of the wedding came like a thief in the night. "Get up," whispered my mother. "Time to get up, sleepy head." An air of buoyancy trilled in her voice. "We have to be at the church by noon. The wedding's at two o'clock. You're going to be the ring bearer. Yes. All you have to do is walk in front of Uncle Everett. I'll be holding his arm. He's going to give me away. Now get some breakfast. Then we'll wash up and get you dressed."

Unbeknown to me, my Aunt Rachel and mother had purchased a boy's long gray Prince Albert jacket, striped pants, black shoes, stiff white shirt, and black tie for me to wear. I must have gone into shock. I winced and wiggled and ground my teeth the entire time my grandmother and Aunt Rachel forced me into the clothes. "Now here's the pillow. Get out there in the hallway and practice marching slowly in here," Grandmother coaxed me from the living room. "But where's the ring?" I objected. "Never you mind," she replied. "Marion will provide it before the wedding."

Uncle Everett came for us and drove us into town in his Buick. People I had never seen before were queuing up at the church door. I was dragged along and placed in line, after everyone had been seated. Colorful flowers filled the sanctuary and bright candles glowed from glass globes placed along the right aisle. From out of somewhere, the organist struck up a flamboyant march. Mr. Chappels and the minister stepped out of a side door near the pulpit. Suddenly, I was pushed forward, and Uncle Everett and my mother guided me toward the minister. I don't remember what was said, or how long the service lasted, but Uncle Everett kissed my mother before he placed her gloved fingers in Mr. Chappels' hands. She dropped her bouquet, to a dither of light laughter. Uncle Everett retrieved it for her.

The reception at home was tumultuous. I strutted around in my stiff costume, enamoring myself to everyone, while the guests filed by to hug my mother and shake Mr. Chappels' hand. Everywhere, everyone balanced ham biscuits on a dainty plate in one hand and clasped a glass of champagne in the other. Aunt Rachel watched these glasses of bubbly essence with an envious twitch on her lips. Nevertheless, she retained a gracious smile and helped Pearl and my grandmother replenish the guests' plates. Three tall white layer cakes were required to satisfy the crowd's demand. The Presbyterian minister appeared to be a little tipsy, but he smiled each time I walked by. His wife had a huge pink orchid in her dress's lapel and chatted familiarly with people. "You will soon be coming to my class," she said.

"Why's that?" I asked.

"To learn the *Children's Catechism*! Hasn't your mother told you?"

"No ma'am," I replied. "What's a catechism?"

"Oh, you'll learn!" she beamed. "It's a beautiful little book, just for children like you."

I must admit I was stunned and not impressed with her sincerity. If it were a book, maybe we had it in our library.

"Yes, you'll love it," she assured me.

If ever a child was shocked, I was totally unprepared for what happened next. Suddenly, people began to congregate in the yard. My mother had disappeared and now came down the stairs with a valise in one hand and her flowers in the other. Outside on the porch, she turned her back and flung the flowers to a group of shrieking women, then raced to Mr. Chappels' car, waved, ran back to kiss me good-bye, then got in the vehicle with him, and drove off. Cans bounced behind the car, and red and white streamers fluttered in the air. I ran across the lawn toward the springhouse. My mother was leaving, and I hadn't the slightest idea where she was going, or if and when she'd come back. "Mama! Mama!" I called to the guests' delight.

I stopped and fought back a well of hot tears that begged for release.

I felt a strong hand on my right shoulder. "It's all right, Tommy," said Uncle Everett. "She'll be back." He rubbed his left hand through my hair. When I glanced up, there were tears in his eyes, too.

CHAPTER SIX

W HEN MY MOTHER AND stepfather returned, we moved to his house
in town. My grandmother had tried to prepare me for the event.

"Now, when they come back, you'll be moving to town. Think of it!
You'll be near your school. The theatre will be only a few blocks up the
street. You'll be able to attend the movies every Saturday. The drug store,
grocery store, bank, post office, everything will be right there. And you
can watch the trains from your back yard. And when you're old enough,
you'll be able to ride a bicycle, all by yourself, anywhere you want. And
you'll be closer to Uncle Everett's, the library, why, everything! And, best
of all, you'll make new friends. You'll be able to play with them, and invite
them to play with you."

"Yes, but I'll miss the creek, and the old cabin," I demurred. "And who
will feed Sally and Fred, the chickens, and pigs, and Jessie's dogs, and ride
the big horses down to water? And will I ever get to go back to Uncle Jim's,
or run in the road, or ride with Uncle Everett and Earl into the Knobs?
And who will play with Pearl? And who will read to me? What will happen to you? Where will you keep my father's picture at night? And who
will sweep the porch and chop kindling and gather the eggs? Why can't I
just stay here and live with you and Pearl?"

"Ah, Tommy! This is harder on me than you. Yes, to be sure! Somehow,
it will work out. Precious little man! Don't fret your heart, dear boy. We
Edmonds have always survived. Besides, you'll be able to visit me every
weekend. Every Friday, Saturday, and Sunday, why you can come here!
And we'll read, rock on the porch, and do all those other things. And just
watch! Come Sundays, you'll be eager to rush back in town, even go to
church, play ball, and show those teachers at school just how bright and
smart you are. Now, I don't want to hear another word. No more pouting
or pitiful curling of the lips! No, sir! We Edmonds must be resolute and
unwavering. Why, as resolute as the old Captain and as calm as Quilly!
Now, run along! Time is of the essence and the bird is on the wing!"

44

She kissed my neck as I went outside to play.

The process of relocating to Abingdon was now immanent. I was asleep when my mother and Mr. Chappels arrived from their honeymoon, but the very next morning, Mr. Chappels hired a truck and several men to transport our clothes and any special furnishings my mother wanted, into town. She kept these to a minimum; however, she determined that our room at Quilly Hall should remain as intact as possible, and ready at a moment's notice for us to use on weekends.

Reluctant to leave the only quarters I had ever known as home, I soon discovered that the move into Abingdon afforded numerous advantages. Marion's house backed up to the Norfolk and Western rail line, and engines and coal cars, passenger trains and flatcars, box cars and cabooses rumbled along its tracks, night and day. A grove of cedars and a high fence, mantled in vines and honeysuckle, muffled the roar of the thundering trains that whistled along the steel rails, or that huffed heavily under the strain of a hundred coal cars trundling by. Marion helped me build a tree house, and from its "lofty heights and perilous deck," as he dubbed it, I could sit and watch the trains pass. "Clank, clank, clank," the wheels thumped along the tracks, as the cars rolled by. Where were the trains going? From whence had they come? Coal soot blackened the limbs of the cedars and sifted through the vines onto my perch. Tiny particles of grit and cinders accompanied billowing smoke.

There was an oil station one block down from our house. Trucks came and went, bearing loads of heating oil for half the town's furnaces and indoor stoves. It served as a filling station as well, and one could buy soft drinks, candy, and ice cream bars inside. And farther down the street, began the first long storage sheds for the county's tobacco harvest, which brought auctioneers and scores of buyers from miles and miles around. In the winter, especially, the mellow aroma of the tobacco barns permeated the air over the entire south end of town.

Marion's property even boasted a barn. An elderly lady across the street kept her milk cow pinned in it and raised chickens and ducks in her own backyard. When she discovered my love for chores, she "hired" me to weed her garden, water her ducks, split kindling, and shoo stray dogs away. The dimes I earned from her purchased the coveted items I so desired at the filling station. No happier child skipped along our street. Still, I missed the farm, my grandmother, Pearl, her father, Earl, and Quilly Hall. I felt bereft without its porches, swings, elms and yard, springhouse, cabin, and, above all, the portrait of the old Captain and the serene German maiden on her pedestal.

From the earliest days of his marriage to my mother, "Marion," as he encouraged me to call him, won my heart more and more each day. Large of frame, but physically fit, with a receding hair line and groomed goatee, his unaffected manner and genteel winsomeness made him a beacon of stability, amidst a family of sometimes emotional turbulence. He loved my mother, tolerated my Aunt Rachel, respected my grandmother, bonded with Uncle Everett, and devoted hours of attention to me. His death in 1952, at age fifty-seven, fell upon us with all the irony and bitter trappings of a Greek tragedy. While visiting the wards of the mental state hospital in Marion, a crazed kinsman of Olan Crawford's family stabbed him with a piece of glass. It severed his jugular vein. He bled to death before anyone could attend to his wound. Hundreds of county residents and members of both the Virginia Senate and House of Delegates stood in the snow for his burial.

He taught me how to shoot birds on the wing, how to lead them and care for the dogs. He took me hiking and camping, fishing and canoeing, and taught me how to drive a car. The hunting we did with Uncle Everett, at both his and my grandmother's farm. The camping, fishing and hiking were products of adventures around Whitetop Mountain and nearby Mt. Rogers. Its rocky ridges and alpine meadows proved no match for Marion's steady stride and muscular frame. He carried the tent and food packs, while I panted and huffed to keep up, laden with my backpack of underwear, socks, and bedding.

We had not resided long in Abingdon before my seventh birthday came around. My grandmother insisted that she bake my favorite cake—devil's food with white foamy icing—and we eat that the coming Sunday with her.

Uncle Everett attended, along with Pearl and Earl, and Uncle Jim and Aunt Viola. Uncle Jim appeared very feeble at the table and had to lie down after dinner. The couple had walked all that morning to my grandmother's and had intended to walk back. "Absolutely not!" my grandmother squelched any such idea. "Everett, will your truck make the journey? The road is harder now. They can't go back on foot! I forbid it!" she addressed her remonstrance to her brother and sister-in-law.

"I doubt it, Mama," replied Uncle Everett. "But we can take them in the wagon. Marion, why don't you and Tommy come with me?"

"Capitol! We'll both enjoy it, won't we, Tommy?"

Thus the decision was made.

We had not quite reached the ridge above the river, when Uncle Jim signaled for us to be silent. Uncle Everett slowed Sally and we sat still and listened. "Somethin' or someone's following us in the woods. Cain't you hear it?" Uncle Jim said in a low voice.

Uncle Everett brought the wagon to a halt. In the stillness of that languorous afternoon, we sat motionless on the buckboard's seats and strained our ears for the slightest noise or movement he must have heard. The hazy mist of drying leaves hung in the treetops above the narrow lane. "Shhhh! There it is again!" he whispered. The faint snap of a fallen branch caught our ears. The woods plunged into silence. Sally's tail swished from side to side and the flesh on her hindquarters quivered. Then it happened. The shadows in the underbrush on the bank above us burst with a crackling sound. Out of the silent darkness lunged a huge opaque form. It landed on the opposite bank without making the faintest sound. Sally neighed and pawed the ground. The big cat hissed and bared its teeth. It's eyes burned with yellow-green fire. It hissed a second time, turned slowly away, slipped into the bramble and vines, and disappeared.

"Damn!" Uncle Everett blurted. "He must be nine feet long!"

I looked about. Uncle Jim was smiling. "I knowed he was up here. He's been spookin' deer for weeks. Must have been waitin' for us to come back from Ginny's."

Neither Uncle Everett nor Marion said a word, but Aunt Viola's face twitched with worry. "We'd better get home, Jim," she urged. "The livestock's not pinned up and Lord only knows where the chickens are."

"Was that a panther?" I asked.

"Yes," Uncle Everett answered softly. "I'm afraid so." He raised the reins and flicked them for Sally to move forward.

"I'm seven, now," I ventured.

"I know," he intoned. "I'll keep my promise."

Two Saturdays later, he came by the house in his pickup truck with his big hounds. Marion was attending a rally in Bristol and had left earlier that morning.

"Why did you ever promise such a ridiculous thing?" my mother reproached him. "That's all this crazy boy has been blabbering about for two whole weeks!"

"Don't get so all fired up!" he rejoined. "He can't hide under your petticoat all his life. And Marion's got obligations all his own. I know what I'm doing. And I know where to go. I've been following that cat since you all moved to town. I know where its lair is. And I promised Tommy I'd take him with me, and, by jingles, I'm here to cash in on my word."

"And my word is 'No!'"

"Mama! Mama!" I cried with tears in my eyes. "Uncle Everett promised! I know how to hold on to the saddle. I ain't afraid. Please, Mama! Please!"

"Don't say 'ain't!' Besides, your stepfather wouldn't approve either. Even he's got more sense than that."

"I hate to tell you, my dearest," Uncle Everett smirked, "but Marion and I have already talked about this. He'd be pleased for Tommy to go. Don't naysay a child's excitement. You know I'll be careful."

My mother turned and stared at me. She shook her head with disapproval, yet with an acquiescence that only a mother's torn heart can grant. "Go! Go, then! But bring him back tomorrow at the latest."

By noon, Uncle Everett and I had saddled Fred and were ascending a trail that deer had made from the Knobs into the orchard. Half-chewed apples, scattered piles of dark pellets, and flattened patches of grass revealed where the deer had foraged. Their trail led up through a stretch of locusts, maples, and poplars, and finally into stands of tall hickories, oaks, and graceful hemlocks. The dogs had displayed little enthusiasm until we came to a rocky ledge that overlooked my grandmother's farm. They began to whine and sniff the base of a gnarled Virginia pine that leaned half-dead over a steep precipice on the opposite side of the ledge. From its open heights, a boulder-strewn ravine dropped off into a thicket of laurel and grove of beech trees below.

"One of its lair's is right down there," Uncle Everett pointed from the saddle. "But the dogs don't seem that interested."

Slowly, Uncle Everett guided Fred down a fresh game trail where the deer had scattered fallen leaves. Toward the bottom of the ravine, a dry creek bed's tiny gravel indicated where spring rains had once gushed as a brook. Several paths branched off, all upslope. Roy picked up a scent of some magnitude and began to weave back and forth. Dixie whined and imitated him. Suddenly, the dogs bolted off in the direction of a huge boulder. The incline was too steep for Fred, so Uncle Everett dismounted and held the reins behind his back as he walked in front of the horse. With tremendous difficulty, we finally made our way parallel with the boulder, where the dogs had stopped to sniff again. While I clung to the saddle horn, Uncle Everett inspected the big rock and its lichen-dappled surface. He looked about the woods to his left, then right, and up the steep slope. He returned and we continued a steady but slow climb to the top of the ridge. The dogs appeared uninterested and, pausing in a grassy gap, we rested Fred before proceeding farther. From knob to knob and ridge to ridge, we followed what trails and scents the dogs seemed to favor. Toward dusk we ascended a rugged stretch of slippery shale and on the leeward side of the descent made camp under a stand of hemlock near a spring. Uncle Everett tied Fred to a nearby limb where the horse could feed on grass blades that poked up between humps of outcroppings. Uncle Everett had said very little all day, and I could sense that he was concealing his disappointment from me.

"No luck, yet!" he smiled, as he spread out a tarp and some blankets for us. He reached in one of the pockets of the saddlebag and handed me a bacon biscuit and fed several to the dogs. "Yes, sir, I thought we'd a treed him by now. But we're near a second lair of his. It's about a half-mile from here. He'll come out tonight to hunt. Might already be around us. So we need to sleep light. If you hear anything in the dark, anything at all, the slightest sound, nudge me. The dogs'll hear it first. Or smell him first. But sometimes even they can fall asleep." He placed his rifle beside his blanket. "I'm going to build a small fire, because it's going to get cold. But, you'll stay warm."

I helped him gather a pile of hemlock boughs, leaves, and dry wood and light the fire. It felt reassuring to hunch beside the bright blaze and rub the big dogs' ears. Gradually, I grew sleepy and curled up close to my uncle's side and stared at the low orange flames. A huge part of me was too terrified to look, even into the woods. Yet, a deeper sphere felt perfectly at home, knowing that nothing bad could ever happen to me, so long as Uncle Everett was alive. That he might get hurt or killed lay beyond my capacity to imagine.

Darkness settled ever so stealthily about us. A pale moon climbed rusty yellow over the Knobs, then disappeared behind clouds. Tree frogs squeaked their nightly vespers with throbbing annoyance; then grew silent. A whippoorwill repeated its cry over and over. I felt warm, snug, excited, but exhausted, and drifted into sleep.

Sometime around midnight or 1:00 a.m., I awakened with a startle. Uncle Everett lay asleep. Roy was licking my face and whining softly. Fred was snorting quietly, shifting his weight from leg to leg, and pawing the ground. I could hear him pulling on the rope where Uncle Everett had tied him to the limb. All else was deathly still. Roy continued to whine, ever so imperceptively. Only a few low flames flickered amid the red embers.

"Uncle Everett! Uncle Everett," I shook him with trembling fingers. "Uncle Everett! Please, wake up!" My throat felt dry, my lips stuck to my mouth. No words were coming out.

Roy rose in a crouched position and burst into wild yelps. A pair of horrendous eyes glowed against the blackness of night. Suddenly, Uncle Everett sat up, swung his body about, and fumbled for his rifle. The snarling cat was almost in his face. He fired his rifle point-blank into the cat's chest. The animal leaped straight up, emitted a muffled cough, and fell silently beside the coals. Both dogs began to rave and claw at the cat. But it was over. It was all over, and when I stood up, I realized my pants were wet, and I was shaking with shock. Uncle Everett produced a flashlight from his saddlebag and shined it on the big cat. The dying animal looked enormous in the fire's glow. Uncle Everett had to pull the dogs off and chain them for the remainder of the night. Blood dripped from the cat's mouth and nose. Uncle Everett dragged it out of sight while my eyes followed his every move. Finally, I rolled up in the tarp again and sank into a deep and marvelous sleep.

The following noon, when we returned to the meadow above the orchard, Jessie, his brother, Albert, and scores of farm people had gathered in the road, awaiting our return. Someone had heard the gun's report in the night and was confident that "Mr. Edmonds had kilt that cat." Marion and my mother were rocking on the front porch when we came out onto the road. We were dragging the big cat behind us, to the happy howling of the tail-wagging dogs. My grandmother came across the road to hug me, as Uncle Everett helped me down. Marion came behind her and carried me into the house. "Whew, Master Thomas!" he teased, as he got a whiff of my pants. "I won't tell anybody, if you don't."

"No, sir!" I beamed, as I clasped his neck.

"What a boy!" he laughed as he mounted the steps and carried me into the hall, passed the stern, silent Captain's gaze and the serene, Fraulein Quelle.

Jessie skinned and nailed the panther's hide to the front of the tobacco barn. The cat measured eight feet in length, from the tip of its nose to the end of its tail. It weighed one-hundred and twenty pounds, dead. Passers-by stopped to gawk at it for the entire next year, until its skin rotted and all the fur sloughed off. What the chickens didn't eat, a fox or some other scavenger finished. Such was the fate of little Ouida's killer. "Just a cryin' shame," Earl would say from time to time.

While visiting my grandmother one weekend not long after that, an elderly widower by the name of Ambrose Stone stopped by the house for coffee. It was early Saturday morning, and Pearl's body had begun to show definite signs of her pregnancy. Mr. Stone noticed but refrained from any direct comments. He wore a clean pair of overalls, a gray flannel shirt, a black, coffee-stained woolen jacket, white socks and brogans. Long hair flowed down the back of his neck and his cropped beard bore the tell-tales signs of tobacco juice. We were seated in the kitchen. It was obvious that my grandmother was hoping that he wouldn't stay long. But, there he was, and her sense of being the grand dame of the Edmonds clan and principal keeper of her father's legacy forbade her from acting in any way other than patient and gracious.

"Ambrose, it's always good to see you. What brings you our way this morning?" she asked the wan, wrinkled figure.

"Ginny," he addressed her. "I cain't sleep well no more. Don't seem rightly fitting just to stare at the walls. Since Eula's death, life's been awfully lonely. I need a new woman," he uttered, as his eyes followed Pearl about the kitchen. "Some'n young with lots of vim, vigor, and vitality left in 'em. An' pretty, too. Like Pearl here." He smiled, as he wiped a driblet of coffee off his beard. His fingers were long and sallow, blue with bruises and brown with age spots. "Pearl, would ya mind thinkin' about it? I'd give ya a good home, and that baby of yo'rns a-comin' would have a place to grow up, all his own."

My grandmother's forearms shivered with goosebumps. Suddenly, she eyed him with a devilish hauteur and twitch of her thin eyebrows. "My, my! Ambrose! How romantic for a Civil War Veteran. You old dog! Why not ask me?"

"Ginny, I ain't no veteran. You know that. I ain't that old, neither," he objected. "I was born in 'sixty-four, not 'thirty-four, like your pa and mine. Sides, you're too refined and educated for me. I ain't nothin' but a mountaineer. What could I offer you? But Pearl, here, I kin offer her a home and food for herself and baby. What's wrong with that?"

"Well, Ambrose, you might succumb before the baby's born. And what would that leave Pearl? What if your own children resented her presence, or denied her inheriting the house?"

"Ginny, they're long gone and left here years ago. They don't even write me no more, or come to see me. I need a wife, Ginny, a woman to cook and care for me."

"Ah! The truth comes out. 'To cook and care' for you! Get one of Albert's sisters to do that. He's got three spinster old maid sisters who'd leap at the opportunity to be your bride. To marry a man of your substance! Especially, Elsie." She smiled at the sound of Elsie's name and folded her hands across her lap with a coy hint of conquest.

"Well, I wanna hear it from Pearl first. Pearl, I'm awaitin'."

Pearl had been mixing flour and milk for fresh biscuits and had been listening attentively as well. Her hair flopped against her back in a long, single, black braid. White flour streaked her apron. Her hairy legs had not been shaven, and the small wart on her right cheek glistened with a smear of lard from her fingers. "Mr. Stone, I'm much obliged and honored," she said, with a tear in her eye. "But I ain't ready to make no decisions like that right yet. I believe Mama Edmonds' idea about Elsie is the place to start. She don't like livin' with Uncle Albert and his people, nohow. And she can cook."

"Well, I kin still raise a garden and turn a plow," Mr. Stone averred. "I reckon, Ginny, you've done me a favor. Yes, ma'am, I thank you and am likewise obliged."

Both women breathed a sigh of relief when the old man left.

"Lord! Miz. Edmonds! I cain't thank you enough!" Pearl wiped her hands in her apron. Then she cut out the biscuits and placed them on a pan. "You always know the right words to say."

My grandmother beamed with confidence, thrilled with the compliment and no doubt in agreement with its veracity.

In less than two weeks, Ambrose had proposed to Elsie.

"Miz. Edmonds, do you mind if we have the weddin' in your front yard? The view from the fence there down to the springhouse is plumb beautiful," Mr. Stone reckoned.

"Of course, Ambrose. I'll provide the cider and some ham. The rest is up to you and Elsie."

"Yes, ma'am."

They wed on a Saturday afternoon in late October. Albert and Jessie played for the wedding. Jessie's fiddle entertained every one with a lively repertoire of mountain music. Albert accompanied him on a banjo, while Earl thumped a taut cord, strung to a tobacco stick, nailed to an upside down washtub.

A country preacher, with gray hair in a long black coat, officiated. "If there be any reason," he intoned, dragging out his words, "why Ambrose and Elsie ought not be married, then let him speak up right now, or forever hold his peace!" He glanced about the crowd of tenants and other guests, as if he actually expected some one to object. "Well, the Lord be honored. Ambrose, you ain't no spring chicken no more, so you take care of Elsie, and don't you lay no lash to her. She's doin' you a favor. And Elsie, you be proud of Ambrose and don't you go foolin' around with other men. You done had plenty of chances to do that earlier."

A general laughter rose from those gathered around. After they exchanged vows, the preacher announced: "I proclaim you man and wife. May the Lord bless you and keep you, and make his face to shine upon you. And may you give him thanks for that, everyday. Amen!"

The three brothers provided music, while their relatives danced. Mr. Stone slapped his thighs and surprised everybody by performing a fast-moving, foot-tapping jig. Soon, the jugs of cider and plates of ham were depleted and the crowd moved on. We could hear their merriment long into the night, along with blasts from a shotgun.

Uncle Everett, my mother, and Marion had attended the wedding, in addition to Grandmother, Pearl, and me. Sadness had enveloped Pearl when the wedding party first left the yard, but her demeanor perked up afterwards.

"Pearl, I don't mean to offend you, but who got you pregnant?" asked Uncle Everett. "If you love him and he respects you, we need to find him and bring him back."

"Please don't do that! He's married, Mr. Everett, and done run off on his own wife. It was trifling of me to do what I done. I just got to bear it the best way I can."

"Well, you can still come and live out at my place, if Mama mistreats you, or you become frightened here."

"Why say a thing like that?" my grandmother challenged him. "Of course, I'll not mistreat her. And I need her more than you. I could not forbear her loss, or live here alone. Not any more."

"Mama, we understand that," said my mother. "Nobody's abandoning you. Nor ever will."

"Of course not," added Marion. "You're like a mother to me, Mrs. Edmonds, 'Virginia,' if I may call you that? You're welcome to live in town with us, if you feel lonely here."

"Oh! I could never leave Quilly Hall! Holman would never forgive me, nor could I forgive myself. This is the family's inheritance, the family's estate. Not just mine. I could never leave it. I could never bear to think of it empty, or without someone to remember its history and care for its rooms!"

CHAPTER SEVEN

J UST PRIOR TO HALLOWEEN, my grandmother and Pearl rode into town
with Uncle Everett. I had just returned from school, when they drove
up in his truck. Grandmother preferred to ride in his car, but there the
three of them were, crowded into his pickup. Grandmother owned a 1939
Ford Coupe, but she rarely drove it. She housed it in a shed near the old
slave quarters. Their unexpected arrival, however, signaled something
amiss, if not worse.

As Uncle Everett assisted, first, Pearl and then my grandmother out
of the truck, my mother came out into the yard. "Well! What a welcome
sight. Come on in! I'll make some tea."

"Please, do!" my grandmother urged. "I'm feeling a little peaked and
could use the stimulant."

While the four of us sat in the living room, my mother prepared
the tea.

"Shaula! We're not really here for a social call," Uncle Everett spoke
up.

"That's right," sighed my grandmother. "We're worried about Jim and
Viola. I haven't seen them in over a month. Nor has anyone on the farm."

"Is that that unusual?" my mother queried.

"It is for this time of year. Jim's not been well at all, and Viola's no
specimen of health, herself."

"If I can talk them into it," Uncle Everett began, "I want to try to
move them to Mama's farm. There's still a nice tenant house vacant, down
the creek, toward town. If Marion's going to be around next weekend, I
could use his help to move them, provided they'll agree to relocate."

"Yes. I'm certain he'll be here," my mother stated, as she brought in
the tray of tea and sat it on an end table near my grandmother.

"Everett's going over tomorrow to check on them, and we'll let you
know." My grandmother placed two cubes of sugar into her cup and stirred
them slowly until they dissolved. "I miss all of you, you know," she con-

tinued. "The farm's not the same without you," she directed her statement toward my mother. "And Tommy, honey! How I miss you!" She sat her cup and saucer down and dabbed her eyes with a white handkerchief, which she had slipped from her purse. "Come here and give Grandmother a hug."

I scooted out of the chair and put my arms around her neck. She kissed me on my cheek. I could feel a hot tear as it ran down my neck under my shirt.

"Shaula, you've got to let this boy stay with me come the holidays. Come Thanksgiving and Christmas." She dried her eyes. "The house gets so lonely without you. The rooms so empty and cold."

"I know, Mama. After all, it's the only home Tommy knew until now, and mine as well."

"Mama, stop dwelling on the past," said Uncle Everett. He rose to his feet, clattering his cup and saucer as he set them in the tray. He glanced intently at my mother and kissed her cheek. "We gotta go," he muttered. "I've got work to do at my own place. Come on, Mama. Time to go. Tell Marion I'll call him as soon as I know anything."

He held my grandmother's arm as she struggled to her feet.

"Pearl, you've been awfully quiet," my mother said.

"Yes, ma'am. Just been thinkin'," she smiled. "Life's kind of hard for all of us, right now. Ain't it?"

"A philosopher in our own midst!" Uncle Everett avowed. "Resolute! 'Resolute's' the word," he announced. "Isn't that what you always say, Mama? 'Resolute!'"

She stared at him in silence and stuffed her handkerchief into her purse. They passed through the living room and foyer and walked to the truck.

"Everett, be sweet to Mama," my mother whispered under her breath.

"I know," he said, with a lost look in his own face. "OK, everybody!" he raised his voice with a smile. "Back to Quilly Hall! All aboard for the Knobs! Nonstop, all the way!" He opened his door, and then suddenly swooped me up in his arms. He gave me a tight hug, set me down, returned to his truck, and slammed its door. Off they drove.

I think Uncle Everett must have been as shocked as my grandmother upon learning that Uncle Jim and Aunt Viola were ready to move. Earl had ridden with him in the wagon to convince them to relocate. According to Uncle Everett, it was Earl's presence and humble spirit that won them.

"Ain't no use in fightin' nature," he told them. "Look at me! I ain't able to live remote, and the Lord knows Miz. Edmonds 'a' been like a sister to me. And you're even kin."

"That's right," Uncle Jim purportedly said. "How I hate to leave here!" he glanced toward the river and the Knobs. "'Twas the best tobacco patch I ever had." He looked up toward the cemetery. "Cain't neglect that!" he moaned. "My whole life was lived right here."

"Nobody's going to neglect their graves," Uncle Everett promised. "We can still come back and raise tobacco, cure it in the barn, and haul it to market. But this house is no place to live anymore, and you're too old to die here from a stroke or something worse and put that burden on Aunt Viola. I'll always come back to check on it."

Earl later told my grandmother how much it hurt him to look back over their farm by the river, as "me and Mr. Everett crossed the ridge. Your brother Jim and Viola had taken to their rockers and was sittin' there in the cold, holdin' hands. Miz. Ginny, it reminded me of Pearl's own mother's death, and how poor we are, though I ain't complain."

Relocating the couple required everyone's help. Jessie, Albert, and Earl each brought a wagon up from the farm. Uncle Everett managed to drive one of his own trucks to the site. It had a flatbed and was used for transporting hay, grain, bailing wire, and heavy farm equipment from locations in town to wherever it was needed at his place or Grandmother's. Many of the women pitched in; my mother and Pearl prepared large baskets of food for everyone. I rode on the truck with Uncle Everett, along with my mother and Marion. Going up, I was able to ride on the flatbed. Coming back, I walked behind Uncle Jim's cow for a while, before clambering up onto the truck again. That Sunday, Uncle Everett and I rode back to retrieve their pigs and chickens. How they squealed and cackled in their respective pins or coops! Earl drove the family buckboard, pulled by Sally. Pearl rode with him and oversaw the packing of Aunt Viola's pantry goods and crocks from the springhouse. Hams and moldering slabs of bacon had been brought down the day before. The old couple couldn't afford to leave anything that necessity would demand of them later. Uncle Jim was too proud to ask for a handout. He remained silent throughout most of the move, as did Aunt Viola.

Grandmother sighed with grateful relief when it was over. Her brother and sister-in-law were now her neighbors, and only a path's stroll away, at that. My mother felt better, too, along with Uncle Everett and

Marion. "At least she'll have them at her elbow," my mother observed. "Thank God for that."

"Now you'll have to take care of all three of them," Marion teased Uncle Everett.

"True, but they're a hell of a lot closer to each other. Maybe we can rest at night now. Plus, they'll have Pearl to look after them, too. Poor girl! Once the war's over, maybe she'll meet somebody decent and that baby of hers will have a father." Suddenly, he grew quiet and glanced down at me.

I instinctively knew what he was thinking. But it was all right. I strained to conjure up an image of my father, but none materialized, other than the photo on my grandmother's mantle. One memory did resurface from time to time. A tall man was holding my hand and we were walking in a park, or at a fair. His grip felt strong. My mother flanked us; a breeze buffeted her hair. She was carrying a sticky cone of pink cotton candy.

"Tommy!" My mother placed her arm about my waist. "Tomorrow's a school day. Time to review your homework before you go to bed."

"Well, time for me to go," said Uncle Everett. We had been sitting in the kitchen. He rose slowly and walked toward the front door and out into the night.

"He needs to remarry," Marion commented. "How long's it been now?"

"Too long," my mother replied. There was a wistful hesitance in her voice, a melancholic glint in her eye. "Far too long."

Just prior to Thanksgiving, Aunt Rachel showed up, uninvited, at the door. Her gay mood and sobriety, however, offset any ill will her unexpected arrival might have caused. Plus, she was my aunt and my mother's sole sister.

"Lord, come on in," my mother greeted her. "We'll all be going to Mama Edmonds' tomorrow, but you're welcome to stay and help."

"What's up?" she asked, as she removed her broad-brimmed white hat, complete with a brown pheasant feather in its band. Her stylish white silk dress tweaked when she sat on the sofa to rest.

"Hog killing time! Remember?"

"Heavens, yes. I know I should have written."

"I'll welcome the help."

"Oh, gads! Cutting up all that hog fat, grinding it into sausage, and rendering out lard! What a grizzly thought!"

"I've got an old dress and scarf you can wear. Or you can stay here in town and flirt with the cab drivers."

"No, no! You know what will happen if I do. I'll tag along and sweat it out."

Hog killing time always coincided with Thanksgiving. By then the weather had turned sufficiently cold enough to kill the hogs and butcher them in the lot beside the slave cabin. Fingers would turn blue and numb, in spite of the long hours and heat from the fires.

Earl kindled one in the cabin's hearth and swung a large kettle over its flames for rendering the fat into lard. Another fire was built outside under a huge cast iron vat. It was shaped like a bathtub. The hogs were dipped immediately into it after being shot. Uncle Everett and Jessie took turns killing them with a .22 rifle. They'd hold the gun to the hog's head and shoot it between the eyes. The stunned animal would squeal and collapse on the frozen ground. Jessie and Albert would hoist it on a pulley and lower it into the vat, then swing it out to scrape off the hair. Hog after hog was butchered in this manner. Earl, Pearl, and several women disemboweled each animal and lifted out the heart, kidneys, and liver for puddings and whatever else. Uncle Jim oversaw the cutting up of the limbs into big white and pink segments for hams, picnic shoulders, loins, bacon, and sausage. Uncle Everett had learned from his father how to salt down the meat and pack it into large wooden casts for storage. Later it would be scraped again and hung in the smokehouse. At least, twenty-two animals were slaughtered that day, to my count. Long into the night and all of the next day saw the continuation of this process. Each tenant family was given a share of the meat for preparing it themselves into bacon, side-meat, hams, and sausage. But the rendering out of the fat into lard remained a communal effort, with its division into tins of lard coming several days later.

We did not celebrate Thanksgiving until the "operation" had concluded. That Sunday afternoon, Grandmother served oven-baked pepper-smeared ham, turkey, sweet potatoes, green beans, canned corn, pickled watermelon rind, relishes of all sorts, canned tomatoes, mashed potatoes, gravy, and biscuits with jelly.

Uncle Jim and Aunt Viola, along with Earl and Pearl, joined us at the table.

"What a blessing to have all of us together!" my grandmother chirped. "The hand of Providence has blessed us once again."

"Please, Mama! No theology! No dogma. Don't spoil such a wonderful day," Uncle Everett interrupted her.

"The Lord giveth and the Lord taketh away," Uncle Jim added, in what was now his squeaky, reed-thin voice. "Who's to say what's providential and what's ain't. I miss the farm."

"That's enough!" Aunt Viola threatened, raising her fork. "Stop sniveling. You sound like an old man. Be grateful and count your blessings."

"Amen!" Marion concurred. He lifted his water glass and held it in the manner of a toast. "To my new family! Its members and Quilly Hall!"

"Amen!" Uncle Everett repeated, clinking his glass against Marion's.

I raised mine with both hands to join in.

"Ah, Mister Biggety!" my grandmother chortled. "To our brilliant scholar in school."

School? That was the last thing on my mind.

Marion smiled and sat forward to touch his glass against mine. A water crystal gleamed on his goatee. He winked, as our eyes met. We had already formed an avuncular bond that transcended words.

CHAPTER EIGHT

THE FIRST WEEKEND OF December that year, I stayed at Uncle Everett's. The ewes were lambing, and sometimes a ewe would die, and its lamb had to be bottle-fed if the little creature were to survive. Uncle Everett had a cabinet full of old Pepsi Cola bottles for this purpose. He, or one of his farmhands (usually one of their wives), would fill a bottle with warm milk, slip a huge rubber nipple over its lip, and feed the lamb. I loved holding the big bottles and feeling a lamb's tug, as it slurped away. Streams of milk would drizzle out, as the lamb pulled hard on the bottle. Its little tail would wag with frenzy. That weekend, I fed four lambs each morning and again before dusk.

That Saturday night, Miles, my uncle's foreman, came to the backdoor. Tall and lanky, of angular and weathered features, he cradled a shotgun in the crook of his left arm. He was bundled in a warm, but tattered coat. The night air felt frigid, and a cold draft entered the kitchen when I opened the door.

"Mr. Everett, bad news. Real bad!"

"What is it, Miles?"

"Dogs! Them dogs from town's been runnin' sheep again. They've done killed five ewes. I found their bodies just before dark. I got a shot at one of the dogs, but it crawled off in the brush."

Uncle Everett drew in a long breath; the muscles in his face twitched at the news. "I'll get my gun, and the boy and I will come with you. Step on in, Miles, till were ready."

Miles removed his cap and entered. His baldhead was almost white in contrast to his tanned face. He waited by the door. I hurried to the hallway and pulled on my coat, cap, and gloves. Uncle Everett donned his hat—a felt Stetson—and coat, and picked up a .22-rifle that leaned against a wall. He kept most of his guns in his gun rack, but always had two or three propped up in the hall.

The night stung us with bitter cold. I pressed my cap down over my ears and ran to keep up with the two men. We skirted the barn, crossed a creek, and struck off toward the high pastureland in the direction of the Laurel Springs. The night burned bright with stars. Frost twinkled on the grass. Miles walked steadily with long, measured strides, as we climbed from hill to hill. Sheep bleated in the darkness, as their ghostly shapes loomed and waned in the night.

After a long climb, Miles began to slow his pace. He shined a flashlight on the ground. Just ahead, dark patches of blood stained a flat outcropping. Others trailed away, off into the brush. He flashed his light in their direction. Suddenly, a pair of eyes glowed in the reflection. A dog's faint whine caught my attention. Uncle Everett approached the wounded animal and waited for Miles to join him. He motioned for me to come to his side. A beautiful salt-and-pepper freckled bird dog lay bleeding in the grass. It lifted its muzzle and whined a second time. Clots of blood had formed around an oozing wound in its side. It lay its jaw back down in the grass, struggled to crawl toward us, and, with big imploring eyes, whined again.

"Here, Miles, exchange guns with me," said Uncle Everett, with heaviness in his voice. He handed his foreman the .22. Uncle Everett stepped back and pressed my face against his hip. He turned his body slightly to shield me from the scene. Miles raised the gun to his shoulder, aimed, and fired. The echo of the report reverberated up the hill, then died with a hollow silence in the starry night. No one said anything as we trudged our way back in the cold, from hill to hill, and field to field, with the frost twinkling in the night's refulgence. Finally Uncle Everett broke his silence. "Sometimes a man has to do things, Tommy, he hates to do. You understand, don't you?"

"Yes, sir," I replied, as we descended the last hill, recrossed the creek, and headed for home.

Christmas was spent with Grandmother at Quilly Hall. Marion had wanted our first Christmas as a new family to be celebrated in town in front of the fireplace, in our own living room. But my mother and he knew better.

"Maybe next year, here," my mother explained, as she bundled me for the ride to the farm. "Santa has left your surprises at Mama Edmonds' house. You'll see when we get there."

Sure enough, there in the hallway, under the boughs of a prickly, tinseled, and lighted cedar tree, lay a stack of brightly wrapped gifts for all of us: my mother, grandmother, Marion, Uncle Everett, Pearl, Earl, and me. I rushed to the base of the tree, almost tipping Quelle off her pedestal. "Oh, my gracious!" my grandmother held her breath. "Careful, careful. Oh, dear God. There's plenty of time."

The one gift that caught my eye more so than any other was a Red Ryder BB gun. "Oh, boy!" I shouted. Packs of bee bees in little red tubes lay wrapped about the tree.

More gifts remained to be opened in the living room. To my surprise, there sat Earl and Aunt Rachel. Her face appeared tired and sallow, her gaze unfocused and hair disheveled. "Give me a kiss," she ordered with slurred speech, as I burst into the room.

"Oh, Rachel!" was all my mother said.

Marion had special ordered a pair of gold earrings for my mother and a huge green lampshade with long silver tassels for my grandmother's favorite lamp, upstairs. He presented Earl with a Hamilton watch, and several bolts of cloth to Pearl. And for all the women, a new sewing machine—each. My grandmother's face expressed only minimal elation. Her mind was somewhere else, preoccupied no doubt with Aunt Rachel's presence.

Toward noon, Uncle Everett, Uncle Jim, and Aunt Viola arrived in his truck. The Christmas meal consisted of ham, corn pudding, pole beans, biscuits, and red gravy. For dessert, my grandmother served slices of spice cake and cups of egg custard, the latter smothered with whipped cream, flavored with brandy.

A joyless silence seemed to engulf us. Very few words were exchanged. Aunt Rachel wanted more whipped cream. "Just bring the damn brandy!" she ordered Pearl.

"Please, Rachel!" Uncle Everett confronted her. "Who invited you, anyway?"

"Everett!" my mother recoiled in protest. "No one's perfect!"

"It's not perfection, Shaula! It's called *decency*. And a little peace this time of year."

"Well, it could start with you," Aunt Rachel retorted, as she belched, leaned forward over her plate, and threw up.

"Oh!" my grandmother placed her hands over her face. "Get a wash cloth! Shaula, get her away. Just get her away."

"Yes, Mama. Come on, Rachel, let's go upstairs to your room."

Later, my mother went outside and wept.

We spent the night with my grandmother. After everyone else had gone home, and we had retired for the evening, I awoke to the sound of breaking glass. No one was in the bedroom, neither Marion, nor my mother. I raised myself on my elbows in the cot where I was sleeping and peered around. Someone was swearing. The angry slurred words seemed to be coming right out of the walls. I hopped out of bed and crept into the hallway. "God, dammit!" the chilling words rose up the stairs. I stole quietly down the steps. There in the hallway, beside Quelle, staggered Aunt Rachel. Her face was distorted; a strap of her nightgown had slipped off her right shoulder. She teetered on unsteady feet. In front of her, in his pajamas, stood Marion, with his right hand extended. My mother and grandmother crowded beside him. Aunt Rachel clutched a pistol in her right hand. "You son-of-a bitch!" she swore. "You damned, sons-of-bitches, all of you." Tears streamed down her swollen face. "You don't know what it is. Not a damned one of you." She aimed the pistol at Marion. Just then, she noticed me. "Tommy! My God, boy! Look at me! It's your poor Aunt Rachel. Ain't I a sight, honey?" She faltered momentarily, caught herself, and pointed the gun again at Marion. "Oh, no!" she half-sang. "No one's gonna tell Aunt Rachel what to do."

"Please," said Marion, as he held out his hand. "The gun. Just hand me the gun. And we can talk about all this tomorrow."

I had come down the remaining steps and was staring up at her. She glanced down at me, then at Marion. A far away look stole across her eyes. Watery eyeslashes veiled her face in a stuporous haze. "Tommy, is that you?"

"Yes, Aunt Rachel."

"I'll be damned," she said. She turned back toward Marion and handed him the pistol.

In the morning, Ralph came for her, and drove her and my mother to the sanitorium in Marion. I spent another two days on the farm, before Marion picked me up and we drove back into Abingdon.

New Years came and passed without celebration. On cold evenings, after I had completed my homework, Marion would read me stories from books in his library, or let me select one that had caught my fancy, then adlib its main contents.

One book in particular that fascinated me was a collection of glossy-colored paintings of Western Indians. "Those are the works of George Catlin," Marion explained. "They capture the Indian's very soul, his heart and culture. His Indians still leap to life in his paintings, don't they?"

Yes, indeed! And they appealed to something latent and equally primitive in me. From the ochre, burnt umber and orange faces, to the tan buckskin, buffalo robes, teepees, and flowing black hair, the call to adventure sounded in my breast. The dancers of the Mandan villages, the warriors in their hideous paint, the green plains swept black with stampeding buffalo, and Indians yelping in pursuit on their ponies, fired my imagination with unbounded ecstasy.

"Are there any Indians still here?"

"Yes. A few. But they live in the Smokies and along the Tennessee around Knoxville. They lived in cabins, like some of ours, but never in teepees or sod houses, like the Sioux and the Mandan."

"Grandmother sometimes mentions them, and so does Uncle Everett."

"Yes. The Cherokee once hunted this area, along with the Shawnee, but after the French and Indian War, the Revolution, and Andrew Jackson became president, they were forced to go West. Before that, however, settlers along the Holston and the New River often fell victim to their attacks. Shawnee from north of the Ohio and raiding parties of Cherokee would cross the mountains and kill or scalp as many people as they could. They captured and tortured families as late as the 1770s. Huge tracts of wilderness still existed when your great-great grandfather and others moved here in the 1790s. We are heirs of all that, Tommy, though I feel sorry for the Indians. It was a different world, and the White man was determined to leave his mark on the land. To seize and claim it for himself, and to turn it into his own empire. I'm afraid both our own ancestors are culpable to the hilt."

"*'Culpable?'* Does that mean good or bad?" I asked.

"I guess neither. Things change, Tommy. Sometimes 'good' and 'bad' don't apply anymore. Like your daddy's death, or your mama's love for you, or your Aunt Rachel's alcoholism! Or Pearl's pregnancy, or your Uncle Jim and Aunt Viola's having to leave their farm! Maybe 'sad' is a better word. Or like these Indians in Catlin's paintings," he thumped one of the pages with his thumb. "Times change; events occur that no one planned. Your grandmother calls that 'Providence,' the work of the hand of God, but it's life, Master Thomas. It's the way we are. Saying it's 'good' or 'bad' doesn't really solve anything, does it?"

"I guess not," I said, as I closed the book and prepared for bed.

One evening, I found him in the library, or "the study," as he preferred to call it, reading a thick, heavy tome with a brown cover and yellowed pages. Lint had collected in its folds and on the edges of its pages. "Tocqueville," he exclaimed, as he lowered the book. "Alexis de Tocqueville's *History of Democracy*. One of the greatest books every written. In time, Tommy, you must read it."

"Does it have pictures?"

"No. Can't say that it does. At least, not in this edition. But its words form pictures. They let us imagine what America was like a hundred years ago. Especially in the South. He was a Frenchman of nobility at a time when France was still not a democracy: a country where the people elect their representatives and make their own laws. And he journeyed South. He saw what slavery did to people. How it made landed slave owners lazy and indolent, even immoral and callous to poor people's misery. Yet, he hailed America's attempt to be just and fair. He tended to credit the North and its Puritan founders with zeal, while describing us in the South as 'coarse' and 'rough,' a land teeming with rogues and independent spirits from Europe. But we weren't, Tommy. Our great-grandfathers did own slaves. Take that cabin next to your grandmother's house, for example— that was just one of several slave quarters. But I can't believe your great-grandfather was ever callous or indifferent. It was just the way it was. The South didn't know how to get out of it. Its wealth was tied up in it.

"Then slavery passed away after the Civil War. And the farms almost went under. Thousands of soldiers returned to lands they no longer owned, or could afford. They became beholden to men like my grandfather and yours. And so they became tenant farmers. Like Jessie and Albert and Earl, or like old man Stone, and so many, many others. They had to work for richer men, and live in old cabins and shacks that should have been razed years ago. And we're still mired in that system. And it's not the best, but it's all we have. Does that make any sense, Tommy? Does that explain anything at all?"

Certainly, I was not precocious enough to grasp the full impact of what had been an earnest, social monologue. But I could visualize Pearl in the kitchen, her father coming in to the table and eating with us, and how Jessie, Albert, Ambrose, Miles, and all the others depended on the farms, the tobacco crops, the hogs and smokehouses; the firewood, flour and ground corn, cows and the springhouses; the orchards and berries, and even the wool production for their livelihood and ours. That we were somehow connected to each other and dependent on one another had become thoroughly engrained. And that somehow their "ain'ts" and "cain'ts," "yes, ma'ams" and "no, ma'ams," "Miz. Edmondses" and "Miz. Ginnys," and "Mr. Everetts" and "Miz. Shaulas" had nothing to do with their intelligence or goodness. That Earl called me "Son" transcended all that. It was our way of life. We needed them, and they needed us. And they never complained, though they suffered more than we did and buried their loved ones in weed-filled graveyards beside country churches, or on nearby hills their families had once owned.

I don't know how I replied. I think Marion understood. He wanted me to know the truth about life, to see it as it is, and not just as my grandmother remembered it, or tended to romanticize it, elevating our family and its past beyond its true role in the founding of our town and its later development. To that extent, he was like Uncle Everett, though more articulate and urbane. Not that Uncle Everett was uncouth, or demonstrated less perspicuity when life hurled its worst his way. He met it head on. It was just that Marion had developed the art of deflection in a less confrontational manner.

CHAPTER NINE

Toward the end of January, dark clouds crept across the Allegany's and hunkered low and silent over the region. A caliginous gloom settled over Abingdon and its farms and swallowed the day-to-day noises of commerce and farm life in its grip. It began to snow, heavy and wet at first, falling from the sky in an ambience of swirling wonder.

"Quick! We've got to get to Mama Edmonds," my mother urged Marion, "before the roads are closed."

"Why?" he asked. "If we do, we'll never get back to town. Why the rush?"

"It's Pearl's time. Her baby's due, if not today, tomorrow. Mama Edmonds will need help. One of us has to be there. You can take me and leave me, and come back later."

"But she can call us. They have a phone."

"I just tried to reach them. The line's dead. The wires must be down."

We packed the car with a few items my mother would need and backed out of the garage. Snow had already accumulated in the road and was falling in a fast whirling cadence. Flake after flake, downy white crystal upon downy white crystal, down, down, they fell. The tumbling marvel fell faster and faster, faster than the windshield wipers could sweep it aside.

Half way there, Marion slowed the car to a stop, put it in neutral, and pulled up the brake. He opened the door and struggled out into the swirling blizzard and began brushing the snow off the windshield with his gloved hands. Time after time, he repeated this action, until we crossed the bridge by the springhouse and commenced up the hill. The tires spun, slipped, caught gravel, and, with a whining-rubber-smelling odor, pulled the car through the drifting snow, before it stalled in the drive. The front lawn lay under a mantle of wintry cover. Darkness hovered everywhere. Overhead, the wind creaked the snow-heavy limbs of the elms and oaks.

We tromped through the snow to the front porch, where Grandmother and Earl awaited us. "Dear, dear get in!" my grandmother exclaimed. "Hang up your coats! Come to the fire and get warm."

"Where's Pearl?" my mother queried.

"In the kitchen, boilin' water," Earl answered. "She's swollen like a cow, ready to bust with a calf. Tearin' up good sheets. Jessie's wife, Leena's, with her."

"She needs to lie down, I keep telling her," said Grandmother, "but the poor thing's too excited to know better."

"Tommy, you stay with Marion, in the living room. I'll go back with Mama Edmonds to help Pearl."

"Fine!" Marion replied, as he helped me with my coat and hung his, as well as mine, on the hall portmanteau.

I glanced up at the Captain. He seemed as self-assured as ever, with a look of resolve and contentment playing about the corners of his mouth. How did he do that? He always seemed to know exactly how to respond, how to look down from that portrait encased in its massive frame, with just the right smile, scowl, aloofness, or disdain. With his hand on that sword! And those eyes, under his bushy brow! Quilly also appeared composed, along with her pigeons. Could any crisis ruffle her eternal calm?

As Marion and I took rockers in front of the fireplace, we could hear the excitement that erupted in the kitchen. "You must get to bed!" Grandmother argued with Pearl. "There'll be no doctor coming. The lines are down. We're going to have to deliver your baby by ourselves."

"Pearl, honey," Jessie's wife intoned, "you're gonna be fine. I had my own at home. So did your mama, and Albert's wife, and ever'one else. You need to lie down and preserve your strength until you're ready."

"I had Hamilton and Everett in this same house," added my grandmother. "In my own bed, with Viola assisting. If it weren't such bad weather, we'd fetch her for you now. You'll be all right."

We could hear them helping her up the stairs. The sound of their heels clacked in the narrow stairwell. A shuffling noise accompanied their assisting Pearl into her room. Someone came clattering back down, then ran back up. "That's your mother," Marion smiled.

Marion and I rocked thoughtfully for a long time. Outside, snow continued to fall. I wandered over to a window and peered out. "Can we build a snowman?"

"What a capital idea! Yes! By George! Let's build one!"

We were midway through our frolic, when Earl waved for us to come in.

"It ain't lookin' good," he mumbled. "It's a breech birth. Leena's never handled one. But Elsie has. If I saddle Fred fer ya, kin you go git her?" he addressed Marion.

"Of course. But where does she live?"

"It's up the road, past where you turn off to go to Mr. Lorran's farm. The next lane up."

"I know where that is!" I volunteered. "Can I go with you?"

"No, Master Thomas, but thank you. I'll find it. But can a horse make it through this snow?"

"Yes, sir! Fred can, but ya ain't got no time to tarry. I'll saddle Fred for ya, now," Earl called.

Marion motioned for me to return to the house, while he followed Earl to the barn. Noon was still an hour away, yet the darkness that accompanied the falling snow swallowed the two in its misty silence as they disappeared toward the barn. I ran to the porch, stomped the snow off my boots, and pushed the big door open. An eerie moan—the cry of a woman in great travail—filtered through the house, its walls, stairwells, and hallway. I hurried into the living room and climbed back into my rocker. The fire had burned low and brilliant coals glowed simmering-red in the hearth. In a few moments, I scooted out of the rocker and threw a piece of firewood onto the fierce embers; then I climbed back in my chair. I don't know how long I had been rocking, when my mother suddenly came to the door.

"Where's your father, your step-father? Did he go?"

"Yes, Mama, with Earl. But they're not back yet."

Strands of wet hair lay matted against my mother's face. "Come! You need to eat something. Pearl's resting now. Her water's broken and the baby's stuck and Pearl's in shock, Tommy. Run in the kitchen and get something to eat. I've got to go back upstairs."

"I'm not hungry, Mama. Can I see Pearl?"

"Not yet. Things will work out," she bent down and kissed me. "Run along now. You need to eat."

I was sitting at the table, when Pearl's moans began to emanate through the house again. They came in waves, with tears and women's chatter. My grandmother came down, sat at the table, and placed her face in her hands. She seemed oblivious to my presence. Lines of exhaustion accompanied the grooves on her cheeks.

There was a stir at the back door, the neighing of a horse, and Elsie rushed in. Snow glistened on her coat and eyebrows. It dissolved in a white dust, when she dropped her coat by the cookstove.

"Thank the Lord, you're here!" my grandmother exclaimed.

"Where's she at?" asked Elsie. "I need some powder and salve on my hands, a'fore I turn the baby. And some hot water."

"Upstairs!" Grandmother pointed. "Tommy, carry that teakettle up for Mrs. Stone, and leave it by the door."

I complied immediately, set down the teakettle, and attempted to stare into the room. "Git on!" some one shouted. I returned to the kitchen. Marion came in, followed later by Earl. We sat in the kitchen and waited and listened. Pearl emitted a long painful cry. Slowly it reached a crescendo, a piercing shriek, then stopped. Moments later, a baby's wail brought smiles of relief to Marion's face. Earl smiled too and wrung his trembling hands, one over the other.

The women came down. Elsie carried the baby on a warm wad of sheets, wrapped in a flannel cloth. "It's a girl!" my grandmother announced. Elsie approached Earl and pulled back a fold of the flannel for the grandfather to take a peek.

"Precious, God Almighty!" he peered down at the child, as he struggled to his feet. "What we gonna call her? I ain't never heard Pearl drop a name."

"What about 'Mamie'?" my grandmother suggested. "Or Eula?" she looked at Earl.

"Mamie is fine," he said, as he reached for the baby and held her in his arms.

"Ain't she a pretty one?" Leena commented.

Earl held the baby for me to see. Its face was red and covered with white powder. There was nothing pretty about the baby that I could tell.

"Can I go out and play?"

"'May' I go out and play?" my grandmother corrected me. "Yes! Bundle up," she smiled. "Just think, Mr. Biggety! You've got a companion, now! A baby girl to read to, to pull in the wagon. Isn't that thrilling? And it's Pearl's."

"Yes, ma'am," I muttered, as Marion buttoned up my coat and winked.

Two days later we were back in town. Albert had to hitch up the draft horses to pull Marion's car out of the drift. But the road into Abingdon had cleared enough for the car to slosh through the slippery mix of melting ice and slush.

Cold weather continued into February. While staying at Grandmother's one Saturday, Earl brought the wagon around to gather more firewood.

"Is it all right, if I take the boy with me?" he asked Grandmother. "He's right handy with a saw. I'll watch he don't get hurt."

"Yes, take him on. He's not much of a baby-sitter, I fear," she feigned, with an ear cocked for Mamie's tears. "Tommy, you do what Mr. Felder tells you."

"Yes, ma'am."

Sally pulled the buckboard away from the house and out into the drive. Earl guided the wagon toward the orchard and up a lane into the woods above the farm. Patches of snow still clung to the dark underbrush, along with leaf-littered clumps of ice in the deep shadows. Deer tracks ran off in several directions. The wagon's wheels cut into the frozen ground, leaving red streaks of mud in their wake. The lane ended near the same outcropping where Uncle Everett and I had stopped to look down the ravine that day. "We'll gather some wood here," said Earl. He pointed to some fallen limbs along the ridge. Several old hickories had tumbled to the ground. Packed snow still lay under their trunks and limbs where the trees had collapsed under the weight of ice. Shaggy bark lay scattered in the snow about them.

We sawed up a number of logs and kindling-size branches. "Son, just leave that rotten stuff there," Earl advised. In my enthusiasm, I had collected an armload of bark and other spongy wood.

"Well! What's this?" he said. "Look, son. This here's bear scat." He picked up a stick and ran it through the dried pile. "Apple seeds! And hair! It's killed itself a deer!"

"I thought bears hibernated in the winter."

"Yeah! I reckon so. But not always around here. There's always a varmint roamin' the Knobs somewhere. They git hungry, you know, just like us. Well, no damage, but we best keep our eyes peeled, case it gets a taste for the hogs, or the smokehouse. They do love bacon! They can smell it cookin' five miles away."

A rush of excitement boosted me; my imagination soared. "Mr. Earl, have you ever killed a bear?"

"Yes. By necessity once't, with an axe. It come at me right out of the brush. A sow. She was defending her cubs, though I never seen them. I swung it just in time to catch her jaw. When she reared back, I clobbered her right in the chest. I split her neck open. She died with a loud gurgle. Couple weeks later, we found her cubs dead. Little fellows had starved, and the foxes had pulled out their meat. Wasn't pretty, son. Killin' nothing's very pretty, not even chickens or hogs. But we gotta eat," he smiled.

"I reckon so," I muttered, trying to imitate Earl.

We loaded the wagon and returned to the house.

One weekend in mid-February, I discovered a false bottom to an old trunk in the loft of the slave cabin. As I lifted up its lid, I could see a long, black, felt-covered box, with gold hinges and a gold latch. A brass plate announced: "Property of Capt. Nathan Edmonds." With curious fingers, I hauled it out and unlatched its catch. "Wow!" There lay two dueling pistols, in immaculate condition. I knew not to touch either, or pick them up, though I doubt I could have pulled back the hammers. A tiny book lay over the barrel of one of the pistols. It couldn't have been more than twenty pages long. Its cover had turned a yellowish brown. The book's faded title read: *Code Duello, 1844.* A hand-written letter, folded and encased in a fancy envelope, poked from a pocket in the lid. I peered in the envelope and slipped out the letter. Its ornate calligraphy surpassed my ability to decipher, but I could make out the word "honor."

I replaced everything in the box and hid it back in the false bottom. Should I tell Uncle Everett or Marion? I wondered if my grandmother knew about the pistols. Would she tell me if I asked her? Or would she huff with indignation and forbid me to play in the loft again? How I wanted to know about the pistols!

When Marion came to retrieve me, I told him what I had found. We were still in the car, riding back for town. He slowed our car, turned it around in the road, and drove back. "Don't say anything to your grandmother. Your Uncle Everett will want them. We'll pick them up and keep them for him. Maybe he knows their history."

My grandmother came to the back door, as we drove up. "Well, well! What did Mr. Biggety forget?"

"Just something he dropped while playing in the cabin. I'll help him find it," Marion said.

"Well, it'll be dark soon."

We could hear Mamie crying in the kitchen. Pearl came to the door. The baby was nursing from one of her breasts. "Sloppy little young'un," Pearl laughed. "If y'all need help, yell."

"Thank you, we will," replied Marion.

I led him up the steps to the old trunk, raised its lid, and lifted the cover to the false bottom. He picked up the box and peeked inside. "Ummm!" he groaned. "What a splendid find!" He tucked the box under his arm, and we returned to the car and drove back into town.

When Uncle Everett dropped by one evening, Marion directed him into the "study" and produced the box. "Shhh!" he warned. "Not even Shaula knows about this. It's a secret between me and Master Thomas."

"I guess so!" Uncle Everett replied. "Damn, but they're handsome." He reached inside and carefully lifted one of the guns out. He held the barrel up and turned the pistol about, admiring its crafted lines and parts. "French made!" he said. "Smooth bore. Uncle Jim told me about these pistols, but he never knew what happened to them. I'll tell you the story, if you'll keep it hushed. Tommy, can you do that?"

"Yes, sir!"

"Well, before the war—the Civil War—Capt. Nathan was sued by a lawyer in town for failure to deliver a promised load of lead from one of his mines around Ft. Chisel. The man called the Captain a 'liar.' The Capt. demanded an apology. The man—a Mr. Patton Roark—refused. All sorts of letters were exchanged, go-betweens intervened, but nothing would satisfy Mr. Roark or the Captain. So, their seconds arranged a duel, east of town, along the Holston. Mama's father, Howard Lorran, was his second. According to Uncle Jim, his father witnessed the whole thing. As the Captain's representative, he dropped the feather and counted the paces. At the count of seven, the two men turned and faced each other. Mr. Lorran fired a small pistol to announce the start. Each man wore a raven vest, white shirt, and light gray trousers. The Captain raised his arm and fired the first shot. It entered Mr. Roark's chest, just under his collarbone. Roark, a large man, winced and, nursing his shoulder, raised his pistol, steadied it as best he could, returned fire, and slumped to the ground. His shot kicked up sand along the river's bank and blinded the Captain for a moment. 'Is your honor satisfied?' Uncle Jim's father asked both men. 'Mine is,' said the Captain. 'I can't speak for the man groveling on the ground.' Roark struggled to his feet, but collapsed again. 'You tawdry bastard!' he groaned. 'Reload my gun for me.' 'Why, of course!' Mr. Roark's second stepped forward. He was a bearded man and bent down to retrieve his principal's weapon. But it was clogged with mud and bits of gravel. 'Here,' said the Captain. 'He can use mine.' The shocked Mr. Roark sat up and coughed blood out of his mouth. 'Nathan, I'll be a son-of-a bitch! Let's just say my honor's been satisfied. Just pay me what you owe.' 'If you'll accept my apology, I will.' The two men shook hands, and that was the end of the duel. Later, Mr. Roark fought alongside Mr. Lorran in Tennessee and around Atlanta. He was killed defending the railroad line from Dalton to Gainesville. After the war, the Captain erected a memorial to him, on the outskirts of town. Several years later, some white trash that lived in the area smashed it up into small pieces to use for chink material around their springhouse. The Captain mustered a group of men from his old Company and late one night rode out to their house, and set the place on fire."

"Well, they're yours now," said Marion. He handed the box to Uncle Everett, who recased the pistol, and closed the lid.

"Tommy! Every man needs to know how to shoot a pistol. When you're a little older, I'll show you how it's done." Uncle Everett brushed his hand through my hair. "You are growing, boy! Like a weed!"

Both men smiled, as we walked back into the living room,

"Well, well!" my mother said. "Aren't you three a secretive group? What about some coffee and raisin-filled cookies?"

"Yes, ma'am!" Uncle Everett uttered. "I knew there had to be some good reason why I stopped by." After he had sipped on his coffee, however, he cleared his throat and looked uneasily at my mother and Marion.

"The truth is, Mama's unhappy. She misses you," he nodded toward my mother and me. "Not that anything can be done. She just wants me there all the time. I can't be at her place and mine everyday. Earl's getting old and Uncle Jim's almost feeble. I don't know what more to do or say."

My mother drew in a long breath and released it slowly. Marion squirmed in his chair.

"I suppose we could stay with her every weekend. I hate to move back, though," Marion acknowledged.

"No! We won't do that," my mother concurred. "I love it there, and Mama Edmonds, too. But Tommy needs to be here in town, and Marion and I, well, we have our own life to live. But I do worry."

Uncle Everett rose slowly, clattering his cup in the saucer as he stood. He picked up another cookie.

"Here," my mother said. "Let me wrap a few in some wax paper for you. Tommy doesn't need to eat all of them, nor you," she said to Marion.

At the door, she ran her hands nervously across Uncle Everett's. He leaned down and hugged her. He shook hands with Marion and went out into the night.

CHAPTER TEN

O N THE FIRST TUESDAY in early March, Uncle Jim suffered a stroke. My mother picked me up at school and drove me to the farm. Uncle Jim and Aunt Viola's "new" house was built against a steep bank. It lay around a sharp curve in the road and across the creek that flowed passed my grandmother's springhouse. One had to drive down a dirt lane to the edge of the creek, park, then cross over a swinging bridge. The old tenant house could also be approached from the hill behind it, but only by way of wagon, or a footpath, and then over rocky outcroppings. That was the route that had been taken when their furnishings were moved in. Grandmother's house was a ten-minute walk away.

I recall staring down into the cold water, as we walked out onto the swaying bridge. Rusting cables, strung from cedar poles anchored in the hard soil and held up in turn by iron pins driven into the rock, provided its source of security. The bridge itself was constructed of planks, fastened to more cables, suspended across the creek.

My grandmother and Aunt Viola met us at the door.

"Shaula! It happened so suddenly!" Aunt Viola groaned. "Jim was eatin' his breakfast, when he put his hands to his head and began to moan. Then his whole body commenced a shakin' and grew stiff. Doctor Wilson come earlier, but said there was nothin' we could do. 'Just rest and hope for the best,' he said. Poor Jim's a pitiful sight."

"It reminds me of Holman's death," added Grandmother. "His was a heart attack. He died in town. We were on horseback—he on his and I on Sally's grandmother. He clutched his chest. 'O Ginny!' he cried. He leaned forward and fell out of the saddle."

Aunt Viola looked at her, somewhat shocked.

"Viola, we're all so sorry," my mother said, offering what consolation she could. "Sometimes people recover. Let's hold out for the best for Uncle Jim."

"Yes. Growin' old's sad, ain't it?" Aunt Viola replied, with a catch of self-pity in her voice.

"Enough of that! We must be strong," Grandmother piped up, in her "resolute" manner.

The three women moved as if one body into a narrow bedroom and stood beside Uncle Jim's bed. I hung back at the door. Dingy wallpaper added to the somberness of the scene. Light from outside illumined the room through a curtainless window. A kerosene lamp rested on one arm of their dresser's divided counter. A large pitcher and washbowl set in a recessed well between the two counters. The dresser's tall mirror reflected the worried looks on my grandmother and Aunt Viola's faces. Strips of mercury had peeled off the mirror's back, lending a streaked effect to anyone peering in. A black-and-red-checkered quilt covered Uncle Jim's feet, legs, and torso. His pale hands stuck out awkwardly from the rumpled sleeves of his long red underwear. Sweat beads glistened under his beard and on his cheeks and brow. He held his left hand out for my grandmother to take.

"Oh, Jim!" she comforted him. "You and I are the last of the Lorrans. Please don't leave me and Viola."

He tried to swallow. His Adam's apple bulged and jerked. He tried to talk, but no sound was emitted.

"Mama, he might not get his speech back for sometime," my mother said. "Uncle Jim, we're all here. We've notified Everett, and he's on his way."

Tears welled in the old man's eyes.

"Tommy," Aunt Viola beckoned. "Please come and hold your Uncle Jim's hand. Let him see you. You've always been one of his favorites."

I approached the bed cautiously and reached down and touched his right hand. He stared up at me with watery eyes and swallowed again. His mouth opened, but no words came out. His fingers were limp, but he was trying to move them. I released his hand and stepped back.

"Did you see that sparkle in his eye?" Aunt Viola said. "He recognized you, honey."

My mother didn't say anything, but she nodded her head, as if to indicate that it would be all right if I went outdoors. I slipped by the bed, passed through the cramped kitchen-living quarters, and out onto the porch. The sky had turned a cerulean blue. The creek's babble and quiet murmur drifted up from the stream. I ran to the bridge and stared down at the water. Just then I heard Uncle Everett's truck and watched him drive down the embankment's lane. I half-strode, half-wobbled across the swinging bridge to greet him. "Uncle Everett! Uncle Everett! Uncle Jim's sick!"

"I know," he said, as he got out and forced his door shut. "Don't get too close to the creek," he ordered, as he crossed the swaying bridge. "Come on back and play near the porch. Then we'll do something special. I promise," he called, as he swayed across the bridge and mounted the steps.

The "something special" turned out to be feeding their chickens, fetching water for their horse, slopping the pigs, and milking the cow. My grandmother sent me running to Quilly Hall to fetch Pearl to accomplish the last chore. She came with little Mamie tied to her back in a sling, which she had cut out of a quilt.

Uncle Everett pitched some hay for the horse from a corner of the shed where the horse and the cow were kept at night. He leaned on the pitchfork and watched Pearl as she drew up a stool, rinsed the cow's udders, and began the process of pressing and pulling each teat. "Are you doing all right?" he asked her. "Is Mama treating you well?"

"Yes, sir! Mr. Everett. Mama Edmonds' a good woman, even if she's hard at times. Elsie helps us, too. Mr. Stone ain't doin' so well, you know. He ain't so perky like he was."

"I'm not surprised. Who helps with the men's work?"

"My daddy and Jessie. Miz. Edmonds seems right pleased. But Daddy's getting old. His hands are all stoved up, and he cain't swing the axe like he used to."

"I'll try to be more helpful. Tommy!" he addressed me. "We need to spend a weekend chopping wood and helping Earl. What do you say?" he smiled.

"I'd like that. Maybe we could go up in the orchard and find a bear."

Both Pearl and Uncle Everett laughed. "Now by George, that would be something!" Uncle Everett chuckled, as he rehung the pitchfork on a wooden peg.

Uncle Jim's condition remained unchanged throughout most of March. One Saturday while all of us were at the farm, Uncle Everett and Marion decided it might be prudent to ride back into the Knobs and check on the Lorran gravesite. "Just in case," as Uncle Everett phrased it.

It so happened that he had brought along a shotgun and two pistols, which he wanted to show Marion and fire as well. Sally and Fred were saddled up, along with an older mare for me. "It's time you learned to ride on your own," said Uncle Everett. "Mayvin's about as gentle a horse as we've got."

At first the big animal intimidated me by the way she snorted and flecked her sides, but she held her ground patiently, while Marion adjusted the bridle and I hauled myself up. I felt all but swallowed in the saddle, but the big pepper-and-gray-spotted mare swished her tail lazily, as I flopped into place. She followed the other horses without ado. Poking out of Uncle Everett's saddlebags were his two pistols, plus the shotgun tethered behind the saddle; Marion's horse carried the axe and bush-hook.

Spring was struggling to sprout into grass along the sunny roadside. The trees' outer twigs formed an intertwined web of swollen red buds. Crows cawed overhead. A hawk's shrill cry preceded its disappearance into the woods. Towhees and brown thrashers scratched in the underbrush.

"Look!" pointed Uncle Everett. "Fresh hoof prints. Somebody's just ahead." He urged Fred forward. "Must be three of them, at least. Come on, Fred, get along."

Just as we mounted the last hill, short of the ridge that dropped down to the farm, we spotted three riders on the side of the road. Their horses were bathed in foam and lather, redolent of fatigue and in need of water. The men wore long coats, cowboy hats and boots, and carried pistols. Their horses trembled under the weight of packs that were covered with rain-proofed oiled-tarps and fishing gear.

"Hello! Partners!" the lead man hailed us. "We hear there's an abandoned cabin over this ridge, somewhere along the river. We plan to camp there, if that's the case. What's your take on these parts?" He exuded a spirit of joviality; his hat was too large and rested on his ears. He had to squint, as the sun struck his face, just under his brim. He must have weighed over 250 pounds. His hands and thighs looked enormous.

Uncle Everett kept riding until we had all three passed them. He turned Fred about and glared at the big man. "My take? You want my take? Is that a fact!" he retorted flatly, with just an edge of sarcasm. Fred neighed as Uncle Everett turned the horse about; he let him prance a little. "My take! Whatta you, say, Marion? Should I tell him?"

My heart began thumping in my chest. I knew instinctively what Uncle Everett was about to do. He pulled out his shotgun and pointed it in the big man's face. "That's my farm over the ridge. And If I catch you on it, I'll blow your face to hell. That's my take!" he swung the horse to and fro. "You wanna hear more?"

"No man talks to me that way!" the lead rider fired back. "I'm Patrick Sullivant from Bristol, and, by God, I know my rights. Where there's a road, I take it!"

"Oh, you do, do you?" Uncle Everett pulled one of the hammers back on his gun. It was a handsome piece, with a pistol grip stock, double hammers, a double-barreled 12-gauge shotgun. Ornate etchings decorated its silver plates. "I've got two shells that say you're turning back, right now."

Just then, Marion swung out of his saddle, with the axe in hand. "If by the count of three, you and your blowhard friends aren't off this ridge, I'll split your horse's face in half." He raised the axe and stepped forward. "One! Two!"

"Well, damn the lot of you!" the big man grunted. "Sorry, son, to be swearing in your presence. We'll leave, but, by God, this won't be the last."

Uncle Everett nudged Fred closer until the double barrels rested against the horse's neck. "For that, I'm going to kill your horse."

"No, no!" the man pleaded. "We're leaving right now. Forget what I said."

"Don't count on it, blubber ass. I know your name, and where you live, and if I ever catch your ass up here again, I will kill you." With that, he raised the gun and fired it in the air. The man's horse reared up, almost hurtling him out of the saddle.

"Out of here!" one of his cohorts shouted. "Hell, let's get out of here!"

"Sounds like good advice to me," said Uncle Everett. He lowered the gun, broke it at the breech, flung out the spent shell, and shoved in another.

The three men swung their horses about and galloped down the lane. Marion remounted, the axe still in his hand. We sat there until the men rode out of sight.

"What do you think?" asked Marion. "Will they come back?"

"Your guess is as good as mine. But I don't think so." Uncle Everett released a long sigh. "Damn, Tommy! They had me scared there for a while. What about you?"

"Yes, sir!" I all but shouted. "I knew you wouldn't back down." I turned admiringly to Marion. "Wait till I tell Mama and Grandmother."

"No, nooo!" whispered Marion. "We'll all be in trouble if you do."

We continued up the ridge and down to the farm. Bramble had over-taken the little cemetery. Sharp briars encircled the wooden markers and covered the base of Uncle Jim's father's grave.

"It ain't very pretty, is it?" Uncle Everett commented.

Slowly we dismounted. Marion and Uncle Everett manned the tools, while I dragged away the brush with gloved hands.

"Well, that's about the best we can do," said Uncle Everett. "God only knows when we'll get back, or have to open a grave."

I think everyone expected Uncle Jim to die within days, but the old man simply wouldn't cooperate with death. By late March, he was able to sit up, bathe and feed himself, and struggle out to the privy with the aid of a cane.

"Jim, this is so wonderful!" my grandmother cooed. "It's not your time. 'Our times are in His hand,'" she quoted from the Bible. "If only you could talk!"

He had not regained his speech, and when he did try to talk, high-pitched chirping sounds fell from his lips. He would "sing" incessantly like a bird, caught in a net of repetitive notes, then stare puzzled at us and cry.

"Poor man!" Aunt Viola would grieve. "What is it you want, Jim?"

"Do! Ab-a-do! Do! Do!" he would reply. After awhile, he gave up trying to communicate with words. He resorted to pointing. "Do! Do!" he would shake his head in frustration. If we picked up the right object, he would sing with enthusiasm, "Do do do do!"

"Tommy, you need to sit with Uncle Jim and just read some to him," my mother suggested. "I've read where that works. It's like a person has to learn how to talk all over again."

For the next few weekends, I was assigned to visit him and read from one of my primer's. I didn't care for them, since I already knew how to read, but I dutifully sat there in the cabin with the old man, and read Dick and Jane adventures to him. I showed him the words and the pictures. His lips would tremble and he would point to a word and rasp out a sound. "Yes, yes!" I encouraged him, just as my mother and grandmother had en-couraged me. By late April, he was saying words like "yes" and "no," "food," "mouth," "hurt," "foot," "sock," and so on. By the end of May, he could speak in short sentences. When my sessions were over, I'd hop off the porch and run out onto the bridge, grab its cables, and make the bridge sway.

Chapter Eleven

O NE MORNING IN EARLY June, I awoke to a strange silence in the house. I dressed and made my way quietly downstairs to the kitchen. Marion and my mother were sitting together in the living room, holding hands. The big Zenith radio near the fireplace droned quietly, its speaker's message interrupted by moments of static-popping sounds.

"Come in," motioned Marion. "A great and horrible event is happening! Our soldiers have invaded France. At last Ike's striking at the enemy's heart."

I had only a vague notion as to what he meant, although I knew the war had claimed my father, somewhere in the Pacific—"just swallowed him alive," as Earl put it. My world was confined to the hills around Abingdon and to the continents, seas, and mountains described in *The Encyclopedia of Knowledge*. Uncle Everett, my grandmother, Pearl, the Knobs, and the Edmonds farms defined my boundaries.

I went to the couch and wiggled in between Marion and my mother. She put her arm around me. "Shhh! Listen. Your Aunt Rachel's ex-husband is over there. Years ago, she stabbed him in a fit of drunkenness, but I know she still loves him."

I sat with my shoulders hunched forward. The crackling news of a far-away war seemed totally irrelevant to my myopic world of backyard trains whistling by and big draft horses straining at their plows. I thought of my father, of the hand that held mine at the fair, of his picture, still on the mantle at Grandmother's. The announcer's voice rose and ebbed with excitement and energy, with horror and shock, of images of bodies awash in blood on some distant beach.

With school out, my mother and Marion asked me if I'd like to spend the summer with Grandmother or Uncle Everett. Both wanted me. I would return to Abingdon on the weekends.

"You could always stay with Mama Edmonds from Sunday night till Thursday, and spend Thursday night and Friday, sometime, with your Uncle Everett," my mother suggested.

"And come home, anytime you want to," Marion insisted. "There are plenty of chores for you to do around here. Besides, Mrs. Hayly needs you to cut grass and help her with her cow."

"I know," I added. "And she gives me money, too."

"Your Uncle Jim needs you, Tommy, first. Then you can help Mrs. Hayly. You're a lucky boy. You have a whole summer to play!"

While at Grandmother's one afternoon, Elsie stopped by to help Pearl put up strawberry preserves. We had picked them at Uncle Everett's on the slope that overlooked his farm by the cedar grove and lichen-encrusted outcroppings, where he and I had stopped for lunch that day.

"Ambrose ain't doin' so well," she reported. "Holds his head in his hands and just mopes about. Says he ain't got no energy no more. We ain't done *you-know-what* since the weddin'."

"I'm not surprised!" my grandmother proffered. "I don't mean to slight you, Elsie, but he's an old man—as hardheaded as can be! Full of himself! Thinking he could please you as his wife! Imagine that? At his age!"

"Miz. Edmonds, Ambrose's a fine man. Shor, we ain't doin' what Adam and Eve done, a'fore they got them leaves. But he's fine company, and we talk a lot. It's jest that I have to do so much work. Cleanin' and ironin' and cookin' for two are all-day chores. But he does tend the garden and feed the hogs. And he's helped Mr. Jim some, too. But them days is numbered. Ambrose's health just ain't good."

Indeed, it wasn't. He died late one muggy June night, after milking his cow. Dusk had formed in the western sky. The scarlet shadows of night had descended, when Jessie came to the back door.

"Mrs. Edmonds, Ambrose is dead. Plumb wore out. I guess it was his heart. Kin we borrow Sally to fetch the preacher? I'll return her in the morning."

"Why, of course! I'm so sorry for Elsie's sake. What will she do?"

"Oh, she's fine. Ambrose ain't got but two daughters and they ain't gonna want his farm. Besides, his tobacco patch ain't yielded nothin' for years."

"Well, be careful. It's late. Why not take the reverend some sidemeat from the smoke house. I'll unlock the door, and you can take him a piece."

"Ma'am, he ain't no 'reverend.' He's just a preacher. A fine man, but just a preacher," Jessie replied.

"Maybe so, but a man of the cloth deserves respect." Grandmother inhaled a deep breath and proceeded outside to the smokehouse.

I followed her into the yard and held the flashlight while she unlocked the door. The odor of smoked hams, bacon, and charred hickory shavings drifted through the dark shed. Row upon row of hams and shoulders hung from huge hooks that were attached to the rafters. Jessie eased down a white-and-brown slab of sidemeat and removed the hook. "Thank you, ma'am," he said. He shouldered the piece and followed her out the door.

As many of us as could, attended the funeral. Grandmother made me wear clean trousers, a white shirt and tie. The sun bore down hot on all of us: Earl, Pearl, her baby, Elsie, Leena, Jessie, Albert, his wife, Uncle Jim, and Aunt Viola. The "reverend" wore a coat and tie. His Bible flopped in his hands, as he read from the Psalms and a passage of the New Testament: "*For if this earthly house of ours passes away, we have a tabernacle eternal in the heavens.*" I don't remember what else he said. The red clay hole yawned wide in front of us. A white pine box, resting on boards, straddled the grave. The burial site overlooked Ambrose's farm, which consisted of his house, barn, pig pin, chickens, garden, corn patch, hay field, and tobacco patch. Far off down the road, I could see Grandmother's house, with its gray stones gleaming in the sunlight and its steep tin roof bright with a silver glare. Just at the last "amen," Uncle Everett arrived from town with my mother. They walked up the hill toward us and offered condolences to Elsie and her family.

"Ambrose had spirit," said Uncle Everett. "He was a true man of these parts. We leave here a noble heart," he comforted Elsie. "As you need help, Mrs. Stone, let me know." He slipped some money in her hand.

Back at the house, in the cool of the big living room, Grandmother turned thoughtfully to Uncle Everett. "That was a kind thing you said to Elsie. 'Mrs. Stone!' Not many people around here have ever called her anything but 'Elsie.' And you gave her money, too! I should be ashamed of myself."

"Mama, their kind won't be here forever. Miles and his family, along with Charlie Mabes, are already asking for more money, for a larger share of the crops, especially the tobacco. I know they need it, but we're barely making ends meet, and your situation's not any better. Marion tells me many sharecroppers are leaving all over the place and finding better jobs in the cities and war production factories. Finding replacements for Miles and Albert, Charlie and Jessie won't be easy."

"Oh, dear! I don't know how I would manage without Albert and Jessie, or Leena or Elsie, least of all, Pearl!"

"Pearl's got to find a home of her own, Mama. You know that."

"I know. I just thought I'd die before I ever saw the need for change. I've never even considered it. How could Quilly Hall be any other way? And what would happen to the farm? Or to all this beautiful land? I can't bear the thought of losing it, or imagining it any other way. I should have died in the twenties, or just after your father's death."

She rose and walked to the window and stared out at the old slave quarters, smokehouse, and hog lot in the distance. Beyond it, ripening corn waved green in the nearest field. The dirt road to the barn angled off to the left. "What will happen to the horses? Do you realize that the Captain himself built that barn, along with Albert's father and Howard's help? God only knows what will become of Jim's place. I don't want to see it, Everett. I don't want to live that long."

"Mama, nothing's going to change here for a while. I spoke out of turn. Jessie, Albert, Earl, the others, there's no place else for them to go. They know that. They're just biding their time, too. But Pearl has a chance for a family. If she'd shave her legs, get rid of her pigtail, and put on a dress, who knows what might happen."

"Everett, I don't like the sound of that. She's not educated enough for you. That's enough of that."

"Mama," my mother interjected, "Everett's right. Pearl's young and pretty. She deserves a new life. With a little schooling, she might have a chance, find a job; attract a good man."

"I can't manage without her. I can't run this house alone. Earl's too old. Let's go sit on the porch and rock. You have agitated me, all of you! It will soon be supper."

"Mama, I have to get Abingdon," said my mother. "Marion will be home soon. Is Tommy being helpful, or do you want me to take him back?"

"Heavens! The boy's a godsend! No, no! Tommy, honey, Grandmother needs you. I haven't baked your favorite cake. Plus, Earl needs to go back in the Knobs to check on Jim's place. You can go with him. What do you say?"

"Yes, ma'am. Then can I go to Uncle Everett's?" I asked, as I looked up at him.

"Yes, sir!" he chuckled. "The fish are waiting, and there's poop to be shoveled in the horse barn!"

"Well, that's hardly an invitation!" Grandmother huffed with a wink in her eye. "'Poop to be shoveled in the barn!' Have you ever heard of anything so ridiculous?"

Uncle Everett ran his hand through my hair. "Next week would be perfect. I'll pick him up next Thursday. OK?" he asked my mother.

"Of course! You know how he loves both of you."

Grandmother wasted no time in baking my chocolate cake with foamy icing. Nor did Earl delay his trip to the Knobs.

On a stultifying muggy morning, he hitched Sally to the buckboard, laid in a shovel, rake, and hoe, along with a pitchfork and a wooden cask of water, and off we drove for the Knobs. Grandmother had prepared a lunch of fried chicken, biscuits, and two wedges of apple pie, all of which she had wrapped in wax paper. Like Earl, I wore a pair of bib overalls, a straw hat, and brogans. Except his hat was felt, with a faded hatband, stained with sweat. He chewed tobacco and occasionally leaned sideways and spat out a stream of brown, stringy juice. "Son, you wanna taste o' plug?" he asked.

"I'd better not. In case Grandmother finds out."

"Now come on, son. You don't think ole Earl's gonna tell on you, do you?"

"No, sir. But, I don't know. I like its smell, though."

"Well, here! It ain't gonna hurt to try none." He slowed the wagon, reached inside his bib, and pulled out a sticky square of tobacco. A yellow and red wrapper protected it from drying out. He cut off a slender edge with his pocketknife and handed the "plug" to me. "Whatever you do, son, don't swallow the juice. Jest let it lay there in your mouth, and then spit once't the saliva builds up. You'll git the hang of it."

I placed the warm lump in my mouth, but gulped as I did. A hot burning sensation attacked the back of my throat. My eyes watered. I coughed and bit down on the plug. More juice squirted against my throat and set my tongue on fire. I thought I would puke. Tears welled up in my eyes, but I said nothing.

"Not so fast!" Earl warned. "Spit any time you need. We got all day."

All day! I thought! I'd be dead by then! The burning inside my throat slid down into my lungs. I gagged, leaned starboard, and spit out as much of the plug as I could.

"Well, son, it takes time. Some things just take time. I got right sick myself the first time. Wanna try again?"

"No, sir!" I squeaked in a tiny voice. "Can I have some water?"

"Whoa!" he called, as he drew back the reins. "Certainly! I could use a swallow myself."

After that ordeal, Earl pointed to the grass along the embankment to our right. "Awful dry!" he noted. "Like tinder. Ain't good back here! This whole mountain could go up with one careless match." He spat a stream of gooey juice in the road. "No, sir! Ain't good a'tall!"

When we arrived at the old cabin, a strong carrion odor drifted in the air. Sally neighed and tossed her head from side to side.

"Bear!" said Earl. "That's a bear you smell. They always smell like somethin' rotten. Probably rolled in it, as well." He slowed the buckboard and pulled on its brake. "Son, hop down and roll a stone under the back wheel. Ole Sally doesn't like this smell."

I complied, and, after securing Sally's reins to a hitching rail, Earl climbed down and picked up his pitchfork. He hadn't brought a shotgun or rifle, which he generally carried. Instead, the wagon bed's floor lay piled with shovels and other gear.

"Wait here, son," he gestured for me to stand beside Sally. "I'm gonna take a peep inside." He ascended the steps and pushed open the door with the tines of the fork. "Whew!" he whistled. "Mr. Tommy, come here, if you wanna see one royal mess!"

I ran to the door and peered in. Bear scat lay in moldering mounds of foul poop. An old chair that Aunt Viola had left behind had been shredded from top to bottom. Window glass lay in sharp shards on the wooden floor. The bear had climbed through the window that looked out into the barnyard behind the house. We wandered through each room, examining the damage. One kitchen cabinet had been ripped off the wall. The larder corner had been chewed to a fine pulp.

"Well, he didn't find nothin' to eat here," drawled Earl. "But his poop shore is fresh. Let's see what he done in the barn."

Outside, we could see his tracks, where he had sauntered off toward the chicken coop and hog lot. The barn door swayed open, almost off its hinges. A path of mauled hay lay strewn about.

"Look at that!" Earl nodded. "Right there, on the ground."

I stared down at something twisted and long, black and half digested.

"That's a black snake's remains, Tommy. He must o' found it in the barn. Poor thing was probably after rats."

We explored the premises some more, saw where the bear had rooted up the hog lot's log rails in search of grubs, and scattered the old nests in the chicken house. The bear had also ripped out several sections of wire screen on the corncrib. Not a kernel remained on the floor.

"I bet it's our friend from up on the ledge," Earl reckoned. "Who knows if he'll come back? But come winter, he just might."

Earl relaxed his grip on the pitchfork and we began cleaning out the house. We piled all the rubble, chewed boards, and chair stuffing into a mound and burned it. The smoke billowed black, straight into the air.

We also weeded the cemetery and walked down toward the river in the direction of Uncle Jim's tobacco patch. A few stray seeds from last year's crop had taken root, and the thin green plants looked dwarfed beside the tall broom sedge and Queen Anne's lace that had reclaimed its former habitat.

The sun had baked the ground hard. Huge cracks appeared in the red clay. Doves cooed in a tall sycamore tree near the river's bank. A line of cedars marked the end of the field and ran upslope toward the house. I glanced up at the cabin's rusting tin roof. An upstairs window had been left open; its faded curtain flapped in the breeze.

"Ain't fit for much now," Earl commented. "But it's a shame to leave it this way. Maybe Mr. Jim's got plans for it, a'fore it goes plumb wild. I shore would like to inherit it."

He let out a long breath. We walked toward the river's edge, toward a copse of neglected apple trees. Large, green sweet apples drooped from the trees' scaly limbs. "Here, let's pick our pockets full and bring Sally down for more," said Earl.

On our way back up the hill, Earl spotted some tracks along the lane. "Riders, at least two or three. See?" he pointed in the hardened mud. He turned toward the Holston. "I'd say they come across the river, up there, by the ford. Ain't been too long ago at that. See where they pitched a tent, or slept on the ground." He walked closer to a depressed area in the grass. Horse turds littered the area. You could smell the manure. "Folks up to no good, I'd say. Either fishin' or poachin' or both." I thought of the three riders Uncle Everett had turned back, of the big man with the pistols. "Just more trouble," Earl sighed.

We returned to the wagon and drove it down to the apple trees and threw as many apples onto the bed as we could. When we finally drove the wagon passed the house, I turned to look out over the rotting cabin, its silent porch, and smokeless chimney. I wondered how much longer Uncle Jim would live and when we'd be making this trip again. As we drove by the cemetery, I could only imagine how much his father—my own great-grandfather Howard—had suffered after the war. "Ah, honey!" as Grandmother so often grieved, "he carried that Minnie ball in his foot until he died 'Couldn't let 'em take it out,' he'd say. 'Cause I know they'd saw off my whole foot.' How he limped, Tommy! My mother would bathe it in Epsom salts and rub it with liniments and oils, but he never enjoyed relief. 'At least I came back alive,' he'd say. 'Along with General Longstreet and the rest of 'em.' How he wanted to attend that great man's funeral in Richmond! Ten thousand Confederate veterans lined its streets to pay homage to his caisson as it rolled by. Oh, Tommy! Think of it! What a shame history's cast all that aside! But not the Edmonds! No, sir-ree! Nor must you! Ever! Never, Tommy! It's indelible. It's in our bones! God Himself placed it there. I believe that with all my heart. Don't you see it, Tommy? It's what makes us who we are. As long as you live, remember that and never despair of your family. The Edmonds or the Lorrans! Never!"

"No, ma'am. I won't." Then I'd steal off to stare up at the portrait of the gallant Captain. If only someone had taken a photo of great-grandfather Howard!

CHAPTER TWELVE

I COULD NEVER PREDICT my grandmother's moods. The morning following Earl's report of Uncle Jim's farm and its deteriorating condition, she went to her rocker and began rocking back and forth. She tapped her right foot each time the rungs dipped forward to keep the chair rocking in a steady, hypnotic motion.

Pearl came into the living room with a tray of fresh coffee and cream and set it on the saucer table beside my grandmother. Pearl clasped her baby against her left shoulder with her left hand. "Miz. Edmonds, you ain't et breakfast yet. I gotta feed Mamie soon, and your cereal's gettin' cold."

"That's all right, Pearl. The baby has to come first," she replied, not missing a tap with her foot. She turned sideways to pick up the cup and saucer. "How is the little darling? Is she gaining weight?"

"Yes, ma'am. She's already wigglin' and startin' to crawl. But I'm afraid to put her on the floor in the kitchen."

"Let me see her," Grandmother looked up.

The baby was clad only in a diaper and messy nightshirt.

"Phew!" Grandmother winced. "Pearl, honey, you've got to change little Mamie's clothes more often. She's a darling, isn't she?" she smiled, as Pearl bent forward for my grandmother to enjoy a better view.

"Thank you, ma'am. She is a pretty one, ain't she?" Pearl glanced at me. "Tommy, what do you think? You're the man of this house, now. Ain't her eyes big and bright?"

I looked up from where I sat beside my grandmother. What an ugly, wrinkled, little black haired creature! "I guess so," I ventured, with a forced smile.

"'Guess so!'" quipped my grandmother. "Oh, Tommy, you have so much to learn. Yes, indeed, Mr. Biggety. Indeed, indeed!"

After Pearl left the room to breastfeed her baby, Grandmother began chuckling to herself. She fingered her cup in one hand and clasped the saucer in the other. She stopped her rocker, poured coffee from her cup into the saucer, and then added the cream. With a tap of her foot, she resumed rocking.

"Grandmother, what do you really remember about your father and his wound? Did it hurt him much?"

She suddenly stopped rocking and stared at me. "Oh, dear! Who is to say? He wasn't a man to cry, but I know it hurt him. He built his shoes up, on his right side, to ease the pain. You could see the bulge under his arch, back near his heel. He feared infection, and, once the wound had healed, he didn't want his foot cut open again. The scar from the bullet ran half the length of his sole. It had turned smooth and white, except where it bulged."

"Didn't he ever talk about it?"

Grandmother continued rocking and stared out the window toward the backyard and driveway. "He did and he didn't. Brave men don't always talk about their wounds. He just accepted it as part of his . . . his fate, of that providential hand that bestows life on some and death on others. It happened along the creek at Chickamauga. He said it was so wooded and swampy, thick and wild, so clouded in the smoke of battle, that he couldn't see more than a few yards ahead. He had just climbed over a fallen tree trunk, when he felt the sting in his foot. He thought a cottonmouth had struck him. He paused to look down, then scurried on into the thicket to keep up with his company. Blood began to ooze through his shoe. His foot became immobile. 'It just went numb!' he said. He paused to reload before dragging himself along. Darkness fell upon the swamp. Men began to fall back on both sides. He could hear the wounded crying and moaning in the night. Two of his friends reached down to drag him to safety. That was on September 19, 1863. The South suffered 18,000 casualties that day, Tommy. Later in November, his unit fought again at Missionary Ridge. That was the saddest battle of all, he said. Because the Yankees were using repeating rifles, while his regiment had only muskets and long rifles. He had bandaged his own foot and made himself a splint of hickory. He wore out his own rifle that day and had to pry one loose from a dead comrade. After the loss of the Ridge, his unit was withdrawn toward Atlanta, where he suffered another wound in his hand. It was minor and healed by the time his company was defeated in the field in front of Atlanta."

She recited all this with a great sense of resignation. Of pride, too, but the veneer of her regal countenance could not match the loss she seemed to harbor in her breast. "I was just a child, Tommy, but I will forever see him for the man he was. He could be jovial in spite of his handicap, but most of the time he kept to himself. He loved to hike the Knobs. He carried a cane and roved the hills to the north and south of our farm, hunted year around, and rode proudly beside the Captain, whenever he'd come over to survey the farm and the woods along the river.

"He was educated, too, Tommy. He could read and write, which many men of his era couldn't do. Your grandfather Holman often discussed politics with him and the rotation of crops. In fact, after the Captain died, my father, Howard, took Holman under his wing and taught him how to shoot from a horse without frightening the animal. He taught him how to log out the best timber and cure hams without smoking them to death. He was poor, but far from dumb. He never owned a slave, but worked as hard as any the Captain ever owned. But then the Captain didn't have that many. Only a handful, as Colonel James didn't approve of slavery. He preferred hardy tenants instead. As soon as the war was over, the Captain manumitted the four slaves he had and paid them wages to go wherever they wanted. They returned to the coast, where relatives of theirs were granted property during Reconstruction. Only one worked in the fields, in tobacco; the other three were cooks and prepared the family's meals in the quarters, right out there," she pointed.

"My father had a secretive side to him. You might even say, 'mysterious.' He once took Jim into the Knobs to hide something. Jim was s big boy, in his teens, and helped my father roll a huge stone over. It was flat underneath and smooth. Jim said our father took out a chisel and carved on its damp under surface: 'Now roll me back and say nothing.' Then they turned the stone over and my father etched on the top of the rock: 'Roll me over and you'll find a treasure.'" Her face betrayed a line of wrinkles about her mouth. "That rock is still up there somewhere, Tommy! Wouldn't it be something to find it some day! My father made Jim swear he'd never reveal its location, or tell what he hid. Your own father often looked for it as a boy, but Everett could have cared less. He was after girls and shooting guns and wanted to earn money to buy a car. What a boy! Your Uncle Everett!"

Her coffee had grown tepid. "Let's tell our fortunes, Tommy!" With that, she poured her coffee into her saucer and turned her cup upside down on the tray. After the grounds had dried, she turned it up and peered inside. "Look! See that face! It's the face of sorrow! It's the face of a woman, weeping. Oh, God! It's your Aunt Rachel! It has to be her! See this figure in the grounds, right there? It's a man. He's fallen. He's down. He can't rise again. He's reaching toward the crying woman. He's dying, but she can't help him. It's William. He…!" but she never completed the sentence. She put her hand to her breasts. "Dead!" she whispered. "He's dead."

I leaned forward and peeped into the cup. On its inside facing surface, I could see the form of a woman, with her hair hanging in her face and her fingers tight against her eyes. In the bottom of the cup, a lumpy edge of grounds formed the outline of a person, with an arm upraised. But how did she know it was Aunt Rachel's husband? I had no memory of him, nor knew who he was. "How do you do that, Grandmother? How do you know?"

"That's a secret. If I told you, I'd lose the gift of fortune telling, of geomancy."

"'Geomancy?'What's that?"

"The gift of being able to read lines and figures. See the figures? The lines? The way the grounds lump up in the bottom of the cup and feather out around the sides? It takes all three of your eyes to read those lines. All three! Your left, your right, and your inner eye."

"'Inner eye?' Where's that? Is it like the eyes in the back of your head?" (Grandmother had often said to Pearl, "Remember, I have eyes in the back of my head!")

"Sort of," she smiled. "No, Mr. Biggety. Your inner eye is in your mind. It's when you see something, or have a hunch about something, or have thought about something for a long time, and then, suddenly, something happens and you 'see' it for what it really is. Like when you've read a Bible verse for many years and suddenly realize what it means. '*Against Thee, Thee only have I sinned, and done that which is evil in thy sight.*' You remember who King David was, the one who killed the giant? Now King David had done a bad thing and had hurt many people. But the real hurt was what he had done to himself, to the voice of God within himself. That he could never repair. Only God could repair that."

I thought about how Uncle Everett and Marion disagreed with her religious views, but as I explored the cup, I could see the lines and figures and imagine people creeping around in the bottom and along the sides of the cup. I was enthralled. I wanted her gift for myself. What a neat power that would be!

"I know what it's like, Grandmother. Like when Earl saw the hoof prints in the lane and knew somebody had been poaching, or camping on Uncle Jim's land. Is that right?"

"Exactly! Earl told me all about that. Remind me to tell your uncle. Everett will know what to do, and how to stop it."

That afternoon, as I was playing in the yard under the shade of the oaks, my mother drove up with Aunt Rachel. Aunt Rachel wore a large white hat with a white veil that concealed her eyes and a portion of her face. She wore white gloves and a black suit, with large white lapels. As she stepped out, her black high heels sank in the soft grass. She turned toward the backseat of the car and retrieved a suitcase.

"Mama Edmonds! You've heard the news, haven't you?" A tone of sadness overlaid her words. "William's dead! He was killed in the assault on Omaha Beach. They've buried him outside a French village, but sent me his dogtags—like poor Hamilton's." She paused and looked toward me. "Tommy, sweet boy! Come to Aunt Rachel. Please give me a kiss. Poor Aunt Rachel's not feeling good."

She bent down and held out her arms to embrace me as I ran toward her. I knew my grandmother and Uncle Everett disliked her, but I loved her, in spite of her cigarettes, booze, and craziness.

"Precious boy!" she hugged me, as she kissed my neck. "My, how you've grown! You're going to be taller than your daddy and bigger than Marion. Strong! What an Edmonds!" She rose to her feet. "Mama Edmonds, may I stay here awhile, until I get my mind straightened out again. I promise I won't drink or get drunk." A crucifix hung about her neck, along with a bright colored red stone. "I'm into the sacred, now. I just don't need to be alone."

"Of course, Rachel!" my grandmother approached and kissed her cheek. "We're all family, here, and nothing more. Tommy, help her with her suitcase, and let's go inside for some tea, or a glass of buttermilk."

"Marion's coming for supper, Mama, along with Everett," my mother added. "I've brought some groceries from town and will help you and Pearl cook supper."

"Yes! It will be nice to be a family, again. Tommy, after you take Aunt Rachel's suitcase in, run to Jim's and Viola's and tell them they're coming to supper. I'll have Earl pick them up in the wagon."

"Yes, ma'am," I answered, excited and eager to tell Uncle Everett about the bear and the hoof prints, and to tell Marion about Uncle Jim's rock. Maybe he would help me find it.

That evening as we sat about the table in the dining room, I listened as Earl began to explain to Uncle Everett and Uncle Jim the condition of the Holston farm.

"It ain't in good repair, I fear to say. A bear broke in and torn up the place and the boy and me found where some intruders had camped near the river. No litter, but you'uns could tell they had been there."

"How fresh were the tracks?" queried Uncle Everett.

"I reckon no more than a week old. I think they come up from the other side, across the ford."

Uncle Everett scrunched up his lips and stared across the table at Marion.

"Our friend, no doubt, from Bristol. Mr. Patrick Sullivant," Marion surmised.

"No doubt! I need to put a bullet in his ass!"

"Everett! Please!" discouraged my grandmother. "What harm can they do?""

"It's just the thought of it, Mama. That's Uncle Jim's land. Our land, to tell the truth! We've a right to keep them off. They've got no business on it."

Uncle Jim had remained silent. His fork trembled in his hand. He tried to speak but could only cough and clear his throat with low grunts. "It ain't worth gettin' hurt over," he finally uttered in a faint voice. "The land is deeded to Viola, and, after that, back to you, Everett. I just don't want Pa's headstone molested, or Mama's."

"Well, they'll not get another chance, if I have anything to do with it," Uncle Everett threatened. "There can't be but so many Sullivants in Bristol. I'll pay him a visit, and that'll end that."

"Everett, don't be so proud, or foolish!" Grandmother glared at him. "Earl, isn't there something less violent we could do?"

"I could put a wire across the road, and signs down by the river. But that ain't gonna stop 'em, ma'am. Only a lesson they'll never forget."

"And what might that be?" inquired Marion.

"You leave that to me, sir! And the boy here, if he'll help me," he stared in my direction.

"Yes, sir! I won't tell nobody, I promise."

"Anybody," my grandmother enunciated the word carefully. "You won't tell 'anybody.'"

"No ma'am, I won't. I promise."

"Well, I wasn't granting you permission. Only your mother and step-father can do that."

"Can I, Mama, Marion? Please?"

"Fine with me!" Marion consented. "I'd like to be part of it."

"Just don't let him get hurt, Earl," Mother conceded.

"Well, I'll take the boy back over there tomorrow, and we'll see what we can do," he grinned. "I like a little trouble myself," he smiled. "So long as we're getting revenge, and they're the ones gettin' the hook."

"Well, 'hook' 'em good!" Uncle Everett encouraged. "Otherwise, it's my plan."

After supper, and everyone had left, Aunt Rachel excused herself and climbed the stairs to her room. Grandmother and I proceeded into the living room and out onto the front porch. We had scarcely taken rockers when Aunt Rachel came down. She closed the door very quietly behind her and sat alone, at some distance from us. The porch ran the full length of the house, wrapped around the end, and back by the dining room and kitchen. She carried a small lamp, no larger than the palm of her hand. Coals glowed from tiny sparks inside it. The odor of incense created a faint aromatic trail. I sniffed the air.

"Ummmh!" Grandmother expelled with disapprobation. "Now what?" she whispered. "Shhhhh! Don't say anything." She began rocking very methodically and staring to her left at Aunt Rachel.

Aunt Rachel appeared very calm and unperturbed. She raised the tiny lamp toward the east and the stars that were beginning to twinkle. She repeated this gesture toward the north and the south. The west lay to our back. She placed the lamp briefly on her head; then held it in her lap. In the growing dark, the thin wisp of smoke formed a white haze about her.

"I guess that's better than alcohol," Grandmother muttered. "I've never understood that girl, nor ever will. Your mama is so different. How they could have come from the same family is a mystery to me."

Fireflies blinked in the darkness over the yard. Their bright green and yellow tails throbbed with syncopation and twinkled in the falling dusk.

Early the next morning, Earl and I returned to Uncle Jim's farm. He had loaded the wagon with axes and tarps, shovels, two hatchets, a tight roll of barbed wire, a fence stretcher, fishing line and stakes. "We're gonna make a bear pit," he said. "It's either gonna catch us a bear, a horse, or scare riders plumb to death. Won't be a pretty sight. But, by George, we'll see what happens."

We arrived at the river just before noon. Earl halted the wagon and climbed out. He walked to the river's edge, down toward its ford, then strode back up its bank into a high stand of reeds. "Here's where the riders come ashore," said Earl. "And where that bear's been feedin', too." He glanced upbank and into a small copse of alders, walked to it, where he found more hoof prints. He strolled back to the wagon and began unloading the bed. I hopped down and helped carry what I could.

He paced off a square area near the river, where the tracks entered the tall grass and bent reeds. "Right here!" he said. "We'll dig right here. Help me spread out the tarps to catch the dirt." I helped him drag the tarps in place. He began digging with a shovel. As he threw dirt up on the tarps, I spread it around and dug what little I had the strength to do. I gathered brush for him, broken reeds, a rotten limb or two, while he continued to dig. We stopped for a late lunch; afterwards, he dug some more. "Fetch me them stakes, now," he said. "You hold them with your hands and I'll drive them in good and stout." We worked for another hour or so placing the stakes. He sharpened them into tapered points with a knife and hatchet. After cutting several small alder saplings, he placed them waist high in the middle of the pit, between the stakes. He coiled barbed wire around the points and filled the pit with it. I helped him stretch the tarps across the narrow chasm. We anchored them with sharpened stakes; then we threw grass and green leaves, alder twigs and broken reeds on the tarps and stepped back. "That ought-er do it," he reckoned. "Now for one more surprise. Fetch that fishin' line for me and the little box beside it." I hurried back to the wagon and returned with the box and line. "Come here, son, and help me untangle it." I held to one end of the line while he unrolled it in his hands. He opened the box and began tying fishhooks in place, along the line. I followed him into the little copse where the horses had passed along the path. "Just in case they come this way," he winked. He spat tobacco juice between his feet, as he strung the fishing line between the alders at the narrowest point. He tied it high, about the height of where a man's hands would be holding to the reins, or at a horse's eye level. "This ain't nice. No sir-ree, but we ain't dealin' with nice people. Now don't you forget where all this is, in case Mr. Everett wants to know. But don't you tell nobody else, 'specially Miz. Edmonds."

"No, sir! I won't," I declared with one hand over my heart.

Earl smiled. "Come on, son. It's late and we ain't out o' here yet."

Chapter Twelve

Darkness fell slowly but steadily as Sally brought us homeward, down the lane, closer to the fields, and out of the Knobs. A huge white owl swept out of the trees from the road's embankment and landed in a pine. It's "hoot" filled me with terrifying loneliness. What if the bear fell in the pit! Or a horse! I felt troubled and unhappy. The moon began to rise, low and orange over the trees, as we trundled out of the woods along the fence beside the big meadow above the barn. I could see kerosene lamps glowing yellow in the windows of Albert and Jessie's house. The moon climbed higher and shimmered bright off the barn's tin roof. By the time we got home, Pearl awaited us at the barn, with her baby in her arms.

"Tommy, you git yourself right in there," she pointed toward the house. "Mama Edmonds is worried sick. Lord, Daddy, we didn't think y'all was ever getting back."

"Pearl, mind yourself! Git on with the boy, and git that baby out of the night air! Even your mama had more sense than that."

It had been a long day. Grandmother made me wash, before I went to bed, but I think I could have fallen asleep, standing in the washtub.

Chapter Thirteen

On Friday I returned to Abingdon with my mother. Aunt Rachel came with us. I could tell that Marion wasn't all that pleased, but he kept whatever misgivings he harbored to himself. After all, she had aimed the pistol that night at him and might well have fired it. He loved my mother and granted her whatever she wished.

Aunt Rachel, however, had seemingly turned a new leaf. Between her bold and visible crucifix and large red stone, which bobbled about her neck and chest, she exuded an air of self-confidence and serenity that emanated peace and warmth. It was fun to be around her. She drove into town frequently with my mother and spent hours shopping for dresses, shoes, and hats. The two would come back laughing and giggling like silly girls. My mother's own tendency toward silence and depression evaporated.

That first Saturday evening, while my mother and Aunt Rachel were reliving old times, Marion and I stole off to the library to read books.

"Marion, has Mama ever told you about Great-Grandfather Howard's hidden stone? The one that he and Uncle Jim scrawled on somewhere in the Knobs?"

"I've never heard about it," he said, his face turning bright with interest. "What did they write?"

"Something about 'roll me over and you'll find a treasure,' and on the other side, 'now roll me back and say nothing.'"

"And just where is this? Where did they do this?"

"Somewhere up in the Knobs. Can we try to find it?"

"Well, you've certainly piqued my interest. Yes. You know me," he toyed with his goatee. "I'm game for adventure. I'm just a big boy like you."

His words delighted me. "When? When can we go?"

"I'll need to ask around some, first. The Knobs take in a lot of territory. Probably better wait until the fall, when the brush isn't so heavy and the frosts have killed back the vines and poison ivy. Plus snakes! I'll talk with Earl or one of his brothers."

Fall! I hated to have to wait so long. "Yes, sir," I mumbled with disappointment.

"Here, let's read about Indians!" he consoled. He slipped one of his many history books off a shelf and opened it to a chapter, entitled: "The French and Indian War." The book had a glossy, red-colored dust jacket of an Indian with a raised tomahawk, about to crash it down onto a blonde woman's head. Her mouth had parted in a scream. Her white blouse was torn open and she was clasping her left hand over her exposed bosom. "This is a popular version but based on true stories." He smiled at my reaction to the dust jacket. "My own father bought me this book years ago. Let's see," he muttered as he turned the pages to a photograph of a log cabin, high on a hill. "Yes. I'll just tell you the story, as the author spends too much time describing the wilderness. We've got enough around here to satisfy our own curiosity, don't we, Master Thomas?"

I knew what he meant, because the Knobs south of Uncle Jim's remained wild and uncharted. Nobody lived there within miles of his place.

"Between 1754 and 1763, the Shawnee Indians allied with the French and fought to keep the British and American pioneers from crossing the mountains. At that time, our state included West Virginia and far beyond. Governor Dinwiddie, King George's deputy, sent George Washington and a contingent of hardy riflemen to the Big Meadows in Pennsylvania to confront the Indians. They got in a skirmish with the Shawnee and Frenchmen and killed about ten of them. General Washington and his men built a fort and prepared for a counterattack. It soon came. Hundreds, if not a thousand Indians swooped out of the woods to assault the fort. Washington realized he couldn't hold out. Finally, a French officer offered Washington truce terms and allowed him and his Virginia militia to withdraw.

"That was the beginning of countless forays and massacres. Indians swarmed across the Allegany's, butchering and hacking pioneers to death. Not even women and children were spared. Their attacks brought them right down the New River and the Holston, and possibly as far south as us. Just north of here, near Meadowview, a whole family was scalped and another woman and her young daughter dragged off. The two later escaped, coming all the way from the Ohio River, back to the New River, and down the Holston. This picture of the cabin is somewhere along the New River, according to the author.

"Fighting went on like that until after the war. The Iroquois hadn't helped matters, because they ceded lands to the British south of their own area, which the Delaware and Shawnee considered theirs. It wasn't until 1768 that a treaty was signed at Fort Stanwix in New York that lands south of the Iroquois' nation were given up to the Colonies.

"But that didn't end the fighting, Master Tom, because the Cherokee in Tennessee were left out of the agreement. So, they went on the war-path next. They claimed the Holston Valley and the mountains around it as their own hunting ground. That took in most of the Knobs. A treaty had to be signed, which forced settlers out of the area. Then came the Revolution! There were too many pioneers settled around Abingdon to pull up stakes. More fighting erupted; the Cherokee sided with the British, and once the Colonies gained independence, that marked the end to Cherokee claims."

He closed the book and ran his hand across the cover. "Not a happy ending, is it, Master Thomas?" He turned with a forlorn glance at his shelves. "Can you imagine how hard your great-grandfather Howard, or the Captain, or even your Uncle Everett, would fight to the death to preserve their land? It's a precious commodity. People don't give up what they love without a fight. Once it's gone, things are never the same. It's like the spirit goes out of a family. That's when they become wanderers, or 'sojourners,' as the Good Book puts it. That's more than you wanted to know, isn't it?" he smiled.

I wasn't certain what to say. But his adlibbed tale of Indians and their horrors, the atrocities they committed, as well as their losses, appealed to me. I wanted to rove the farm just then, stand on the ledge that overlooked the orchard and Quilly Hall. I imagined myself with Uncle Everett, seated on the rough outcroppings by the cedars, with his own land stretching below. That any of that would ever have to be given up was beyond my credulity. Why would that ever have to happen?

"Won't it always be ours?" I objected.

"Who's to say, Master Thomas? There's no magic ball to predict that far ahead."

"What about Grandmother's coffee cup? She sees all sorts of things in it. Like when you came, and Uncle William's death."

Chapter Thirteen

"She's a wonder, all right, isn't she?" he grinned. "I guess I'd be impressed, too."

Sunday evening saw me back at Grandmother's. I wanted to ask her about the farms and why anyone would ever want to take them from us. But I held my peace.

It had become very dry; no rain had fallen in several weeks. The corn shriveled in the heat. Its green blades drooped and yellow tassels fell to one side. The young tobacco plants fared even worse. Their leaves hung wilted and all but touched the hot soil. Albert and Jessie were loath to disturb the rows for fear that hoeing either the corn or tobacco would hasten the drought conditions. The creek ran low, though the spring continued to gurgle with fresh cool water. Earl had to cart water in large vats for the horses and hogs, as the cistern for that purpose ran dry. The cattle grazing near the Knobs broke into the orchard and sought shade beneath the apple and pear trees. The wheat had been harvested, and its chaff-blown soil looked like an abandoned airstrip between rows of sagging fence line and barbed wire. Even the bramble and thistles in the meadows and crisscrossed cattle paths had turned dark tan.

"How we need a rain!" my grandmother lamented. "The Lord giveth and the Lord taketh away, but how we need Him to send rain!"

"It don't look likely, anytime soon," Earl rejoined, as he searched the blue vault overhead for the thinnest wisp of cloud.

As the week progressed, the days grew hotter and hotter, drier and drier. Jessie and Albert worked mainly around the horse barn, hauling out manure and refurbishing the stalls with fresh hay. They let me climb up into the loft and pitch forkfuls down for them to rearrange. "Lordy, Lordy!" Albert groaned, as he wiped huge beads of sweat from his forehead. He had taken off his hat and the top of his head was white and growing bald. Deep tanned wrinkles ran the length of his face. They disappeared into scraggly whiskers of graying beard, before continuing down his neck. His red bandana dripped with perspiration. His flannel shirt lay open at the breast, revealing a large chest of more gray hair. The aroma of tobacco hung all about him. He walked outside to roll a cigarette and sit down in the shade.

"Watch where you fling your match," Jessie warned. "This whole barn could go up, just like that!" he snapped his fingers. "Tommy, son, why don't you go fetch us some clean water. This here's done got hot," he pointed to the wooden cask. He picked it up, removed its corncob stopper, and took a swig. He swished the liquid about in his mouth and spat it on the ground. He handed the small cask to me. When I returned from the spring, both men were stretched out beside the door, asleep. I set the cask down beside Albert and stole back to the house.

That night, just before dusk, a line of thunderheads rumbled into view. You could hear and feel the reverberations of the distant thunder. Lightning flashed yellow and white behind the convoluted mounds of towering darkness. On they came, looming ever closer and ever louder. Erratic veins of lightning crinkled against the black sky. A stiff wind picked up and began swirling dried leaves and bits of gravel from the driveway. In the front yard, the oak and elm limbs began to sway. The excitement was contagious. I ran off the porch and zigzagged across the lawn, holding my arms out, like a bird or airplane. The force of the wind literally lifted me off the ground. I lost balance and fell backwards. I struggled up and repeated the game. "Weeee!" What a marvelous wind! Where had it come from? "Lord! Git in here!" shouted Pearl. She had come to the front porch and was standing on its steps. Leaves and stinging particles of debris struck my face. She tugged at her apron, to keep the wind from blowing it off her waist. "Hurry, boy! There's a tornado coming! Git in here, quick!" Suddenly, drops of rain began pelting the ground and the leaves overhead. I ran as fast as I could. The wind bore down even harder, with gale-force intensity. Ice began hitting my face, hands, head, and body. It was hail! It fell with unleashed fury. Pearl ran toward me and grabbed my hand. Leaning into the wind, it was all we could do to reach the porch. The roar of the hail on the roof was deafening. Grandmother held the door for us, as we fell into the hallway. "Quickly!" Grandmother said. "We must crouch by the fireplace. Tommy, crawl inside the hearth. Pearl, where's Mamie? Lord, where is the child?"

"Upstairs, Mom!" she shrieked. "Asleep."

"Run. Get her! Bring her down as fast as you can. There's no time to lose!"

I crawled into the fireplace, while Grandmother snatched up a cushion to place over our faces. A horrendous roar descended. Darkness swallowed the room. Lightning crackled in the tress outside. A horrific thump shook the house as a huge tree trunk came crashing down. Pearl squirmed in between us, with Mamie tucked in her arms. The child was still asleep, her mouth twitching, as if her lips were searching for milk. "O, for the soul of me! Look at that!" smiled my grandmother. "We ought to be ashamed. That's the Lord Himself looking after us."

My knees were beginning to sting, but I didn't dare move. If God was watching us, I sure didn't want to appear ungrateful, or afraid.

The storm rumbled on. The wind died down. An eerie calm fell about the house. The sky grew light again, and dusk returned. A bright seam of pink stretched across the east, filling the Knobs with a languid, russet glow. Then darkness. The lights blinked and went out. "Get the candles and lanterns," Grandmother said, "or we'll not be able to see a thing." I ran with Pearl into the kitchen and helped her light several kerosene lamps. I was afraid to carry them, but she brought them into the living room, while I followed her with candles. "Thank God we've been spared," said Grandmother. "Tomorrow, we'll have to assess the damage. Poor Jim! I wonder how they are!"

Just then, Earl came to the back door. His hat and brogans were wet, but he himself appeared dry. "Miz. Edmonds, we was plumb lucky. You ain't lost nothin' but a tree. I was up at the barn when the wind struck. The Captain shore did build that thing well!" he stated with pride. "It never quivered once't, though some of the tin blowed loose. But we can fix that. Yes, ma'am!"

"Thank God!" replied Grandmother. "Do you mind going over to Jim's to check on them?"

"They're fine, ma'am. I done that before I come here. I know you too well," he grinned. "Frightened a bit. But otherwise, they're fine."

"Let's have some sherry!" she proposed. "We all need to settle our nerves before we go to bed."

"Lordy, ma'am! Look how my hands 'er tremblin'!" Earl feigned with a big smile.

Early the next morning, my mother and Aunt Rachel drove out to the farm.

"You should see Abingdon's Valley Street! Trees are down every-where, along with power lines. The whole sides of houses are swept away, shingles strewn all across town! Yet our barn escaped damage. How odd!" My mother's face looked pale; she had failed to comb her red hair.

"It's a wonder anything is left," added Aunt Rachel. "We haven't heard from Everett. We tried calling, but the phone lines must be down."

"It's Valley Street!" Grandmother commented. "If the tress are down there, he can't get into town, unless he drives half-way back to Tazewell."

"Mama, I hate to tell you," said my mother, " but Uncle Jim's bridge is out. The wind must have snapped it."

"I was afraid that might happen. Least, he can get out across the field. Earl says they're all right."

The young tobacco plants and corn had taken a beating. Many stalks of tobacco had been stripped of their leaves by the hail. The corn didn't fare much better. "Might as well turn the cows loose in there," Albert muttered. "Ain't good for much else. Don't know what the livestock will live on come winter. The hay ain't no better, either."

Grandmother quietly wrung her hands and retreated to the sanctuary of the living room to rock in front of the damp hearth and its drafty chimney. As the week progressed, I watched Earl and Jessie saw up the large elm that had crashed near the porch. They dragged it off, section by section, with the big draft horses. They let me ride the animals down to the creek for water. When the horses bent forward to drink, I almost tumbled over their heads, save for the knobs on their harness gear.

Finally, the sky clouded up, and, after a brief night thunderstorm, a gentle rain fell for the next two days. The drought had been forestalled. The cornfield revived. Fortunately, a tobacco patch on the border of the Knobs had escaped damage. The farm would survive to witness another season. We went up in the orchard and harvested what pears had been spared, and Grandmother, Pearl, and Elsie washed, peeled, cooked, and canned them in huge blue jars and carried them to the apple house.

The week following the Fourth of July, the farm slowed its pace and Grandmother declared a holiday. Jessie and Albert broke out their instruments, and on a Wednesday night of that week, we celebrated our nation's one hundred and sixty-eighth birthday. Uncle Everett, Marion, Aunt Rachel, and my mother joined us in a hand-clapping, festive occasion. Only Uncle Jim couldn't attend. His body had begun to swell around his chest and his legs wouldn't move.

Midway through the next week, Uncle Jim passed away at the age of eighty-seven. "Congestive heart failure," Marion explained. Only my grandmother was left, now, of a family that could trace its lineage back to the Campbells of Scotland and their descendants who had spilled into the Virginia wilderness as early as the mid-1700s. Aunt Viola wanted the country preacher to conduct his funeral, but Grandmother insisted on the Reverent Dr. G. Carlton Wells, the Presbyterian minister, to "preach" his funeral. I rode with Earl and Uncle Everett to the Lorran family plot to dig his grave. I stood beside my great-grandfather's headstone, while Uncle Everett and Earl bent over their picks and shovels, with sweat pouring from their brows, and opened the grave. Reverend Wells rode out with my grandmother and Aunt Viola in Uncle Everett's truck. They sat in the front seat with him. Marion, my mother, and I rode horses. I held to Marion. Pearl, her father, and others rode in the buckboard.

Uncle Jim's body had been wrapped in a white sheet. He was buried in a cherry coffin that he had prepared for himself. How beautifully that coffin reflected the sun's rays, as Uncle Everett, Marion, Jessie, and the others lay it across a row of rough planks! I had always thought of Mr. Wells as some kind of irrelevant figure, although I couldnot have articulated it in those terms at the time. Preachers and ministers, their wives and their ways, seemed foreign and subversive. What was their purpose, anyway? But on that hot July afternoon, I learned otherwise. While Aunt Viola dabbed a handkerchief to her eyes and my grandmother wept quietly, the minister opened a green book, and began to read:

> *O Lord of boundless love, the only Comforter of the afflicted, send, we beseech Thee, Thy peace into the hearts of Thy sorrowing servants, Viola and Virginia Katherine. As they earnestly seek Thee, turn the shadow of death into the light of morning. Lift up their hearts above earth's darkness to the light and love of Thy presence, that where their treasure is their heart may be also, through Jesus Christ our Lord. Amen.*

He went on to say other things, about Uncle Jim, the Knobs, the brevity of life, the beauty of the mountains and the hills. I looked out across the sagging frame of the cabin that Great-Grandfather Howard had built himself, and the flowing Holston beyond. "*What is man that Thou art mindful of him and the son of man that Thou dost care?*" quoted Wells. I experienced a small shock at those words. My own eyes filled with tears, as I stood between my mother and Uncle Everett, with Marion holding my mother's hand.

After the service, Marion, Earl, Albert and Jessie filled in the grave. As they did, Uncle Everett bent down beside me. "Tommy, where is that pit?" he whispered. "Can you show me?"

"Yes, sir!" I whispered in turn. "Follow me."

Uncle Everett took my hand and we strolled thoughtfully passed the old cabin and down the lane toward the river. As we neared the bottom, I pointed in the direction of the high reeds and alders. "There! Somewhere in there."

He walked slowly toward the area, stopped and peered around. "Pretty good," he said. "I pity the bear or 'creatures' who wind up in it. They'll think twice. Hopefully, they'll never come back. That's for certain! Come on. Let's get out of here," he said, with a grim set of his jaw.

CHAPTER FOURTEEN

THE REMAINDER OF THAT torpid summer slipped wearily into Dog Days. On both farms, the men cut tobacco and speared the stalks onto splintery sticks, before hauling them off to the barns. I was too young to lift the heavy loads of sticky tobacco, or hand them overhead to the men who straddled the rafters. In stead, I sat in the wagon and steadied the steaming horses. Tobacco gum turned everything black: your hands, sticks, reins, bib-overalls, even your shoes. Whatever the big, green leaves touched, they blackened with their indigenous tars and gums. The aroma of the freshly cut crop had a powerful pungency. It mingled in with the smells of sweat and body odor and the brown foam that lathered up on the horses' withers. Working alongside the men gave me the feeling of being grownup. When suppertime came, I too could scrub my hands with the bars of brown lye soap and splash water in my face. How good the fried chicken, gravy, biscuits, corn on the cob and slices of apple pie tasted!

"Biggety, Biggety! Mr. Biggety!" my grandmother chortled as she watched me eat. "Oh, how Holman would be proud of you! You're going to be as big as the Colonel when you grow up!"

I wasn't confident that her acclamations represented a compliment. The portrait of the Colonel depicted him as a large man: in chest as well as girth. Plus, he had that white wig cocked on his head, which didn't flatter him, either.

"Ah, Tommy! Thomas Hamilton Edmonds! What a wonderful future awaits such a hard-working lad! How your English and Scottish ancestors would thrill at your height and mettle. Few boys are made of nobler stuff!" And so her praises ran, whenever Providence smiled her way.

With the coming of school, again, I returned to my mother and Marion's house in town. I had been allowed to skip the first grade and now I was enrolled in the third. Math, reading, writing, and geography continued to be my favorite subjects. Spelling less so! I enjoyed music as well, but when offered the opportunity to take piano, I ran outside to watch trains. Marion elected to let me go. "Maybe next year," he shrugged it off to my mother.

"We'll see," was all she replied.

My eighth birthday arrived with enormous welcome. Cold nights and frosty mornings had turned the land and its fields dry and brown. Now Marion and I could search for the rock.

"It won't be long!" he said. "Snakes are still out there, but they'll be searching for cover and dens of their own. Then we'll go."

Throughout this time, Aunt Rachel had continued to live with us. She had given up her apartment in Roanoke. More puzzling was the fact that Uncle Everett began inviting her out to dinner and accompanying her to the Barter Theatre. I thought he didn't like her. I wondered why I had seen so little of him, until school had restarted and I moved back into my room in town. He had been dating her most of the summer.

Aunt Rachel had taken on a new glow.

"God, he is quite a man!" she revealed to my mother.

It was on a cold Saturday morning. I was about to enter the kitchen. I hesitated at the door.

"You're not telling me anything new. I remember what he was like before I dated Hamilton. Suave, but impulsive! If not impetuous! He drank then, too. Mean! He enjoyed teasing girls and had only one thing in mind."

"I know. I haven't been the best baby sister."

"Watch it! He's not over Sylvia, yet!"

"Whatever caused that break up, anyway? I've always wondered."

"Alcohol. He couldn't leave the bottle alone, and she couldn't stop bitching him out. I can't blame her, though."

"Why hasn't he remarried?"

"Who's to say? Everett's just Everett! That's all."

I stepped into the kitchen and slipped into my chair by the window. I could see out across the backyard and the dead vines that clung on the fence beside the railroad tracks. In the shadows, a heavy frost glistened on the grass.

"Marion plans to take you out to Mama Edmonds' today. Remember?"

"Yes ma'am! We're going to look for Uncle Jim's daddy's rock."

"Sweetheart! That old tale should have died long ago. Your father spent half his boyhood searching for that stone. If it exists, nobody has the slightest idea where it is."

"Marion and I will find it! Where is he, anyway?"

"Getting gasoline. Our rationbook's running low. He took a dozen eggs with him," my mother smiled, "just in case."

"Will it work?"

"It did last month. I needed new tires, and Frank gladly *found* some, after I showed him a side of bacon."

"Won't he get in trouble?"

"Not in Abingdon. We all have to do it. Plus, if you're a farmer, or your job's farm related, you get extra cards, anyway."

The two women talked on, as I ate my cream of wheat and toast. I could hardly wait for Marion to get back. When he came in, he slipped out of his coat and tie and donned a woolen shirt and warm jacket. "Better get ready!" he smiled. "Shaula, let's buddle him up good. The temperature's liable to drop before we get home. Besides, the Knobs always seem colder."

After driving out to the farm, we visited Grandmother for a few minutes, warmed our hands by the fireplace, and subsequently hurried to the barn. We saddled the horses, Marion on Fred and I on Sally.

"Which way, Master Thomas?" Marion grinned. "Up behind the orchard, or off toward the river?"

"There're lots of rocks behind the orchard. Big ledges and smooth cliffs! Ravines and ridges." I wanted to see the ledge again.

"My! You don't forget a thing, do you?"

"No, sir!" I replied with excitement. "I've been up there too many times with Earl and Uncle Everett."

"Then, maybe that's not the direction to go. Maybe we should try down by the river."

"Grandmother thinks it's in the Knobs."

"Well, who am I to dispute Mama Edmonds? Goodness! I'm just an interloper anyway. Come on, then. To the orchard!"

With a nudge of his heels, off he rode. I followed him at a low gallop on Sally. By the time, however, we climbed up through the orchard, and made our way along the trails through the fallen leaves, the sky had begun to turn gray. We stopped to rest the horses at the overlook. A damp wind picked up and stung our faces and numbed our hands. Steam from the horses' breath escaped their nostrils. We ducked off the ridge and began descending the trail to the bottom of the ravine. Rocky walls and lichen-splotched boulders towered to our south. The underbrush had died back; limp ferns lay shriveled about the base of rocks. I could see far up the hill, through the stands of poplars and tall lean oaks. Only holly trees, thickets of laurel, and Virginia pines presented us with swaths of green. We peered about for a man-sized stone, or rock, that looked like it might qualify, but none appeared as a candidate. We rode slowly along. Up, up we climbed, and down several ridges. "Nothing! I don't think it's here," said Marion.

The woods grew colder. Wind soughed in the pine trees about us. It began to drizzle. Mist formed and cloaked us in its gray mantle.

"We'd best move on, Tommy," Marion stated, as he stared up at the darkening sky. "We'll try another time. OK?"

"Yes, sir," I replied with dejection. "I know it's up here," I reassured myself. "Don't you think so?"

"Oh, yes! Stories like that are hard to invent. I believe it happened, just as sure as we're riding these horses."

I felt better listening to his words. I nudged Sally, as I followed him and Fred back across the ridges to the orchard and Grandmother's farm.

It wasn't long after that that late one October Friday afternoon, Albert came down to the house, rather breathlessly. My mother had dropped me off and had returned to town. Uncle Everett was there and was about to leave, when Albert came to the side of his truck.

"Mr. Edmonds! Mr. Everett. Two horses with saddles a jarrin' just come out of the Knobs! There's blood on one of the horses and it's limpin'. The other'n's got claw marks all over it. I think they was jumped by a bear."

"You don't say! Where are the horses now?"

"Up at the barn. Jessie brung 'em in. They're right scared and fidgety."

"Get in, and I'll take you back."

Uncle Everett turned the truck about and headed toward the barn. I ran behind him and Albert.

Jessie was holding onto the two horses by their bridles. He and Earl had taken off the saddles and were examining their wounds. Uncle Everett parked the truck. Then he and Albert got out.

"Plumb hurt and skittish, if you ask me," said Earl. "They're hurt right bad. I'll git some liniment on 'em."

"I believe I recognize them," said Uncle Everett. "Whatta you think, Tommy? Don't they look like the horses those men from Bristol were riding?"

I took a good look. "Yes, sir! That big black one looks like the one the man with the pistols was riding."

"I think you're right. Well, well! Earl, let's care for these horses, then tomorrow we'll ride up toward Uncle Jim's and check things out. It's too dark and late to do it now." A worried smile played uneasily about his mouth. "What do you think, Earl? You think your pit got them? Or a bear? Or both?"

"That shore would be somethin' if-in it was both! But somethin's happened! That's for sure."

"We'll find out tomorrow. No point in risking life or limb in the dark. Though I must say, I pity any rider out there tonight. We really should do something. But, they'll just have to wait. Tommy, let's get some sleep. Mama loves company, and tonight she'll have us both!"

"Can I go? I can ride alone now. I know how to keep up. Please!"

"Goodness, boy! I guess so. I wouldn't want you to miss this. Besides, you were part of the posse that stopped them the first time." A faint smile creased his lips in the light of the lantern that Albert had lit. It's glow filled the barn's entrance with warmth and soft light. "You men get some good sleep. Jessie, you might need to go with us. You won't mind?"

"No, sir! I'll meet you here in the mornin'. You jest say when."

"Oh! Let's let it warm up a little. Say, 7:30? OK?"

"Yes, sir! I'll be right here, rearin' to go!"

Uncle Everett reached up and patted the right shoulder of the mare closest to Jessie. "A beautiful animal. What a shame we might have to keep it."

Jessie, Albert, and Earl all enjoyed a nervous laugh.

"Till the morning, gentlemen!"

By eight o'clock the next morning, we were saddled and on our way. Albert and Earl rode in the wagon and Uncle Everett and I were mounted. A heavy frost bent the grass in the meadows and sparkled in the morning's yellow glow. The road to Uncle Jim's was slippery with ice where the sun's rays hadn't burned the shadows dry. A pale sky heralded a clear cold day. Just before ascending the last rise in the road, Earl pointed high in the sky. The eastern sunrise made it difficult to see what had caught his attention, until the circling, floating objects dropped closer along the horizon. "Buzzards! Lots of 'em!" Earl stated. "We got us somethin', for sure."

"Unfortunately, so," Uncle Everett concurred.

As we crossed the final ridge, we could see the mist above the river. We could barely make out its banks and the alders and reeds along its edge. We rode closer to the scene and passed the cemetery and buildings on our right. As the bottomland came into view, big buzzards lumbered slowly out of the wet grass and took heavily to air. Albert stopped the buckboard and held loosely to the reins. He pointed down in the dirt to a frost-covered pile of bear scat. Uncle Everett motioned for me to remain with Earl and Albert, while he approached the river's banks. He turned in the direction of the pit, stopped, and dismounted. He walked the several yards to the area. I watched him remove his hat and stare down. He waved his hand for us to join him. There, in the bottom of the pit, lay two men. One appeared still to be alive, but blood covered his throat and neck. The larger man, Sullivant, lay face down, where his horse had thrown him onto the stobs and barbwire. He was dead. Uncle Everett lowered himself into the pit and examined the wounded man. I could see the whites of his eyes as Uncle Everett attempted to lift his face and neck off a stake. As he did, the man's eyes stared up, blank and gray. A low gurgle slipped from his lips; his body sagged limp.

"We ain't in trouble, are we?" asked Earl. "They was trespassin' warn't they?"

"Yeah! But you can't kill a man for that, unless he means you harm. I'd say we're in deep trouble." He held a hand up for Earl to help hoist him out of the pit. "Whatta ya think happened?" he asked Albert.

"I ain't no judge of that, sir. Earl's always been the hound dog."

"What do you think, Earl?"

"Well, I've been glancin' about. Lots of commotion here. You can see it in the grass. This is how I figure it. That bear had sniffed this pit out. He warn't no fool. Them fellows come across the river and surprised him. He jumped up and scared the horses. They reared back and threw the fat one in the ditch. His friend probably fell in, tryin' to he'p him, or might have been throwed in, hisself. The bear lunged for the horses and they run off. See all this scat! That bear had been sniffin' around here for some time. Eatin' apples and grass. See the seeds! But he knowed somethin' was in the air. They don't like to be fooled. Them black bears, 'specially the males, ain't dumb."

Chapter Fourteen

"Ahhh!" groaned Uncle Everett. He had put his hat back on and had taken it off again. "Shit!" he hissed under his breath, then looked at me. "Mr. Edmonds, Jr., 'hush' is the word, boy. You hear me?"

"Yes, sir."

"Good."

"Mr. Everett, I've been thinkin'. Why don't you jest leave this here to me and Albert." Earl glanced up into a nearby walnut. A black cluster of vultures hunched on the tree's limbs. "Why not let them fellers do their chore for a week or so. Then, me and Albert will return. Nobody'll ever know. It's a good gravesite. I'll clean it up right nice." He waited for Uncle Everett's reply.

"Tommy! You heard the man. I like his idea. But you mustn't tell anybody. Not Mama, your mama, Marion, Pearl, or anyone. Hear?"

"I won't tell. Promise."

"That's right. A promise is a promise. Let's head on back, then." He shook Earl's hand, along with Albert's. "I'll see you're rewarded for this. Both of you."

"That ain't necessary, Mr. Everett. Mrs. Edmonds an' you have always looked after us. It's our turn now to he'p you. Futhermore," he pointed to the large's man's belt, "me and Albert would sure love to keep them pistols. They ain't gonna do him no good no more."

Uncle Everett didn't reply. Instead, he simply nodded, then helped me remount, and we left the brothers behind, as they slipped out the pistols and began stripping the dead men of their clothing to enable the vultures to hasten their task.

CHAPTER FIFTEEN

IN MID NOVEMBER, MARION and I returned to the Knobs to search again for Great-Grandfather Howard's rock. On a pleasant fall afternoon, we found ourselves descending the woods toward the river. We were north of the old homeplace and had been riding all morning up and down ravines and gentle coves, staring down at rocks.

"I wonder how large this stone is, anyway?" Marion mumbled. "We've been looking for a large rock. Maybe it's quite small. Still, if it took both of them to turn it over, who's to say?"

At the river's edge, we dismounted and ate lunch. Grandmother had prepared several pieces of fried chicken, along with a jug of coffee for Marion. She had included a jar of milk for me. It was fresh and cold, with lumps of golden cream floating on the surface. I had grown to prefer creamery milk from town, but since it was autumn, the milk tasted rich and sweet, seeing it contained no wild onions.

We lay on the river's bank where the sun could warm us. A bright blue and white kingfisher darted over the water in search of minnows, or whatever. Behind us, a flock of turkeys crept through the dry hickory and oaks leaves. I could hear them scratching the ground for acorns and bugs.

"Should have brought my shotgun," said Marion. "We need to be hunting, not looking for a rock," he feigned with disgust. "No offense, Master Thomas. What do you say?"

"I'd love to shoot turkeys. Is it hard?"

"Well, yes, to be frank! You have to lie still and wait for them to come in range. Morning's the best time, when they're just coming off roost. That's when the gobbler gobbles for his hens. They like to roost in oak trees at night; then hop down in the morning. If you think you know where they are, then you can set up for them before dawn. But it's a long way back to here. We'd have to camp out some Friday night to be ready.

Maybe next year. Maybe ole Santa will bring you a .410 this Christmas. You could handle that gauge."

Something stirred in the woods behind us, and the turkeys took to wing. I could hear their feathers whipping the air as they scattered into the trees.

"Let's investigate," Marion whispered.

We tethered the horses to the low limbs of an alder and walked quietly upslope. "I'll be!" mumbled Marion. "Look!" he pointed uphill.

I strained to pick out the movement or listen for a sound. "I see," I whispered. A fat skunk was scurrying along, kicking up leaves in pursuit of the flock.

"Don't move! Don't make a sound!" Marion warned. I could hear his heart beating and feel my own.

We stood motionless in the shadows of the trees and watched the big skunk waddle by. He came within thirty yards of us; he appeared to be right at our feet.

"Whew!" Marion expelled a sigh of relief.

We could hear the horses neighing quietly behind us.

"Time to move on," surmised Marion. "Next time, let's try south of here. We'll not give up, till we find it."

"Yes, sir!" I agreed, my enthusiasm for the day compromised by the huge skunk's sudden debut.

Marion smiled at my wisdom. We remounted and rode down river by way of the farm. We passed the "grave" where the trespassers lay. No one could have known anyone was buried there. We actually rode passed the alders and reeds where Earl had dug the pit. All was smooth and covered with leaf litter and small limbs. I looked down. A bear track as large as a man's hand shimmered in the gravel by the river. "Look!" I pointed it out to Marion. "That's the bear Earl keeps talking about. Would my .410 kill him?"

"Not hardly! Don't every hope you'll meet up with him. He must feel quite at home here. Probably the apples," he nodded toward the gnarled trees. "They must be gone by now. Maybe that will change his tune for a while."

We turned on the lane and rode back over the ridge. It was suppertime before we returned to Grandmother's. Marion left me for the weekend, as he drove off to rejoin my mother. I watched him drive away in the dusk.

"Come, now!" Grandmother said. "We've got a lot of catching up to do." She put her arm across my shoulder and we repaired to the kitchen.

The following morning, my grandmother and I were waiting for Aunt Viola to drop in, when a deputy's car pulled up in the drive. Grandmother knew the man, as Uncle Everett had also been a deputy, and still accompanied the sheriff's deputies into the Knobs, whenever they needed him. A short, bald, and overweight man struggled out of the car. His gunbelt wouldn't stay on his hips, since his waist was rather rotund. He had a kindly face, however, and showed great respect for my grandmother.

"Miz. Edmonds, I hate to disturb your Sabbath morning, but we've received a missing person's report at the office. Seems some riders came up this way and got lost. You ain't seen nobody who'd fit that description have you?"

"No, I haven't," she placed her hands over her chest. "They're not dangerous, are they?"

"Oh, no! Just two men from Bristol. They've been missing several weeks, now."

"Well, Earl and Albert did find two loose horses on the road. They're in the barn now, recovering from a bear mauling. You don't suppose there might be a connection? We've just been caring for the horses, until we heard better."

"Well, that's just what I figured a fine family like yours would do, ma'am. You don't mind if I look around and talk to the men, do you."

"Why, heavens, no! We'd sure hate to loose those horses, though."

"Don't you fret none about that. Your mother cared for mine, long ago, and we Pattersons don't forget things like that. They'll not even show up in my report. I just need to look around."

"Well, go right ahead. I know Earl won't mind your asking a thing. He's up at the barn now, feeding and watering the animals."

She watched him carefully as he opened his door to re-enter his car. "Tommy! Quickly! Run to the barn and warn Earl. I'll hold Mr. Patterson here a few more minutes. Go out the front door."

I obeyed her instructions and found both Earl and Albert caring for the horses. "The sheriff's coming!" I blurted. "He wants to look at the horses and ask questions."

Earl peered over my shoulder at the deputy's' Plymouth, as it made its way up the road in the cold dust. "Git up there in the loft and hush yourself."

"Yes, sir!" He helped me reach the first rung of the loft's ladder, and I scampered up into the hay. From there, I could look down and listen.

"Well, well, Melton, what brings you out here, today?" asked Earl. "You ain't lost?" he teased him.

"You know better than that. What are you two grooming there? Them two fine horses? Especially that one with a scar? She ain't one of Everett's, is she?"

"Maybe and maybe not!" Earl answered with his dander slightly annoyed. "What right you got coming in here anyway? This here's private property."

"Come on, Earl. If you're hiding somethin', let it out. We ain't enemies. I'm here to care for you more than lock you up. Whatta you know about the fellows who was riding these mounts?"

Earl glanced toward his brother. "Ain't no use in playin' dumb, I reckon. Here's what happened, Mel, and it's the truth. Albert and me was up here at the barn when these two horses showed up in the road. They was scared and rearing up. We seen the marks on their flanks where they had been mauled. It was dark, so we put 'em up for the night, then come morning, we tried to ascertain where they'd come from. Their tracks led back into the Knobs. But we lost them by the river. We never seed a thing! That's the full, gospel truth. I swear it, Melton. Save some bear tracks. If I knowed anymore, I'd tell you."

"Albert, is that the truth? You got anything to add?"

Albert studied the deputy's face, before turning sideways to wipe his hands on a dirty cloth. He offered it to the deputy. "I wished I could add somethin'. We done all we knowed to do."

"I can't blame you for that," rejoined the pudgy man. "Ain't no use in me trying to out do you fellows. You know these woods better than I. Thanks for your time. Tell Miz. Edmonds not to worry about these horses. There wasn't any report on them. They ain't officially missing," he grinned. "Might want to ride one, sometime."

"Well, you just come right on!" Albert piped up. "We'll be glad to go back with you, anywhere you want to. We ain't hidin' nothin'."

"I know you aren't. But I've got to make my report. You all saw 'nothing'—pure and simple. But if you ever sell one of them horses, let me know."

The deputy climbed back in his car and drove off toward town.

"Can we trust him?" asked Albert.

"No further than I can spit. But we might have to give him one of them horses, to shut him up."

"Bastard!" Albert groaned. "Least, the sheriff didn't come. He's harder to fool than Melton."

"I know. Tommy!" Earl called up to me. "You best tell Mr. Edmonds, a'fore they visit him."

I hurried down the ladder and ran back to the house.

As Thanksgiving approached, Pearl became ill. Her baby was tiny, seven or eight months old, and she was still nursing the infant. Little Mamie could crawl and almost pull herself up, but it was apparent that she was underweight.

"Pearl! You've got to see a doctor," my grandmother fused. "Your milk's not nutritious enough. You've got to put that child on real food. Poor little thing! She looks worse than a muskrat."

"I have, Mama Edmonds! I've been mashin' cereal and beans for her. I just feel weak all the time."

"You're working too hard. Caring after me's enough. But having to look after Viola and milk her cow, has got to stop."

"Yes, ma'am. But who's to do it! Pa's too old and hates milkin' anyway. He just wants to take care of livestock and chop kindling. And tend them horses! They'll be the death of him yet."

"Pearl, don't talk like that. The word 'death' always brings bad luck."

"What about Elsie? I heard her say that Ambrose's daughters want his land back, and house, too. She ain't got no place to go, except to Albert's and Jessie's."

"Excellent! We'll ask Elsie to stay with Viola! And help you, too. But until then, I'm going to call Dr. Wilson to come and see you. You need iron pills, honey, or something more powerful than that. We can't let Mamie starve anymore. Or you get any weaker."

I happened to be there the Friday night Dr. Wilson came out. He drove up in a black Ford that had high running boards and curved front fenders. He was tall and slightly slumped over at the shoulders. He came in the house with a black, alligator skin-covered handbag and a gray Stetson. Grandmother hung his hat on the portmanteau while he adjusted his watch and slipped it back in his vest pocket.

"You're too fastidious!" Grandmother addressed him. "Didn't the University of Virginia teach you doctors any etiquette? We've got a sick child here, and her baby's not in the best of health, either. And here you are admiring your watch!"

"Goodness, Ginny! I've known you for seventy years or more! What's gotten in to you? You used to offer me sherry," he smiled, with a wink toward me. "Tommy, it's been awhile since I've seen you. How's the healthiest boy in town? You must be five feet tall!"

"He's going to make one fine man," Grandmother commented. "Come on, Brodus, the girl's this way."

Grandmother led the doctor toward the kitchen and Pearl's bedroom upstairs. I remained in the parlor, looking through some of my grandfather's old books. I found the yellowed sheet of an invoice in one, but I couldn't make out the words. It had something to do with money. I could see a list of things with dollar marks in front of them. Suddenly, I realized it was an inventory of equipment my great-grandfather, the Captain, had purchased for Great-Grandfather Howard's A Company. He had outfitted the Company with guns, belts, shoes, and ammunition.

When Dr. Wilson and my grandmother came back down, both appeared embarrassed. "I think you should give some to the boy, too, though he looks healthy enough," the doctor smiled. "Won't hurt him any. Two doses should be sufficient. But I'd wait till tomorrow."

"What about that sherry, now?" she asked. "I could use some myself."

"Thank you, Ginny, but I'd best head home. Perhaps, next time."

She handed him his Stetson, he tipped his hat, and left by the way he had come.

"What's that I'm supposed to take?" I asked.

"Castor oil," she replied, without smiling. "You'll need to be near a potty. Pearl's got worms and the baby, too." She inhaled a deep breath and we went upstairs for bed.

The Castor oil came in a tall brown bottle. Grandmother made me take two tablespoons, followed by biting into an orange. Pearl had to do the same. Grandmother ladled out only a tiny amount for Mamie. I had no idea what to expect, but within an hour my stomach began to growl and intestines gurgle. I barely made it to the bathroom in time to squat on a chamber pot. I stared between my legs. There in the bottom of the enameled pot squirmed a white coil of pinworms. Yuk! I ran out, only to have my grandmother force me to go back and empty the chamber into the commode. As for Pearl, her health improved, along with the baby's.

Thanksgiving's hog-killing ritual occurred without a hitch. All the farmhands, their wives, Elsie, and people I'd never seen before, joined in to help Grandmother and Uncle Everett butcher the hogs. Aunt Viola sat in the old slave quarters by the huge iron kettle and stirred the melting fat. Whenever I grew too cold, I'd run in to watch her, then hurry back out whenever Albert or Uncle Everett shot another hog. Marion helped Jessie and Earl scrub the carcasses, but he observed more than he worked. He was fascinated with the salting and rubbing down of the pieces of meat, which the men stored in salt barrels. My mother and Aunt Rachel helped in the kitchen. The women had formed an assembly line to fry pork chops, which they sealed in jars of hot lard.

Whatever satisfaction the butchering brought, the sheriff's visit the following Saturday tempered.

He came in his official car, complete with a six-pointed star on his driver's door, and a court order to retrieve the two horses. While he explained this to my grandmother, a horse van showed up. The sheriff directed the van toward the barn, and with Earl's reluctant assistance, they loaded the two horses onboard. I watched from the corner of the corncrib. The sheriff kept putting his finger to Earl's chest and pushing him around. I began to tremble, but then the trembling stopped. I ran toward Earl and wiggled in between the two men. "I'm going to tell Uncle Everett on you!" I blurted. "You're just a bully, like boys at school. Don't you touch Mr. Earl again, or I'll whup your ass!" (I had heard boys say that at school and, nine out of ten times, it worked.)

"Ohhhh! You will, will you! You little brat!" he swung the back of his hand at me.

Just then I saw a pitchfork out of the corner of my eye. I grabbed it and rammed it into his buttocks. It must have struck his billfold, however, as it glanced off.

"Oh, my God!" he shouted. He started to reach for his pistol.

At that point, Earl stepped forward and clobbered him with a shovel. The handle broke as it hit the man's face. The sheriff slumped, unconscious, to the ground. Blood ran from a cut along his cheek.

"Jesus Christ!" the van driver whistled. "God Almighty!" he smiled. "He's pushed hisself into trouble all his life. Well! You'd better call Melton to come get him, 'cause I shore ain't goin' touch his ass."

About that time, Grandmother came out to the barn. She had wondered why I hadn't returned.

"Oh, dear God, what's happened? Earl, what have you done? Tommy, run, quickly, fetch me a cold cloth and that bottle of sherry. Hurry! This man's hurt!"

I complied and ran back with the goods as fast as I could. Slowly, the sheriff came to.

"Mrs. Edmonds! I ought to arrest the whole lot of you. But I can't blame you for what your young'un did." He patted his sore rear-end and ran his fingers over the bruises across his face. Earl helped him to his car, along with the van driver's assistance, in spite of what the latter had sworn.

When Uncle Everett learned of these events, he demanded that the County Commission dismiss the sheriff. The Commission refused but required the sheriff to apologize.

He drove out to the farm and came up on the porch. I was standing with my grandmother when he did. Black bruises covered the side of his face that Earl had struck, and he walked with a limp. I could tell his buttocks were sore.

"Mrs. Edmonds, I profoundly regret the incident," he extended his hand. "I had no right to push Mr. Earl about or threaten your grandson." He stared at me, without a smile.

"Your apologies are accepted, Mr. Wright. Yours is a demanding profession, and we fully understand."

"Thank you, ma'am." He turned and limped off the porch and back to his car.

However much the men hated loosing the horses, Earl felt vindicated for the moment. Albert and Jessie felt relieved. "Boy, you shor done the right thing!" Albert assured me.

Grandmother was proud of me, too. But my mother was aghast.

"Marion, Tommy could have been killed! Where did you learn behavior like that?" she grilled me. "The only violent person in our family is Everett. Wait till I see him! Marion, no more hunting in the Knobs for that rock, until Tommy settles down. I won't have him growing up like a heathen. No more BB gun shooting for you, Mr. Biggety! Do you hear?"

Aunt Rachel had been listening. She put her arm around me. "Shaula, he's just a boy! Big, yes! But still a boy! You don't want him to grow up a sissy. He can't have a daddy dying in a war, or a grandmother filling him with Civil War stories, and not inflate his ego. And please don't fault Everett. Everett and I are going to marry. He asked me last week. Yes! We were going to keep it a surprise until Christmas. But, here I am letting it out." She said the last three sentences without drawing a single breath and ended by kissing me.

"Oh, goodness!" my mother clapped her hands. "Why didn't you tell me earlier? When is the date?"

"We haven't set one. I might just go out there and live with him until we do."

My mother's countenance fell. She had not meant her squabble to alienate anyone, or offend her sister. "Rachel! Please, don't. There's too much to do between now and then to get ready. Plus, Christmas is coming."

"Congratulations!" Marion managed to get a word in. "Everett will be happy, I know. And you, too."

"After all these years, at least one of us deserves it," she replied. "I've sworn off alcohol for good, and it's made all the difference."

"Yes," my mother concurred. "What a fall this has been!"

When Uncle Everett came by the house that Sunday afternoon, he placed a large diamond on Aunt Rachel's finger. "Look at that, Tommy!" he said. "That cost a lot of tobacco leaves." He kissed Aunt Rachel's lips.

My mother squirmed in her chair. A flicker of jealousy flashed briefly in her eyes. She reminded me of the woman in the story from the Bible that Grandmother had read to me one night. Someone else had had a baby for this woman, and the other woman was looking at her with contempt. It made the woman sad, and she made her husband send the woman away.

"Why don't we just get married Christmas Day?" said Uncle Everett. "That'll settle a lot of logistics right there. Only one meal to cook. No need for extra gifts. Savings all around for everyone!"

"Fine with me," Aunt Rachel smiled. "I've never been big on ceremony anyway."

Thus it came about that on Christmas Day, in Grandmother's house in Quilly's hallway, Dr. Wells conducted their wedding and pronounced them "husband and wife." Once again I stood beside Quelle and glanced up at her serene eyes. The pigeons behaved without a ruffle of their feathers. The old Captain looked down from his gold-framed portrait and bestowed his familial blessings.

My grandmother wept; so did my mother. Pearl withdrew to her room to nurse Mamie. Aunt Viola rocked in front of the fireplace, as the rest of us roamed about the house and living room, eating turkey and ham and date pudding. Marion and Uncle Everett drank champagne. Aunt Rachel stayed away from it. Earl, Jessie, Albert and their families were guests, too. A number of Marion's friends from town dropped by as well. A bright fire blazed in the downstairs hearth until late that night.

After the bride and groom and all the guests had departed, Marion and my mother called me back to the Christmas tree. We had opened our gifts earlier, but now the two harbored big smiles on their faces. "There's a package you forgot to open," my mother said.

I peeked under the tree. I hadn't missed anything, to my knowledge. But there lay a long box, wrapped in red paper and decorated with a yellow bow.

"Well, open it," said Marion.

I unwrapped it as fast as my fingers would move and lifted the long box's lid. "Oh, Mama!" I looked up. "Thank you, Marion. Thank you!" I reached in and proudly cradled the handsome .410 in my hands. I pulled it up to my right shoulder and sighted down the top barrel. It was an over-and-under shotgun/rifle: a .22 long rifle top barrel, with the .410 beneath.

"You must be careful, Tommy! You're still just a boy. I don't want you getting hurt with this thing, or shooting just anything, or hurting someone else."

"No, Mama, I won't. I'll be careful." I leaned up to kiss her. Her lips were wet and soft. There were tears in her eyes. They reflected the lights on the Christmas tree: green, red, amber, blue, and white. She turned sideways to kiss Marion, and both hugged me.

Chapter Sixteen

With the coming of the New Year, Mrs. Wells dropped by the house to leave a booklet. That afternoon, upon my return from school, my mother presented it to me. With excitement I opened the envelope in which the minister's wife had placed it. My enthusiasm drained immediately when I saw the pink cover and read its title: *Catechism for Young Children*. I knew what it meant. "Mama, do I have to?"

"Yes, Mr. Biggety! It won't hurt you to study it. Thousands of children have survived it before you."

When Marion came home that night, I showed him the book. "Ah! So they hope to make a theologian of you! Luckily as a child, my Episcopalian mother despised Presbyterian doctrine. I suppose there's no escaping for you, Tommy. We'll work through it together. OK?"

That certainly sounded better. To have a compatriot in suffering soothed my feeling of having been singled out for torment.

As the winter nights crept by, he would ask the designated questions for the coming Sunday, read the answer to each, and wait for me to repeat it. Mrs. Wells' class advanced only two pages per Sunday, so the assignment was easy enough. But the questions! And their answers! Half the time I had no idea what their import implied.

"Who made you?" Marion asked.

"God!"

"What else did God make?"

"All things."

"Why did God make you and all things?"

"For his own glory."

"Let's stop there," Marion moaned, looking up from the page with discomfort. "Tommy, do you have any idea who God is?"

"That's on the next page?" I answered. "I read ahead yesterday."

"Oh! And the answer?"

"God is a spirit."

"And what's a spirit?"

"I guess it's like a ghost. Grandmother says that a ghost once haunted the barn."

"Well, I haven't heard this one. What kind of ghost was it?"

"I don't know, but Grandmother says it moved into the barn after Grandfather's father's death."

"The Captain's?" He set the pink booklet aside. "What happened?

"Grandmother says that after the Captain's death, a loud knocking could be heard in the barn. It happened a week after he died and only at night and lasted for a month. Then the ghost went away."

"That sounds very reasonable. Quite credible! Probably his favorite horse kicking the stall, or the wind blowing one of the doors back and forth."

"Grandmother says it was a ghost, that there wasn't a single door or window open."

Marion studied my face and eyes thoughtfully. "Tommy, you and I are a like. Abstractions are not our forté. Think you can remember your answers till Sunday?"

"Yes, sir! I get a gold star for every page I answer correctly."

"Well, now, that's one, sound, theological incentive, if I ever heard one! We'll just fill up the whole book." He shook his head, from side to side, good-naturedly. "What do you say this Saturday we go back and look for the rock?"

"Can I take my gun?"

"Not yet. Let's wait till you've practiced a little more. There's plenty of time. Then you can carry it."

That Saturday, as he promised, Marion and I returned to the farm to look for Great-Grandfather Howard's rock. A light snow had fallen the night before, and a cold wind moved crisply though the trees. We rode rather rapidly up the road to Uncle Jim's. Near his farm, wet turned off on a ridge to the south. I followed Marion into the woods. A mixture of hemlocks, holly trees, and hickories dominated the crest. The clear sky rose straight up, like a wall into the vault of heaven. Sunlight flooded its blue dome with magnificent splendor. An inch of snow or less covered the ground. As we moved downslope, we passed one rockslide after another, each glistening under a glaze of icy crystals. We halted the horses in a protected copse of hemlocks and sat on a gray boulder that overlooked a steep gorge below. After eating a piece of fried chicken and crunching down on our apples, Marion said:

"Let's tether the horses and explore on foot. There must be a thousand rocks around here. This might just be the trove."

We tied the horses to a low hemlock bough and began walking cautiously among the rocks and dry ferns. Occasionally, Marion bent down to sweep off ice and snow from a promising rock or small boulder. The afternoon passed all too quickly. We walked back to the horses and rode out to the road and down the lane toward Grandmother's farm.

"*Resolute!* Isn't that your grandmother's credo, as well as your Uncle Everett's favorite word? Master Edmonds, our resolve must remain 'resolute.' What do you say?"

I smiled, holding to the saddle horn and reins with all my strength since Sally had begun to lope. The cold air had quickened her own resolve to return to the barn and the warmth of her stall.

"We'll be back!" Marion promised. Once to the barn, Marion patted Fred, then we brushed the horses down and fed them some oats and hay.

January continued to be cold and inclement. Other than caring for the livestock, bitter winds and frigid conditions kept the farmhands confined to menial chores and routine duties. The lambing season brought its usual spate of killings, the tobacco auctions their anticipated rewards, and the cold mornings and evenings their thankless tasks of milking, egg-gathering, and slopping the hogs. Whenever possible, Marion carried me out to Grandmother's to assist Earl complete many of these smaller tasks.

Earl's age had begun to take its toll. His knuckles ached with arthritic pain, his muscles stiffened and limbs went numb. His fingers dropped gloves, axes, hatchets, and pitchforks full of hay. Stooping to gather kindling became a cruel game. His left arm would collapse, and the firewood would tumble out of his hands. He bore it with stoic patience, knowing that time spares no one, least of all the poor of the earth, the humble, or the old.

After a particularly bad Saturday of repeated fumblings, he sat on the steps of the corncrib and placed his hands under his armpits. His lips turned blue; he began shivering. His face turned clammy, his eyes milky and tongue thick. "Tommy, son! I don't feel good." He looked up at me with sunken eyes. Dark, enflamed patches of fire burned in his sockets. His skin looked gray, his wrinkles white.

I had been scattering feed for the chickens. Their clucks resounded in my ears. I was holding the small pail in my hands, when Earl's shoulders slid forward and he collapsed silently by the steps. I ran to his side. "Pearl! Pearl!

Grandmother! Grandmother! Earl's sick! Earl's not moving! Grandmother! Grandmother!" I nudged his body; his eyes rolled up, watery and red. A terrible odor escaped his mouth. His fingernails turned blue.

I looked about. Pearl was running. Little Mamie stood in the entrance of the back screen door. As it slammed shut, it frightened the child and she began to cry. Grandmother picked her up and stared down the dirt lane toward us. Slowly she came out into the yard. She must have reasoned what had happened, because she stopped, wrapped her sweater about Mamie, and listened to Pearl's sobs.

Earl's body lay in a box for three days. The ground was too frozen to open. Albert and Jessie, along with Uncle Everett and Miles, built fires over the site of his pending grave. Soft snowflakes fell as his coffin was lowered passed the frozen mush that lay beside the hole. An icy wind cut through the mourners' clothes as people huddled about his grave and sought to comfort Pearl and one another. My mother held my hand. Grandmother looked on, grim and silent. A black veil covered her eyes and nose. No "preacher" had been summoned for his burial. As Pearl sniffed back cold tears, Marion read from the Bible. "*Blessed are they that mourn, for they shall be comforted. Blessed are the meek, for they shall inherit the earth. Blessed are the pure in heart, for they shall see God.*" Marion closed his brief service with "The Lord's Prayer." Uncle Everett, Aunt Rachel, and my mother joined in, along with Jessie and Albert. But my grandmother remained aloof, withdrawn. Her lips appeared to be praying. But only the fine-tuned ears of Eternity could have heard her whispered thoughts, or the resident spirits of Quilly Hall harkened to her lament.

Toward mid-February, a young stranger stopped by the farm. Grandmother had been in the process of deciphering one of Pearl's dreams when he showed up at the back door.

"It's called 'oneiromancy,'" she explained. "I learned it from a psychology book I read in the 'thirties. Marvelous book!"

Pearl had been having a series of dreams in which she awakened hot, sweating, and "feelin' strange and wonderful."

"I'd be careful not to mention that to just anyone," Grandmother remonstrated. "You're hungry for a man. That's all it means. We'll have to examine our grounds some morning."

These words had scarcely escaped her lips, when we heard the knock.

"Tommy, honey, run, see who that is," Grandmother directed me.

I scooted out of my chair at the kitchen table and opened the door onto the porch. "It's a tall man in a soldier's coat," I announced. "He's got a patch over one eye."

The man smiled. The collar of his olive green jacket had been pulled up to protect his neck from the cold. A faded army cap partially covered his black hair. He wore no gloves. A notable scar ran along his right cheek and disappeared beneath a green army shirt. His bib-overalls were new, but his shoes looked old and used. They were army boots.

"Is Miz. Edmonds home?" he asked. He removed his cap. "I'd like to speak to her, if she is."

Grandmother had been listening and watching. Pearl noticed him, too. Mamie was holding on to the table leg and munching a dried piece of bacon.

"Yes!" Grandmother piped up, with interest in her voice. "Tommy, bring the man in."

I opened the screen door and waited for him to step inside the porch.

"I'm much obliged, Miz. Edmonds," he called. "Mr. Everett said I'd find you home."

"You know Mr. Edmonds?" she replied with hesitancy.

"Yes, ma'am. I walked out yesterday to his place. He said he didn't need nobody but maybe you could use an extra hand. I got a medical discharge on account of my eye, but I can work. I ain't particular where I sleep. I ain't got no job. I just need work and board till I get my self together." He twisted his cap while awaiting her reply. His eyes roved about the kitchen; he noted Pearl and Mamie. "Mighty pretty child," he nodded, with embarrassment, reluctant to appear any more ingratiating than he had to.

"Pearl, pour the man some coffee and fry him some eggs. Please, come in and sit down. Indeed, I could use a man. We've just lost this child's father," she pointed to Pearl, "and we haven't gotten over his loss yet."

"I'm sorry to hear that." He took a seat and watched Pearl pour a cup of coffee. "Ma'am, I don't need to eat. Mr. Edmonds let me stay in his barn last night and his wife fixed me a biscuit a'fore I left. I come with Mr. Edmonds into town. He drove his truck and brought me as far as the tracks."

"Earl did a lot of chores for us and his brothers. We're all getting old here. They could use you in the fields. Let me see your hands."

The man held his palms out for Grandmother to examine.

"Calloused enough! What did you do in the army?"

"Trained to be a machine gunner. They're pretty heavy weapons."

"What did you do before that? And where are you from?"

"From Fincastle. My folks are sharecroppers, ma'am, tenant farmers. I volunteered the day I turned seventeen. I got this patch in a hedgerow in Normandy, from a grenade. My arm got busted up, too. But I can work, ma'am, and work hard. I won't be a slacker. I'd appreciate whatever you can do."

"I don't pay any wages, except at sell-off time! And that's mainly tobacco money, a little wool, some corn, and cattle. You'd have a garden patch and a cabin, but no furnishings, other than a stove and springhouse. That'd be the best I can do. What's your name, anyway?"

Pearl served his coffee and placed Mamie on her hip and began to busy herself about the kitchen. She had set a biscuit filled with a wedge of sidemeat in front of him.

"Thank you, Miss," he smiled at her. "You're all so kind." He took a deep breath. "My name's Henry Long, from Fincastle, like I say. Ain't much more to add." He bit hungrily into the meat and dipped his biscuit in the coffee.

"Well, if you want the work, you can move in today. Do you have a suit case or clothes or anything at all?"

"Yes, ma'am. I left all that at your barn."

"Tommy, run up there and find Jessie or Albert and ask them to show Mr. Long the old Breckenridge cabin. The flue needs cleaning out before you start a fire, but you're welcome to stay in it. Once you get your feet on the ground, we'll see how things work out."

"Thank you, ma'am. I'll strive my best."

"Everett will check on you, too. Any money that's coming to you will always come through him."

"I understand. You won't regret this, Miz. Edmonds. All I need is a chance." He finished his coffee, smiled again at Pearl, and followed me off the porch and into the backyard. I ran ahead to the barn, and, from there, Albert took over and led him up toward the Knobs to Grandmother's third and oldest tenant shack. It lay just beyond a ridge, behind a fence line of cedars, near a small spring. Three hundred yards or so separated it from Albert and Jessie's place, and the shed where Earl had slept at night. The Breckenridge cabin, as it was called, had been constructed of logs and rested on uneven rocks. A stone chimney leaned out from the tallest wall, and a rusted flue poked out of a boarded kitchen window. Chinks of mortar had fallen out between the logs, and sections of the tin roof needed repair or were simply missing. I had followed them to the edge of the yard, or what was left of a yard (a rail fenced-in area, bordered by apple trees and a privy, with a garden patch out back). The tall man entered, stuck his head back out the doorway, and waved to me. I waved back, then turned, and ran most of the way home.

One of the first tasks that needed attention was firewood. Although Quilly Hall enjoyed the benefits of a coal furnace, Grandmother preferred a cookstove in the kitchen and the comfort of fireplaces, day and night, during cold weather. Accordingly, the next weekend I spent at Grandmother's, Mr. Henry and I were appointed woodsmen and sent off to gather more firewood. "Mr. Henry," as I called him, hitched up the wagon, while I searched for the axes and saws that Earl had kept in the tool shed.

With Sally harnessed, we began our ascent into the Knobs. I wanted to see the overlook again, so I directed Mr. Henry toward the lane that wended its way slowly to the top. We came to a cove whose trees had sustained heavy ice damage and stopped to fill the bed with limbs. We also cut up a few logs. Hanging on to my end of the crosscut saw thrilled me enormously. Mr. Long was impressed, too. We got back in the wagon and rode on. As we climbed higher, I said: "Mr. Henry, see right there! Earl once found some bear tracks in the mud. We set a trap for it, but the bear never fell in."

"They're very clever, Mr. Tom. I'm not surprised. But old bears don't like to come too close to humans. Somewhere deep down in that bear's memory, someone shot at him, or dogs chased him, or just nature sent him packin' elsewhere. I wouldn't worry about him, if that's on your mind."

I sat in silence for a while. I didn't want to appear afraid of any bear. Secretly, I had hoped we'd come across more tracks, or see fresh signs of its presence.

At the crest of the overlook, we stopped again and climbed out of the wagon. We both stood on the edge of the ledge and looked out across the farm. Quilly Hall's roof gleamed in the morning sunlight. The twig ends on the orchard trees in the distance below blazed garnet red. Fallow fields stretched town ward in rolling humps of dormant land. Pastures covered the lower hills, where sheep and Hereford grazed.

"A beautiful sight, ain't it?" Mr. Henry declared. He turned and looked down at me with his one good eye. The black patch across his right eye bore flecks of sawdust on it. I noticed how large his hands were.

"Are machine guns heavy?" I asked.

"You bet!" he clenched and unclenched his hands. "But these," he held them up, "come from milkin' cows. I worked on a dairy farm, as well as in the fields. I hope I never have to milk another cow again," he smiled.

We gathered more limbs, sawed up a load of hickory and oak downfall, and prepared to descend the lane. A red-tail hawk screamed overhead and plummeted toward the woods to our east. Moments later it climbed slowly into the sky, clutching a snake. I shivered at the sight and watched the hawk wing heavily across a rocky rise.

"I'd thought it was too early for snakes," the new farmhand surmised. "Learn somethin' new all the time. You might warn Miss Pearl to look out, herself. And for the baby, too. How come she's not married? Or is she? Do you know?"

"She's not. The man ran off. Her daddy's dead, too. And so is her mother and brother. Albert and Jessie are her uncles."

"I'm sorry to hear that. She seems like a mighty fine woman. Where does she live?"

"With us. With my grandmother."

"Ummm! You don't suppose your grandmother would mind my stoppin' by from time to time? Maybe Miss Pearl would do my laundry for me."

We rode on and discharged the firewood near the chopping block beside the smokehouse. It was past lunch, as my stomach's growling reminded me. Just then, my grandmother came to the screen door.

"Mr. Long! Take Sally on back to the barn and come in for lunch. Pearl's fried plenty of chicken and there's ample for you. Tommy, get in here and wash your hands."

That was the third weekend of February. By the end of April, Mr. Long asked Pearl to marry him. My mother drove the two of them into town, where a justice of the peace performed the ceremony. I stayed on the farm with Grandmother and Mamie until they returned. I recall no celebration, flowers, or rings, other than my grandmother and mother presenting the couple with a basket of flatware, a kettle of cooking utensils, and some clean white sheets. Grandmother did give Pearl two sides of meat and a picnic shoulder. Leena, Elsie, and Albert's wife gave them a sack full of dried beans and flour, along with jars of canned apples, pears, and peaches. Uncle Everett and Aunt Rachel bought them a bed and springs, an icebox, a washtub with a ringer, and new crocks for their springhouse.

With the defeat of the German armies that Spring, hope of the war's end soared on the farms. I was too young to understand the economics, but Charles left Uncle Everett's farm to work in Johnson City, which only compounded Miles's obligations. Now, all of the plowing, planting, cultivating, hay mowing, and suckering of tobacco fell on Miles. Aunt Rachel's duties doubled, too. She became the main organizer of the wheat harvest lunches, the berry picking forays, and canning operations.

Mr. Henry worked especially hard to prove his worth. Pearl continued to help my grandmother while Elsie assisted Aunt Viola. More was expected of me, too. Pitching hay and suckering tobacco made me feel like a man. I wanted to be a farmer like Uncle Everett.

Reprieve from the hot weather and toilsome labor came only in the evenings. Grandmother permitted me to steal off into the high meadows to shoot groundhogs. The fat varmints had created labyrinths of tunnels in the soft red clay. A network of their holes lay along fencerows, thus producing hazards for the cattle. I would slip out and follow the road back toward Uncle Jim's until I was parallel with Albert and Jessie's place. Behind their cabin, on the steeper hills, I would lie in wait in the shadows of the meadows and watch for the groundhogs to emerge. Inevitably they did. I would kneel quietly on one knee, bring the bead of the rifle's barrel in line with a groundhog, and pull the trigger. I gave the meat to either Leena or Pearl, depending on whose place was closest to the kill. One evening, Pearl wanted me to stay for dinner. She had roasted a groundhog from the night before and had baked some cinnamon-filled sweet potatoes to complement the dish.

"Lord! Mama! I can't believe you let Tommy go up there and eat that!" my mother protested. "You've never served anything like that, to my knowledge."

"Shaula! Hush! This is the Knobs! The Middle Fork of the Holston! Many's the evening my mother had nothing to feed us, save groundhog. Yes, we're refined, but life's hard for Henry and Pearl."

"Mama! I know. But the thought of *groundhog*! That's another matter."

"Shaula, honey, just remember what the Good Book says: '*Let the days own trouble be sufficient for the day.*'" She sighed deeply, smiled, and rocked methodically in front of the fireplace's cool hearth.

My mother kissed me and gave me a tender hug, before heading out to her car. "Watch for snakes," she warned, as she shut the car door. "Henry told us about the hawk. Be careful with your gun. And do whatever your grandmother asks. You hear?"

"I will, Mama!" I waved, as she rolled her window up and drove down the driveway toward town. Fireflies blinked in the night. Their incandescent glows filled the darkness with the soft throbbing of yellow points of light. Overhead the first stars of evening twinkled into view. The heat of another day was yielding to the cooling whispers of night. I ran back to the porch and sat in the swing and watched the darkness fill the lawn. With imperceptible deepening tones, it settled between the oaks and elms, while starlight glistened on the somnolent dew.

Finally, Grandmother came for me, and we went inside to go to bed.

CHAPTER SEVENTEEN

Toward early June, Albert showed up at the kitchen porch one morning with a bloodstained shirtsleeve in his hands. "It's Jessie's!" he moaned. "He was up in the Knobs fetchin' ramps and never come home. Mike was with him and brung this back. Poor dog's hind leg's broken and face scratched near death. Either a big cat or bear's done got Jessie. Ain't sure which. Kin you call Mr. Everett?"

"Of course!" my grandmother raised her hands to her chest in horror. "I'll call him immediately."

Within an hour, Uncle Everett arrived. He brought his own tracking dogs and saddled Fred as quickly as possible. "Come on, boy!" he signaled to me. "Bring your gun, if you've got it. Albert, help Tommy with Sally! Can you follow us on one of the draft horses?"

"Yes, sir, Mr. Everett! I'll be right behind ya! I'll bring my rifle, too."

Uncle Everett had strapped a pistol to his hip. A rifle poked out of his gun sling along the saddle. "Fall in, Tommy!" Albert released the dogs, and off they lunged down the road.

We set off at a gallop and followed the dogs to a narrow path that led off into the woods. After about thirty minutes, we crossed a brook and started climbing. We could hear the dogs yelping and baying ahead. Uncle Everett slowed Fred and studied the ground for Jessie's tracks or any sign of his having passed that way. Nothing! Not an upturned leaf, disturbed twig, or anything. "Keep coming!" Uncle Everett motioned to me. "Don't miss a thing!" he said, as he stared at the ground.

We rode for twenty minutes or so, crisscrossing our search area, looking for any clue: whether a dropped piece of cloth, bloodstain, shoe, or whatever. Again, nothing! Albert caught up with us and took the lead. His big horse shouldered its way through the underbrush and laurel, huge ferns and sodden leaves. Uncle Everett's dogs had totally disappeared, swallowed by the silence of the Knobs.

"Damn, I wish I knew where they were!" he stated.

Toward noon, we paused to rest near an outcropping on a high crest that overlooked a neighbor's farm to the south of Grandmother's. We had dismounted but were still holding to the horses' reins.

"Look!" pointed Albert.

Below us, toward the east, we could see big Roy; he appeared to be wagging his tail. Dixie ran excitedly beside and around him. They began to bark.

"Hurry!" Uncle Everett blurted.

We remounted and made our way cautiously down a steep slope to a rocky area near a stream. Ferns grew prolifically along its banks. Dog hobble and galax scented the way. We crossed the narrow stream and looked up.

"I'll be damned!" snorted Albert.

There was Jessie, high in a cleft on a rock wall, clinging to a trellis of vines. His shirt was missing, along with his brogans. Blood oozed from claw marks on his back.

"Great day'n a'morning! I didn't think y'all would ever find me," he called down with exhaustion. "I surprised a sow bear. She done her best to kill me."

"Well, drop down and we'll catch you!" his brother hollered.

"Wait!" said Uncle Everett. "Just stay right there." He urged Fred across the spongy ground and placed him against the surface of the rocky wall. Water dripped from its crevices and seeped into the wet mosses under Fred's hoofs. Fred's fetlocks sank into the soft mud before his hoofs found firmer footing. Jessie was still ten-to-twelve feet above Fred's head. Uncle Everett stood in the saddle and reached up for Jessie's feet. Jessie placed them on Uncle Everett's shoulders and slowly descended the rock. Lacerations, a patchwork of tiny cuts and bruises covered Jessie's feet.

"Well, by Granny, you shore had me plannin' yer funeral!" Albert feigned. "I bet ya never plucked a stinkin' ramp!"

"So What? You ain't man enough to eat 'em, nohow!" Jessie retorted.

Albert held his hands up to steady Jessie as Uncle Everett passed him down. A big smile spread cheerfully across Albert's bearded face. Jessie said nothing to his brother. Once off the rock, he winked at me.

"Jessie, ride behind me," Uncle Everett offered. "Do you have any idea where you lost your shoes?"

"No, sir! If anywhere, they're in that bear's mouth. She chewed the hell out of my shirt. Just think what she'ens might o' done to my ass!"

The three men laughed, as we turned the horses about and guided them out of the bottom and up the slope for home. The big dogs dropped behind. They wagged their tails with satisfaction and each rolled over in the stream to cool off.

That Friday afternoon, when Marion picked me up, I repeated the story. Marion's eyes lit up, as I reported each detail.

"Just maybe that's the area we need to search. I'm not sure where that is. Could you find it again?"

"I think so. It was farther back in the woods than we've ever gone. We could see another farm before we rode in to it."

"Your tracks should still be visible. Three horses and dogs make quite a trail. Tomorrow morning, we'll drive out and try again."

By late morning, Marion and I had saddled the horses and had traced our way back to the ridge where I had heard the dogs bark. We paused to look out over the neighboring farmland, before descending the steep slope to the rocky face above the spring.

"So that's where he found sanctuary!" Marion smiled. "Look at all these rocks. They're strewn everywhere."

One could peer up the hill where rocks had slipped off its spiny slope eons ago. Half buried in moss and ferns—most covered with humus and leaves—the rocks poked up along the ridge like fins on some pre-historic reptile's back. We rode up through the protrusions and studied their surfaces. Many were iron dark, rust colored. Others sparkled with tiny facets of mica and quartz. "I bet there's an old mica mine around here someplace, Tommy. It's either just above these rocks, or down by the stream."

We rode through the ferns along the steep slope but found nothing of note. We returned to the bottom and followed the seeping springs that oozed along the base of the rock wall. Droplets of water dripped in cool streams from its hanging vines. Tiny translucent spiders had made their home in the dense web of intricate vegetation.

"Up there!" Marion pointed. "See! Just below the ledge of the rock. Can you make that out? What is it?"

I sat forward in the saddle and patted Sally's neck. I strained to look up. Hidden under festoons of brush, there appeared to be an opening. "A cave?"

"Yes! Let's check it out."

We guided the horses around the base of the rock, until we could negotiate a trail up passed the rock's face. We dismounted and examined the dark hole.

"Just a depression where some tree fell long ago," Marion surmised. "I still bet there's a mine up here somewhere." He looked at his watch. "It'll have to wait till another time. I'm beginning to doubt if we'll ever find Howard's infamous rock." He expelled a sigh of disappointment.

While dismounted we ate our lunch. We rode back down to the springs, watered the horses, and let the horses amble slowly out of the Knobs.

"Do you think maybe Uncle Jim just made up that tale?" I asked.

"Wish I knew! Your grandmother insists it's true. We'll come back another time. Defeat's not in our vocabulary," Marion frowned, with a tight grimace about his mouth. Tiny beads of sweat sparkled on his goatee. "O, such a tawdry day!" he half-hollered, half-winked at me. From somewhere out of the Knobs his echo bounced back. He laughed aloud and spurred Fred faster. Both horses galloped all the way back to the barn.

One weekend while staying at Grandmother's, Marion and my grandmother fell into a heated discussion over a host of questions and answers in my *Children's Catechism*. I had earned gold stars on every page and qualified to be confirmed for the Eucharist, but both my mother and Marion felt I was too young for such a formidable step.

"There are some I approve," Marion emphasized, as he discussed them with Grandmother. "Like, 'Can you see God?' Or, 'How do you know you have a soul?' Or, 'What becomes of you at death?'"

Their answers were: "No, but he always sees me," "I can think about God and the world to come," and, "The body returns to dust, and the soul goes into the world of spirits."

Marion had found these statements acceptable. "Any religion or religious person can espouse them," he said to her. "There is a sense in which we are perceived beyond ourselves. All human beings wonder about God and death. And who's to say that, long after death, our spirits aren't taken up into the realm of memory, just the way we remember our ancestors? Plus, they live on in our genes. But, Mama Edmonds, to insist on more than that, borders on fanaticism, and do we really want Tommy to grow up brain-washed?"

"You sound, oh, so modern! So insouciant!" she glared at him. "There's nothing theologically incorrect about believing in God, or his only-begotten Son, or our need for a Savior."

"Mama Edmonds, I don't' disagree about believing in God or the need for some transcendent dimension that encourages us to be our best. But those answers about sin and God's punishment defy logic and universal goodness. To punish a literal Adam with literal death, to indoctrinate a child's mind with the dogma that he's been born into a 'state of sin and misery' that deserves the 'wrath and curse of God,' which in turn requires God's own Son's suffering and death to assuage this divine ogre's wrath, is a horrible, if not an unforgivable, piece of madness. If God exists, he cannot be evil; he cannot entertain wrath, nor exact it to satisfy some twisted notion of retribution. That's what upsets me, Mama, and that's what I want Tommy to be spared. Yes, let him grown up humble before the Infinite, in love with the farm and its people, along with the glory of the Knobs! But to overlay that with a poisonous darkness contradicts the very wonder of Quilly Hall. Don't you think so? In your own heart of hearts, Virginia, don't you agree? Don't you believe that yourself, when it's all said and done?"

My Grandmother's rouged face tightened. She continued her rocking as her hands massaged each other in transparent distress. Her eyes darted back and forth, sometimes looking at him, sometimes at me. "You know too much for your own good," she muttered. "No amount of universal goodness, as you allude to it, has ever transformed any life. Oh, it may sound good in famous books, shelved away somewhere in our libraries. Holman preferred to remain a pagan. I hated it, but came to respect him. At least he was honest. It's poor Everett's fate, too. But I don't want Tommy growing up a pantheist. Yes, a pantheist! I'm not a theological moron. I've read Emerson and Thoreau and all those other Transcendentalists. And I don't believe in a quasi-spiritual realm, where every soul is condemned to wander some untrodden path, inaccessible to truth and happiness. The Bible makes it all so clear. We need a Savior; we need divine guidance. Marion, our own goodness is worthless, when goodness really counts. God knows the Edmonds are far from perfect! God knows the sufferings my father bore, the poverty we endured year after year. The hand of God's wrath was laid against us. Lincoln was right. We still struggle under God's curse. But thank heavens for the farm!" She sat forward in her chair. "It's beyond good and evil, and so are the Knobs. I am too old to change. I have lived too long to doubt otherwise. I will leave this world with no illusions. However you define God, God exists, Marion. And, yes, God is good. Perhaps the 'wrathful part' is wrong. But I don't want Tommy believing that his own goodness is sufficient, that he won't need God at some point in the future, that he'll always succeed in everything, and that the Edmonds pride and resoluteness are all he'll ever need. I may be an old woman, but I'm not a fool."

The rungs of her rocker made a soft squeaking sound. The muscles in her face relaxed. She sat back in her chair, smiled, and reached a hand toward me. "Tommy, always love Marion," she advised, glancing tenderly at him. "He's the best thing that's happened to this family in a long time."

"Mama Edmonds! You're one hell of a devil's advocate! Tom, let's saddle up and search for that rock again."

Soon afterwards, we were riding out of the barn and down the road that led back to the Knobs.

We returned to the site where Uncle Everett had rescued Jessie. We rode slowly through the dense undergrowth of galax, ferns, and dwarf laurel. We climbed several steep slopes and descended more ridges. The woods of hickories, oaks, and poplars shaded our search and protected us from the sun's torpid heat. Humid and muggy air settled about us and covered the horses with a coat of rank lather.

"We'd better head for the river," said Marion. "We ought not be far from it, any way."

We climbed another ridge, whose long crest lay under a mantle of moss and smooth rocks. We could hear the Middle Fork of the Holston purling gently ahead.

"Better rest them a tad," Marion stated, as he brought Fred to a halt and dismounted. He held to Sally's reins, as I dismounted, too. "Look at these nice rocks," he pointed. "Let's scrape the moss off a few."

We broke off a cluster of hemlock boughs and began sweeping the rocks back and forth. One large stone in particular caught Marion's attention.

"Help me with this one," he said.

We scrubbed its surface of moss and crusty lichens and ran our fingers across it.

"Hey! I've got something!" Marion said with excitement.

We scrubbed harder until we could make out a series of clean grooves in the stone.

"It's somebody's initials!" Marion leaned forward and brushed the stone clean with his hand. "Look!"

I peered over his shoulder. My heart thumped in my chest. I could feel my body cavity shaking. On the stone I could see a set of clean, beautifully carved initials: "H. C. L."

"Howard Campbell Lorran," Marion uttered. "Help me roll it over."

I knelt down and pressed my knees into the damp leaves and dark soil about the rock and grasped it with Marion. We tugged and tugged, each time improving our grip, until we rolled it over. Nothing! Not a mark lay on its under side. Earthworms and brown centipedes struggled to burrow themselves anew, as they sought escape from the forest light.

"Here! Let's set it upright," Marion suggested. "We'll have to come back with a tarp and drag it out."

We set the stone up, like a grave marker, and packed leaves and clumps of earth around it. Marion stomped the soil with his boots, until the stone stood erect, with Great-Grandfather Lorran's initials clearly visible. We angled the stone to face the river.

"Now, to find our way out of here," Marion glanced about.

We mounted the horses and descended toward the river. To our left, or north, we could see a clearing in the distance. We headed in its direction and came out just above Uncle Jim's old orchard.

"I'll be! Maybe that stone's closer than we think."

Marion guided Fred toward the river, as I followed on Sally. We rode toward the ford and let the horses drink.

"What do you think, Master Thomas?" Marion inquired with a huge smile. "I think we're going to find it soon. What about you?"

"I sure hope so. Wouldn't Uncle Everett be surprised?"

"Surprised, indeed!" The words had scarcely slipped from his lips when he looked up toward the old house and its outbuildings. "What a shame! What a crying shame! We've got to do something about this, before it all rots and sinks in the ground. And look at the fields, the tobacco patch, and garden! They worked too hard to let it go like this."

He turned slowly in the saddle, tugged on the reins, as we guided Fred and Sally out of the river and up the lane. We stopped at the house, went inside and peered around. "Need to replace these windows," said Marion. "And get a new stove. Wouldn't hurt to fire it up come this fall. Maybe we could camp out here some this winter and hunt for turkey, or maybe that bear."

I followed him about the house, the lots outside, the old chicken coop, and barn. We walked up to the graves and pulled weeds from around

Great-Grandfather Howard's stone. Uncle Jim's grave mound had sunk. A groundhog had begun digging a hole nearby but appeared to have abandoned the effort. "I bet a fox got him," Marion pointed to some dried hair in the weeds. "For all its glory, there are no happy endings in nature," he stated with a vacant stare. We returned to the horses and rode back along the dusty lane to Grandmother's farm.

One evening the following week, Uncle Everett and Aunt Rachel, along with my mother and Marion, came out to Grandmother's for supper. Aunt Viola and Elsie joined us, too. In fact, Elsie did most of the cooking, along with Pearl, before Pearl returned to her own cabin. Elsie and Pearl had prepared two fryers, corn on the cob, tomatoes out of the garden, peas, biscuits, and two apple pies. The table seemed empty without Earl, Uncle Jim, Pearl, and her baby, but we fell into our meal with the usual clatter of forks on porcelain and the scrape of knifes and serving ware on the large oval platters.

"I tell you, Everett, Tommy and I are getting closer and closer to finding Howard's stone. We located one he initialed and sat it upright. It's not all that far from his home place. I'd like to drag it down here with a tarp and set it up in the yard."

"Oh, don't do that!" Grandmother brooded. "Just leave it there, for others to discover from time to time. If my father had wanted it set up in the yard, he'd brought it down himself."

Uncle Everett wiped his lips with his napkin and turned to Marion. "Forgive me, Marion, but I don't believe that story about Mr. Howard's rock. If it existed, someone would have found it by now, or Uncle Jim would have dropped some clues, before he grew too old to remember its location. But I agree with you about restoring the house and barn and maybe finding someone to live there again and farm the place. What do you think, Aunt Vi?"

The old woman brushed back a strand of gray hair that had stuck to her face while eating corn. Her blue lips appeared smileless, her brow heavy with age, her eyes watery. "I don't know. It's in your hands, Everett. I'd love to live there again, before I die." Her narrow shoulders seemed almost unable to support her disheveled hair and petite head. "We only pass this way once. I don't want to be buried in town, but out there with Jim, and the children we lost in childbirth, and his father, Howard."

"Nonsense!" huffed Grandmother. "You can't go back! The place is unlivable! Besides, where you and Elsie are now is vastly superior. Your springhouse is clean, running with fresh cold water, your cow gives milk, your garden's right at your fingertips, and all the help you need just for the asking. I'd worry myself sick if you went back."

"You would be lonely and isolated," said Uncle Everett. "But if that's what you want, that's what we ought to do."

"I'd go with you, Miss Viola," said Elsie. "Them orchard apples is some of the best in the Knobs, and the spring colder than ourn. Plus, we could raise a passel of pigs and chickens, and maybe even sell some. I'm still strong, and I ain't plannin' on marryin' no more. Old Ambrose broke me of that."

Everyone smiled. "Hear, hear!" chimed in Aunt Rachel. "Don't ever rule out love," she smiled at Uncle Everett.

"Ma'am, it wouldn't be love. Just the need for he'p and a body for comfort from the loneliness and cold."

"Well, I don't want to hear of it!" Grandmother rejoined. "Life's hard enough around here without all of you being so maudlin. If it weren't for Tommy and the summers, I'd be lonely, too. My time's limited." She stared at Everett. She uttered her words with challenge and remorse.

No one replied immediately. Finally my mother broke the silence. "We've been talking about that, Marion and I. You're more than welcome to stay with us during the winters, or we could look for a permanent resident, a widow herself, to lodge with you."

"Absolutely not! I have no interest in attending on anyone else. I'd rather have Viola and Elsie."

"Well, we'll not be resolving this tonight," Uncle Everett stated. "The summer's young. Let's enjoy what's left of it. Hopefully, the Japs will be defeated in another year. Who knows what lies ahead for any of us, especially the farms?"

"How very true!" Marion concurred. "We'll soon find out, I fear."

On that uncertain note, we finished our meal in silence, all but forgetting about the luscious pies. I ate my slice later, after everyone had left Quilly Hall.

"Don't you fret, Tommy!' Grandmother exhorted, as we rocked on the porch. "All this doom and gloom talk about the war and what's going to happen. I have no intention of abandoning this farm. It would be nice, though, to see Jim's place raised phoenix like to its glory again. My own poor mother slaved to keep it warm and dry. She died in its kitchen, Tommy, with her hands in the dough tray. She outlived my father by less than a year."

CHAPTER EIGHTEEN

THE NEWS OF THE Japanese surrender brought jubilation to the farm. Grandmother pronounced the following Saturday a holiday and allowed Albert, Jessie, and Henry to help themselves to a smoked ham, each. In addition, she provided fryers for a picnic celebration on the Hall's lawn. When Albert and Jessie discovered that Henry could replace Earl on the base tub, a dance was organized and Knob folk came from adjoining farms to participate in the festivities. Grandmother rocked on the porch and Aunt Viola actually quick-stepped to a mountain jig. Marion, my mother, Aunt Rachel, and Uncle Everett also attended, along with some of Marion's legislature friends and members of the town council.

The latter, however, brought fifths of whiskey with them. Not aware of Aunt Rachel's previous history, the mayor asked her for glasses for himself and his buddies, and Aunt Rachel, all too innocently, obliged. I noticed that Uncle Everett seemed edgy and displeased with Marion's friends, but out of a spirit of congeniality, he accepted a drink when they offered him one. So did Aunt Rachel. As twilight blended into dusk and dusk into the shadows of evening, one after the other of the fifths was emptied. Aunt Rachel's speech became slurred. One glass led to another. Grandmother became agitated, fidgety, and, finally, alarmed.

"This has got to stop!" she admonished Uncle Everett. "Marion, it's time for these people to go home! Look at Rachel! I won't have any more of this. Act quickly, or I will embarrass all of you. This has got to stop!" she repeated.

Uncle Everett rose slowly to his feet. He walked to the edge of the porch, descended the steps, and ambled good-naturedly toward the musicians. He motioned to Albert and whispered something in his ear. Albert nodded, swept his fiddle bow across the strings with a flourish of jovial notes, then he brought it down in a swift and curt squeal. "Gotta milk cows come mornin," he announced. "Y'all be good, now, and thank

Mrs. Edmonds a'fore you leave. And the good Lord for endin' this war! Halleluiah!" he shouted.

On that declaration, the music ended. The revelers gathered up their baskets, children, and other possessions and came by the porch to thank Grandmother. Marion's friends bowed awkwardly, tipsy to say the least, and broke off to leave as well.

When all were gone, Uncle Everett turned uneasily toward Aunt Rachel. Her face had resumed that look of old. A sallow chill possessed it; swollen glossy eyes glared at him. "Come, Rachel. I'm sorry this happened. Are you all right?" He extended her his hand.

"Hell, no!" she retorted. "What do you think? I want another drink. Where's the bottle? Where's the GD bottle?" she cursed. "Where's my glass?"

"You're holding it. Here, give it to me!" Uncle Everett said. Sadness and disgust twitched about the corners of his mouth. "Take my arm. We'll get back on track tomorrow."

"Like hell!" she replied. "I've been too damn good, too damn long. I wanna be me again."

"Oh, Rachel!" my mother pleaded. "You can't mean it!"

Aunt Rachel rolled her eyes and dropped her glass. It shattered as it struck the hard porch flooring.

Mother and Marion came to Uncle Everett's side. "I'm so sorry for this," said Marion. "I had no idea this would happen."

Uncle Everett waved his hand, as if to dismiss Marion's culpability in any way. "Please, it's not your fault," he said, with gruff impatience. "I'm to blame, too."

Grandmother sat rigid in her rocker. "Just get her out of here," Grandmother demanded. She placed her hands to her face and began to cry. "Oh, Hamilton! Hamilton! Where are you, dear son? Where are you, dear boy? Why did God take you? What wrong did you ever do? I want to be left alone, to cry," she suddenly said. She looked up at all of us, patted Viola's forearm, and dabbed a waded handkerchief to her eyes. "Go on. Just go on! Shaula, take Tommy to bed. He's our only dear hope. If only his daddy were alive!"

I looked up at Marion and Uncle Everett and my mother. Uncle Everett ran his fingers through my hair and patted the side of my head. Marion's face sagged with grief. He took me by the hand and led me into the hallway. I could hear my mother helping Uncle Everett pull Aunt

Rachel out of the chair. "God damn all of you!" she kept cursing, as they assisted her off the porch and out into the yard toward the car.

Marion and I sat down on the Napoleon seat beside Quelle. I glanced up toward the gallant Captain's portrait. The old Captain's head seemed bowed itself, his countenance humble.

"You love this hall, don't you?" observed Marion. "You mustn't let your Aunt Rachel's profanity upset you. It's an illness, Tommy. A disease. Some people have it and some don't. You and I are the lucky ones," he smiled.

"Does she mean what she says? Doesn't she know she's hurting Uncle Everett? And Grandmother, too?"

"No. Tomorrow, she won't remember a thing. That's the horrible part about the disease. She'll never know, or fathom, the heartaches her words cause. Life's strange like that, Master Thomas. You hurt people, not meaning to, and never realize what you've done."

We sat there awhile, until my mother came in and took me up to bed. After tucking me in, she wrung her hands momentarily. Tears glistened in her eyes. Marion took her hands in his, bent down, and kissed my forehead. "Good night, Tommy. One day we'll find that stone, just you and me. And we'll give a big party afterwards, just the two of us. For ourselves. And we'll be like your great-grandfather Howard and Uncle Jim. We'll keep it a secret in turn."

I liked that idea very much and could hardly wait to fall asleep to awaken to a new day.

Early the next morning, I awoke to an eerie silence. I could hear the chickens clucking in the driveway, but the usual hum of the house was absent. No sounds from the kitchen, or stir of skirts in the hallways slipped up the stairs. Bright, summer daylight streamed through the window glass, causing the ever-present ubiquitous dust particles to somersault lazily in the warm air. Birds twittered in the nearest elms by the porch. An uneasy silence permeated the house.

I slid out of bed, slipped into my clothes, and hurried down the stairs to the hallway. Quilly's shadow formed a restful pattern against the wall; the old Captain's face shimmered in the sun's glare. The hand on his sword trembled in the fierce light. I opened my grandmother's door and peered into the living room. Her rocker's rungs squeaked softly, as she pushed herself back and forth with the sole of her left foot. My mother was seated beside her.

"Mama! What's up? Summer's not over, is it? I don't want to go home yet."

"Hush! Tommy!" she whispered. Large tears glistened in her eyes. A low sob broke above the methodical squeak of Grandmother's chair. "Come here, Tommy. Your Aunt Rachel's dead." She held out her right hand for me to take.

I felt numb, curious, and deeply sad. Death I understood. It meant people never returned. You never saw them again. They went off to heaven, I supposed. Or at least their spirit did, according to the *Catechism*. I walked slowly toward my mother and took her hand.

"She killed herself, Tommy. With a knife, when they got home last night. Your Uncle Everett took her to the hospital, but it was too late. She bled to death in the car. The police listed it as an accident. She fell on it, Everett said, after she placed it against her chest. He's at the funeral home now."

I sat on the edge of my mother's lap and stared at my father's picture on the mantle. My grandmother had yet to look up. She simply rocked, with her hands folded acquiescently across her lap, her chin slightly raised, her eyes cast down. She must have rocked like that for ten minutes, before she suddenly pursed her lips, glanced about, and stopped rocking. She focused her gaze on me.

"That's a terrible thing, Tommy! Terrible for her! Terrible for Everett. The hand of Providence has found us, again. Holman once said, 'If ever a family was forged in hardship and hammered on the anvil of adversity, the Edmonds were.'" She paused momentarily and resumed rocking with a push of her right foot. "My father never complained. He suffered in silence and bore his infirmities till he died. Your grandfather Holman was equally stalwart. How far we have come from their day! How little we have added to what they've left us. Where will you bury her, Shaula, or has Everett even thought of that?"

"I suppose in Wytheville, beside our mother and father, unless Everett has other plans."

"Well, he'll be coming out soon. There are only three plots left in town. One for me, one for Everett, and one for you, if you want it."

"I'd rather not think about that." My mother sat forward. As she did, I scooted out of her chair. She brushed her skirt off and smoothed out its wrinkles. "Tommy, you need to have some breakfast. Then let's go outside and wait for Marion and your uncle to return."

Aunt Rachel's funeral was held in Wytheville. Only a handful of the family attended—Uncle Everett, my mother, Marion, and I. Grandmother stayed home on the farm, along with Aunt Viola, Elsie, and Pearl. We rode the train from Abingdon to Wytheville. Uncle Everett sat in the mail car, to accompany the casket. Marion and my mother sat silently together, opposite me in a coach car. I sat by the window and watched the passing landscape of woods and meadows, bright cornfields and green hills, steep granite embankments and rugged ravines, and listened to the engine's whistle and the rumble of the wheels. I could feel the sway of our coach and the dip and rise of the rails on the crossties. "Clack, clack, clack" trundled the cars. The swoosh of crossings, the clang of bells, and the crescendo and diminution of passing objects added their spell of mournful empathy to our ride. At the graveside, a Catholic priest from Roanoke presided. His black and white vestments and gold-tasseled stole reminded me of the old Dominicker rooster that loved to strut and crow in front of Jessie's cabin. The priest read from his missal in Latin. Uncle Everett stood gaunt, emotionless, grim. My mother slipped her arm through his to comfort him. A tear formed in his left eye. He raised his hand awkwardly and wiped it away, clenched her gloved hand, and kissed her neck. After the service, Marion put his hand to Uncle Everett's shoulder. "I'm so sorry," said Marion. "Please forgive me." "Enough, enough," Uncle Everett replied. "I don't want to hear another word like that." Moments later, we returned to the station and caught a through-train to Marion, Abingdon, and Bristol. We had supper in the dining car. A crisp white creased linen cloth covered the table. Nickel-plated flatware and shiny white dishes attested to the elegance of the Pocahontas line. Water sloshed in the glasses, as the coach car swayed from side to side. A tall black waiter came to our table. His polite demeanor and cheerful smile transformed my sadness into an experience of grace. I had seen so few black men. When he brought us finger bowls, I dipped my entire hands in with a huge smile.

With the coming of fall, I returned to the house in town, to live with Marion and my mother. My leaving Quilly Hall proved especially daunting for Grandmother. Her usual ebullience, which had been slowly eroding since Uncle Jim's death, sank to a low ebb when my mother picked me up for the ride back to Abingdon. It was a late Sunday afternoon. A dry, brownish red sky foretold of the glorious coming sunset, reflected on the leaves in the Knobs. Grandmother, my mother, and I were seated on the porch that overlooked the vast lawn. An arid hue had settled in the orchard across the road.

"Shaula, if you only knew how lonely I feel!" Grandmother stated, as she rocked. "I'm embarrassed to complain. Me and all my talk about fortitude and resolve! If it weren't for Pearl's and Elsie's help, I don't think I could bear it."

"I understand, Mama. It must gnaw on poor Everett, too."

"Yes, I think so." She continued to rock.

I rocked with them, fascinated by the creak of the rungs and the rhythmic spell it cast. Grandmother could be so erudite, aristocratic, genteel, and, on occasion, even boisterous and overflowing with rollicking stories and joy. Yet, equally, she could be cold, superstitious, and fearful of the unknown. Her hypnotic rocking and long garment of black gabardine only added to her inaccessibility that day.

"Oh, well!" she sighed, smiling toward me. "You must come and stay with me every weekend. Hear? Grandmother will fete you with all your favorite delights. Egg custard, apple pies, big yellow cakes with chocolate icing, biscuits, ham, ladles of thick milk gravy! Ummm, umm! Even I can hardly wait," she chortled, in her good-natured manner. "Shaula, you must bring him! I'll see he does his homework, every Saturday night. I won't send him back ill prepared. No, siree! Not this Grandmother! And we'll read in the library and listen to Bach and Beethoven and all your favorite bands. Nothing but the best for Thomas Hamilton Edmonds! That's a strict guarantee! Yes, sir! You have it on my word. So help me! And that's a promise. Yes, siree!"

Promise or no promise, Marion and my mother kept their end of the bargain.

Frequently, on Fridays, Uncle Everett would be at Grandmother's by the time the school bus let me off near the springhouse. I'd climb the stile and run up the gravel path, pass the apple shed, and mount the back steps to the kitchen. Sometimes Pearl would be present, either cleaning house, or cooking for the weekend. She and Grandmother would bake lemon layer cakes and two to three apple or berry pies, place them in a corner china cabinet in the dining room, and keep them locked until Saturday or Sunday. The layer cakes were Uncle Everett's favorite dessert. Now that Aunt Rachel was dead, he stopped by Grandmother's three to four times a week, especially on the weekends. He had returned to his former self, if that's possible, nursing a forbidding smile and talking to himself. This was uniquely the case, if I found him sitting alone on the porch. Otherwise, he would be pacing the kitchen and half-arguing with, or gruffly contesting, whatever Grandmother was attempting to say. His best frame of mind he reserved for the horse barn and conversations with Jessie and Albert, as displayed one Friday in mid-September.

"You think Sally's good for one more foal?" he asked Jessie. "She and Fred are both getting old. What do you think?"

"I rightly don't know, Mr. Everett," Jessie replied. "But I wouldn't pair her up with Fred. He ain't got stamina no more. Look at the poor critter! Even his face is gray and fetlocks all matted stiff. Poor thing can hardly budge till mid-mornin' or afternoon. But he's done his share, I reckon," he patted the stallion's gray neck.

"Mr. Marshall up the valley's got a spirited stud," Albert volunteered. "We could take Sally up there and see what happens," he grinned. "I'll take her Monday, if'n Marshall agrees."

"I'll give him a call and see," Uncle Everett rejoined.

Early the next morning, on Saturday, I found Uncle Everett seated in the living room with Grandmother, both sipping coffee out of their saucers.

"Mama, you haven't told my fortune in years. Just what the hell's in store for me now?" He heard me come in, smiled, and mopped a strand of black hair out of his face. "Boy, just how tall are you? Mama, look at him. That kid must be five-five! And he's how old? Eight? Nine?"

"Eight!' I stated proudly. "But I'll soon be nine."

"Run get yourself some breakfast," Grandmother ordered. "There's oatmeal on the stove and milk in the ice box. Eat heartily. Everett's going to find that rock for you, just as soon as you eat."

"Is that true? Do you know where it's at?"

"Oh, Tommy! Thomas Edmonds! Don't say 'at'!" Grandmother reeled forward, as she set her saucer down and covered her face with her hands. "Your speech is unbelievable. Everett, don't let him talk like that!"

"Yes and no!" Uncle Everett laughed. "Just do what Mama says. We'll leave directly, once it warms up."

"Yes, sir!" I replied, as I hurried to the kitchen. I found the milk in the refrigerator, which Grandmother continued to call "the ice box"— though we had one of those, too. It stood on the side porch, near a second kitchen entrance. It was reserved for fresh milk, blue john, buttermilk, and cream. After downing a half-bowl of oatmeal, I returned to the living room.

Grandmother was rocking softly, but she was bent forward, with her gaze fixed on Uncle Everett's cup's contents.

"Maybe my eye's failing me, or Gypsy's mind on furlough," she smiled, "but I don't see a thing worth noting." She handed the cup back to my uncle. "It's just as well. You've been through enough."

He peered in the cup, himself, and grimaced a little. "Think I'll run for sheriff one day, Mama. Miles can run the farm himself. Hell, he's better at it than I am. It's a lot better than wringing my hands and pacing the farm and driving mindlessly all over town."

"And dangerous, too. You'd make a fine sheriff, but they're too many thieves and cutthroats roaming the county, bootleggers, and shiftless trash. You'd get killed. But you'd make a good one. Your great-great Uncle Willis was sheriff, back in the 1830s, and the riff-raff were just as abundant then. I'd hate to see you get hurt."

"I'm a good shot, Mama, and I'm not afraid of anyone. It's the administrative duties that'd get me down. That's all. Besides, I'm good at sizing up people. There are plenty of soldier boys coming home who'd make great deputies. Plus, we're facing a new era. This county is going to grow. Maybe from sheriff, I could run for the Council, or even for Congress. I'm tired of corrupt, inept assholes representing our district. And Marion's happy where he is. He'd support me, he said. The bank's going to grow too. Hell, Mama! Maybe I could become someone after all. You've always wanted that."

"You already are! Don't talk like that! There's not another family equal to ours. That's a fact. It's history. It's right there in Mr. Summers' book," she pointed toward the library. "'The most distinguished family of Washington County,' he says."

"Mama, that's history. That's the problem. It's *past history*. It's the 1940s. And farms like ours are on the way out. Sharecropping days are over. There'll never be another Miles, or Jessie, or Albert to work for nothing again, for just a cabin and place to live. Henry Long's a miracle, Mama. Men like him are rarer than hen's teeth." He suddenly sprang up, as if bewildered and miffed, if not forgetful of where he was. "O God, I should have been the one killed in Guadalcanal. Maybe Hamilton would have known what to do. Jesus! Holy Christ, Mama! What am I to do?"

Ordinarily, Grandmother would have blistered his ears for his profanity, but she sat, rocking, clutching her cup and saucer, as lost in thought as he. "Well, we'll not solve it this way," she heaved with a heavy breath.

"Just let me know when you run for office. I'll host the announcement party, and try to get back into social circles. It's been years since I've worn anything other than black. It would be good for me, too. '*Mrs. Edmonds, at home*,'" she pretended to scribble on a card. A huge smile transformed her face and filled it with soft radiance.

"Thanks, Mama! Well, boy!" he grinned, his eye finally focusing on me. I was standing quietly by the window. "Get on your jacket, and let's head for the Knobs! Jessie's already got the horses saddled."

Soon thereafter, we were mounted and riding hard on the road toward Uncle Jim's place. Uncle Everett led the way but, after thirty or forty minutes, brought Fred to a halt. The big horse stopped, snorted with gratitude, and rested beside the lane. The sumac leaves had turned a purplish red, along with the foliage of sweet gums. The scarlet hues of the dogwood embraced us. Their limbs draped over us and over the dusty weeds that hugged the embankment. I reached up and pulled a limb down and plucked off a handful of leaves. Titmice and chickadees flitted about, as I released the branch. I examined the bright foliage and turned the leaves over delicately in my hands before letting them somersault to the ground.

"Tommy, just where is this place you and Marion found Grandfather Howard's initials? Are we anywhere near it?"

I sat forward in the saddle and wiped a stream of perspiration from under the band of my cap. Sally shook the reins and swished her tail against my legs. "No, sir. It's almost near the farmhouse, back on a ridge. We could hear the Holston in the distance and rode down to it."

"Well, let me know when you think we're near it." He nudged Fred's sides with the heels of his boots and led off again.

We rode for another thirty-to-forty minutes along the dry road. Near the high embankment where the cat had bounded out of the woods, I called to Uncle Everett and pointed to my right. "About there, I think."

Uncle Everett slowed Fred and swung him about to climb the embankment. Up, up struggled Fred, but he reached the crest and shook his mane, sending slobbers all over me, as Sally and I were right behind him. "Whoa, boy!" Uncle Everett patted his neck. "Better rest again. Which way, now?"

"Straight ahead. Up on that ridge," I pointed again. "There were lots of rocks around, mostly flat, but some big ones, too."

"You're the boss," he smiled. "Just take them at a slow pace. Yell when you think we're near."

The woods felt wonderfully cool and restful. Many oak leaves had begun to turn brown; the hickories had already lost their foliage. All this was from dryness, however. No frosts had burned the leaves, at least, not in the Knobs. A few birches had turned a fuscous gray on the edges of their serrated surfaces. A lone maple tree glowed blood red in the forest light. Otherwise, the dusky air filled the woods with a dusty film of yellow and green colors.

As we crossed the next ridge, I recognized the cant of the hill and the leeward lip of the crest. "There! Right there! It's right there! See it?" The edge of the flat stone caught my eye, its upright position still facing Uncle Jim's farmland that rolled away somewhere downslope and over the hills below.

Big Fred's right hind leg almost kicked the stone before Uncle Everett saw it. "I'll be! Look at that! As big as day! Thank God it isn't a snake!"

Uncle Everett dismounted and tied Fred's reins to a laurel bush. He bent down and examined the stone. "Those are his initials all right. Look at 'em! As smooth as a stone cutter's." He ran his fingers gently across the grooves. "Maybe it's true after all. But I'll have to see it with my own eyes." He looked up, as if studying the crest of the hill, its other rocks, and gnarled brush and fallen leaves. "Let's scout about. Whatta you say? Here, slip off your horse," he reached for my reins.

I slid off the saddle while he tied Sally's reins to a hemlock bough near Fred. Cool air drifted across the ridge. A towhee flew up from a patch of leaves where it had been scratching for a meal. Its rufus sides, black head and back, and white chest made it imminently visible. A nuthatch with gray feathers and a white breast hopped about, upside down, on a hickory tree just past the laurel.

Uncle Everett had noticed my interest in the birds and the fact that frequently I pulled down branches to feel leaves.

"Tommy! You ought to be a forester, or study forestry. I did years ago but dropped out of school, like a fool. You're a natural. Most of the Edmonds aren't. You take after your Uncle Jim and Great-Grandfather Howard. They were mountain men, rangers of the Knobs, hunters and farmers, but woodsmen foremost. I think I got a little of their blood in my veins. Your daddy, though, was more like Mama. Intelligent, well-spoken, well-read, eager to leave his mark on society! He might have made governor one day, or at least become an attorney—like our father before us, and our grandfather before him. Those men were entrepreneurs, determined to obtain fame and fortune, however it might be gained. They amassed great wealth but made enemies in the process. People of lesser ambition got jealous. It's called 'spite,' Tommy. Damn if anybody needs to wallow in spite. If you do something wrong, Tommy, admit it. And if somebody's better at something than you are, don't envy them. Don't say mean things about them or try to hurt them behind their back. That's what 'spite' is. Envy and spite! They've sent more people down the road to hell than alcohol or hanging out with bad women." A smile slipped past his thin lips. "There is so much to learn, Mr. Biggety. Take it from me. Life is just one long classroom of 'shouldn't have done this' and 'ought to have done that.' I should know," he studied my face for my reaction. "I've learned it all the hard way."

I liked hearing Uncle Everett expound. Grandmother's monologues always came across as a little too heavy, a little too obviously pedagogic, as if she were trying to impress the family's history and greatness on me, in spite of its flaws and sorrows. We were superior to others, in her mind. People in town knew this but were just too common to acknowledge the truth. Uncle Everett was straightforward. He said what came into his mind, nothing more and nothing less, direct and unfiltered. He relished such talk and so did I.

"Well, we'd best be looking about, Tommy. Let's reason this out. If it took both men to roll it over, it has to be a large stone. And if it was soft enough to scratch words on it, it has to be of limestone or sandstone or some kind of granite. Take this small rock here," he bent forward and handed it to me. "That's what you call 'conglomerate.' It's just a hard mass of compact clays and what have you. It'll break up if you strike it with a hammer." He shook his head with doubt. "I wish I knew." He stood up and stared about at all the loose rock, the dark outcroppings of granite that poked up under the leaves, and at the larger stones that time had heaped on top of others. Many—over the eons that it had taken to form the Appalachians—had rolled, or slid, downslope. "Wish Marion hadn't moved the slab," he sighed. "Its original lie might have told us something. But don't you tell him that. He's a good man. Let's eat lunch," he suddenly grunted. "Then we'll gawk about a bit."

We sat on a large rock that overlooked a patch of laurel, ate our biscuits and a slice of cake that Grandmother had provided, and afterwards began our exploration. I searched the area along the ridge, while Uncle Everett roved through the rocks that littered the slope.

"It ain't here, boy," Uncle Everett concluded. "Or if it is, it's buried in leaves, or under tons of undergrowth. Yes, it would be something to find!

You know, Grandfather Howard might just have put a treasure under it. That's what Jessie believes and so does Albert. A broken pistol, or something! Or his regimental buttons! Mama said he always had a penchant for the unexpected. Got nervous and fearful. Grieved a lot, too. He survived while many of his friends hadn't. It was the War that did it to him. He was never the same. Your grandmother likes to romanticize the past, but Tommy, there's nothing romantic about killing. Whether it's Indians or settlers, thieves or cutthroats, Yankees or Rebs. Like the way Marion and I went after Crawford. That's not something to brag about. Or the way Earl dug that pit, and we, yes, I say, 'we'—he and I—killed those two men. That's just between us. Nobody else. OK?" He looked directly into my face. His dark eyes drilled through my own. "OK?" he repeated.

"Yes, sir," I replied lamely, somewhat disappointed and confused. I liked it when Uncle Everett had said, "Where's the son-of-a-bitch hiding?" That was the Uncle Everett I wanted to be.

He removed my hat and tussled my hair. "Here, boy," he handed it back to me. "Time to mount up and head home."

I wanted to see Uncle Jim's place, to look out across the river, search for any good apples in the dying orchard, and stop by Great-Grandfather Howard's marker. Uncle Everett sensed as much.

"Can you hear the river?" I asked. "I know it's down there somewhere."

He smiled. "Can't say that I do. It's near fall, and the river's down. Probably bubbling over nothing but rocks and moss-covered outcroppings. There'll be other times."

We mounted the horses and threaded our way slowly back through the hickories, oaks, and poplars, passed the laurel, down the embankment, and out into the road. Fine reddish-brown dust particles coated the sumac bushes and dried grass. A red-tailed hawk glided across the tree canopy overhead, no doubt searching for rodents or small birds along the sides of the lane. His cry sent a lonely note, sounding to the depths of my own heart. It left an empty feeling in my stomach. I prodded Sally with my heels to quicken her pace, to keep up with Uncle Everett. Lost in his own worries and troubled thoughts, he never glanced back once toward me. I kicked Sally's sides to catch up. "Uncle Everett! Uncle Everett!" I called. But he kept riding, sending Fred into a trot. We were almost galloping by the time we reached the meadows and yellow corn stalks. It would soon be time to harvest their ears and stack them into shocks. Smoke curled from Pearl and Henry's chimney. The gray needle-like wisp rose in a thin straight spire. Darkness would not arrive for several hours, but Saturday night meant reprieve from the never-ending drudgery of tenant life.

We put the horses up, rubbed them down, watered, and fed them, and walked to the kitchen. Grandmother had already set the table. Marion and my mother came out on the backporch to greet us.

"Well, well, look what the cat's drug in!" Marion teased. "Any luck?"

"Nope! It's all yours again!" said Uncle Everett. "But I enjoyed the day with Tommy. Timber man Tom!" he laughed. "He's one stalwart partner. I hope to live to see what he becomes."

Grandmother came to the door. "We're eating in the dining room. Get washed and behave like Edmonds! I've set the table with china, with real Sterling from England, and my crystal from Bavaria." She untied her apron. She had combed her hair back and pined it up with a pearl tiara. She wore a black rayon skirt and a silk, cream-colored blouse. I had never seen her that stylish on a Saturday night before. She smiled with a twinkle in her eye. "Come on, now! Hurry along, both of you."

"Yes, ma'am!" smiled Uncle Everett, as he stepped passed Marion and winked at my mother.

From somewhere in the living room, the Victrola played a wobbling record of "the Blue Danube." I could hear the faint "thump" of the platter, intermingled with the violin notes of the waltz.

Chapter Nineteen

Fall ushered in the shucking of cornfields, the disking of others, and above all, dove and quail season. Uncle Everett and Marion supervised the hunts and placed me in the safest corners of the fields when dove hunting. When quail hunting, they stationed me to the far right of both of them. It took a box or more of .410 gauge shells to hit my first dove. I had watched it circling from the far end of the field that bordered the road that led to Uncle Jim's. The barn was to my back. The swift bird fluttered drunkenly toward me. I raised my gun, sighted down the blue steel barrel, put the bead just in front of the bird, led it a little more and pulled gently on the trigger. A puff of pink and gray feathers exploded around its body. The bird plunged downward. It thudded into the corn stobs with an audible "thump." I raced out and retrieved the first dove I had ever killed. Its soft feathers felt warm and fluffy; a drop of blood dripped from its right eye. Its neck slipped between my fingers and dangled broken. I was enthralled. By late afternoon, I had shot seven more. Uncle Everett, Marion, Jessie, Albert, and Henry bagged an additional sixty or seventy. They piled them up in the field. "You boys take what you need. We'll keep Tommy's and a dozen more," said Uncle Everett. "Nice shootin'," he congratulated everyone. "They're pretty birds, aren't they?"

"Yes, sir!" replied Jessie. He bent down, picked one up, and weighed it in his hand. "Nice and plump." He ran his fingers across its craw. "Enough corn in here to plant a field," he grinned.

"Jessie, you and Albert and Henry crack down on these birds any time you want to. The land may be Mama's, but the birds?" he glanced up at the sky, "I guess they belong to the Man up there, and anybody who can hit them."

I watched the men divide the birds. Albert laid out a dozen of the nicest ones for us. He, Jessie, and Henry stuffed their shirts with the rest. The sun set in a swath of reddish-orange clouds that filled the Knobs with a deep crimson hue. We picked up our share of the dove and walked home. After we cleaned them, Grandmother soaked them in salt water, placed them in a pan in the icebox on the porch, and prepared them the next evening. She rolled them in peppered flour, patted them with butter, sage, and salt, and slow steam-fried them in a large, iron lid-covered, skillet that took up two eyes on the cook stove. Uncle Everett, along with my mother, Marion, Aunt Viola and Elsie hunkered down about the kitchen table to savor the feast and its luscious "with-its," as Elsie called them. The latter consisted of sweet potatoes, corn pudding, biscuits, gravy, and green beans. For dessert, Grandmother served apple pie, coffee, and a glass of cider for each of us.

The quail hunts proved more daunting. Marion and I drove out to Uncle Everett's on Saturday afternoons for the hunts. Uncle Everett's harrowed wheat fields, hay rows, and bramble-lined fences, especially in the corners, harbored numerous coveys. Uncle Everett's big salt-and-pepper bird dogs—skinny to look at but muscular and big jawed—ranged across the fields with amazing swiftness. They pointed covey after covey. Up the birds would flush in an explosion of speckled color. They would sail like fat darts into the thickest bramble, however close or far away. Uncle Everett's .12 gauge La Salle would roar as the quail rose in mass, and down one or two would tumble with each shot. Marion would be the second to fire, and if any flew off to the right, then I'd aim, trying desperately to smother the bird's flight with my bead, before pressing the trigger. I was more shocked than they with my first kill.

Getting the birds from the dogs required a stern will. "Drop! Drop!" Uncle Everett would order, after the dogs had retrieved the birds and placed them in his hand. The excited dogs didn't want to open their muzzles. Instead, they wanted to clamp down on the birds with their large drooling mouths. Uncle Everett had to rap their jaws with his hat to get them to release the quail.

Grandmother would prepare them in a style similar to the dove, rolling them in fresh butter and flour, sprinkling them with salt and pepper, and cooking them in the steam-frier with huge ladles of more butter to add sweetness and flavor. We ate them with biscuits and grits and little else, lest the "with-its" should detract from the delicate taste of the quail.

In the evenings that fall, Marion read stories to me about the American West, its Plains Indians, mountain men, wildlife, and Rocky Mountains. I wanted to be a fur trapper, Indian scout, coureur de bois, adventurer and explorer, like Meriwether Lewis and George Rogers Clark. Tales of Jim

Bridger and Kit Carson's exploits stirred my imagination, so much so that they inspired me to slip off one Saturday morning at Grandmother's to explore the Knobs alone. I left a note in my bedroom, disclosing my intentions and route, so as not to frighten her. I pulled on my boots and cap, warm corduroy jacket, and crept down the stairs. Darkness still filled the hallway with deep shadows. I couldn't help but touch Quelle's right arm and glance up at the old Captain. "Are you sure you should be doing this?" I could imagine him whispering in a gruff voice, as his eyes glowered at me. "I bet you did the same," I thought, as I groped for the doorknob of the hall's closet. I felt inside for my gun, lifted it out, and slipped a few shells in my jacket pocket, then quietly closed the door. I opened the living room door and stole toward the kitchen. After rolling several ham biscuits in a square of wax paper, I pulled on my gloves and crept out the back door, down the steps, and ran across the frosty gravel of the driveway. Starlight twinkled off the tin roofs of the outbuildings. I headed toward the road in front of the house, climbed the fence to the orchard, and strode as manfully as I could through the tall grass and wet broom sedge. Cradling the gun in the crook of my left arm created a sense of invulnerability. As I passed along, I plucked a yellow overripe apple from one of the trees and paused to look back. Grandmother was still asleep, I reasoned, as I could see no lights. Elsie hadn't gotten there either, nor had Pearl.

Just as I turned to resume my adventure, a loud stirring of feet set my heart to racing. In the starlight, a small herd of deer bounded off in different directions, leaping through the grass and flipping up their broad white tails. I caught my breath, crunched down on the apple, and walked on. What if I should encounter a panther? Or a bear? I was Kit Carson! George Rogers Clark! Uncle Everett! Great-Grandfather Howard! I would know what to do! Still, my heart pounded wildly beneath my jacket. As I jostled the gun in my arm, I guessed it was all right to be afraid.

By the time I climbed to the overlook, the new moon was sliding off to the west; starlight was growing faint. A thin sliver of dawn split the sky to the east. The woods across the Knobs hovered in cold darkness. Quilly Hall remained shrouded in night. As bravely as I could, I turned and entered the woods and quietly wandered downslope into the ravine in the morning darkness. All was quiet, damp, and hushed. As I walked along, the glow of dawn filtered through the trees. Squirrels became active; a woodpecker fluttered its wings and swooped into a nearby tree. An owl hooted and from somewhere up-ridge, a gobbler responded. Wouldn't it be something to shoot a turkey! I headed in the gobbler's direction, slowly climbing across rocks and up through the brown ferns. By the time I made it to the ridge, the gobbler had gathered his hens and crept on. I could see where they had clawed up the leaves the day before in their search for acorns and grubs. Warm sunlight began seeping through the trees, turning the ridge into a glowing seam of white and yellow light. I paused, sat down on a rock, and wondered what to do. My forehead was wet from perspiration, and I was panting for breath. I wanted to find the copse of trees where Uncle Everett and I had spent the night he killed the panther. That's where I wanted to eat lunch, before walking back out to the lane and home again. At least, that was the plan on the little map I had drawn for Grandmother.

Just as I rose off the rock, I thought I heard a low grunt. I froze; my heart thumped in my chest. I heard the grunt a second time. With trembling arms, I clutched the gun's barrels tightly in my left hand, and placed a shaking finger on the trigger. A strong odor of carrion drifted in the wind. Whatever the creature was, bear or cougar, it was upwind. Slowly I backed up against a hemlock and crouched beneath its boughs. With one knee in the damp soil, I listened and waited. In the distance, flies swarmed in the sunlight about a dark hump in the brush. Suddenly, the forest shook with ear-splitting cries, as the hump rose in a black specter of fur and red paws. The animal had been digging under a rotten log, and its fur was covered with reddish-brown bark. The huge bear roared with displeasure and raked its claws against a hickory tree's shaggy trunk. It sniffed the air, whimpered with a snort, and lumbered off at a slow trot down the ridge to the north. My hands were shaking as I laid the gun down, crawled out from under the hemlock's boughs, and took an instant pee. I thought the stream would never stop.

By noon I located the ridge where Uncle Everett and I had camped. The circle of stones we had gathered for our fire lay just as we had left them. I walked toward the hemlocks where Uncle Everett had tied up Fred and looked out across the gap in the forest. The poplars had all turned color and glowed bright yellow in the sunlight. A light breeze set them trembling. The brown leaves of the hickories and oaks formed soft rills of muted wonder. Maybe I should be a woodsman, I pondered. A wanderer of trails and forests! I sat beside the hemlock and stared out across the Knobs. It was time to eat lunch.

How good the ham biscuits tasted! I wished I had plucked a second apple! I replaced the wax paper in my pocket and stood up to stretch. As I did, I noticed a large black rock just beyond the hemlock. It jutted out of the earth and was covered with layers of lichen. Moss grew about its base. It was long, jagged, and appeared to have settled into the ground over the years. Sodden, moldering leaves had blown under its protruding ledge. I walked toward it, climbed out on its lip, and sat down. My feet dangled over its edge. From there, the crest of the ridge broke off sharply. A drop off of twenty feet or more loomed below. Scraggy Scotch pine and wild blue berries grew on a lower ledge. A few berries remained on the stems. I could see their dark cobalt marble shapes. With the gun in my left hand, I stood up, peered over the ledge, and decided to climb down to the berries. Just as I turned to jump off the rock, its weight shifted. The enormous stone slipped forward and hurtled me down the face of the cliff into the pines. I could hear it crashing through the brush overhead. The berry bushes broke my fall, but cut deeply into my jacket, legs, arms, and hands. I could see the blue sky. I was still clutching the gun, when the huge rock took one more tumble and came to rest against one of the small pines, pining my right leg under it. Slowly the rock settled, coming to rest just inches above my chest. I could smell the pine resin, fresh dirt, and moldering leaves. My right ankle hurt; my neck ached. I blinked as a sudden surge of sickness drew me into its black pit. I lost consciousness.

Twilight had fallen upon the Knobs when I awakened. I ached all over. I peered to my left and right. Dried streaks of blood covered my hands and curled about my fingers. I tried to move, to crawl, but couldn't. I squinted out beneath the rock. Tiny beads of moisture glistened on patches of moss near the bushes. The faint sound of water trickling off rocks and crinkling on leaves made a pleasant patter. A light drizzle had fallen across the Knobs; mist drifted in fine gray tatters. A cold breeze slipped up the mountain and with it, the scent of carrion and feces. A deep grunt sifted through the woods, accompanied by the annoying buzz of flies. It was the bear! My skin tingled and ears burned with every sound. It was grazing in my direction. I could hear it pulling down the bushes and crushing the berries and stems in its mouth. Suddenly, it stopped, sniffed the air, and released a series of low growls. As I looked out into the wavering night, aglow now with the first stars, I held my breath and quietly placed my fingers to my throat. Would it claw out my eyes, gut me alive, and no one every find me! I wanted Uncle Everett. I wanted to whimper, but didn't dare.

From somewhere across the Knobs, the broken yelps of a hound's bay rose and fell in syncopation with a second hound's baleful howling. Like a mountain ballad of wistful song, the baying grew louder and louder. The bear rose on its hind feet, staggered toward me, laid down, and swept a paw under the rock. I could see its yellow teeth in the starlight. It grunted, rolled over, and sauntered away in the darkness. Within moments, the hounds came crashing by. Big Roy whined, stopped, crawled under the rock, and licked my face. I tried to hug him, but couldn't reach him. He backed out, yelped, then raced on in pursuit of the bear's scent. Minutes later, Albert, Jessie, and Uncle Everett burst into earshot, their big flashlights sweeping the darkness aside with gigantic, lonesome swaths.

"Damn a'mighty!" Jessie blurted. "He's under this rock. You hurt, boy? Plumb pinned down. Albert, come on! Give me a hand!"

Strong arms, smelling of sweat and tobacco, and hands stained with nicotine, lifted the rock slowly. Uncle Everett reached down and pulled me out.

"You all right, boy?" Albert queried. "If you ain't a mess. Them hounds a' got somethin' treed, Jessie. Hear it! Come on!"

Away they slipped in the darkness. They followed their flashlights' beams, with guns in hand.

Uncle Everett towered over me in the night. I could see the outline of his hat, though not his face, but he was there. He swept his flashlight over me, bent down, and felt my arms and legs. "You all right, son?" he whispered. "Damn, Tommy, you had me scared to death, boy!" There were tears in his eyes.

"Yes, sir," I whimpered, with a flood of sobs. "I'll not do it, again. I swear!"

I could feel him release a long sigh. "You're alive. Thank God!" He put his hands under my shoulders and helped me up. "Can you walk?"

"I'll try," I sniffled. "My right ankle hurts, but I'll try."

"We'll make you a crutch," he said. "Marion's waiting for us on the lane with Sally and Fred. You can make it that far."

By now, the dogs had treed the bear. We could hear it, as it clattered its way up the trunk. There was no mistaking the sound.

"They gonna kill it?"

"I reckon so," he replied, as he put his right arm around me.

The night shook with an explosion and flash of powder. A second explosion quickly followed. In a frenzy of baying and barking, the bear crashed to the earth. A hot, hollow sorrow filled my chest. Warm tears trickled down my dirty cheeks. Uncle Everett took me by his left hand and ran his right hand through my hair. "Come on, Tommy. Let's check it out, then head for home."

I limped behind Uncle Everett toward the flashlights' beams. There lay the huge creature, stretched out under its robe of silky black fur. Its red tongue dangled to one side between its yellow teeth. Its small black eyes stared into the night. The dogs were licking a wound in its neck. It was dead.

"Mr. Everett, me an' Albert, here, wanna skin this critter. Tote back some of its fat and meat. You don't mind if we stay behind and come in later?"

"Of course not! Me and Tommy will be fine. Just be careful. Thanks for finding the boy."

The two men smiled, and Uncle Everett and I ascended a neighboring hill and followed its crest to the road. Marion was standing beside the horses in the moonlight. He came forward, lifted me in his arms, and set me behind the saddle on Sally. In silence, Uncle Everett pulled himself up into Fred's saddle, as Marion mounted Sally. I placed my arms around his stout waist, and away we trotted. Pale moonlight illumined the lane and the dogwoods along the forlorn banks. In the faint glow of the evening, we jolted to the sound of the horses' hoofs, as starlight twinkled on the weeds and sedges. Not once did either man scold me, nor my grandmother when we arrived, neither then nor the following morning.

Chapter Twenty

As fall progressed, Grandmother began scheduling "teas" in the afternoons for the town's illustrious ladies, patrons of the arts, and Abingdon's theatre guild. Being at school, I missed these events. My mother, however, and Marion would discuss them at the table, or in the den, while I was engaged in homework.

"She's in her element!" my mother joked with Marion. "Back to wearing beige and pink blouses, navy blue skirts, pearls, bracelets, her hair lightly powdered and with a touch of lipstick! Really, she's quite stunning for sixty-eight!"

"She truly wants Everett to succeed, doesn't she?"

"Oh, yes! She had such hopes for him! But his dropping out of college set them both back."

"Maybe he resented Hamilton, or needed to rebel. To be different! It's a shame he's never been able to focus on anything. What if his sheriff bid fails? How will he take it?"

"He'll manage," my mother mumbled. She looked uncomfortably toward me. "He's been a blessing for Tommy. Along with you!" she smiled. "It would be nice if he could succeed at something other than farming. You know, he was a deputy for a while and is still deputized, or authorized to wear his badge. He's even been called up when needed. That's at least one thing in his favor."

"Well, I need to do more when the time comes. I've already discussed it with some in the legislature and with the commissioner over our district. Everett would make a fine sheriff and bring pride and some old aristocracy to the office. Plus, I know of no one who is really qualified to run against him. Nor has anyone announced."

Winter arrived in a blast of bitter cold, with heavy, hoary frost bending the grass down white, and winds raw with biting snow. It came in frigid swirls, in small tiny flakes, accompanied by freezing temperatures that cut through coats and jackets, caps and gloves, and sent me running to the fireplace, or barn, when visiting Grandmother.

Jessie and Albert had nailed the bear's hide over the entrance to the horse barn, but later had to remove it before it dried, as neither Sally nor Fred would abide it. They kicked at their stalls and neighed for days, until the men took it down and tacked it, in stead, on the inside of the tobacco barn. It was frozen stiff, but after it dried, they reversed it, and I would climb up on a tobacco pallet to stroke the old bear's fur. "Poor fellow, he was just being a bear," Mr. Henry allowed.

Grandmother's "teas" began to include church members, gentlemen farmers and their wives, and any merchants who were free to come, especially if she held them on Wednesday afternoons. Aunt Viola and Elsie served tea. Pearl saw that the fire was stirred, while Grandmother bragged about Abingdon's history, its role throughout the Indian era, and "valiant defense during the Federal raid of 1864." My mother continued to report on these events, sometimes with laugher and often with a touch of melancholy.

"She's a wonderful hostess, really! But constantly reminds her guests—'You know, my father was wounded at Chickamauga. Yes, shot in the foot, and carried his wound to the day he died. He often spoke about it when he'd read where one of his comrades had passed away. Such a horrible battle! Men rushing through the woods and thickets, crossing creeks and dirt roads, firing in deafening volleys at the enemy, only to be driven back, exhausted, dragging their wounded compatriots' bodies amid the cries of the dying, and fields strewn with shattered limbs! The bloody stumps! He collapsed and fell, he said. He dragged himself to safety until his friends could bear him back. Oh, yes! And he and the Captain, my husband Holman's father—you passed his portrait in the hall—they were the best of friends. It was he who rallied the town's brigade that repulsed the Federals on the courthouse hill. The two really devoted themselves to Abingdon and its progress, right through the worst of times.' Now, how often can you tell that story while pretending to be objective and interested in others? Especially when promoting your own son?" My mother's freckled face would break out in a smile, but in a smile of concern, at best.

During this period, Uncle Everett kept a low profile. On Saturdays, however, he managed to make himself visible, particularly at the stockyards and around the train station in town.

I was with him one cold Saturday when he made his rounds. We had just pulled into the stockyards and climbed out of Uncle Everett's truck.

"Well, Everett!" a stout, middle-aged farmer, with a balding head and cigar butt in his mouth, greeted him. "What's this I hear about your runnin' for sheriff? You know you've got competition now? Or haven't you heard?" His nose had turned very red and his rough hands were chapped.

Several men had gathered about. Most owned farms like Uncle Everett's. They loved to speculate on cattle and often assembled at the stockyards. Their unpolished brogans and cowboy boots showed signs of wear. Mud and smears of red clay streaked the bottoms of their faded overalls. Tobacco juice stains had collected in the corners of their mouth. Some wore handsome Stetsons; others were bareheaded. All had warm coats on, although some had left them unbuttoned. I stood shivering beside Uncle Everett.

"Says he can beat you! In more ways than one," the first speaker continued.

"That's right, Everett. I've heard him braggin' the same," a second man voiced.

"Yeah!" a tall, leaner man confirmed. "He's an ex-Marine. MP, he claims. From over near Meadowview! Big man! Says he's more qualified, more experienced, and tougher than you. Doubts that you could corral a real criminal, or man twice your size. Claims he can. Says, he'll challenge you to prove it, if you don't believe it."

Uncle Everett smiled at me and ran his fingers through my hair. "Tommy, don't believe everything you hear! Especially, from a braggart! That's 'Lesson one,' from your new sheriff," he tipped his hat toward the men.

"He's serious, Everett. We're on your side. You might not be able to avoid him."

"I've taken my share of riff-raff down," Uncle Everett replied.

I noticed his hands were trembling. He placed his right hand's thumb in his belt loop.

"It's like calling you incompetent or a coward," the second speaker half-mumbled. "I don't like it anymore than you. Several of us are prepared to back you, if you'll take him on."

A gray pallor formed about Uncle Everett's face. Any flesh color of pink or tan drained away. He glanced at me, placed his right arm around me, and pulled me to his side. "What do you have in mind? Speak up! You know me well enough. I've never backed down from a fight. But I've never provoked one either."

"Let the word out that you ain't afraid of this braggart. That Abingdon's bigger than any buffoon! That'll put the ball in his court! If he's half as witless as we think he is, he'll jeopardize himself."

"All right! What the hell! Come on, Tommy, let's check out the steers and the big sows," he winked. "Old Mildred's litter's getting smaller each year."

Word must have traveled quickly, because it wasn't long until one weekend Uncle Everett came by the farm for Sunday dinner. All of us were gathered about the table, including Aunt Viola and Elsie.

Grandmother put her fork down and stared at Uncle Everett. She always sat at the head of the table and Uncle Everett opposite her, at the other end. "What's this talk in town I'm hearing about you and some body by the name of Westley Holt? It doesn't sound flattering, in the least."

"It's not, Mama, but you needn't worry. He's just a windbag."

"Maybe so, but the county deserves more than two roughnecks boasting about who's the toughest. He'll just drag you and our name into the mud. You can't let him do that," she stated, as she resumed eating.

"I know that, Mama. But sometimes a man has to do things he doesn't want to do, or he stops being a man."

"Everett's right, Mama Edmonds," Marion replied. "The town won't forget Holt's words, or how Everett responds. It just has to be done with class, with a touch of élan. And Everett's certainly capable of that."

"What are you suggesting?" asked Uncle Everett.

"I've been thinking about it. What are you best at? What do you know you can do that he probably can't match?"

"Shooting! I don't miss clays. I can put a revolver of slugs within a silver dollar's diameter at twenty yards. I can hit a deer or groundhog with a .30-30 at one hundred yards, if not farther. I've decapitated copperheads on horse back with one shot, while still controlling the animal. But fist-fighting all depends on how fast the other man is. If I can stay clear of him long enough, I can bring him down in time."

"Accept his challenge and challenge him in turn to a shootout with shot gun, pistol, and rifle. Pick a safe public place, and announce to the county that you are only doing this on behalf of its law-abiding citizens and as a display of your resolve to bring professionalism and justice to the county. I'll see that it's published in the paper and even in the *Bristol Star.*"

"I like that!" Grandmother smiled. "Why not have it here! The orchard would make as fine a place as any. You all could fire into the clay banks behind the trees. I could serve cider and pie to the onlookers. Albert and Jessie, along with Henry, could set up the targets. I relish the thought of it! You in your handsome boots, leather jacket, and tie, seated on Fred! Marion in his tweed coat and polished boots, handing you the guns, and Tommie holding the reins! That would allay any appearances of rough-housing and keep it from degenerating into a spectacle."

An expansive smile slipped across Uncle Everett's swarthy face. He shook his head in positive agreement and helped himself to another cup of coffee. Marion winked at Grandmother, who smiled graciously in turn.

By March, news of Uncle Everett's acceptance of Holt's hearsay challenge had led to several of the latter's ads in the local papers. He assured the county and its citizens that, as a former Marine and experienced MP, he could offer a level of "appropriate force" to dissuade any of the "county's bootleggers and potential crooks from thinking they can continue milling in and out of Abingdon with impunity."

"The bastard!" grunted Uncle Everett. "He makes it sound like we're already under siege. I know most of the bootleggers around here! Not a damn thing wrong with them that a soft word and an occasional visit can't turn around. He'll create far more harm than good."

Toward late May, Holt accepted Uncle Everett's offer to demonstrate his shooting prowess, but at a site of his own choice: in town at the fairgrounds! It would be limited to pistols and hand-to-hand wrestling, the winner being the first to handcuff the loser.

"Shhhhhit!" hissed Grandmother, in a rare display of profanity. "There go our best laid plans!"

Marion and I accompanied Uncle Everett to the event. Grandmother and my mother thought it best not to attend the "outing," as Grandmother dubbed it. "Everett, you've got the whip him and whip him good! There'll be no second chance. I will not rest till this is over!" she advised him with a hug.

"I know, Mama! I've been practicing on the farm. My hands are steady and trigger finger relaxed. I've been wrestling with Miles, too. I'm as ready as I'll ever be."

The fairground stands looked out across a dirt track and a green inner field. The latter was crowded with onlookers and steeplechase jumps, placed as bleachers for the hardy and the able and for anyone else who cared to climb them. The event began at 2:00 p.m., with speeches from both men. Uncle Everett won the coin toss to speak first. My heart pulsated in my throat, as he stepped up to the shiny microphone to address the crowd.

"Citizens of Abingdon, it is an honor to represent you. You know me and my family's past, its long history and devotion to this county. As my mother has often said, 'There can be no substitute for *resolve*, nor excuse for failure.' Our forebears possessed that resolve and struggled to make this county progressive and successful. They protected it in time of peril, fought for it in all our wars, and built its schools, banks, theatres, and businesses in the belief that honest men and women always prevail. I promise to continue allegiance to that commitment and will never, ever, let you down. I will be honest, frugal with your funds, professional, and respectful of all our county's residents, rich or poor, farmer or tenant, townsmen or mountain folk, and those least among us, those folks from the Knobs. I will resolve never to let you down, regardless of what happens here today. Thank you for every opportunity you've given me to make this town my home and highest place of joy."

A warm sustained applause rose quietly from the crowd. Many people who were seated in the stands stood up, as they applauded. My heart continued to race wildly. I reached up for Marion's hand. He gripped mine with equal excitement and uncertainty. I could feel it in the tremor of his fingers and warmth of his palm.

Mr. Holt slowly approached the microphone. He drew his chest up and planted his feet squarely in the dirt of the racetrack. He seemed twice as large as Uncle Everett, though not as tall. He placed his hands together and pressed in on his palms. "I assure you that we from Meadowview equally share our commitment to this fine county, named for our first president, and the gateway to Tennessee." There was a light smattering of applause at his mentioning of "Tennessee." "Men like Daniel Boone, who passed so frequently through here, deserve a sheriff's department, manned by our very best. My record of service in the Marines, my decorations from Iwo Jima and Okinawa, where I served briefly as an MP, and my military experience in general, well qualify me, I believe, to oversee the law enforcement needs of Washington County. Today's criminals and thugs represent a threat unlike any in the past. I can appreciate Mr. Edmonds' love for his county and his family's past contribution, but more than love and family ties are required in this era of crime and radio technology. I have the skills to bring new technology to the sheriff's office, as well as the strength and muscle to overpower any resistors to the law. Today's little demonstration will leave no doubt in your minds." He turned toward Uncle Everett and extended him his right hand. Uncle Everett gripped it and backed politely aside.

Human silhouette targets had been fastened to heavy boards about thirty yards down the track in front of the stands. A target had been set up for each man. Mr. Holt was carrying an Army semi-automatic pistol of some heavy caliber. Uncle Everett was wearing his favorite arms-piece, a Colt .45, with inlaid walnut grips, with a gun barrel of at least nine inches long. It had belonged to my grandfather Holman and hung in its holster on Uncle Everett's portmanteau in his hall at his home. He sometimes wore it when he and I had gone horseback riding, but I had never seen him draw it or fire it. Uncle Everett pushed his Stetson back slightly and stood calmly in his designated place.

"Mr. Holt! Please fire first," Uncle Everett motioned with his left hand. "Six rounds each?"

"You've got it!" said the confident big man. He pulled the hammer back on his pistol, brought the gun up slowly with his right hand, gripped its handle with both hands, and methodically squeezed off six shots. The gun leapt only slightly in the big man's grip. He smiled and stepped back. He gestured for Uncle Everett to take his turn.

Uncle Everett paused for a second, glanced quickly at the target, drew the huge pistol with a smooth, sweeping motion from its holster, and fired six shots, hip level, palming the gun's hammer with his left hand. He stopped, re-holstered his gun, and released a tense breath. A smile spread across his thin lips and tanned face; he knew he had bested Holt on the match.

The silhouettes were taken down and shown to the crowd. Mr. Holt had placed four shots in his target's chest, another in its abdomen, and one in its left arm. He bowed as the crowd applauded. "They'd all have killed him!" he boasted.

Uncle Everett's target was held up next. A large, ragged hole, near the silhouette's heart, was all that could be seen. The man holding the target shoved his fist though the hole and wiggled his fingers. "All six right here!" he announced. "He didn't miss a shot!"

The onlookers cheered and whistled with satisfaction. "Do it again, Everett! Do it again! Do it again!" they chanted. "Do it again!"

Mr. Holt appeared breathless, if not stunned. "Hell, that had to be luck!" he exclaimed to a man at his side. "Just sheer luck!"

Another set of targets was fastened to the boards. "You, first!" Holt pointed.

Uncle Everett reloaded his gun, spun the cylinder, and raised the pistol. He aimed toward the silhouette and, this time, with deliberate two-to-three second intervals, squeezed off the shots. I looked toward the silhouette. No hole or holes appeared around the heart. Where had he placed them?

Mr. Holt, sensing new hope, smiled and repeated his performance a second time. I could see a tighter pattern around the sternum of his target's chest. One had missed again, but landed in the neck. Now that I knew how to look for them, they were easily visible. But where were Uncle Everett's?

Once again, the targets were unfastened and displayed. "Oh, look!" someone shouted. "In the head! The forehead! Look!"

Indeed! A small white ring appeared in the target's forehead, just over the nose, in the middle of the brow. The corners were chewed up.

"Oh, God!" someone shouted. "Look at that! Look where he put 'em!"

Suddenly, others began to moan; a few laughed nervously. Uncle Everett had placed a bullet hole in each eye and the other four in the target's forehead.

Marion gripped my hand. "Dammit!" he whispered. "He might have gone too far, Tommy. That makes him look bad?"

"Why? Didn't he outshoot the big man?"

"That's not the problem."

"Well, some fancy shooting, I do admit!" said Holt, as he addressed the crowd. "A bit cruel! But, good shootin', to be sure." He handed his pistol to his closest comrade. "Here, I wanna know what sort of man I'm dealin' with! We got a right to know. I wouldn't want my brother, if he got drunk, treated that way. Shot up for the sport of it."

"Git him!" some supporter of the Marine's bellowed. "Show us what you can do, big man!"

A ripple of laughter slipped uneasily through the crowd.

"Everett, your gun!" Marion stated. "Use your gloves."

Uncle Everett handed Marion his gun. He fumbled inside his denim pockets for a pair of tight-fitting, leather gloves. He handed me his jacket. The Marine swung at Uncle Everett but missed. Uncle Everett pulled the gloves on his hands, dodged a second blow, and ducked a third. The man hit Uncle Everett in the chest with a left jab and sent him reeling back. Uncle Everett stumbled but regained his footing.

"Smart ass! Just a fancy smart ass! That's all you are!" blustered the Marine.

"Hit him, Everett! Dammit, hit him!" Uncle Everett's friends called out in support.

People in the stands rose to their feet. They were yelling and cheering on the two contenders. "Show him!" shouted the Marine's supporters. "Beat his ass, good! The showoff!"

"Stand up to him!" shouted Uncle Everett's friends in turn. "Don't let him bully you around! You've already out-shot him! We know who's right! Who'll make the best sheriff! Give it back! Let him have it!"

And so the two men slugged at each other, the burly Marine pummeling Uncle Everett's forearms and chest, while Uncle Everett sidestepped and waited patiently to throw the ideal punch. Uncle Everett went down, rolled to one side, and sprang up quickly again. He jabbed at Holt's sweating face, catching him in the right ear. Blood spurted out and ran down the man's neck. "Shit!" the latter hollered, as he swung again. Uncle Everett dodged and punched him in the jaw. Sweat coursed down Uncle Everett's face and broke out in stains under his armpits. He was wearing a white shirt, stained now about the neck with blood drops and dust.

The big man lunged for Uncle Everett, caught him around the waist, and hurled him to the ground. I could hear Uncle's Everett's head hit the dirt with a thump. He grunted and struggled to free himself. The big man sat astride his chest and reached in his back pocket. Suddenly he produced a pair of handcuffs. "It's over, Everett!" he said for the crowd to hear. "Mr. Edmonds, it's over!" he added with a raised voice.

"Marion, do something!" I pleaded. "Can't you do something? Can't you pull him off?"

The ex-Marine heard me and chuckled. "Boy, there's nothing you can do for this man. Nor nobody else! He's not fit for it! That's what I had to prove! He just ain't got the resolve."

At that word "resolve," Uncle Everett glanced up at me, then turned his eyes away. The big man from Meadowview had managed to place a cuff on Uncle Everett's left wrist, but he couldn't snap it. His fallen contender was refusing to cooperate. With a mighty grunt, Uncle Everett raised his legs, locked them about Holt's neck, then sat upright, somersaulting the man off his chest and slamming him to the ground. Holt's entire weight crashed down about his face and neck. He rolled to one side and let out a pitiful groan. Uncle Everett had broken his nose, if not his neck!

My mouth fell open with joy. Uncle Everett raised himself on his elbows in the dirt and sat up. He seemed as surprised as anyone. He shook the handcuff off his wrist. Marion rushed forward to help him, but others beat him to Uncle Everett's side.

"I'll be damned, Everett, if you didn't do it!" a townsman congratulated him. "That was one hell of a good speech, too. You Edmonds know how to do it. I swear to God! Congratulations."

People on the track, as well as in the stands, made their way forward, some to congratulate him, others laughing and congregating about the targets on display. "Would you look at that? Damn! That was some show! I've always heard he was good. But damn, that's excellent!" And so the kudos ran.

Mr. Holt's friends helped him to his feet. He had apparently sprained his neck, but his nose did appear broken and mashed to one side.

Uncle Everett offered him his hand. "There'll be a need for good deputies," he said to Holt, "unless you still wish to run against me."

"I'm not ready to concede," Mr. Holt replied. "I'll have to think about it." He shook Uncle Everett's hand and slapped the dust off his trousers and shirt. He was feigning disinterest, but I could tell he was humbled by Uncle Everett's offer. He left with his friends but not before waving to the crowd. Many people clapped and followed him to his car.

"We'll not forget you," someone said. "You'll be back and running for something. There's plenty of room in this county for men like you."

"Thank you," he mumbled, somewhat crestfallen. He rubbed his neck and felt his nose. He tumbled into the backseat of his car, and his friends drove him away.

When Grandmother learned of the details, she was not pleased. To the contrary, she was appalled. "The eyes! Why the eyes? And the forehead! Were you trying to be cute? The point was to be professional, not stupid!"

"Mama, I did my best. I did what made sense at the time. I was trying to put him in his place. That's all!"

"Everett! Oh, Everett! It was you who got put in place—last place! You made a fool of yourself. Called attention to yourself! Whimsical, petulant, unpredictable! That's what people will think of you. Not how calm you were, or the fact that you out shot him!"

"Don't be so hard on him, Mama," my mother came to his support. "Everett was having to prove himself. You should be proud of him, not angry." My mother bent forward from where she was seated (in the rocker in the living room beside him) and reached for his hand. She took it and held it momentarily in her own. There were tears in her eyes. "Everett, you did the right thing. You did what instinct told you to do. You stepped in and did it. Right on the spot! No indecisiveness! Just, *pow!* Bang! He had challenged you. You had to put him in his place. Which you certainly did! Mr. Grundy, the butcher, was there. He said you were superb. 'Quiet, steady, unflinching.' Those are his words. His assessment. Marion said the same. The whole town's still talking about it. Wait till the newspapers report their stories. They'll all be on your side."

Unfortunately, that was not quite true. The local papers were, but not the *Bristol Star*. Marion read me the article that the editor had written himself. "*Cocky, two-fisted, gun-totin' candidate brawls his way into the limelight,*" it began. "*Did the better man win the match? Are either qualified? Certainly, the rugged, lean Edmonds of Abingdon captured the crowd's attention, but is a gunslinger what they need? Is it what we need, on the edge of our sister county? To be true, the county has its pockets of rough necks, boot-leggers, and petty thieves. Its bars in Damascus are notorious for brawls. But if the town hopes to retain its status as a tobacco Mecca and crossroads of culture, theatre, and the arts, it clearly deserves more than either Edmonds or Holt has to offer.*"

Marion laid the paper to one side and smiled at me. We were seated in the library at home. "Master Thomas, destiny requires me to respond. A letter to our erudite editor of said newspaper," he nodded in its direction, "is about to be born!"

I had no idea what he meant, but the following week's paper carried a long and tongue-in-cheek reply to the editor's article. "*Oh how we bumpkins of Washington County are so indebted to our wise and considerate brother to our south! And just whose county is rife with boot-leggers and petty thieves? Where else in America can you die of thirst on one side of the street, but cross over and drown in cheap whiskey on the other side? And who has to bail them out? Whose sheriff picks up the pieces when they roll in drunk to bumpkin town? And who stands vigilant over our small but progressive banks? Our commerce, residents, and farmers? Oh, for a two-fisted, square shootin', gun-totin' star of finesse and swagger for the* **Star** *to herald! Jealousy! Envy! Arrogance! Shame! That's what your editorial reeks* of! 'But as for me and my county,' as a famous Virginian once put it, 'give me Edmonds, if you want peace!'"

No one else came forward to contest Uncle Everett's candidacy. That fall he won the election and became the county's new and youngest sheriff. Not since the 1830s had an Edmonds held the position. Uncle Everett threw himself into the office with a determination to succeed, while still overseeing his farm and looking after Grandmother's and Quilly Hall.

CHAPTER TWENTY-ONE

FOLLOWING UNCLE EVERETT'S RUN for office, a series of memorable occasions unfolded. Perhaps the happiest involved Sally's giving birth to a little red colt, a frisky fellow we named "Mac." Since he was born in the fall, he stayed in the horse barn, or hay barn, most of the time, but followed Sally about, whenever Jessie or Albert let him out. I wanted to name him "Red," but Jessie explained that he'd soon lose his curly coat and darken up like his father, into a chestnut brown.

A deep snow fell the second week of lambing, in late December. Many ewes had remained in a high pasture that saddled a rocky hill, just beyond Pearl and Mr. Henry's cabin. The hill faced north, and though protected by wild plum bushes, chinquapins, and higher up, a fencerow of cedars, the cover proved insufficient against the ice and plunging temperatures that sank below zero. The night before, Henry and I had herded a score or so of ewes down the hill to a bottom, aglow in frost, and into a sheep shed. But no one anticipated the storm's intensity or that the snowfall would be so deep. The lambs simply froze beside their mothers, whose own dirty yellow, woolen carcasses lay buried under the two-foot mantle of ice and snow.

"I've seen a lot of sadness, but nothin' like this, Miz. Edmonds," Henry commented. "Their little bodies was just matted with ice, frozen clean through. Wasn't nothin' nobody could have done. Unless we had knowed earlier."

"That's quite all right, Henry. You did your best. The hand of God is testing us. Somehow with trust, we will make it through."

Mr. Long looked at Grandmother with seasoned incredulity. "I reckon so," was all he replied.

After the snow melted and the ice grudgingly gave up its grip, spiraling circles of vultures glided in descending coils to feed on the black rotting remains.

"Why would God have done that to the little lambs?" I asked Marion. "Grandmother said that God was testing us, but why them?"

"Sometimes your Grandmother doesn't say quite what she means," he replied. "I think what she meant is that without the lambs and their mothers, there'll be less wool to shear; and if that's the case, then the farm won't generate as much revenue, or money, as it might have, and, all around, things will become economically harsh. Farming's a hard business, and banks hold thousands of mortgages on thousands of farms. It's a tough time and a tough business. She needs every penny the farm can earn."

He attempted a reassuring smile and sat forward in his leather chair. "You know, we never did go back to see that rock that fell on you. When the snow's gone, and the weather's warmer, we ought to go back. What do you say?"

"Yes, sir! I'd like that! That rock came crashing down with a roar like a freight train."

"I bet it did," he smiled. "What about the bear? Didn't that scare you? It would have me."

I didn't know how to reply. Yes, it had scared me. Just the thought of it filled my mind with fear. Yet, now that it was over, I felt braver. "Yessss!" I began. "But I was trying not to be afraid."

"Tommy, it's all right to be afraid when danger's near. We're made that way. It helps us survive. It's all right to run when you have to run, and fight if you have to fight, even if you're afraid. But 'fear' is a kind of friend. It warns us when we need to take flight, or figure out what to do."

"Like when you shot Mr. Crawford? Were you afraid? Uncle Everett was mad. Does he ever get afraid? I want to be brave like him."

"Oh, he's brave, all right! But I imagine he's been afraid. He just doesn't show it. Plus, he's got a will, a stubborn streak of determination, to keep on going, no matter what. As for myself, I hadn't thought about Crawford like that. That is, in terms of fear! He meant to kill Everett, or wound him, at least. I know Crawford too well. My heart was beating fast, and I was sweating under my coat. But I knew I had to be calm, that I had to be watchful. I don't think fear entered my mind until after I pulled the trigger. Then I realized I had shot the man. And I felt sad about that. Bad, Tommy! I felt bad. But I knew it was justified, that I had done the right thing, and that somehow things would work out. Actually, I felt relieved that Everett hadn't shot him, or killed him, for that would have gotten him in trouble. He would have been charged with 'manslaughter,' that is, killing a man in a fight out of rage or anger. Does that make any sense, young fellow?" His goatee prickled, as he wrinkled his chin.

"I guess so," I mumbled. "Do you think my father was ever scared? Was he brave, like Uncle Everett?"

"Tommy, I didn't know him that well. But, he was brave all right. He volunteered and served in the Army, in some kind of liaison capacity with the Marines. He didn't have to go. He could have gotten a farmer's exemption. He could have stayed home. I imagine hearing the mortar rounds bursting in the jungle about him and the sound of bullets hissing in the grass would have made any man cringe. But 'fear?' I suspect he was still clutching his rifle, ready to fire it, when he was killed. Bravery and courage are strange virtues. They require fear and danger to evoke them. But once they rise up and join hands, they can overcome the most perilous situation—provided they are guided by common sense." He leaned forward and nudged my head with his big, friendly, balled up fist. "Reason! Your mind! That's where bravery comes from. Thinking ahead. Being prepared. Knowing what to do if danger strikes. And not backing off when you don't have to! It's inside you, Tommy. You're already a brave boy. And almost as tall as a man! You would have never trekked off into the Knobs alone, if you weren't brave. Don't worry about it, son. You're going to be fine."

One cold Friday when I got off the school bus to stay at Quilly Hall, Aunt Viola met me at the door. I had tromped up the back steps of the porch, still icy with patches of snow, when she heard me. Actually, Elsie opened the kitchen door. "Boy, git in here!" she ordered. "We've been awaitin' on ya. Your granny fetched us to watch for you. Git on in!"

I entered the kitchen, stomped off the remaining icy crystals on my shoes, and searched about for Aunt Viola. She had already disappeared. "Where'd she go?"

"She's in the parlor," Elsie said, referring to the living room. "She's nippin' on that sherry of Miz. Edmonds, but I've got some cocoa for you. Git on, and I'll bring it in."

I hurried toward the living room and dropped my coat and book satchel in the dining room along the way.

"Now you pick that up right now!" Elsie barked. "Your granny raised you better than that."

I placed them on the floor beneath a window and slipped into the living room. A crackling fire sang in the fireplace. Tiny coals popped onto the hearth. The room glowed from the warm bright embers. All else was dark, but I could make out Aunt Viola, rocking in Grandmother's chair. She saw me enter and motioned for me to come to her.

"Come over here, Tommy. Your grandmother's in town at the doctor's office. She's not feelin' so good. Everett'll be bringing her back directly." She sat forward in the rocker and held her hands out to me.

I had never been with her alone, except when helping Uncle Jim regain his speech. Her smile, wrinkles, and thin face did nothing to enhance her beauty, but goodness from somewhere deep within her gave her cheeks a warmth and softness that made her attractive. I clasped her hands, which were hard and cold,

"What's wrong with Grandmother?"

"Her feet's been a'swellin' and she's been short of breath. She plumb exhausted herself helpin' Everett and not carin' for herself. But that's your granny."

I sat in the rocker beside her and began swaying in cadence with her. I was tall enough now that I didn't have to climb into the large rockers, plus my own was too short and tight for me.

"Boy you have grown!" she noticed. "You're gonna be as tall as Jim. Taller than your daddy or Everett. Maybe even as tall as your great-grandfather. Now, he was tall and lean. Your Uncle Everett favors him. But he was even taller. And loved the Knobs. If he hadn't been wounded, no telling what he'd have done. He wanted to be a timber cruiser. Work up around Whitetop and Damascus. There was lots of timber then, whole mountain sides of it. Big pines and chestnuts. But his right leg just couldn't take the pounding of walkin' all day and dragging limbs and wrestlin' with the horses and mules. He did work in a sawmill for a while, one of your grandfather's, but Holman lost that during hard times, seeing he was short of cash after his father's death."

Elsie came in with a huge cup of hot chocolate and a biscuit topped with strawberry jam. "This ought to hold you, boy, till supper," she smiled. "Miss Viola, are we eatin' here or back home? I'm fixin' some pork chops and fried apples and heatin' up a jar of carrots."

"I'm sure Ginny will want us to stay for supper, along with Everett. But in case she's too tired for company, we'll just wrap somethin' up and take it with us. Ginny won't mind."

"Yes, ma'am," she replied, as she returned to the kitchen.

"Aunt Viola, did Great-Grandfather Howard really get shot in the foot, like Grandmother says, and carry the wound till the day he died?"

"Yes, honey. Though, that ain't the whole story. He tried removing the bullet, but only hurt hisself all the more. It ached worse in cold and rainy weather. He'd limp from room to room, or just roam the orchard by the river, or whittle in the shed. He liked taking oak strips and weaving them into baskets. He made all sizes: from tobacco baskets, which he'd sell in town, to baskets for carryin' eggs and corn, chicken feed, and whatever. He made a lot of spending money that way."

"Do you remember what it was like when he came home?"

"Sweet boy, I was just a girl, living on the east bank of the river. My daddy and Jim's was good friends and fought together. Only my daddy didn't make it home. He's buried north of Atlanta, in one of them Confederate cemeteries. My mother, Jim, and I went to visit his grave, when Jim and I got married. We thought about having him dug up and brung home, but it didn't seem fitting to yank him from his resting place and away from his fallen comrades. They was all there together in peace. Mr. Howard wanted to go with us, but he had hurt his back ploughing and couldn't stand the ride into town, let alone the trip to Georgia.

"I was a girl of five or so, when Abingdon was burned. Smoke hung over the town and warehouses for days. The Yankees set fire to the warehouses, because they was full of supplies. Abingdon was an important rail center. It was the main line from Culpepper to Chattanooga, the only one. There was hospitals in town, too, to care for the wounded. Lots of soldiers passed through. I can remember my mother, Mrs. Lorran, Jim, the Captain, and me meeting the trains to supply the troops with baskets. Cornbread, fried chicken, cakes, and pies! Those boys was hungry. They looked so homesick and dirty. They was heading for Tennessee to fight before Grant could get there. But they was too late. Later, my father and Mr. Howard's Company left to join them. They was to meet up with General Longstreet's army to fight under General Bragg. Of course, they did. That's when the battle took place, and Mr. Howard was wounded, and my father killed."

I had never heard these details. My cocoa had grown cold, and I had scarcely nibbled on the biscuit. My rocking had intensified, sometimes almost toppling me, while at other times ebbing and coming to a halt.

"We've not recovered yet," she continued. "The government had to levy supplies. The Captain was constantly having to send wagonloads of corn, beef, salt, and pork into town, where it'd be shipped off to Richmond, or wherever. Slaves were levied, too. The Captain sent all but two families of his own. That was earlier in the war, when they was needed around Richmond to dig trenches. But I don't remember much of that. By the end of the war, most of the blacks were gone. They never came back. There was hardly anything left for the white boys to come home to. That's when your great-grandfather, Captain Nathan, willed Mr. Howard his land by the Holston. Your grandfather Holman kept it in his name for a while, till Mr. Howard could get on his feet, then transferred it to him. But he never got it out of debt." She released a long sigh and without saying anything, got up and walked to the kitchen.

Darkness was less than an hour away. I pulled on my coat and hat and slipped out the front door and walked back to the smokehouse and old slave quarters. As dusk fell, I climbed the steps to the loft and peered out toward the apple house. Its stone exterior glowed pink in the faltering rays of the sunlight. Toward the Knobs, darkness had already swallowed the orchard and its meadows. I searched about the dusty boxes, sacks, and cracked leather harnesses, more out of boredom than anything else. I retrieved my tobacco stick. My sword! My link with the past, our family, and, above all, the Knobs! That wilderness of redemption and terror! Haunt of bears and panthers! Home of Uncle Jim's farm! I raised the stick and pointed it toward Tennessee. "Take that!" I thrust toward the imaginary enemy in blue. "And that, and that, and that!" I swung my sword wildly, stabbing at the shadows and scarlet rays of dust. I paused, stood quiet at attention, placed the stick over the narrow, lint-encrusted mantle, and descended the stairs.

Lights approached in the driveway. Uncle Everett and Grandmother had come home. Little was said at the table. Uncle Everett's holster was visible. Its latch was snapped just under his gun's hammer, holding his pistol in place. He ate with his black leather jacket unzipped. I could see his sheriff's badge on his left shirt pocket whenever he leaned forward to eat. His demeanor had changed. He seemed worried, pre-occupied, even weighed down. We ate the pork chops in silence. Uncle Everett drove Elsie and Aunt Viola back to their cabin, while Grandmother retired for the evening.

"Tommy, if you read any, don't add any wood to the fire, and cut out the lights before you go to bed. Grandmother doesn't feel well. Perhaps tomorrow, she'll feel better. Now, come and kiss me," she said in a weary voice. She held out her arms and put them around me. Her lips were wet and strangely cold.

I rocked for a while in front of the dying embers, then turned off the living room lamps, and stepped quietly into the hallway. Grandmother had left the light on and its orange, ornate globe filled the hall with a sallow hollowness. Even Quilly appeared subdued and the old Captain reticent. I climbed the stairs, turned on the light in my own room, glanced at my father's photo on its stand, and switched off the hall light. Later I crept back out into the hall and placed my father's photograph on the spindly table beside my bed. His cap covered his brow, but his sparkling eyes, soft features, and tanned face beamed with a radiance that warmed the frigid room. I snuggled down between the cold sheets of the feather bed, pulled several heavy quilts about my shoulders, wiggled my feet until they were warm, and fell, almost instantly, asleep.

As the snows melted in the higher Knobs, Marion and I made still one more foray in search of the rock. Early one cold, February morning, we saddled Fred and Sally, and headed up the lane toward Uncle Jim's farm. The thin, raw air numbed us. Steam rose about the horses' nostrils and off their necks and manes. My fingertips felt frostbitten, in spite of my thick, red woolen mittens and deep coat pockets in which I could slip them, when not having to guide Sally.

"I want to see that slab that almost crushed you," Marion said, as the horses clopped along. "Maybe we've been looking for the wrong kind of rock. Not round but flat and smooth. Like ledge rock, or some huge sheet of stone. Long and layered, but heavy enough to require two men to roll over! How does that sound, Mr. Thomas?"

I'd been wondering about that myself, ever since falling off the ledge, but didn't know how to express it. "Yes! Exactly!" I shivered, rubbing my shoulders and sides with my gloved hands.

"We'll turn off at that bend," he nodded, "and work our way back toward the ledge. Whew! It is cold, isn't it? We'll need to build a fire, once we get there."

I liked that idea immensely. My enthusiasm for the ride had already dissipated; my feet felt like clumps of ice in my leather boots.

Toward late morning, we arrived at the slide where I had fallen off the ledge and had come to rest under the rock. The huge stone had crushed the small trees supporting it, and it now lay flat on the ground, covered with a crusty mantle of ice and soggy lichens. We dismounted and tied the horses to a small pine. Marion walked slowly toward the stone.

"Tommy, you were lucky! Just plain, downright lucky!" he shook his head in pensive amazement. "Yes, sir! What your grandmother would call, 'Providence.' But luck is more like it. Let's take a closer look."

We bent down, scraped off some ice and snow, and tried to budge the stone. It had settled in the earth, sinking heavily through several layers of rotting leaves and frozen humus. "Ummmm!" strained Marion, as he attempted to shift it. For over ten minutes, we continued to scrape frozen debris from the face of the rock, in hope of finding some clue, some scratch or lettering, or just anything Great-Grandfather Howard might have left behind. "Nothing!" Marion uttered. "Mr. Thomas! We've been foiled again. Let's lead the horses up the ridge and lunch there. And build a fire!" he added, as he swung and pumped his arms from side to side to keep warm. He stood erect and glanced about the woods. Streams of cold sunlight illumined the slopes. In places, the latter were knee deep in fallen leaves. A numbing draft of air settled all about. "Thomas, we must not give up! Somewhere, on one of these hills rests a stone, with Mr. Howard's message engraved on it. Our task is to find it. He meant it that way! That's why he hid it. And to find it, will be like finding him. Whether there's a treasure under it or not. What do you say?"

"Yes, sir! Can we build that fire now?"

The big man tugged at his goatee and smiled. "A realist, Tommy! You're a realist! A dreamer, but a realist." He looked upslope and back at me. "Come on. By the time we build a fire, eat, and get warm, it'll be dark here. What will it take to find that stone? I wish I knew!"

We led the horses in a roundabout way to the ridge, hobbled them so they could forage on moss and lichens, and built a fire. Its low blaze emanated shafts of soft red light off the rocks about the fire's base. Never had greasy bacon stuffed in cold biscuits, or hard rusty pears tasted better! I sat on a rock with my feet toward the fire. We kept it small and low. Around mid-afternoon, we scattered its coals, covered them with old ashes, and stamped out any remaining sparks. The ride back proved as arduous as the ride in. The bitter cold had settled in the hollows and ditches along the lane. The pale light of the sun provided minimal warmth, and darkness awaited us at every bend. Sally plodded along slowly, heavily, her head down, shaking the bridle, as it cut into her sore mouth—thanks to the cold. Fred (as old as he was) trotted ahead, eager to return to the shelter of the barn. In the distance, toward town, the sun began to sink in a streak of crimson, scarlet, and dark gold. Suddenly, its somber colors glowed bright yellow, as shafts of light peeked out from under a line of gray clouds that drifted over the hills toward Abingdon. I expelled a stream of warm breath that turned to instant vapor. Moments later, we trotted out of the woods toward home. Back at the barn, the all-day tiring search and adventure slipped into the realm of memory. I hugged the fuzzy Mac and watched him nurse on Sally. Old Fred looked on, as Marion rubbed his flanks with a wire brush and knocked the ice off his muddy fetlocks.

CHAPTER TWENTY-TWO

THE YEARS PASSED. I had turned sixteen. Grandmother seventy-eight. Aunt Viola was in her early nineties. Jessie had died, along with Elsie. So also Sally and old Fred. Mac's companion was a silver mare, named Nimble for the perky way she behaved as a colt when first brought to the farm. Both were great horses to ride. Mac loved to race, and looked forward to my weekend stays with Grandmother. He had learned to recognize the sound of Marion's tires, or car, and would neigh and kick the boards in his stall as soon as the vehicle stopped and I opened the car's door. I often had to walk to the barn and comfort him before returning to greet Grandmother.

Grandmother's hair had turned a silvery white. Her shoulders slumped, and with them her fine posture and erect stature. Still, her spirit reined high and her word ruled the house and farm's affairs. Amazingly, Aunt Viola possessed more physical stamina than Grandmother, but she deferred to her in all matters that counted. They lived together now at Quilly Hall, Aunt Viola having moved in following Elsie's death. That winter Elsie had complained of a pain in her side, which then moved to her back. Dr. Wilson's replacement, a Dr. Arnold, prescribed an elixir to combat her spells of nausea. He recommended hot pads to alleviate her pain. She died just after the first jonquils began to bloom.

Elsie was buried beside her husband in the fennel-filled cemetery beside his old house. The graveyard's picket fence had rotted, its gray boards lay scattered about the ground, and its rusty nails exposed. I held to Aunt Viola's arm while Marion and my mother assisted Grandmother. Uncle Everett's duties prevented him from attending.

A preacher from across the Knobs officiated at the grave. "The Lord giveth and the Lord taketh away," he droned. "Blessed be the name of the Lord!" He cast his dark eyes about us, exploring each of us carefully. He was of diminutive stature, clad in a soiled brown coat, un-ironed white shirt, and dusty gray trousers. Tobacco juice stained the right edges of his mouth. It was April, still cool, and a mist had formed along the hayfield beside the graveyard. Albert and his family, Mr. Henry and Pearl stood to the left of the preacher. "God ain't to be mocked! If there's any here with sin in his heart," he eye-balled us sternly, "you'd best repent now. The grave's ain't no place to do it. *'I am the resurrection and the life,'* says the Lord. *'Whoever believes in me, though he die, yet shall he live, and whoever lives and believes in me shall never die.'* Elsie's with the Lord and our good brother Ambrose. Ain't for us to judge none. God has a way of pityin' them that die poor, that ain't proud, nor hung up on themselves. But our days are few, like the twinklin' of a star at night, or the passin' of a cloud in the day. Elsie never had nothin' but the clothes on her back. We know she worked hard. It's for God to decide. We ain't got no say in it. But, brothers and sisters, would he pick you, if'n you was here instead of Elsie? Would his voice raise you from the dead? Like our Lord done with Lazarus? Would he?" He dropped his gaze and stared at the grave. "Let us praise the Lord! 'Now ashes to ashes, an' dust to dust,'" he intoned, as he stepped toward the open pit and crumbled a fist full of red clay into the hole. I could hear it pelting her coffin, as the soil tumbled about the box.

Not long after that, Marion and I spent the next Saturday fishing in the streams above Damascus and camped along the river that night. Many swift-moving creeks created great trout fishing, and April brought numerous trout to the surface in search of gnats and flies. Marion had purchased the latest in fly-casting and wading equipment. We each wore a vest, whose pockets bulged with handsome tins of trout flies and nymphs. I caught five browns and six rainbows. Marion caught ten, all told. We released all but the fattest five. Toward late evening, we set up our tent near a copse of laurel and basked the trout over a bed of hot coals. As the embers glowed in the darkness and starlight rippled on the gurgling stream, we crawled into our sleeping bags and stretched out for the night.

"Tom, you've never said what you hope to do when you finish school. Your mother and I have been talking and think you might like Harvard, or maybe the University of Virginia when you're through. You're certainly bright enough for either. And funds are available for you to go."

"I haven't really given it that much thought," I said. "I just love the woods, the Knobs, and all that goes with the farms. Uncle Everett's and Grandmother's. Maybe forestry. I've often thought I'd like to study forestry. I hear there's a good school at VPI? Plus there's VMI and West

Point. The coach says I could easily get a scholarship in football or track. Grandmother would like that."

"Tommy! You've got brains to spare. Not just brawn. You love history, reading, science, music, adventure. You love a challenge. There's nothing you can't do. The farms will all be yours, for sure. But you've got this wonderful brain to use. You can easily be a doctor, or lawyer, or banker, or anything you want. Please give it more thought. We only want what's best for you."

"Don't tell Mom this, but Uncle Everett's promised he's going to ask her if he can hire me as a deputy this summer. It will only be part time, cause he knows Grandmother needs me on the farm. But it would be exciting and provide something worthwhile to do."

"I should say! I don't know. That's a tall order. And dangerous! I'll keep it a secret. But don't forget what I've proposed about Harvard or the University? You'd thrive at either and love both. Well, just keep yourself open. You've still got another year, but time is important. Think about it and let me know."

"Yes, sir! I'm just not sure which way I'm leaning at the moment. But I'll let you know."

I can't say that my school days were particularly memorable. I never tired of reading, loved math and science, and toyed with poetry and short fiction. Adventure was what I craved. Riding back into the Knobs. Hunting, fishing, and camping on Whitetop with Marion. Racing Mac. Wrestling, football, and running cross-country. I lettered in all three, but sports represented merely a side attraction. It was the Knobs that appealed to me: their hollows, dark ledges, outcroppings, lichens, and deep green mosses; their pines, hickories, oaks, poplars and sourwood trees; their flaming colors in autumn, crisp snows in the winter, and dogwood and laurel blossoms in the spring. That's what summoned the muses in my soul. I could never get enough of their solitude, their silence and wonder, or the thought of one day finding Great-Grandfather Howard's stone. Where was it? Was it a truth or fiction? A legend or a fact? "A tale told by an idiot, full of sound and fury, signifying nothing?" Or was it for real? Marion and I had given up any hopes of finding it. My forays into the Knobs consisted now of revisiting Uncle Jim's farm house, searching for an occasional apple in the old orchard, or wandering along the Holston's banks, where Earl and I had dug the pit that had claimed the lives of the riders from Bristol.

There was a girl I had grown excessively fond of, if not fallen in love with—if love is ever the *mot juste* at that age? Her name was Julie. Lanky and tall, her long brown hair and sensuous curves fired my pubescence into maturity. At six-foot-two and weighing one hundred seventy-five pounds, I was the perfect match for her. Holding hands soon led to necking, and necking to heavy petting, and finally to consummation late one spring afternoon in the haybarn.

She was a cheerleader, and on the way back from games, we'd sit together in the rear of the bus. The night of our consummation followed a track meet against a Holston team. Marion had let me drive his car out to the farm for her to meet Grandmother. We stopped at the barn first. Her eyes glowed with a softness that transcended passion. We laughed as we paused by the stalls to pat Mac and Nimble. Then I held her hand as we climbed the ladder to the loft. The smell of the hay encompassed us; its aroma provided our aphrodisiac; her kisses melted my tongue as her own explored the back of my mouth; our hands found each other's; our bodies met. "You won't get pregnant?" I mumbled in a nervous whisper. "Shhh! No," she placed her fingers over my lips. Our bodies united, sighed, and heaved softly. Never had I felt so vibrant, excited, alive! Later we lay beside each other in blissful rest, amid heavy breathing and light sweat. She smothered me with kisses; I kissed her eyebrows, eyes, eyelashes, and lips.

"Oh, Tommy! She's beautiful!" Grandmother explained. "You must be Elton Patterson Hobert's daughter. I knew his mother. She and I attended the Girl's Seminary together in the late '80s. How delightful!" she reached for Julie's hands. "Do stay for supper! You are staying, aren't you?"

"No, ma'am! I promised Mama I'd come right back. But Tommy and I have a date tomorrow."

"Well, he certainly knows class!" Grandmother chortled. "It's an old family trait, you know. Our Tom here inherited it straight from his father and grandfathers before him."

"Yes, ma'am!" she rolled her bright, sparkling eyes at me. Her deep hazel irises radiated love.

How I wanted to kiss her again!

"Well, sweet girl, you'd better get that hay out of your hair before your mama sees you," Grandmother smiled, "or I'm certain Mr. Hobert won't be letting you or Thomas see each other again."

"Oh, goodness!" she raised her hands to her head. "Please Miz. Edmonds! Don't tell Daddy. He'll kill me if he finds out. I mean that we stopped by the barn," she said with flushed cheeks.

I pulled out a few broken sheaves of hay and brushed off her shoulders. I looked proudly at Grandmother.

"Don't you dare smirk like that!" she scolded me. "But you make a handsome pair! Indeed, you do!" With that, she kissed Julie on the cheek. "Come back, honey, as often as you want. You'll always be welcome here. And the same for your mama and daddy! Your father's a fine man. My Holman knew him when he was a boy and bought supplies from his father's store. Do you still own it?"

"No, ma'am! My grandfather sold it before he died. That's how Daddy got the money to finish school and open his law practice."

"Yes! Yes! Now I remember! Tommy, be careful taking her home. There're no lights on the roads. Call me when you get home."

"Yes, ma'am," I promised.

"Will you be coming back?"

"Not tonight, unless Marion brings me."

"Well, tell him I need you. Viola and I have a lot of cleaning out to do in her house. Someone's got to drive the wagon. I can't ask Henry and Pearl to do everything all the time. Viola's spending the night over there herself, packing boxes and cooking ware."

"I'm sure Marion'll bring me."

I leaned forward and kissed Grandmother's cheek. It felt soft and pubescent, covered with pink powder and the slight tint of rough. She placed a trembling hand on my right forearm and pressed it. "You're all I have, Tommy! Be careful."

"Yes, ma'am."

That night Marion drove me back to the farm. The next morning I rose early and walked out to the barn. The air was chilly and my light jacket was insufficient for the weather. Still, I saddled Mac and galloped him up and down the road for about half an hour. He bowed his head and pawed the earth, shook the bridle, snorted, and wanted to race. My cheeks burned red from the cold; my hands felt numb; my breath created a thin vapor, and my lungs ached from the rush of air. "Sorry, ole boy, but not now. Maybe later today. We'll have to see."

Hitching Nimble to the wagon proved no easy task either. She preferred to trot along the road, or gallop through the meadow behind the barn. But her primary purpose—however utilitarian—was to pull the buckboard, now that Sally was dead and Fred but a memory. "Come on, Nimble, stop stalling and back up in this harness! Come on! That a girl! You know what to do. Good girl!" I patted her neck and stroked her long face. "What a beautiful horse!" I reassured her.

After several trips in the wagon for Aunt Viola's furnishings and cooking items, I was pleased to discover Uncle Everett's car in the driveway. We had just pulled up with the last load. He had driven his sheriff's car, a Dodge sedan, to the farm. He stood leaning against it, as Nimble strained up the slight incline with Aunt Viola's washtub and dishes clattering in the back of the wagon.

"Everett! What a nice surprise!" Grandmother hailed. "Can you stay for lunch? It won't take but a moment to fix something."

"Mama, I wish I could, but I can't." He stood free of the car and walked toward the wagon. "Boy, I need your help. Mama, you've got to spare Tommy for the rest of the day." He glanced up at me and shifted his Stetson back slightly on his forehead. "Tommy, I've got to deputize you right now. Raise your right hand and repeat after me. 'I solemnly swear that I will fulfill the duties of deputy sheriff, according to the sheriff's orders, and desist all services the moment I am told so.'"

I raised my hand and repeated the oath.

"Good! Mama, there's been a shooting near the river toward Damascus. I need Tommy as a back up. He'll carry my shotgun and remain in the car. So help me God, I won't get him hurt. I need him, Mama. I can't get anyone else on the phone. I've had to arrest this man before. He'll come peacefully, I trust. I won't know till we get there. Tom, come on! Leave the wagon here, and I'll take Nimble back to the barn. We can't tarry any longer."

"Well! Just like that! Everett, for the life of me!" Grandmother protested. "You're being impulsive. Have you thought this out? Shaula will never forgive you, if he gets hurt. If you're not back by dark, what should I do?"

"Call Julie!" I blurted. "Grandmother. Please call her and explain."

Uncle Everett unhitched Nimble. "Tommy, get a heavier coat and gloves. It might turn cold," he said, as he took Nimble by her halter and headed for the barn.

"Don't I need a badge?" I asked, as we drove along.

"No! You don't need a damn thing!" Uncle Everett gripped the steering wheel tightly and sped down the gravel road. We passed Pearl and

Henry's cabin, the sheep shed and the end of the farm, then turned onto the old road to Bristol, but headed in the opposite direction. "You're gonna see a part of this county you never knew existed! People in rags and living in hovels! Poor as dirt! They're out of work. Down on their luck, Tommy. It's a damn shame. Ignorant as Hell! Stubborn as mules! Lying around drunk. Living off the land, poaching, bootlegging, cock fighting, beating their wives and children. I try to leave them alone. Stay out of their lives. Civilization's encroached on them. They don't take lightly to strangers. God only knows what's really happened."

We drove across several ranges of the Knobs. The gravel gave way to a dry dirt lane. We passed a rushing brook that babbled swiftly over rocks in a narrow gorge. Hemlocks cast dark shadows across the road. It grew narrower and narrower. Uncle Everett slowed his car. He turned on its red dome light. "Keep the gun in your lap," he said. "We'll soon be there. Just stay in the car. I'll do the talking. Don't get out until I tell you to."

"Yes, sir!"

"You've got buckshot in those shells. They do a lot of damage to flesh. To boards, or doors, or anything else! You'll know when I need you."

He slowed the car as we came around a sharp bend, flanked by prodigious thickets of blackberry bushes. Suddenly, the cabin came into view. Its rusted tin roof and rotting planks cast even darker shadows about the place. A front glass window gaped shattered from a gun blast. A man lay on the side of the road, where he had been dragged from the cabin's front porch. A pool of blood still glimmered on its worn boards. A rifle lay beside him. He had been shot by someone, probably from within the house.

Uncle Everett stopped the car, but left the motor running, as the dome light pulsated bands of light across the scene. He opened his door and stepped out cautiously. "Coop! Come on out! Don't make me have to come in. The deputy's got your door covered. Let's don't make this anymore painful than we have to."

I rolled my window down and laid the gun barrel across the edge of the door's windshield. A rustling sound could be heard within the cabin. A frightened woman appeared at the door. Her black hair was pulled back behind her head; her hands clutched something beneath her apron.

"Mae, for God's sake, don't try anything stupid!" Uncle Everett warned.

Suddenly, a gruff hand brushed her aside, and a rotund man stepped out on the porch. Black stubble covered his face. His long white underwear appeared stained and soiled. He clutched a pistol in his right hand. "I done it, Mr. Edmonds, before I could think. He's been intimidatin' Mae for months. Comin' up here, sneakin' pussy." Two small children stuck their heads out the door. "Git back in!" he threatened them with his elbow. "A man's got a right to defend hisself an' his family. I didn't do nothin' wrong. So help me God! Ain't that so, Mr. Edmonds? Tell me it is!"

I could see his thumb moving slowly toward the gun's hammer.

"Don't mean you no harm, Sheriff. Ain't nobody don't like you, Mr. Edmonds. Just back off, please. Me and the boys know whut to do."

Just then two other men appeared. They were bearded, barefoot, and dressed in overalls. Neither carried a gun. All three men looked worried. They hadn't planned on it ending this way.

"Coop! I'm not the judge, or the jury. I'm just sworn to uphold the law. God knows I don't want to harm you, or the Mrs. Please come with me. You know you'll get a fair trial. That's all I ask. The boys can stay here. It's better than festering a feud. Who's the victim, anyway?"

"Gordon Hester's boy, Ralph. Just no count, Sheriff. I seen it comin' to this from way back. He had it comin'. Mark my words. And him bringin' a gun at that."

"Keep your thumb away from that hammer!" Uncle Everett ordered. "You boys, back off. Mr. Lynch, please. Deputy, watch Mr. Lynch. I've got to handcuff him. You might want to step out of the car. Hand me the gun, Coop. Please! Let's end this standoff alive! Nobody needs to get hurt."

Slowly, the big man relaxed his thumb on the hammer and handed the pistol to Uncle Everett. As he did, Uncle Everett nodded for me to step out of the car and take the gun. Carefully, I opened the door and approached Uncle Everett. He handed me Mr. Lynch's pistol and turned the man around to handcuff him. I stepped back a pace or two, keeping my eye on his wife, her apron, and his two sons. A rush of adrenaline surged through me at the sound of the handcuffs locking Coop's wrists in place. Then, relief! I held the shotgun on my hip, while Uncle Everett escorted Coop to the car. He opened a back door and assisted the big man in. Mr. Lynch's fire had subsided. His complexion paled; his eyes filled with sadness and fear. Uncle Everett ordered the two boys to place Ralph's body in the trunk of the car. He retrieved the man's rifle and laid it beside his body. He tied the trunk door loosely with the dead man's belt.

It was well after dark before Uncle Everett drove me home. Grandmother had called Marion and my mother, who anxiously awaited our return.

"Everett! I don't know what to make of you! Honestly, I don't," my mother wrung her hands. "I know you needed Tommy. But, my God! You haven't changed, have you? You're still as reckless as ever!"

"Shaula! For Heaven's sake!" Marion interrupted. "Tommy's a man! Everett needed him. He had to have somebody he could trust. Everett, you owe us no apologies. You did the right thing! Come on, Shaula! Everett's our brother-in-law. The least we can do is support him."

My mother's eyes were swollen and wet. Her small hands trembled. The freckles on her face had lost their dark pink color. She reached up and kissed Uncle Everett on his cheek, then burst into tears. When she learned later that he wanted me to work for him over the summer, a tide of resignation ebbed about her. She lost weight, argued with Marion against it, but, in the end, acquiesced. "Why do I even bother!" she was wont to declare.

The remainder of the school year passed quickly. Julie's infatuation had ebbed as summer drew near. We had walked to the drugstore after school and were seated in a booth in the back. The light that streamed coral through a side window filled her face and eyes with a radiance of Wordsworth's "Lucy." I began to quote it.

> She dwelt among the untrodden ways
> *Beside the springs of Dove*

"Tommy, we've got our whole lives ahead of us," she interrupted. "Aren't you afraid and ashamed? My daddy didn't like your uncle's deputizing you and taking you off like that. 'It's not a good sign,' he said. 'The Edmonds are a violent people. Still living in the past. Just one step above sharecroppers! That's right, honey. Just glorified white trash! I don't want you seeing that boy again.'"

"'*White trash!*' I can't believe he'd say a thing like that! We're as much a part of Abingdon as any family. We've been here since the Revolution. And no telling how far back the Lorrans go!"

"Well, that's what he said," she repeated, as her eyes filled with tears.

"Julie, I love you. I can't be ashamed of that, or of my family." My heart ached to have to say the words. My stomach burned deep within my torso, sending its gasses and hot flames along the walls of my esophagus. My chest felt heavy and numb. My world, with all its proud beliefs, had never been so shocked or turned on its head before! "*White trash*! Julie! Don't believe that! I'm crazy about you. Please, Julie! Believe me, I am!"

She put her hands to her face and cried softly. "I love you, too," she whispered.

Early that summer, her father accepted a partnership with a large law firm in Roanoke, and Julie and her family moved away.

Chapter Twenty-three

WORKING FOR UNCLE EVERETT as a deputy turned out to be less thrilling than I had imagined. It did have its high moments, but they were few and far between. The County Commissioner and his staff demurred over Uncle Everett's having "deputized" me. Before they would approve of my being hired, they requested that the two of us meet with them.

We met the first night of June in the courthouse, in one of its chamber rooms. The Chairmen of the Commission was clad in a white suit, red suspenders, and loosened black tie. Ordinarily, the senator under whom our district fell oversaw the Commission, but owing to his absence, Mr. Erwin Aldridge filled in as pro tem in his place. He owned and operated an insurance company near Meadowview. Windows were open in the chamber room, but the muggy night breeze scarcely stirred the curtains behind him. Ribbons of yellow cigar smoke drifted in layers under the dim light of the chandelier. "Everett, for God's sake, he's still a boy! He's under age. It's against the law." He puffed on his cigar and turned to me. "Damn, boy, but you are tall! Son, how tall are you?"

"Six-two, maybe three."

"Weight?"

"About one hundred eighty, or so."

"Well, you look fit enough. Have you ever fought with your fists? We've got some rough people in this county. Some of 'em would just as soon kill ya as spit at ya! You know that?"

"It wouldn't surprise me, sir. I've had my share of fights at school. I'm on the wrestling team. I think I'm fit for whatever capacity the Sheriff needs me, sir!"

"Well! Everett, we don't need him totin' no gun, unless an absolute necessity. And he needs to be where he can get hold of you, at a moment's notice. How many deputies do we have on duty at any one time?"

"Other than the clerk who doubles as dispatcher, three per twelve-hour shift. I can use Tom both in the office and running surveillance. He'd need a gun for the latter, but he'd be in a car the entire time."

"What kind of surveillance? We got criminals we don't know about?"

"No, sir! But the office receives daily bulletins from Tennessee and North Carolina, describing any number of wanted people, all running from the law. I often receive good descriptions of their automobiles and license tags. If and when they pass through here, I'd like to know."

"Reasonable enough. Well, your request for young Edmonds here is granted, unless there's any objection," he glanced around the room. "Hearing none, you've got a new deputy. But, damn, if he gets hurt, Everett, it'll be your ass, not ours! And don't blabber about his age! There ain't another person we'd do this for."

"I fully concur! Remember, gentlemen, young Tom's my nephew. I've raised him from a boy, as much as his mom and step-dad have. But we're short of funds, and I need his help!"

"And how much are we paying him?"

"Seventy cents an hour! Two days a week! More, if a crisis develops. You have my word."

"Well, you can hire him up to four days a week, if you need him. The county's growing. We hope to attract industry. Improve accommodations. Law an' order's essential!"

"Indeed, Mr. Aldridge! I ran on that platform and pursue it every day."

"Thank you, Everett. We know we can count on you. Best luck to you and the boy!"

Luck was hardly on the agenda. Helping Uncle Everett file reports consumed my first week's energies and at least one day a week every week thereafter. Investigations of burglaries, responses to calls for assistance, disturbances of the peace, requests for detective services, domestic violence cases, the transporting of violent offenders to Richmond, and dozens of other related chores created a shocking awakening that first day I sat in front of his three, green file cabinets, beside an antiquated typewriter, whose keys had been worn smooth a decade earlier, and listened to one or the other of his two telephones ring about every twenty minutes. If that weren't enough, typing and storing everything in triplicate only added to the numbing effect of a sheriff's pared-down force. And all this to do in spite of his secretary! Dumpy, coarse, with long eyelashes and huge breasts, brown stockings, and flat black shoes, Gail came in every morning, puffing on a cigarette and grinding it out in an ashtray that hadn't been emptied all week.

"Tommy! You should meet my niece. She's perfect for you, honey! Built like I am, but younnnng, and sweeeeeet! Oh, how sweeeet she'd be! I'll bring her picture sometime." All this she said in a deep smoker's voice.

"That's fine, ma'am! I've got a sweetie I'm hot on, myself."

"Well, all's fair in love and war, you know! Ain't that the truth! That uncle of yours ain't so ugly himself."

"I wouldn't know," I tried to avoid her gaze.

A disquieting event did occur my second week on the job. I had stopped in town at the drugstore to quench my thirst with a Coke. Since I had been riding surveillance in the county, on an especially dusty road, a fine film of red mist covered my shirt and trousers as well as the toes of my cowboy boots. Moreover, since my revolver was holstered and snug against my waist, I hadn't bothered to unbuckle it or leave it in the car. I had just stepped out of the vehicle.

A crowd of boys and an older man, whom I recognized as a clerk at a fertilizer store, were hassling a utility worker in a ditch across the street from the drugstore. He was trying to avoid muddying the sidewalk under the ornate balcony of the downtown hotel. A pipe had burst, and sewage was gurgling out into the street. The worker was straddling the ditch and trying futilely to dig around the pipe in hope of finding the break. The bubbling mess reeked of raw, fetid waste. A woman on the hotel's balcony had come out of her room to observe the fuss. Her long dark red hair caught my attention. She looked like my mother, but was taller. She peered down over the balcony's rusty iron grill and smiled at me. All the while, she drew a pink brush slowly through her hair.

"Hell!" the clerk droned. "That man don't know the difference 'tween shit and a shovel."

The pack of boys laughed and gathered behind the clerk. "Whew! You like that work, boy!" they mocked the man in the ditch.

I glanced up at the woman, then walked over and stared down at the worker. About that instant, he stared up at me.

"Mr. Tom! Is that you?"

It was Charles! Uncle Everett's former sharecropper! Waste muck soiled his overalls' leg bottoms, and flecks of feces clung to his boots. His tanned face filled with a flush of shame, as he stared at me and I at him.

"Mr. Charles! How may I help?"

"Just shoo these gawkers away! A man cain't work with them a jeerin' him, Deputy! I see you're a deputy! I sometimes wish I was back on the farm. Don't tell Mr. Edmonds you seed me like this. Don't let him know I'm doin' this. He gave me a cussin' out the day I left. Well, not really, Mr. Tom! But I seen it in his eyes."

"All right, you people. Stand back now. Let's let this man work," I said. "You wouldn't want to be jeered at, either. You boys! There's plenty of trains to watch and yards to mow, if you're willing to work."

"I say you gotta know shit from a shovel," the clerk repeated. He spat a stream of clumpy tobacco juice into the ditch, near Charles.

With that I stepped toward Charles. "Sir," I addressed him, "may I see your shovel a minute?"

He stared up at me, embarrassed, but with a smile that stretched to the edge of his sunburned ears.

I took the shovel, scooped up a wedge of waste on its lip, and slopped it against the clerk's shoes. "I'll be damned!" I said. "I've always been clumsy. You'll have to pardon me. But that's '*shit*,' and this," I clutched the handle, "is a '*shovel*.' Isn't that right, Mr. Charles?" I smiled, as I returned the implement to him.

Charles suppressed a yellow grin and began digging again. The woman on the balcony applauded, while the clerk stared up at her. The boys looked stunned, smirked sheepishly, and scurried off. The man glared in fury at me but backed away. "You son-of-a-bitch!" he grunted. "I oughtta take you over my knee."

"Sir, let's just leave it at this." I placed my right hand on the back of my belt, where the handcuffs hung. "Sir, you may be my elder, but don't you ever call me a 'son-of-a-bitch' again. Is that clear?"

He eyed me angrily, wiped his shoes against the back of his trouser legs, and trudged off defiantly.

"Mr. Tom! If'n it'll please you, I'll even the score with that bastard myself. You don't need to do no grovelin' afore him. I'll take care o' him after work. A shovel up his ass is all he needs."

"No, Charles. But thank you! Let's just let him be. OK?"

"Yes, sir! Please don't tell Mr. Edmonds. That's all I ask."

"You have my word, Mr. Charles! Thank you for the offer."

I glanced back up at the balcony, but the woman had re-entered her room.

Two weeks later, a group of men, clad in Klan robes, appeared at the clerk's house, late at night. They dragged him from his bed, tied him to his own porch's post, and whipped him with a buggy whip, until his back and legs bled. Neighbors heard his cries and could see the cross, burning in his yard. After the flames died down, they called Uncle Everett at home.

When he came to the office the next morning, I noticed clay on his boots and blood on his trouser cuffs. "Damn Klan!" he muttered. "Gail, get me that FBI file! There's been another rally somewhere. Couldn't sleep a wink last night, from all the calls."

Gail stared at me. She hurried to one of the dusty file cabinets and brought him a form.

"Just put the usual in it," he said to her. "'Klan roughs up resident, thought to be troublesome. No lasting damage or property lost. End of case.'" He dropped the form on her desk. "Come on, deputy!" he smiled. "Let's go get some coffee and check out the fairgrounds. They're supposed to be racing out there today."

"Should I wear my gun?"

He thought for a moment. "Yes! Wear it. Walk tall and proud, and don't pay a damn bit of attention to anyone, or what they say. We'll look around, look important, smile, but be friendly. It won't hurt to lean up against the rails for a while. It pays to be seen, now and then. Especially after the Klan's met. People get nervous, edgy, afraid. Our being there will quell a lot of nerves. Ah, me! We've along way to go in this County, Mr. Tom! Justice isn't always what it appears to be."

"Now, that's a fact!" stated Gail. She shifted her brassiere with her thumbs and sat down to type up the report. "Well, don't stare at me!" she blurted. "Y'all get on out of here."

"Yes, ma'am," teased Uncle Everett. "If anybody calls, tell them where we'll be. Come on, deputy! We've got work to do."

One night late, while staying at Uncle Everett's, Carl, his oldest deputy—heavy set and slow of speech—came by the house to report a death. "A man's died just beyond the Bottom. Poisin'," said Carl. "Liquor poisin'! Got it from somewhere in the mountains. Here's the jug. I did seize it as material witness." He handed Uncle Everett the glass jug. It was dirty and chipped about the lip.

"I know where he got this. I'd recognize it anywhere," Uncle Everett replied, as he handed it back to Carl.

"I've filled out the report. They plan to bury him tomorrow. Won't say where they got it. Scared. Just plumb scared."

"Can't blame them. I'm sure they got it at Macky's still, up near Tazewell. It's in our county. The Feds won't go up there anymore. You available to go tomorrow?"

"Yes, sir. Just say when."

"Be out here early. Say, before five. The boy and I'll be ready. We can be there by six and surprise them when they come up the cove. I know exactly where it is. I used to buy some from him," he grinned.

"They say it's the best."

"Used to be. But I warned Macky when I became sheriff. 'You ever distill a bad run, and I'll have to haul you in. Won't want to, but the risk will be too great.' He promised he wouldn't. But he's been known to use old radiators instead of copper tubing. Who's the victim?"

"James Craig. Used to work on Glenn Fields' farm. Until Fields sold out."

"Well. Bring your shotgun. No telling what we're liable to run into."

The ride early the next morning took us high into the hills, beyond the Laurel Bottom, and close to the edge of the county line. Carl sat in the front seat with Uncle Everett; I sat in the back. The interminable curves and washboard ruts on the dirt roads filled me with nausea. Dawn struggled to peek through the mists along the creeks and around the shoulders of the wooded hills. Gradually, we climbed higher and higher. Finally, the sun broke through, just as we came upon a wagon track that angled back into a stand of white pine and young hemlocks.

"Let's turn off here," said Uncle Everett. "We'll walk in the rest of the way. Mackey will be coming up from his place, about at that gap," Uncle Everett pointed.

After pulling the car off into the shadows of a berry thicket, we slipped out, opened our double-barreled shotguns, and dropped the shells into the chambers. We each wore a pistol. We crept quietly along a damp trail, passed through a grassy knoll, and hid behind a rampart of honeysuckle vines. I could see the still below us and hear water dripping from a pipe. It ran from a shallow spring into an old water heater, passed into coils of tubing, and into a radiator. We crouched behind the thicket until my legs ached and arches burned with the strain. An hour passed. The sun climbed above the treetops. Crows cawed overhead. A huge buzzard circled high in the sky and drifted away. Then we heard footsteps: soggy twigs being crunched softly beneath feet. Two men appeared, almost simultaneously, out of the brush. They were thin, of medium height, unshaved, and clad in overalls, flannel shirts, and brogans. They stepped quietly toward the still and prepared to light a fire under the large, rusted, water tank.

"All right, boys!" Uncle Everett stood up, revealing himself and his gun. "Mackey," he addressed the older of the two men. "I warned you. Old James is dead. Died from your run. I'd know your glass jugs anywhere. You did sell to him, didn't you?"

"I ain't got to answer you, Everett. You ain't got nothin' on me. No proof. None whatsoever!"

"I've got his jug, one of yours! That'll provide all the circumstantial evidence I need. Plus, I'll carry some of these along," he tapped a few, near the base of the water tank, with the toe of his right boot.

"You ain't man enough to take us," Mackey snapped. "'Sides, me an' George can pay you off, if'n that's whut you come for." He backed slowly away from his still, toward a shotgun that poked out from under a tarp. "Ain't worth dyin' over, or shootin' a' body over. You ain't that kind of a man, Everett. We can make this up. Me and George didn't mean no harm."

"Carl! Tommy! Come on out! Handcuff them. Let's get on back. Hell, Mackey! I don't delight in doing this. I warned you. A man's dead. I've got no choice. You're coming with us. Or I'll blow your foot off," he aimed his gun toward the older man's left foot.

Carl and I stepped out behind the bushes. I pointed my gun in the air, resting the stock on my right hip.

"Damn ya, Everett! You ain't got no cause to do this. What'll they do to us?"

"Maybe nothing! Mr. Craig bought it on his own. He knew the risks. I'll plead your side. You've never done anything else wrong. Now, come on! Turn around. Let's get this done."

With reluctance, the two men turned about. Carl handcuffed them, and we led them to the car. I rode between them in the back seat. They were tried, found guilty of operating a still, were fined thirty dollars each and thirty days in jail, then released. Uncle Everett was ordered to destroy their still, but he delegated that responsibility to Carl. If Carl destroyed it, however, he never mentioned it. Gail simply recorded the order.

"Tommy," explained Uncle Everett, "you've got to understand. Most of these people have been chaffing against authority since their grandfathers fought in the Civil War. They're as penniless now as they were then. And even less educated. Remember that, if you hope to get along. Maybe it'll change one day, but I doubt I'll live to see it. As for the rooster fighting they do, I just have to turn a blind eye. Hell, I even bet with them, myself, from time to time."

When not on patrol, or on assignment at the courthouse, I'd slip down to the library and browse its holdings on the War. A variety of histories of Abingdon had been written by Confederate veterans, and their books were housed in a special room, along with diaries by an ex-general and several privates. The general had served under Lee, but the privates were enlisted men and members of a large brigade in the Army of the Tennessee. They had fought in almost all of the major battles from Shiloh to Johnston's surrender to Sherman in Greensboro in April of 1865. Reading their diaries began to satisfy that curiosity that had been building in me since Grandmother and Aunt Viola had first spun their stories of Great-Grandfather Howard's regiment and his presence at the Battle of Chickamauga and "in the field before Atlanta." It was demoralizing to read them. How proud, brave, and unconquerable their Corps, Divisions, and Brigades had been, until their defeat at Missionary Ridge. At Chickamauga, they had swept through the woods, firing and reloading, until at last they had taken the Ridge—thanks to Longstreet's Corps, under whom Great-Grandfather Howard's Regiment served. They had taken heavy casualties and spent the night searching for the wounded amidst the piles of maimed and dying soldiers. The dairies described how men's bodies lay twisted, torn, and stacked, eyes dangling from sockets, brains scattered in the grass and weeds, entrails bulging beside bloating bodies, blood and mud intermingled, and fallen horses, gutted by shells, but still alive. Later they pursued Rosecrans' Federals back into Chattanooga and watched them from Lookout Mountain. How they chaffed when their generals made them form columns to cheer President Davis and his staff as they galloped by! "Massa Jeff! Massa Jeff! Won't you feed us hungry boys? Can't you see we're poor and hungry?" They described their terrible defeat at Missionary Ridge and how bewildered and frightened Bragg appeared. Their stragglers fell farther and farther behind. Wagon after wagon passed them, laden with the wounded. To the whiz of Minnie balls and the thump of cannon shells falling around them, they retreated to Chickamauga Station, then to Dalton, where they wintered. They hated Bragg yet felt sorry for him. He had deprived them of the very food and clothing they needed to stay viable in the field. After Chickamauga, I could see why their spirits slumped, how defeat had eaten into their pride, and that, cold and demoralized, they now realized their cause was lost. My heart ached to read their entries. Great-Grandfather Howard's ghost wavered in the dim light that fell upon them and over their campsites on every page. This was his book, his war, his loss, his sorrow that he must have carried till the day he died. Not just his wound! How could any of them have forgotten the comrades they left behind, the notes they penned for each other, the prayers they whispered, the cold, fatigue, wounds, hunger, and filth they endured every day? Was that why Grandmother behaved, spoke, and rocked as she did? Why her favorite word was "resolute?" Why Aunt Viola bore her poverty without ever murmuring, as if assigned to her by God himself? I read on and on: of the shelling of Atlanta, of the Federals' repeating rifles that ripped through the ranks of the 63rd. Of Johnston's attempt to lure Sherman into a frontal attack. Of his desperate gamble to mar Lincoln's re-election. Of Davis' dismissal of the old general and of Hood's new command. Of the skirmishes around Atlanta. Was that when Great-Grandfatther Howard was wounded a second time? Was he in the city when it burned? How did he manage to escape? Was he taken by ambulance to Augusta? When did he finally make it home? Back to his beloved Knobs and sacred hills along the Holston? Was he swept up in the retreat from Atlanta? Stymied along the clogged roads? Helpless but helping the old men and women who carted what few belongings they had, as Sherman pursued the Army of the Confederacy toward Savannah and into South Carolina? Did he ever share that with Grandmother, or Uncle Jim, or Aunt Viola? I knew enough now to ask better questions, but how could I get them to tell me what they knew? What I knew was in books. What they knew was existential, beyond expunging from their hearts: such as his battle-seared stare, his long fingers and sallow hands, his lapses into silence, his eternal and painful limp, his withdrawal from society, and escape into the Knobs. Did they remind him of Missionary Ridge? In his dreams, was he still searching for his fallen comrades, for Aunt Viola's father? I wanted to steal the diaries and take them home. I always put them back. No wonder Uncle Everett paced Quilly Hall as often as he did, why he never seemed satisfied or self-fulfilled, drank coffee, as if on the run, and taught himself to outshoot the best marksmen in the county. I sank in waves of grief whenever I opened or read the diaries. My strength would return, only after I had left the library and hurried up the hill to the courthouse and Uncle Everett's office.

"We've had another complaint," Gail said. "From Jeannie's millinery shop. She's upset with the traffic upstairs."

Uncle Everett paused beside her desk. He let out a slow breath. "What's it this time? The girls, again?"

"Yes, sir. Though I don't think Sarah's to blame. Probably her cohorts."

"Cohorts? 'Co-whores' is more like it," he smiled. "They're an innocent lot. Keep a passel of transient salesmen happy. They even buy hats and gowns from Jeannie. She ought to keep her trap shut."

"We'll, she's not. Threatening to go to the Commissioner, if you don't act."

"The hotel's in town. Let Chief Bailey handle it."

"He's tried. Arrested them twice. Booked them, too. But they go right back at it."

Uncle Everett glanced at me. "Call her and tell her I'll send someone down. Thomas, shine your boots, tuck in your shirt properly, and comb your hair. You're going to be my liaison with the hotel." He picked up a sheet of official paper, scribbled a brief message on it, folded the sheet, and placed it in an envelope. He wrote a room number on its face. "Go to this room. Knock politely, and hand this note to the person who'll come to the door. It should be a red-haired lady, with pretty eyes and dark features. If a man opens the door, tell him this is for 'Miss Sarah.' You got it?"

"Yes, sir." I knew he meant the attractive woman who had been brushing her hair and observing the ditch-digging scene of a month ago.

A thin smile formed about Uncle Everett's lips. A sparkle gleamed momentarily in his eyes. "She'll understand. Then tell Miss Moran—that's Jeannie—that all's well."

"Yes, sir."

I drove downtown and parked on the street that paralleled the hotel. It stood a block from the railway station. One entered the hotel's office next to a door beside the millinery shop. But once in the hotel's lobby, one had to go back out to climb a flight of metal stairs to enter the rooms.

I paced the balcony several times before finding Miss Sarah's number. I had never been upstairs before. All this was new to me. I was confident that eyes were watching me. A curtain twitched in a room near hers. I stood outside Miss Sarah's door, collected my wits, and knocked.

All was silent. I took a deep breath and knocked again.

The door opened. I saw the woman's long hair and smelled her perfume before she glanced around the door's edge.

"My! You're Everett's nephew. Aren't you? Come in."

She opened the door, and I entered a rather confined room, with yellow and pink flowery wallpaper, a handsome writing desk, a tall mahogany armoire, a narrow bed, and two curved-back sitting chairs beside the room's lone window.

"Well, you like it?"

"Yes, ma'am," I blushed. "Uncle Everett," I caught myself, "the sheriff's sent me with this message." I cleared my throat and handed her the envelope.

"Does he expect a reply?"

"I don't know. He didn't say. He said you'd understand."

"Sounds like him," she mumbled. "You're younger than I thought." She unsealed the envelope, unfolded his note, and read it in silence.

"Shhhit" she hissed in a low whisper. "Don't tell him I cussed," she laughed. "He's very fond of you. Proud, I should say. You know that?"

"I've suspected as much."

"Oh, you have! Sonny, you're as good-lookin' as Everett. Don't be so bashful. You know why he's sent you, don't you?"

"I guess he didn't want to come in person."

Her eyes twinkled. "God, another charmer!" she laughed. "How many more like you are there? There's more like me but younger and here every Saturday night. How old are you, anyway?"

"Nineteen," I lied.

"I'd say more like twenty," she leaned forward and kissed my cheek. "Tell him I understand. The girls'll be quieter. I'll pay a personal visit on Miss Nosey Ass, herself. All she wants is a bribe. Hats ain't in style like they used to. And don't tell him I flirted with you," she winked.

"It'll be a secret, ma'am. He'll never know."

She pursed her lips. Her gaze shifted, drifted somewhere, as if far away, to another place, and another time. "Tell him I miss him. I won't disappoint him," she whispered. She clutched my hand, squeezed it, and leaned against the open door. "Thanks for coming."

"I'll relay the message." I backed away, nodded respectfully, and clambered down the metal steps to the millinery shop.

An anorexic woman in an elegant green velvet dress, with a white lacy collar and lacy sleeves, was standing behind the shop's glassed-in front door. I could see its curtain jerk as she peeked out. I almost struck her nose, as I opened the door. Her face looked like a wrinkled map. "Ma'am, I'm so sorry. If you're Miss Moran, the sheriff's sent me. He said he's taking action on your complaint. I didn't mean to pop in so abruptly."

"Oh, he is? I just bet he is! I saw you go up those stairs first. I'm no fool, young man! There'll be an election soon. Remind him of that. You're his nephew, aren't you? I know all about you Edmonds. You can't fool me. I know your grandmother. Miss Hot n Tot! Runs off to Bristol to buy her goods. Braggin' about that farm and house of hers! Like she was some lord's lady."

"Ma'am, I've just come to deliver a message! That's all."

Her jaw fell open. "Well, I have never! How dare you snub me! Young man, I am for real! And I'm tired of your Uncle, the famous sheriff," she scowled, "ignoring my pleas. I don't like a whorehou . . ." she caught her breath, "a *brothel* over my business. Nor does the town support it. Nor would you. I want it stopped. Stopped!" she repeated. "Do you hear me?"

"Yes, ma'am!"

"Then tell him that! I won't have him dying here the way your grandfather did."

"My grandfather?"

"Yes, your grandfather! I don't suppose your lady Grandmother told you that! Did she?'

I glared at the woman, I guess in shock.

"That's right, Mr. Edmonds. Your famous grandfather, Holman, died upstairs, right above my shop, my mother's shop," she motioned with her eyes, "in the arms of a whore! A whore! Just like your uncle will."

I backed away slowly. I tucked my chin against my chest, nodded respectfully out of habit, and rushed into the street. I stared up at the balcony as I passed in front of the car, opened the door, and climbed in. My hands were trembling as I turned the ignition switch. I drove out toward the Bristol highway, turned at the Pet plant, circled back into town, drove passed the old cemetery where my grandfather is buried, then returned to the office.

Gail was filing her nails as I entered. Her huge breasts sagged under her white blouse. They almost touched her typewriter's keys. "Well!" she said, as she glanced up. "You look like you've just seen a ghost! That Miss Moran is somethin', isn't she? Or was it Miss Sarah?" she raised her eyebrows with a knowing smile. "Huh! Cat got your tongue? Mr. Tommmmmmy! Was it that bad? Or that gooood! Come on, boy! Speak!"

I wiped a line of sweat off my brow and twiddled my hat in my hands. "They were both something!" I feigned a smile. "I delivered the note, but Miss Moran sure let Uncle Everett have it. Called the rooms upstairs a 'whorehouse.' Just mean! She was mad and mean."

"Don't worry, Tommy. The red head will know what to do. She's got a crush on the sheriff, and she's not about to lose him, if she can help it. She's sweet on him. But, alas! He just totally ignores me!" she crooned in a high-pitched comical voice, while twitching her eyebrows all the while.

"His loss," I smiled. I was so grateful not to have to divulge more.

Died in the arms of a whore! Was that really true? Or just another myth? Like Great-Grandfather Howard's stone? Or, even worse, an unmitigated rumor, or out-and-out lie? And if true, how would I ever find out? Would his death certificate include the cause? Or was it even recorded in the courthouse? I set about to find out, located his death certificate, but it listed his cause of death as "heart attack, October 11, 1922." It gave no further details.

That Saturday, while staying at the farm, I managed to steal a moment all to myself with Aunt Viola. She had come out on the front porch to rock. A warm summer breeze stirred the leaves of the great oaks and elms. I could hear their limbs creaking against each other.

"Aunt Viola, how did my grandfather Holman die? Was he shot? Did he die here? Was Grandmother with him?"

While still rocking, she turned and glanced suspiciously at me. "Why do you ask?" she inquired softly.

"Just curious!"

"No you're not! Somebody's told you something, ain't they?"

"Yes, they have. Said he died in a whore's arms, in the hotel in town."

"Moran! That hussy Moran told you, didn't she? She's always hated us. Her father was a two-bit Yankee carpetbagger from Illinois. His people came south to buy up the town. All they got was her shop. Your Great-Grandfather Nathan and later Holman exposed them for what they were—greedy illiterate trash! She's as venomous as a copperhead! Stay away from her. Don't believe a word she mouths."

"But is it true? I'm going on seventeen. Or soon will be. What if he did? He's still my grandfather. I'd rather know the truth and shrug it off, than lie about it."

She rocked in silence, annoyed, visibly perturbed that I had stumbled onto something verboten. It took her several minutes to regain her composure.

"There are things that family's don't pass on," she mumbled. "They're meant to be kept secret. His dirty laundry's our business. Kate's suffered enough. Ain't nobody else's concern. He was a good man and loved Jim's father. Ain't nobody free of total vice. Nobody knows for sure, Tommy. But the rumors broke Ginny's heart. She resolved to rise above it. To be a lady, to act like a lady, talk like a lady, and manage her affairs without whining. That's the truth, Tommy. The stark ugly truth! But don't betray it, or throw it up to your grandmother," she rocked with vigor. "Tommy, he owned all kind of property, but lost it gambling. He just couldn't stay away from alcohol, cards, horses, and women. That was the fate of so many boys of his generation. They wasn't old enough to have fought in the war. All they had was memories of men who'd come home: poor, broken up, crippled, diseased, determined to survive the best they could. The economy was horrible: farms foreclosed and men became tenants who hadn't already. Kate was a savior to them. That's when Earl and Jessie and Albert hired on. It's not over yet." She rested her head against the back of the rocker and reached for my hand. I stopped rocking and sat forward in my own chair to clasp it. It was hard, boney, and gnarled about the knuckles, sallow and purple with bruises.

"I'll not say anything," I assured her. "Thank you for telling me the truth."

"You're a good boy, Tommy! It ain't fittin' that we've put so much to rest on you. When I'm dead, promise me you'll visit my grave and keep it clean. The thought of briars and snakes crowding it sends shivers up my back. I can't even remember when we cleaned Jim's grave last. Can you?"

"No, ma'am. Maybe I'll ride out there today. Take a scythe and rake and see what I can do."

"God bless you! I'd give you a dollar if I had one."

I squeezed her hand gently. "Think I'll find Grandmother and head for the Knobs."

I spent the remainder of the day riding back into the Knobs to survey the old farm. Mac knew the way and followed the lane at a slow trot. I let him amble up the hilly grades, then gallop down hill. Fennel, weeds, and sumac grew along the edge of the lane. In places, Princess Anne Lace and bluets graced the road.

I was unprepared for the neglect I saw. No one had checked on the farm since Uncle Everett had become sheriff and Jessie had died. As I came up over the last rise, I could see where a section of the cabin's roof had buckled. Swallows swarmed out of the chimney at my approach. Field sparrows and meadowlarks took to wing. The graveyard lay choked under a heavy tangle of briars. The orchard in the distance looked blighted; many trees had lost their leaves. Bramble grew where the land had once grudgingly permitted corn, wheat, and tobacco to flourish. It had at least sustained a grateful, aging couple, whose children were long gone, or lay in the graveyard on the hill. I dismounted and set about my chore. Before leaving, I walked down to the river and skipped a stone across the ford.

Grandmother had a pan of hot cornbread and fried apples waiting when I returned. Aunt Viola had steam-fried a fat rabbit that Henry had killed while mowing below the sheep shed. He had cut into a nest of yellow jackets, just when the rabbit jumped. Henry had come down to the house for some cornstarch to rub on the stings, since he and Pearl were out. She gave him a box to take home, and he left the rabbit with her. "She did give him a side of bacon," Aunt Viola added, as if to even the score.

Chapter Twenty-four

THE LAST WEEK OF that August, Marion made reservations on a Pullman for the two of us to tour the University of Virginia and the Harvard Campus. We took the train to Boston first. Marion had booked a nice room in a hotel along the Charles River. We enjoyed a visit to the historic area, then the next day, made it out to Harvard. After introductions in the Admissions Office, we were provided a leisure tour of the campus. The library, with its marble steps under the dome and its lofty reading rooms, the lecture halls where the philosophers James and Whitehead had taught, and the ornate Annenberg Hall appealed to me the most. Marion and I were both chagrinned, however, to discover that the Hall's bronze plagues to the Civil War fallen honored only its Union alumni. "Well, welcome to *veritas*," Marion growled. Before leaving the campus, we stopped by the dean's office. He and his staff were very polite and encouraged me to apply. We left with a catalog and a folder filled with application forms.

Back in Virginia, we rested a few days in Charlottesville, visited Jefferson's Monticello, before touring the university. I fell in love with its double rows of old dorm rooms, still heated by fireplaces, and its gracious grounds and rotunda, designed by Jefferson himself. This is where I wanted to study, to attend college. Besides, Abingdon would only be a day's ride away on the train. Moreover, I could take a bus to Lexington, whenever I wanted to explore Washington and Lee, or VMI, and their collections of Civil War records. Marion seemed relieved that my matriculation plans for the future appeared resolved. "Let's head for home," he announced. "Your mother will be as pleased as I am—though Harvard would have been a great choice, too," he added with a note of disappointment.

Once home, Uncle Everett stopped by the house one evening to present me with my last paycheck of the summer. He and Marion had retired to the library to chat, while my mother and I rummaged through a chest of drawers of clothing I had outgrown. "You'll never be able to wear these again," she said, as she held up a variety of sweaters and pants. "They're too good to throw away. Let's save them for Henry, or Miles, or some of his grandchildren. It's a shame to waste good garments like these. Well, let's check on your uncle and Marion. They're probably ready for some pie about now."

I helped carry several small plates of lemon pie into the study. My mother brought in the coffee.

Uncle Everett appeared relaxed. Marion sat slouched in his favorite leather chair. "Good news, but sad news!" Marion addressed us.

"What is it?" my mother asked.

"The sheriff'll have to tell you. It's his to explain."

My mother turned to him, with a slight hint of apprehension, and handed him his coffee. "Well! What is it?"

"I'll not be seeking re-election next year. Ten years is enough. Half the county's irked that I haven't raided enough stills, and the other half's furious that I've destroyed the few I have. But that's not all. The town's not made the progress the Council wants. They're hinting that maybe I'm too lenient on certain types, like the rooster fighters, drunks, the crowds at the race tracks, and the girls downtown." He bit his lips at the mention of the latter and glanced up at my mother with a vacant cast to his eyes.

"Cream?" she offered, in a cool voice.

He shook his head no.

His remark about "the girls downtown" nipped my mother's playful banter, to say the least. "Who'll take your place? That ex-Marine? He still interested?"

"Don't know and doubt it. I need to get back to the farm. Miles's days are numbered. Tractors have taken the place of draft horses and mules. Don't need to raise all those crops anymore. Plus, nobody's around anymore to replace men like Miles and Charles and the others, anyway."

"But can tobacco and cattle, wheat, hogs, wool, and hay, still turn a profit?" Marion questioned. "We have farmers drifting into the bank, almost everyday, having to mortgage their farms and equipment, just to make ends meet."

"I'll still remain a deputy," Uncle Everett replied, as he cradled his cup and saucer in his hands. "I want to put Jim's farm back into cultivation. His tobacco allotment alone will pay for everything else. Mama's farm needs refurbishing, too, and Henry can't handle it alone after Albert goes. There's a chance to place some sheep on Whitetop and its meadows, I've learned. The government's going to open its lands for grazing, and nobody's signed up for the project yet. I stand to make a handsome profit, if I can find a mountaineer who's willing to watch the sheep."

"Maybe I could check on them," I volunteered. "That'd be like camping out on weekends and during breaks."

"Dream on!" Uncle Everett dismissed my offer. "It'll be nothing but drudgery and hard work. Something that only a hardy old hermit would do. Besides, you've chosen the soft way out. UVA! That's for doctors, lawyers, and Indian chiefs. What will you major in, anyway?"

"I've been researching that: biology or the natural sciences. Who knows, I might wind up at VPI yet. Forestry's still my first love. But history and science run a close second, and Harvard and UVA would be nice to attend."

Uncle Everett clattered his cup in its saucer, rested them on an end table, and rose from his chair. "Tommy, we'd all be better off if we could just forget these farms. Just let them go. The land's been nothing but a burden all our lives. It's never recovered since the 1860s, or ever will. A man can't make money on family farms anymore. Not enough to count. Go on to Harvard, if you can. Or UVA. I'll still be here when you get back, and you'll inherit the whole damn thing. If you live along enough, you'll understand what I mean. Sorry to be so pessimistic." He adjusted his holster, kissed my mother on the neck, and left.

Toward the middle of November, Marion and his friend, Allan Templeton, a fellow legislator, drove to the state hospital in Marion to review its policies governing the mentally ill. While visiting a ward for the criminally insane, one of the inmates became unusually agitated, attacked Marion, and killed him. According to Mr. Templeton, the man asked, "Who are you? Why are you here? I'm tired of being doped up and kept a prisoner to please the likes of you."

"I'm Marion Chappels, chairmen of the state's committee on the mentally ill. If you're being mistreated, tell us how."

"Chappels? You said, 'Chappels?'"

"Marion Chappels. That's correct. From Abingdon."

"You any kin to the Chappels that killed my cousin, Olan? Are ya?" he demanded in a surly voice. "Are you?" he all but shouted.

"Marion backed away," said Mr. Templeton. "'Is there a staff person here?' he asked. 'Better get one! I don't want a confrontation. Not with him.'

"'Let's leave,' I was about to say, when the man suddenly broke a window pane with his fist, picked up the largest bloody piece of glass he could find, and stabbed Marion in the throat. He died before we could get him off the ward. The man would have stabbed me, except an orderly, passing by, heard the commotion and tackled him to the floor."

All this Mr. Templeton explained while Uncle Everett, my mother and I, along with Templeton, were at the funeral home, selecting a casket. We buried Marion in the Chappels plot, near the crest of the cemetery that overlooks the mountains to the west. Snow had fallen the night before, and a cold wind numbed the air. My mother wore an entirely black outfit, with a thin black veil, as did Grandmother and Aunt Viola. Numerous townspeople and legislator colleagues attended the services and burial. My mother kept her grief to herself. Uncle Everett sat beside her and held her hand. After the committal, she placed her head on his shoulder and wept. That night, we stayed alone at the house in town. After my mother went to bed, I sat in the library. I could feel Marion's presence amid the room's richly bound books and dim lamps. Finally, I climbed the narrow steps up the hall stairs, tip-toed solemnly passed my mother's room, and prepared for bed.

It took the longest time for my mother to recover from Marion's death. School activities, sports, and an occasional date kept me occupied. Mother spent her time tidying the house, canning a few apples and pears with Grandmother, Aunt Viola, and Pearl on the farm, or just whiling away hours shopping aimlessly in town. Uncle Everett would stop by, two-to-three evenings a week, before going to his own home.

"How do you take the loneliness?" she asked him one night, when he dropped by for supper. "You're as far out in the country as Mama and Viola. I know you're dating that woman in town, but, do you really love her?"

Uncle Everett had removed his holster and was seated at the kitchen table. He sat his fork down and hugged his mug of coffee in his hands. Over the years, gray furrows had formed across his forehead. His hands were swollen and knuckles chapped. Deep lines ran perpendicular along his cheeks, accentuating his tanned nose. He stared at the dishes on the table, smiled at me, then her.

"That's a big order. Loneliness? Love? I'm not sure I'm qualified to talk about either. I did love Rachel," he stared off into the room's shadows. "She was fun, sweet, unpredictable, but aloof and depressed most of the time. I could never move her beyond her darkness. As for loneliness, I guess I've always felt lonely. Mama's never been able to love anyone without qualification. Ham and I always had to measure up. Until he met you!"

he said softly. A faint smile twinkled in his eyes; it warmed my mother's face and the room. He glanced uncertainly toward me. "Tom, you've had it lonely yourself. No brothers or sisters, or even cousins, just you."

I didn't know how to reply. I had never thought of myself as being lonely, or feeling alone. I liked everything as it was.

"What about that woman?" my mother touched his hand. "Do you really love her? Would she marry you, if you asked her?"

Uncle Everett appeared stunned. "Love her? I guess I do, but only for," he hesitated, "for escaping from loneliness. She helps lots of men like me escape. Tom, you understand what I mean? What I'm trying to say?"

"Yes, sir."

"I guess I'd better be going." Uncle Everett pressed my mother's hand. "You're always welcome to stay out at my place. Certainly, Mama would love to have you at Quilly Hall. Have you thought about that?"

"Not really, but yes! I do love my freedom, and everything I need's right here in town."

"This is Tom's last year, before he goes off. Maybe after that, you'll want to reconsider," he released her hand.

"Maybe," she replied softly.

She walked him to the door. He re-buckled his holster. She helped him into his black leather jacket. She ran her fingers over its silver star. They both glanced over their shoulders at me. I turned away, but I could hear her kiss his cheek, as he put his arm about her waist. Together, they stepped out into the night. I returned to the table to help with the dishes.

Chapter Twenty-five

M Y SENIOR YEAR EVAPORATED. I dated a little girl whose father owned a farm near Glade Spring. I loved her lusty kisses and shapely body, the softness inside her mouth and her warm cuddly breasts. I wanted to take her to the hay barn, but Julie had made the loft special in a way I wanted to keep inviolable. Brenda, the new girl, had short black hair, green eyes, and dark eyelashes. She loved long skirts and cashmere sweaters, white socks and two-tone oxfords. I would bring her home after ball games, and we would embrace, fondle, and kiss in Marion's cozy library. Mom would steal upstairs, but stay awake until I took Brenda home. Her light would still be on when I returned. One night when I came back, she was seated in the library, waiting for me.

"Tommy. This thing with Brenda's moving too fast. Don't get too involved. I know she's sweet and all. But you've got your whole future before you."

"I know Mom. I'll be careful."

"You, you haven't been having sex, have you?"

I hesitated to answer, not knowing how to reply. All my silence did, however, was to exacerbate her alarm.

"Tommy, she's not pregnant, is she?"

"No Mom. I promise. I'm sure she's not!"

"Oh, Tom! I don't want you to be like your Uncle Everett. He could have been so much more in life. Maybe a governor! The whole family was capable of that."

With the coming fall, I enrolled at Harvard. I did it as much for Marion as for myself. I knew that's where he wanted me to attend. Besides, it was his money that was sending me; the farm certainly couldn't afford it.

At Christmas, I returned home. Mom met me at the train station. "We're going out to see your Grandmother first. Don't be surprised if she seems cranky or a little testy," Mom glanced at me with a worried frown.

It was good to drive out the old road again. The harvested and fallow fields lay cold, barren, mantled in winter's seasonal rest. Mists rose above the creeks and seeping springs. Cattle munched on trampled fodder and humps of scattered hay. Vapor formed thin clouds about their mouths and huge nostrils. Skiffs of light snow hugged the higher crests of the Knobs.

We found Grandmother and Aunt Viola huddled in shawls and rocking before the fireplace. Grandmother tried to rise to kiss me, but collapsed back in her chair. "I'm so feeble," she moaned. I kissed her and Aunt Viola.

Suddenly, Grandmother's face grew stern. Her eyes narrowed, her furrows deepened above her eyebrows. She cleared her throat. "Sit down, Tommy," she pointed to one of the empty rockers. "You, too, Shaula."

I looked toward Mom. A desperate cant filled her eyes. We both sat down.

"Has she told you?" Grandmother glared.

"Ginny!" Aunt Viola interjected. "Leave her alone. She ain't doin' nothing wrong."

"He needs to know," Grandmother snapped. "Tommy, your Uncle Everett and mother have been living together. It's the whole talk of town. It's not natural. I'm so upset." She shook her gray head with profound woe. "If that's what they want, they need to marry. Haven't we suffered enough grief?"

I turned toward Mom. I felt shock and joy, wonder and surprise. My lips parted, but I didn't know what to say. She reached for my hand. I held hers while Grandmother continued.

"Marry! That's what you ought to do! Otherwise you only shame yourself and our name. Yes, our name! I have striven so hard to uphold our name. The family name! The Edmonds name! Doesn't that mean anything to either of you? Don't you care?"

"Mama, of course I care. You aren't the only one who counts. Don't you ever grieve about Everett or wonder how he might feel? Everett and I were going to tell Tommy. We just hadn't figured out the right time."

"Well, the right time is *now!*" she emphasized with vehemence. "Get married! I want this settled, once and for all! You can have the wedding here."

My mother looked at me, stunned, obviously a bit angry, and yet relieved. "Tommy! I wanted to tell you. We wanted to tell you. We just weren't sure how or when."

"Mom! That's OK! Uncle Everett has always been special."

My grandmother beamed with sardonic pride, just short of a rueful smirk. Aunt Viola smiled, but never looked up. Mom's face paled with tired acceptance, but with a radiant peace in her eyes.

With only days to spare, Mom set about to plan the wedding, all by herself. She scheduled the event for the early evening, following Christmas Day. Uncle Everett never equivocated. "Oh, what the deuce!" he muttered. "Might as well make it public."

Actually, the announcement helped Uncle Everett return to something of his more buoyant self. His cocky, gruff nature resurfaced. A jovial flush brought new color to his cheeks, along with a healthy, ruddy boldness. Their grayness had disappeared. Even the lines in his face had softened. Dressed for the wedding in a modest tuxedo, he reminded me more of the Captain—suave and commanding—than the lanky sheriff and rugged farm man I knew him to be.

Mom looked as great as ever. Petite, short, and red-haired, she wore a pale pink dress, with pearl earrings, and long white gloves. Uncle Everett had to slip off her glove to slide her wedding band on. The Reverend Dr. Wells officiated. He had returned from retirement to participate in the occasion. The ceremony took place, naturally, at Quilly Hall, with guests standing in the foyer, living room, and library. Fire blazed in the big hearth. Pearl wore a black dress with a starched, white apron. She stood in the library, just behind me, to watch the wedding. Henry and eleven-year-old Mamie stood behind her. I served as the best man. A rich punch of brandy, rum, and eggnog, capped with peaks of whipped cream, slaked the guests' thirst. Ham, turkey, rabbit, and quail garnished the main platters. Home-canned watermelon rind pickles, beets, and artichoke hearts served as side dishes. Mom and Uncle Everett went off to Roanoke for their honeymoon. While they were away, I stayed with Grandmother and Aunt Vi.

There was so much I wanted to know about my great-grandfather Lorran: when and where he was born and all that had happened to him. I determined to pique their memories one more time.

In spite of her sometime acerbic nature, Grandmother's health was beginning to fail. Aunt Viola was clearly aging more and more each day. After coming in late the morning after the wedding—following a brisk ride on Mac—I approached them as nonchalantly as I could. I wanted to be disimpassioned, and I wanted them to feel relaxed. They were seated in the living room, rocking in front of the fireplace. Taking a seat between them, I turned to Grandmother first. "Grandmother, please tell me all you can about your father. I want to know every detail you remember. Aunt Viola, please add whatever you remember, too."

Grandmother looked up at me with annoyed indifference, if not riled displeasure. "My mind's not there anymore. I've told you all I know. Looking back doesn't bring comfort like it used to, Tommy. Just pain! Seeing him suffer was hard to bear. I was just a girl. The war was a distant past, yet you would have thought it was still going on. My mother bathed his foot with liniment every night. And often his shoulder, too. That was in the early '80s. He never said much about the horrors he witnessed. Still he was proud. So many men had died for their 'country,' as he put it. Apology was not on his mind. Just sadness. So many had left family and friends and come back wounded, hungry, and penniless. We were on the border of starvation, except for the Captain. He had lost a lot himself, but had kept my mother and Jim alive for all four of those years." She paused for a moment, before continuing. "My father was born right there in that house, overlooking the Holston, in 1832. His father had worked for the Colonel, who died in the 1840s. My father craved solitude, even as a child, he said. The war changed none of that. Afterwards, he still plowed alone. He'd work a haystack all by himself, even when Jim was helping. In the late afternoons, he'd take a walk in the Knobs. In the summer, I would carry water to them in a wooden bucket. Jim had quit school, but each fall, I'd ride my pony into Abingdon, and stay at the Captain's sister's house to attend school. On the weekends, I'd ride back. That went on until I married Holman at fifteen. Viola here knows the rest. She knows more than I do. Viola, you tell him," she deferred to her sister-in-law.

I turned toward Aunt Viola and waited for her to speak.

"It ain't as pretty as folks remember. I'd be playin' at Jim's when the old man would come out and sit on his porch after lunch. He'd take a nap, if he could, before commencing to hoe or plow again. That's when he might drop a word or two. Jim was the main instigator of them reveries. I think Mr. Howard told the stories to ease his own pain, more than to tickle us.

"He and the Captain had been great friends before the War and hated that they wasn't in the same regiment. Mr. Howard was just a private, but he respected all them officers he come to know. He'd remembered both generals in the battles he fought: Johnston and Hood. Both was good men, he said, but Johnston was the kinder of the two. He had a goatee, like your stepfather had, was short, perky, and full of himself. But after he took command from Bragg, he kept retreating toward Atlanta, givin' up Dalton along the way. 'We was already becoming dispirited,' he said. 'We had won so many skirmishes, only to give up ground after ground.' That winter, they spent four months at Dalton, diggin' trenches and buildin' pits and log defenses. At near starvation, too. Groups of them took turns foraging. 'We was just robbin' the poor to feed the poor,' he lamented. It made him sick. Then came the order for retreat. To fall back. That's when the men's spirits really commenced to sagging. They was frustrated, hungry, many wounded and discouraged. Davis relieved Johnston and Hood come in. Mr. Howard said he was a towering man, blond, with a long beard. Looked like some cadaver, right off the battlefield. But he had spunk; he was spoilin' for a fight. Ready to attack Sherman, which he did. Right in front of Atlanta! Orderin' the men to come out of their trenches, marchin' them all day, havin' them do fancy flanking movements, until they was sent into battle. They was in a valley, thick with pines and oaks, when the order come. Up they marched at the double-quick, Minnie balls and cannon shells whizzin' and bursting all around them. You didn't dare look back, or to the left or right, he said, cause it was a horrible thing to see a man cut in half and others crying and falling into pools of their own blood. But they won that battle and routed a whole company of Yankees. Then toward the end of the day, Mr. Howard got struck, right in his shoulder. Limpin' like he was! Climbin' that hill! Firing and loading his rifle and fixin' his bayonet for the final charge! Indeed, Hood was hurt right bad, himself. He'd gotten shot in the leg at Chickamauga and wasn't in the best of health, either."

"How did he survive? How did he make it back? It's a wonder he wasn't killed!"

"Wasn't easy, he allowed. Thousands lay on the hill dead, thousands more wounded and cryin'. He was carried into Atlanta on a cart. They plucked a ball fragment from his right shoulder and seared it with an iron. They wanted to amputate his foot, but he snook away and hid in a carriage house. As Sherman came closer, Mr. Howard's brigade retreated. Alone and frightened, he remained in the carriage house, until Sherman made all the people leave town. The family that owned the carriage house had to flee, too. They discovered Mr. Howard and felt sorry for him and hid him under a pile of blankets and cookin' pans. They left the city a'fore the fires burned it down and headed for South Carolina. Onc't across the

Savannah, Mr. Howard thanked them and slipped away. He was scared, he said, an' certain he was goin' to die. He hid by day and traveled by night. But he made it up across the mountains, down passed Erwin and Johnson City, and finally come draggin' in late one cold snowy mornin'. His feet was bleedin' and raw from sores. I was standing with Jim by the river when he come limpin' home. We didn't know who he was, till he got to the porch, dropped a bag he was carrying, and collapsed at the door. 'Daddy!' Jim shouted. 'Viola, it's Daddy. Mama!' he hollered, 'Mama! Pa's home!' That was in December of 1864.

"We was all so hungry, Tommy. And he was so broken! He feared he'd be charged with desertion. Captain Nathan felt sorry for him and added his name to his Company's roster. He gave him one of his mounts and a fresh uniform. Lord, just in time! That's when the Federals, coming up from Bristol, swept into town. It was the night of the 13th or 14th. The Captain's troops were overrun. He was wounded and the town burned. It was Mr. Howard who brung him home. Both were bloody and exhausted. There were three hospitals in town, runnin' over with wounded boys. Some of them got out of their beds to fight the Federals. Smoke hung over the town for days. Once the Captain recovered, he hired Mr. Howard to help on the farm, but poor Mr. Howard wasn't fit to do no laborin'. It was all he could do to manage his own garden and tobacco. He and Mr. Nathan did like to shoot together, hunt, and ride horses. Come Jockey Day, they'd ride into town and watch the races. The Captain, himself, would race, if he had a good horse. Sometimes, he let Holman be the jockey. But he and my father was bosom buddies, played cards together, sat out there on the porch, and drank the Captain's brandy and berry wine. The farms ain't been the same since them."

I stared at my grandmother. She had not ceased rocking throughout Aunt Viola's tale. Her shawl had slipped off her shoulders and her chin rested on her chest. She was on the verge of falling asleep. Aunt Viola's own gaze focused somewhere far beyond the hearth and the fire's blaze. I rose slowly, stirred the fire with a poker, and went outside for an armload of firewood.

Before my mother and Uncle Everett returned, I saddled Mac one morning and rode up into the Knobs. I hadn't done that since summer, and I wanted to re-experience the ride. Decembers could sometimes be warm, or, if cold in the mornings, by noon the sun's rays would actually feel pleasant. It was not so that day. The sun's perigee barely broke above the treetops. In many coves, its wan light never penetrated the woods at all. A cold dampness had settled in the air. Mac's nostrils streamed with wisps of vapor. The sodden frosty ground crunched beneath his hoofs. A numbing chill stung my face and fingertips, although the latter were stuffed in warm gloves. I guided Mac along the lane toward Uncle Jim's, until parallel with the incline that led upslope and to the stone that bore Great-Grandfather Howard's initials. Finding it again and sitting beside it provided a solace that walks along the Charles in Boston had only occasionally equaled. The tweaking ice on the tree limbs, the frost heave about the rocks, and under the leaves, constituted something primordial, primeval, that nature alone awakened within me. I sat there, contemplating that un-bracketed mystery, wondering what my own future held.

The day before my mother and Uncle Everett's return, I drove into town in Mom's car to visit Marion's grave. It was still early morning and pockets of frost sparkled in the shadows on the ground. I parked under an ancient elm and walked out to his stone. The clear sky stretched blue from east to west in a canopy of cold, winter glory. Warm sunlight reflected brightly off the rounded markers and granite monuments. A brisk breeze fluttered the Virginia State flag and the Stars-and-Stripes that flapped beside it. They were to my left, at the highest point of the hill. I could hear their cords slapping noisily against the poles. I paused in front of his grave and stared down at his stone. I removed my hat. "Marion! You were quite a man. In truth, you were one hell of a good man!" I looked out across the cedars and leafless oaks toward the mountains to the west. Uncle Everett's farm, the Laurel Bottom, and the old Whites Mill lay in their direction. A flock of foraging common grackles took noisily to wing, rose above the cedars, and disappeared in a purple swirl beyond the rise. I leaned forward and touched the top of Marion's curved monument. "Farewell, dear man!" I replaced my hat on my cold head and returned to the car.

That afternoon, Henry and I went hunting. Albert's last bird dog, Pepper, raced ahead of us for the first hour or so, then slowed to a walk beside us. His jowls dripped saliva and his paws and tail oozed bright red with blood. He was a big salt-and-pepper-spotted pointer. He'd look up at us and whine. Still, we killed a dozen or more quail, mostly around bramble patches and areas parallel to cedars along the fencerows; sauntering back home, we added two rabbits to the take. "Henry, keep the rabbits and just let me have three quail. It's been a great hunt," I shook his hand.

"Yes, sir, Mr. Tom. Much obliged! Mamie loves rabbit. She's learnin' to cook as good as Pearl."

Mom and Uncle Everett returned from their honeymoon the day before New Year's Eve. We celebrated it with Grandmother and Aunt Viola. Mr. Preston, the bank's sole trustee now, and a widower himself, joined us for dinner. Grandmother went out of her way to prepare a lavish spread. Rising early that morning, I helped her boil a ham in an iron kettle outside; next we cut away the thick skin and excess fat. She baked it in an oven with cloves poked into the remaining fat, which she thumb-printed with pepper patches. For dessert, she served plum pudding and eggnog. Grandmother had made the latter herself, but she commissioned me to "spike it." I poured in a liberal portion of brandy and rum, with a splash of bourbon.

Mr. Preston reminded me a little of Marion, with his portly frame, graying mustache, and wide shoulders. His handsome velvet black coat and fine-tailored woolen trousers gave him the air of a refined gentleman, which he was. After all, his ancestors had settled around Abingdon prior to our own. After dinner, he and Uncle Everett and I sat by the iron stove in the library.

"Now that is one beautiful Fraulein," he commented as we passed Quelle. He paused and looked back over his shoulder at the Captain's portrait. "God, what a man! He should have been with Lee or Jackson! Or served with Ike! Damn, look at that face, his eyes, that coat and sash! It's a shame such chivalry's dead! Did you know him at all?"

"No! He'd passed from the scene by the time I'd come along," said Uncle Everett. "I think he was more dash than dare, but he did the best he could with what he had. I can't walk up the courthouse hill by the Rebel monument without thinking of him."

Once seated by the stove, Mr. Preston turned toward me. "Thomas, what are your plans after Harvard? I could use you at the bank, if you're interested. You'd be the first person with a real degree since its founding."

"Thanks, sir, but I'm not certain what I'll do. Forestry's still my first love, but who's to say? Maybe I'll try surveying, or timber cruising, or teaching biology, or run for sheriff. Who knows?"

"What a waste that'd be!" Uncle Everett frowned. "Tom here's gonna be one hell-of-a whatever he wants to be."

Mr. Preston eased back in the deep leather chair by the stove and twiddled his thumbs about the eggnog cup he had carried in with him.

He looked at Uncle Everett with no small amount of consternation before he spoke. "Everett! I've got bad news about your sheep adventure. I should say 'ours.' I can't keep funneling money into a losing enterprise. You understand, I'm sure."

"I've been expecting you to say something. No need to apologize. I need to give it up. I know that."

"What's gone wrong?" I asked. "You began it with such zeal."

"Two things, mainly, Mr. Biggety!" Uncle Everett glanced over at Mr. Preston and smiled. "We call him that since he's so damned spoiled and smart. Been that way since childhood. Well," he began afresh, "If you really must know, in the first place, our mountaineer shepherd's been drunk most of the time and his dog's not worth a fart! And second, disease, cold, and wild dogs have decimated the flock. I lost two hundred sheep the first winter, and this present season doesn't look any better."

"I admire your realism, Everett," Mr. Preston said, as he licked the insides of his cup. "Let's just sell off whatever you have left and call it quits. Let me know when you plan to corral them and bring them down to the stockyard."

About an hour after Mr. Preston left, there was a knock at the back door. Mom and Uncle Everett had returned to town. I was ladling myself one last cup of eggnog. I took a sip and opened the door. It was Henry. I realized he had walked all the way down from his cabin in the bitter night air. His denim coat was buttoned tight about his throat. The gray scarf that Pearl had knitted for him hugged his neck. He rubbed his chapped hands against the cold.

"Come in! Have some!" I held the cup up for him to see. "There's plenty more."

"Much obliged, Mr. Tom, but old Pepper's died. Had a stroke. Guess he wasn't fit to hunt no more. Albert came up to the cabin to tell me. Grounds too hard for him to break up, he said. He left the dog with me. I brought him down here. I hate for Mamie to watch me burn him. Don't know what else to do."

Not that! I thought. I should have known better than to exhaust the dog. "Please, Henry, come in."

"Better not! Goin' home with liquor on my breath would upset Pearl. I promised her I wasn't the drinkin' type. No offense."

I thought for a moment. "Leave him in the old slave quarters and close its door. I'll think of something to do tomorrow and find some place to bury him."

The next morning, on New Year's Day, I saddled Mac, placed Pepper's stiff corpse in an empty feed sack, and rode up into the Knobs. I rode up behind the orchard and through the woods and dismounted beneath the overlook on the ledge. I untied the sack and rolled the dog's body down into a thicket of laurel and dried honeysuckle vines. Foxes would find it, if not vultures. I'm sure Earl would have approved. I missed him and his humble, comforting ways. Surely, Jessie would have granted his blessings, too.

"Thank you, sir! I knew I could count on you," Henry said, when he dropped by the house that evening. He had brought Grandmother some pear preserves, which Pearl had canned.

"Let me get my wrap," Grandmother said to him. "Tommy, come with me." I helped her down the back steps and held her arm. "To the smoke-house," she pointed. She gave me the keys to unlock it. She stepped in with me. Its musty redolence of hickory smoke greeted our cold nostrils with all its pleasant odors. She picked out a fat shank of white side meat for me to let down. She pointed toward a smoked shoulder, too. "Take that to Pearl," she ordered Henry. She pulled her shawl tightly about her shoulders. "And take that one to Albert," she nodded toward a dark, shriveled, mold-covered ham.

"Thank you, ma'am. Thank you!" Henry repeated.

The day after New Year's I boarded the train for New England. The long ride back to Harvard brought me into the Boston station two mornings later. It felt good to be on the Yard again, crunching through the snow, attending lectures, burying myself in the reading rooms on cold winter nights, and later guzzling beer at nearby pubs.

Spring arrived and, soon, summer and once again I was back on the farm, in town with Mom, and working for Uncle Everett.

"Damn! Double damn!" he moaned to Gail, as he opened a telegraph wire.

She and I both looked up from where we were seated.

"It's a notice! Crawford's cousin has escaped from his ward. Cut right through his cage with a coil of mattress springs. Is on his way here. Dated, this morning. Oh, what the Hell! We'll just watch our guard. Would love to nail that bastard—crazy or not."

A week passed without incident or sightings. During that time, I helped Henry and Albert on the farm, and even Miles one afternoon. In both cases, we weeded and hoed young tobacco seedlings, and replaced a few that had suffered frost. "Lord knows we need a good crop!" Miles asserted. "Ain't like it used to be, Tom. Market's still good, but ain't as many companies showin' up as used to. Plus the new allotments ain't that favorable no more. Mr. Everett's cut my own back, to match his. Workers ain't that abundant. My own grandchildren won't help. Share croppin's a poor man's gate, straight to the grave."

Late that Saturday night, Uncle Everett came to the front door at the farm. Grandmother and Aunt Viola had long since retired and were sleeping soundly. Uncle Everett, who had a key to the door, let himself in and stepped into the hall. I could hear its boards creaking. I had taken off my boots and was seated in the library. I sprang up the instant I heard the noise.

"Shhh!" he whispered, hearing me get up.

"What is it?"

"Somebody's out here somewhere. A motorist reported a man hiding near the springhouse about dusk. Said he looked dazed and wild. Up to no good. Could be Crawford's cousin. I got the report only thirty minutes ago. Get a gun and follow me. I'll be on the porch."

I pulled on my boots and slipped into the hall. I reached for a shotgun and pistol in the closet and joined Uncle Everett at the door. We locked it behind us as we crept out.

"I parked my car at Viola's old cabin, by the road," he whispered. "I think he might be at the apple house. I saw movement there in the moonlight as I came across the branch. I'm going around the back of the house," he nodded in the dark. "You ease around the porch and come down by the kitchen. Crouch there for a while. I'll be down by the creek. I'll light a match, if I see him, or when I want you to run toward the place."

"Yes, sir!"

I waited until Uncle Everett had slipped out of sight, then I crept along the porch, toward the back kitchen steps. At the bottom landing, I sat down and peered toward the apple house. Moonlight cast an eerie sheen about its old tin roof. Its limestone outer walls reflected the milky night. I could see Uncle Everett, where he crouched near some willows by the creek. No one in the apple house could have seen him, as the rock building rested behind a rise, which blocked the view of the creek.

The June night air began to cool. Luckily, I was wearing a long sleeve work shirt. Its sleeves were rolled up, but I soon rolled them down. The Milky Way and a million other stars twinkled in the night. A pale sliver of the moon slipped behind a band of thin clouds. The night grew darker. I strained to make out Uncle Everett's crouched form. Nothing moved. The night deepened. The air grew warmer as the clouds thickened. Then I heard a noise, faint at first. A man's figure appeared in the upper window of the apple house. He was letting himself down on a rope. Just then, a wan ray of moonlight broke through the clouds. It illuminated a glistening object, tucked inside the man's belt. He dangled in mid-air, stopped his descent, and looked around. Darkness swallowed him again, as the moon's light faded and disappeared. I could see nothing now. Nor hear a sound. Other than the throbbing of my heart, hot in my chest. Was he coming this way? I couldn't tell. I couldn't see. Should I move? Should I crouch beside the steps? I froze and sat motionless. Slowly I brought the shotgun up and aimed it toward the fence. Whoever it was, would have to climb the fence. He'd have to mount the stile. At that instant, I saw Uncle Everett's match flash in the darkness by the tree. It sputtered for a second, flickered, and went out. A stirring of feet in the weeds erupted across the fence. Someone was climbing the stile. I could see their silhouette and hear their breathing. It wasn't Uncle Everett's. I held my breath, pointed the gun at the figure, and waited. He jumped down and began sprinting toward the house. I stood up, cocked the hammer back, and fired. The big, single-barrel, 12-gauge roared with flames and spewed birdshot in his direction. The pellets caught the man in the neck and chest. "Uhhh!" he groaned, as he stumbled toward me. I reached for the pistol, but before I could cock it, he was on me. A knife's blade glinted in the darkness. I tried to fire the pistol, but he knocked my hand to one side. Blood glistened on his face and neck, as a faint seam of moonlight passed over us. He raised his blade to sink it in my chest. A second explosion rocked the night. It was Uncle Everett's Colt .45. The man staggered off to my right and fell against the steps. Uncle Everett crossed the fence near the stile. "Tommy! I thought for sure I'd hit you. Are you all right?"

"Yes," I replied, as my pistol went off, spending its bullet into the fallen man. I had forgotten that I was still clutching it. My hand trembled, along with my voice. "I didn't know what to do, except shoot."

"You did the right thing. Roll him over."

We rolled him face up.

"That's the man. He even looks like Crawford. Jesus God!" Uncle Everett sighed. "That's the only man I've killed in the line of duty." His hands were trembling, too. He re-holstered his pistol and bent down to close the man's eyes. "I believe he'd killed you, Mama, Aunt Viola, and anyone else in the house. Son-of-a bitch!" he whistled softly. "Help me drag him to the car."

Numerous other adventures filled the summer, but the most frightening occurred the last week of July.

"Preston's been shot!" a man shouted, as he entered the office.

I recognized him as Mr. Lotz, the senior vice president of the bank. Short, corpulent, and almost bald, he bent forward and placed his hands on his knees to catch his breath. Coursing sweat had turned his white collar a soiled yellow. The buttons on his shirt had popped off and his gray vest gaped open. He plopped in an empty chair and mopped his forehead with a crumpled handkerchief.

"They just got away! Forced us on the floor. Cleaned out the vault and every drawer. Even took my watch. Cut the phone lines before they left. I think Preston's dead. Mr. Hollingsworth's carrying him to the hospital."

"How many were they? Did you see what they were driving?"

"Yes, sir! Two! A faded yellow Packard, with rusted running boards! I rushed out after they left. They headed out North Main Street."

"Gail! Check the hospital! Tom, call Wally's station. See which fork of the road they took, if he knows.

"Mr. Lotz, I'll have a deputy down there as fast as I can. Close the bank and keep the tellers away from any fingerprints."

The rumpled man rose from his chair and hurried back to his car. I called Wally's and waited for the operator to connect me.

"I hear there's been a robbery," the operator said. "It's all over town."

"Yes, ma'am," I replied.

As soon as someone picked up the receiver, I handed the phone to Uncle Everett.

"Hello! Wally? That you? You have? Did you see them? Good! Which way? Left! Out Valley Street. Good! Yes! Probably. I'm leaving now. Thanks! Bye!" He hung up and turned toward Gail. "Anything on Preston?"

"Can't get through" she said. "Everybody in town's on line."

"Keep trying. Call Carl, or any of the other deputies, and have them check out the bank. Tommy! Come on! We're heading out toward the

Laurel Bottom. That's where Wally thinks they've gone. Grab a pistol. The shotguns are in the car!"

Within minutes, we were turning off Valley Street and left onto the old mill road. In five more, we were squealing tires around the curves east of Uncle Everett's farm, and, minutes later, approaching the Laurel Springs Bottom. A chicken lay dead in the road, opposite Miles's tenant house, and his wife had come out to the fence to retrieve it. Uncle Everett slowed the car and rolled down his window.

"Has a yellow Packard passed here in the last hour, or so?"

"Yes, sir, Mr. Edmonds. They killed two pullets and this chicken," she pointed in the road. "They almost overturned, a'fore goin' off toward Miss Waters' place. They've been up there a week. They told Miles they had your permission to stay there."

"Thanks! Noreen, tell Miles to stay clear, but come up if he hears shots."

He rolled up his window and we drove on. Near a sharp bend in the road, we turned off onto a clay lane that paralleled the Bottom and led up to the old Waters farm. There in a thicket of blackberry bushes and trumpet vines, we could see the back of the Packard. It had been pulled in as far as it could go. Its windows were down and occupants gone. It bore Virginia license plates.

"I'll be damned. I'd sworn they were from Tennessee or Kentucky. They must have been hiding here for some time."

We parked our car behind theirs and armed ourselves with shotguns. I had strapped a standard .38 police revolver around my waist earlier. I cradled the barrel of the shotgun in the palm of my left hand and double-checked the safety.

"This way!" Uncle Everett motioned. "The old farmhouse is just past the springhouse. No one's lived there in years."

Uncle Everett took the lead. I followed along the creek bed. He ducked under tangles of laurel that bent out over the stream. Moments later, he dropped down quietly onto its sandy bank. The creek had worn a deep ditch over the years and its high banks concealed us from anyone above. It also concealed the farmhouse. We passed a number of rusting drums and debris in the creek, a bed springs, broken chair, child's doll, bottles and rusty cans. We slipped around a springhouse and sprinted quietly uphill to the main house's backyard. Wireless clotheslines leaned in the damp darkness under a stand of young pines. The path to a gray, peeling, outside privy showed signs of recent use. Cautiously, we approached the rear of the house. Uncle Everett stood to one side of its back door and, with the barrel of his shotgun, nudged the door. It swung open in swollen silence. He entered and waited for me to do the same. Together, we stood there, in what had once been a washroom, and listened for voices. Within seconds, we could hear them, and smell tobacco smoke, as well. A moldering Army blanket, strung along a wire, separated the room from the rest of the house. Uncle Everett slid the blanket back with the tip of his gun. I had raised mine, ready to fire it, if necessary. Two men sat on crates near a gutted sofa. Rats had totally destroyed the old couch's cushions and inner stuffing. The men were sharing a bottle of liquor together, between puffs on cigarettes. They were laughing and counting bills on a third crate between them. Two bags of stash lay at their feet. A kerosene lamp cast a sallow glow across their faces.

"Up! Up with your hands!" Uncle Everett pointed the shotgun toward the nearest man's face.

I took the safety off mine.

Just then the second man turned and fired a pistol. As he ducked for cover, I shot the man in the side of his head, just above his neck. His whole head lifted, as if slapped by a board, and his brains splattered against the wall. Gray cranial matter and blood dripped onto the sofa. The lamp crashed to the floor and the man's body sank across it. The other robber leaped to his feet. Burning kerosene spread rapidly up his pants and into his face. He reached for a pistol in his belt. The roar of Uncle Everett's shotgun deafened the crackling flames.

"The money! Grab the money! Grab as much as you can!" Uncle Everett shouted.

Together, we lunged forward, each fumbling for a bag.

"Out! Hurry!" Uncle Everett raised his forearms to shield his face from the heat. Just then, the rotten floor beneath his feet gave way. He sank through the hole, but his arms caught on the flooring. Red flames crackled all about.

I threw the bag down and reached for Uncle Everett's right arm. He was still holding the other money sack. I tugged on him as hard as I could, but his waist was caught in the floor. I took off my shirt and began flailing the flames. Uncle Everett covered his face and tried to drop through the hole. The blanket! The moldering blanket behind me! I yanked it off its wire and threw it around Uncle Everett's head. I found another one and began slapping wildly at the fire. The flames had totally consumed the crates, couch, and wallpaper, and were beginning to lick into the rafters. The two men's bodies sizzled in the heat. The smell of burning flesh filled me with nausea. I covered my mouth but vomited. Smoke poured out of the ceiling. I reached again for Uncle Everett's arms and dragged his head, shoulders, and chest out of the hole. Still, I could not wrest his waist free. "O my God!" I mumbled. I thought of Grandmother's words about Providence and of her tiffs with Marion! Burning wallpaper fell from the ceiling. I didn't want to die, or lose Uncle Everett.

I felt a hand on my back. I looked up. It was Miles. He bent over me and pulled Uncle Everett from the hole. As lanky and old as he was, he lifted him onto his shoulder, and, with his left hand, pulled me from the burning house. Outside, we collapsed in the damp grass and watched as the flames consumed the rafters, the roof, and upper walls of the house. That night when we returned to town, we stopped by the hospital, deposited the two bodies at the morgue, and drove home in the dusk. Mom was delirious with sobs and kisses, with anger and joy! "Everett! Everett! Will you ever learn? O Everett! You could have gotten Tommy killed! And yourself as well!"

Uncle Everett, Miles, and I became instant heroes. At least, according to the *Bristol Star*. Mr. Preston recovered, but his left leg remained paralyzed. The paper's stories, however, blew my "cover," and the Commission's state senator, who oversaw our district, reprimanded Uncle Everett for having a deputy on his staff under twenty-one. Of course, he already knew that but was trying to deflect further criticism from himself. In any event, no one seemed to mind, or even object. Just when I thought it was over, I received a phone call. I was at the office, engaged in typing a report. Gail answered the phone. "Yes? Yes! He's right here!" She handed me the receiver with a wink and a roll of her eyes.

"Hello! Yes! *Julie!* Where are you?"

"In Roanoke. The Roanoke paper has been carrying your story for two weeks. I told Daddy I had to call. Are you hurt?"

"No! I'm fine! You know me! Plus, Uncle Everett did all the talking. He'd arrest the Devil, if he passes through here."

"I want to see you. Where are you going to school?"

"Harvard! It's a little place up North."

"Stop it! No really, where are you in school? VPI? VMI? I'm at Longwood. I miss you so much."

"Can you come and visit me? I'm sure Grandmother will let you stay on the farm. You can tell your dad that I'll stay in town. If you could stay just a couple of days, that would be wonderful!"

"I know. When do you have to go back?"

"In another three weeks, at the latest. What about you?"

"The same. Oh, Tommy! Here's my number. Ask your grandmother and call me back."

I wrote her number down. "Yes, yes!" I uttered, as I handed the receiver to Gail.

"Ohhhhh!" she mimicked me, as she hung the receiver up.

What did I care? My heart soared to my head. The back of my throat burned and pulsated with joy. My body ached for Julie. My sighs erupted into gasps, much to Gail's amusement. "Oh, Tommy!" she teased. "'I'll stay in town!' Like hell, you will! Stay in town? Oh, Tommy!" she shrieked. "You and your Uncle Everett! If you two aren't cut out of the same cloth, then I'm a monkey's uncle!"

That Friday, Julie arrived by train. I met her at the station, caught her about the waist with my right arm, and kissed her in full daylight. "Tommy!" she scolded me. She glanced about, before she kissed me in turn. She looked as gorgeous as ever! Tall, but with shorter hair, delightful curves, and soft gray eyes. I kissed her again, placed her suitcase in the car, and drove immediately to Quilly Hall. I wanted so much to stop by the barn, but I knew Grandmother would be watching for us as I came up the lane. We embraced again in the car, before we got out. I carried Julie's valise to the porch.

"Oh, Julie! You've cut your hair!" Grandmother fretted. "I liked it long! But, it's still lustrous and 'sexy,'" she whispered.

"Mrs. Edmonds! No wonder Tommy's such a romantic!"

"Well, come in, dear! I'm putting you in Pearl's old room. It's small, but you'll like it. Dinner's at seven. Viola and Shaula will be joining us. Tommy, show her upstairs."

"Yes, ma'am!"

"And don't tarry! You come right back down! You hear me, young man? No hanky-panky!" she wagged her finger in my face.

Julie smiled and followed me through the living and dining rooms, into the kitchen and up the back stairs. Once out of Grandmother's sight, we embraced and kissed as we ascended each step.

"I'll wait for you downstairs," I whispered.

Chapter Twenty-five

"Why are you whispering?"

"Cause Aunt Viola sleeps in the next room," I nodded toward her closed door. "She's probably taking a nap right now."

"OK!" she puckered up her lips for one more kiss.

Though almost five o'clock, the August sun's rays had scarcely reached the peak of their fierce heat. When Julie descended, she was clad in white shorts, toeless white sandals, and a green blouse. As she took my hand, her presence aroused every nerve ending in my groin.

We slipped out the screen door, walked hand-in-hand passed the old slave quarters, and hurried for the hay barn. Henry and Albert were still in the fields, suckering tobacco one last time.

"Tommy! Are you sure we should do this?" she hesitated at the barn door. "I want you, too. But, I'm afraid."

"Why! I love you. I'll be careful."

"I'm having my period. You know what that means?"

"Ohh! So what! We can clean up by the stream. Grandmother won't think anything about it. It's as hot as hell, anyway."

"Please don't swear. I don't want you to swear. I don't want you to be like your Uncle Everett. You're so handsome, Tommy! You don't need any vices other than, than, what we're about to do." She put both hands in mine and pressed her lips to my neck. "Kiss me! I don't ever want to lose you again. Take me up the ladder. Hold my hands. They're trembling already. See?"

"So are mine."

Quietly, we climbed the ladder. We kissed at the top and crawled into the loft. The aroma of the dark sage-green hay rose about us. I kissed her again. We felt around for the most comfortable spot possible; we lay down in the hay and rolled sideways. She slipped off her shorts, as I ran my hands under her blouse. I unbuckled my jeans, slid them off, and lay against her hot body. "Oh, God, Julie! I never thought I'd see you again."

"Shhhh!" she kissed me. "Don't say any words."

I buried my face against her lean slender neck, nibbled her soft perfumed ears with my hungry lips, and brushed my eyebrows against her glossy, cropped brown hair. O precious God! O Julie! The rush of ecstasy bore me beyond Paradise!

For the next year and a half, Julie and I dated, wrote letter after letter to each other, and visited one another's schools. She had never been to Harvard and fell in love with its Yard, its campuses, its library, its surrounding neighborhoods, bookstores, and pubs. She came every fall and spring, and the winter of my junior year. After running and laughing and floundering through the snow, we sought out a coffee shop to revive our spirits. She ordered cocoa; I hot coffee. Her eyes dazzled in the mauve glow of a fireplace, near the kitchen.

"I have something I've been wanting to give you," I said. I reached in my right parka pocket and produced a small black velvet box. I fumbled it nervously before placing it in her hands.

"Tommy!" she whispered, as she took the box, turned it about, and pried its tight lid open. "Ohh!" she groaned, as tears slipped down her cheeks. "Tommy!" She leaned across the table and kissed me.

"Will you marry me? You're all I've ever wanted, Julie. Just you."

"Of course!" she sniffled. "I wanted you long before you ever noticed me. Don't you know that?"

I kissed her hand and her ring finger. "May I place it on?"

She handed the box back to me. I pulled the ring out and slipped it on her finger. "It's only a third of a carat, but one day I'll replace it with a bigger one."

"No you won't. I'll never let anything replace this!" she beamed, as she held her hand up to the firelight, as the diamond's facets sparkled with blue, silver, and pink light. We kissed again and hurried back to the boarding house where she was staying. We snuggled against each other, long past dinner and early into the night. When she boarded the train the next day for Richmond and Longwood, I felt a pang of happiness that transcended every previous joy I had known.

Chapter Twenty-six

WITH THE COMING OF the summer, I took a job with Marion's old bank. Mr. Preston introduced me to investments, bonds, and his loans division.

"You're capable of doing this," he said. "Just read over our offerings. Become familiar with our percentages, fees, and forms. Whenever in doubt, just call for me, or Mr. Lotz. We don't give loans to anyone under twenty-five, or," he looked away painfully, "to farmers or tenants. They just can't repay them. That's the sad truth, Thomas. Like it or not! We could foreclose on a dozen farms right now. Even your Uncle Everett has borrowed money to buy the Laurel Bottom, but don't you dare let on that you know."

"No, sir! I won't. But why would he want it? It's all he can do to manage his own place, or rather all Miles can do to keep it up. Besides, he lives with Mom in town now."

"Value! The Bottom's one of the most coveted properties in the county. Its timber's worth the price of the land, and its tobacco patches yield some of the mellowest leaves in the Southeast. I'd buy it, but what use do I have for it? I'm a cripple anyway, and who knows when the meat wagon'll be coming for me? It comes for everyone, Thomas! First it was Crawford, then Marion, and who knows who'll be next!"

He had been leaning against his cane all this time, pointing to various sheets as I had been sorting through the forms. I was seated, but rose respectfully after his melancholic speech.

"Where'd you get your class, anyway? From Marion?"

"I suppose so. And Grandmother."

"How is she? I haven't seen her but once or twice since the wedding. Everett does most of her banking for her. And that's another story I could tell you. But one's enough, I guess." He studied my face for any expression of surprise or doubt, and with a feigned disinterest of his own.

I had learned the word "prufrockian" in one of my literature classes. As I stared down at him, he fit most of its details: a bit indecisive, haunted by unfulfilled aspirations, with a twinge of timidity, all of which he masked behind a veil of refined but gruff speech.

While at Grandmother's, early one June evening, I asked her at the kitchen table, "Grandmother, how's the farm? How are Albert and Henry? Should I be helping you, or stay at my job in town?"

"Well, now, you know the answer to that!" Aunt Viola interjected. "Ain't no need for pretense here! Ginny needs every able-bodied worker that comes around. Ain't that so, Kate?"

"Hush, Viola! No need to overburden Tommy! Yes, we could use you, but you've got a future of your own. When do you and Julie plan to marry? I'm fading, Tommy! Your old grandmother's not going to be around much longer. I feel it in my bones, my chest, my arms. I have premonitions every night and even in my sleep. Viola, here, will outlive me," she turned to her right and stroked Aunt Vi's arm.

I had never witnessed my grandmother display lavish affection for anyone, although she certainly had for me. I looked at both women, where they slumped in their chairs: their silver hair pulled back, like Quilly's, their frail hands discolored with purple and blue bruises and old-age spots. The wrinkles about their lips and eyes, and furrows along their neck and chin, provided a visible commentary on all their years, as well as on the strain of enduring childhoods that had been formalized in the harsh decades of the last quarter of the 1800s. That their lives actually went back to that harrowing era horrified and fascinated me. Feelings of pride and sadness, gratification and sorrow, simultaneously washed over me. Aunt Viola was ninety-eight, or ninety-nine, my grandmother, eighty-two.

"Grandmother, I'm going to ask Mr. Preston to let me work less for him. Only three days a week. That'll give me Fridays-through-Mondays to help here at Quilly Hall." I reached out and put my right hand over both of theirs.

Her reference to her "premonitions," and Preston's remark about the "meat wagon," had sounded a bell of mourning in my heart. As I observed the two women, its peals knelled softly in the back of my mind. I bent forward and kissed Grandmother on her lips, and Aunt Vi, too. Grandmother put her hands up to my face and kissed my cheek. "O Tommy!"

In mid July, Julie came for a week to visit. Mr. Preston allowed me to go home early on the three days I worked for him, so I could be with Julie. His father had been a good friend of her grandfather's, and her father was borrowing Julie's college money from the bank.

"Julie, you gorgeous woman!" I greeted her at the bus station. "Why didn't you take the train?"

"It's so slow, anymore," she lamented. "Look!" she raised her ring finger. "I had it cleaned yesterday!" She turned her fingers and wrist about, causing the diamond's sparkles to gleam all the brighter.

We kissed and I drove her to the farm.

The following afternoon, I saddled Mac and Nimble and took Julie for a ride into the Knobs.

"So these are your Knobs!" she chuckled, as she rode beside me on the lane. "They look so much less imposing than they do from the road. Bright and not so dark."

The sun's hot rays shimmered off the dusty sumac and laurel leaves that hugged the banks. Trellises of wild grapevine and honeysuckle shadowed us along the road. Sparrows flitted up and took to wing as we passed their nooks and hideaways. A hawk cried overhead, before disappearing over a ridge.

"True. It's much clearer in the woods, and cooler, too. We'll go off in a minute. I want you to see my great-grandfather Lorran's inscription. He carved his initials on a rock not too far ahead. They've been there close to a hundred years. Still deep and vivid as ever! He also hid something under another rock. But no one's found it to date."

"Tommy, it is hot! My face is blistering in this scorching heat!"

"We're almost there. Hang on to the saddle horn and let me take your bridle." I reached over for Julie's reins and goaded Mac up the embankment. Nimble followed, her hoofs slipping in the damp soil under foot. "Hang on!" I repeated. "It's just ahead."

Up we rode, climbing the hill to its crest. The woods broke free of underbrush, and a gentle breeze cooled us as we approached the stony copse of hemlocks and laurel. "There it is!" I pointed. We dismounted to examine the stone.

"Oh, they're so neat and clean!" Julie noted, as she ran her fingertips across the old veteran's initials. "'H.C.L.' Just as plain as day! Is this where he's buried?"

"No. That's farther on, toward the river. Hear it? If you listen closely enough, you can hear it."

"I do. It's like the wind. Soft, purling in the distance." She stood up and peered all around. "It's so quiet and beautiful. Maybe we could build a cabin here someday!"

Her eyes looked deeply into my own. I took her hands, cupped her long fingers into my own, pressed her bosom against my chest, and kissed her. "Uncle Jim's old cabin is just down the ridge," I pointed. "Wait till you see it. It needs a lot of work, but we could transform it into something special."

"This is already special enough. Why didn't you ever bring me here before?"

"I don't know. Never thought you'd care to see it, I guess."

We remounted and negotiated our way down the ridge, through its ferns, and over its gray mantle of matted leaves, passed its age-old rocks. A pair of towhees, scratching for insects near a mound of moss, noisily ignored us. Clusters of monarch butterflies drifted lazily about a rotting stump. Or was it something else? "Look!" I pointed down. "That's bear scat! They're still coming in here, after all these years."

"Couldn't we get killed? Or mauled? Are you sure we should go on?"

"Don't worry! I've got a pistol in the saddlebag, and any bear would run before he'd attack us. Mac wouldn't hesitate to kick him. Or Nimble!"

We rode on down the slope between the mixed woods of poplars, oaks, and hickories. As we came out behind the house, Julie tugged on her reins and stopped. "Oh, Tom! It's so bleak! Deserted! So sad!" She shook her head from side to side, distraught with what she saw. "How did anyone ever live here?" She turned in the saddle and glanced up at the weathered logs and hole in the tin roof. "Who lived here? And how long ago?"

"My great-grandfather, his family, my great-Uncle Jim and Aunt Viola. Nobody's lived here since the late '40s. Marion was going to repair it, and Uncle Everett too, but they never got around to it."

"Can we look inside? It's so wild, isolated! Forgotten!"

"Come on!"

We guided our mounts toward the barnyard and tied them up in the shade. Julie followed me around to the front porch and passed the half-rotten, sagging front door. The odor of must stung our nostrils. The air inside was stifling. A snakeskin lay draped across the soiled back of the exposed padding of the moldering armchair. Rat pellets and bird droppings littered the floor. The brittle curtains had rotted and collapsed in dirty threads across the window sash.

"Oh! Thomas! What a filth hole! That people actually lived here!"

We piled outside into the fresh rays of the sunshine. Its light almost blinded us. "Come. Let's run down to the river. There's an old orchard there. Come on!" I reached for her hand.

Together we ran toward the Holston and stopped on the banks of its stony course. Always low in the summer, its current gurgled and purled quietly by. Mossy stones lined the bottom of its bed. The redolence of decaying sunken leaves drifted over its babbling current and slate-green water.

We walked to the orchard. Fallen limbs and broken branches created a maze of obstacles between the trees. We found a few gnarled June apples, covered with rotten spots and dark brown wormholes.

"No thank you!" Julie shuddered, as I brushed off one for her.

I felt a raindrop strike my head, then another. I glanced up. Black clouds had slipped in across the Knobs. A downpour appeared imminent.

"Hurry! To the barn!"

We made it just in time. The patter of the rain on the barn's roof grew to a thunderous drubbing. We fumbled with the horses' reins and guided them in as well. Lightning struck somewhere close, and the horses pulled nervously on their reins. Streams of water coursed off the roof and splashed loudly onto the clay pan of the barnyard. The air grew cool. The sky roared with thunder as torrents of rain fell in opaque sheets. Lightning strikes lit up the outside in the midst of all the darkness. Suddenly, a crackling noise sundered the air. An explosion rocked the barn. Debris from Uncle Jim's house slammed against its sides. Lightning had struck the house and set it on fire. Its tallest chimney burst into pieces, hurtling its ancient stones everywhere. Then, all grew still. Once again, heavy sheens of rain began to fall. They slammed against the barn and house, drenching everything, including the fire. A cold calm followed. The storm had passed.

Julie and I opened the barn door and peered out. The entire west side of the house was smoldering. Its chimney had collapsed. The odor of crushed, singed rock stung my nostrils. The strong smell of ozone wafted in the air. We held hands and stepped out amid the debris.

On our way home, I took her by the cemetery. Rivulets of water still trickled through the weeds among the thorns. I pulled some bramble away from Uncle Jim's grave and around the base of my great-grandfather's marker.

"So this was your grandmother's father, yes?"

"Yes! He was wounded at the battle of Chickamauga and later in front of Atlanta."

On our return, the road proved slick and muddy. The horses plodded along, sliding in the clay mire from side to side. Wind-blown leaves cluttered the lane. We passed a dead sparrow beside a leaf, and a field mouse that had drowned in the downpour. Its tiny gray body had washed against a clod of mud. Mac all but stepped on it, as he slogged along. But we made it back and out of the Knobs and into the sunlight in time for supper.

Later, Julie and I sat on the front porch and gazed out at the coming night. The darkness throbbed with fireflies. The huge yard glowed from end to end. We held hands and rocked.

Grandmother came out with a shawl about her shoulders and offered one to Julie.

"You'll catch the death of pneumonia!" she warned, as she dropped it in her lap. "Viola's not feeling well! She's been running a fever since supper. Her forehead's hot, but her skin's cold and clammy. You might have to fetch a doctor, if she doesn't improve."

"Yes, ma'am!" I replied.

"Won't you sit with us?" Julie asked. "I saw your father's marker today. It's so sad back there. Isn't it?"

"Please, honey! This old woman's had all the sadness she can bear. Life is for the young, you know. Memories for the old! God's right hand has been kind. But his left hand has its work to do, too." She stared off into the darkness across the road, toward the orchard. "Like sorting through the good and bad apples when they've fallen to the ground."

I slept with Julie that night, in the room above the kitchen, next to Aunt Viola's. Toward two o'clock in the morning, we heard a crash in Aunt Viola's room. We got up to investigate. Starlight revealed what had happened. The old woman had rolled out of bed. She was lying on her side. I bent over her, to put my arms under her neck and head. Her thin hair had fallen across her face. Her mouth drooled saliva. Her eyes stared at me, lifeless. They were without emotion or any sign of recognition.

"Aunt Vi! Aunt Viola! Are you all right?" I tried lifting her, but my foot caught in her night robe. I slipped my foot free, picked her up, and laid her in the bed. She felt practically weightless. Like a child in my arms!

"Tommy!" Julie whispered. "She's not breathing. Turn on the light. Here, I'll do it." She groped for the switch, found it, and turned on the overhead light bulb. It's amber glow filled the room with an eerie starkness. "Tommy! The poor thing! Better get a washcloth to wipe her face. Look at her eyes! So black! So cold!"

"So dead!" I uttered in a hush.

Two days later we buried her beside Uncle Jim, near his own father's marker. Henry, Uncle Everett and I opened the grave. Albert was too weak and lame to help. Midway through the digging, Charles came down the lane. "Kin I be of he'p?" he asked. "Here, Mr. Edmonds, let me have that shovel. You've got more important things to do."

Uncle Everett climbed out of the grave and handed his shovel to Charles.

"Thank you, Mr. Everett, for what you done to he'p me. T'warn't no way to treat a man, was it? I know you done it. I'm much obliged."

"Charles, you don't ever have to thank me for anything. Wish you were still working for me."

"I'd like to, Mr. Everett. So he'p me, God, I would. If'n you ain't mad at me?"

"Of course not! Nothing's changed. Miles needs you. And this house?" he pointed toward Uncle Jim's blackened cabin. "If you can fix it, repair it a bit, you can live here, too. I've been meaning to fix it up for a long time. If you can help Henry and Albert, you can stay here on days you do. Raise a garden, prune the orchard, have the tobacco allotment. Whatever you earn, will be yours!"

"Yes, sir!" he replied, as he dropped into the hole and began digging. Henry and I rested, then resumed our task as well.

Thus we buried Aunt Viola in the cemetery, above the Middle Fork of the Holston, where her grave overlooks the cabin that she and Uncle Jim lived in all their married life, save for their last years. Pearl, Henry, Mamie, Grandmother, Charles, Albert, his wife, Mr. Preston, Uncle Everett, my mother, Julie and I—together we laid her to rest. We recited the 23rd Psalm and the Lord's Prayer. Charles stayed behind to fill in the grave.

Grandmother sat the entire time in Uncle Everett's truck. This had been her home, too, her family's burial ground—save for her husband's. She dabbed her eyes with a wadded silk, white handkerchief and stared out across the river. A pair of doves lighted on the barn's roof. A single bird in rapid flight fluttered over the distant cedars that bordered the edge of what had once been Uncle Jim's cornfield. "I have lived too long," Grandmother allowed, as Uncle Everett started the truck.

"Mama, you'll feel better, after you've rested," he replied. "Tommy, I'll see you and Julie back at the house. Your mother will be riding with Mr. Preston. You can ride with them, too. Charles can bring the horses back."

"Thanks, but I'd rather ride out." I looked toward Julie.

"I, too," she nodded, as she fondled my hand.

"That's probably just as well. He barely made it up here in that old Ford of his. Better follow them out," Uncle Everett nodded toward Preston's car.

"We will."

I watched him drive off and helped Julie mount Nimble. Pearl, Henry, and the rest followed in the wagon. Julie and I brought up the rear.

Two weeks later, I took the train to Roanoke to visit Julie and her parents. I had scarcely arrived, when I received a phone call from Uncle Everett. "Tom, can you come home? Your grandmother's suffered a stroke. Mama's not expected to live. She's in and out of a coma."

My stomach rose in my throat. Not now, I wanted to say. Hasn't there been enough death? Doesn't death ever take a holiday? The back of my throat felt swollen, my tongue thick and heavy.

"You're her pride and joy, Tom. You need to get here immediately."

"Yes, sir! I'll be there. I'll take the five o'clock train."

My mother met me at the station. Darkness had already enveloped the town. Street lamps cast their somnific spell along Main Street and out to the hospital. Old sycamore limbs arched silently overhead, their tan and white bark reflecting the car's headlights as we sped along. The drive to the hospital passed in silence. Mom's mind was as preoccupied as mine. We parked the car and went straight to Grandmother's room. Grandmother had aroused briefly, we were told, but had slipped back into sleep or unconsciousness. Uncle Everett was still on patrol. I stood in the doorway. A white sheet covered her feet, legs, and torso. Only her head, face, and arms were exposed. I edged quietly toward her bed. Her silver hair lay in damp strands about her forehead. Her breathing was audible and labored. Her face looked swollen, pasty: a dull ivory. I lifted her right hand and stroked it softly in my own. My mother pulled up a chair for me to sit in. Grandmother's breathing grew lighter; there was a stir in the bed. Her eyes opened as she stared up at me.

"Tommy, is that you? Is that you, Mr. Biggety? I can't see. Come closer."

I rose and bent over the bed. "Yes, Grandmother. I'm right here," I whispered, as I continued to hold her hand.

She raised it with great effort and ran her fingers across my mouth, my lips, and face. "Tommy!" Tears filled her eyes and ran down her cheeks and onto the bedding. "Tommy!" she whispered. "Where's Everett?"

"He's coming."

"Tell him I'm sorry for all the hurt I caused him as a boy."

"Grandmother, please! Rest. We're all here."

My mother came to the bed. "Mama, it's Shaula. Everett's on his way." She leaned forward and wiped Grandmother's clammy brow and dabbed her cheeks with a tissue. "Mama? Are you all right?"

Grandmother grew very still, suddenly stretched her legs out in the bed, gripped my hand tightly, released her fingers, and expelled a long, slow breath. Her lips quivered. "Are my feet cold?"

I placed my left hand over her tiny, hardened, diminutive feet. "No! Grandmother! They feel fine."

"Tommy, don't lie." Her eyes closed. She tried to swallow. Suddenly, her eyes clicked open. A rancid odor slipped passed her lips, from deep within her lungs. Her sphincter muscles failed. The shadow of death descended. The redolence of waste filled the room. Her mouth fell open. "*I am no respecter of persons!*" Death whispered in my ear.

"Grandmother! Grandmother!"

We buried her beside my grandfather Edmonds in the cemetery behind the Baptist Church in town. By the time I returned to Harvard, I felt emotionally exhausted. At night, I would wander the Yard and sit under its various gates. I could hardly wait to graduate. Once I did, Julie and I married. I took a position as Vice President of the Highland's Bank; Julie hired on in a neighboring district to teach school. With excitement and love, we settled into Quilly Hall. The future was ours, as Grandmother had said. It was time to lay memories aside. Time to modernize the farm and build a family. Time to laugh and sing! Time to forge ahead.

Chapter Twenty-seven

WHILE RIDING OLD MAC the spring of 1966, I guided him toward the rocky ledge above the orchard, reached its summit, and dismounted. I tied his reins to a laurel bush, aglow in white flowers, and turned to look out over the blossoming apple trees and the alfalfa meadows that bloomed purple in the distance below. My position at the bank had allowed me to replace many of the orchard's older fruit trees, as well as re-equip the farm with tractors, a corn harvester, a threshing machine, and numerous other implements. Julie could not have been happier, and our family had grown by two: a little boy, Hamilton Howard, and a precious baby girl, Ginny Patterson, named for Grandmother and Julia's mother's maiden name. All was well. Save for one person! Namely, me!

Vietnam would not go away. I was twenty-nine. I could not be drafted. I had passed the age for that. But it was my generation's war. Had not my father volunteered for World War II? And what might the Captain think if he could step down from his portrait? Or Great-Grandfather Lorran, if he should come limping in from the grave?

I sat on the ledge and stared off toward town. Three of her sons had already returned in body bags. One was Mr. Lotz' grandson. I fell into a kind of psychotic dialogue with myself, with that ancient Tempter within. "You don't have to go!" he whispered. "Your father would understand. After all, look what happened to him, and to you, because he did? And your mother? Is that what you want for Julia, or little Ham, or Baby Ginny? No father to remember, no father to be proud of them? Just photographs on a mantle? No one will question your manhood. Your age sets you free."

"Yes! Still, it's my generation's war!"

"That's nonsense! Generations don't choose wars. Politicians blunder into them. Don't say I didn't warn you. Pride is the Devil's joy, you know. Why make me happier?"

"It's myself I have to please. I'm the one whose conscience is the issue."

"Have it your way then. I win regardless."

That night I stood beside Julia and helped her wash the dishes at the sink. The children were playing on the screened-in porch.

"Julia, I've been thinking. This war will probably be over soon. I can't just stand by. It's in the family, you know. What do you think?"

"Thomas Edmonds, it's not the Civil War. You don't have to go! I want you here."

"I've thought about all that. I assure you."

"Tommy, the children need you. The farm needs you. Your mother and Uncle Everett need you! Please, I don't want to hear it again!"

"Sweetheart, if I don't go, I'll always feel bad inside. Like I betrayed my father. Going would be like going to find him, to be with him. He was killed in a jungle. Troops are better trained now. And today's medical corps is better equipped. It would be a catharsis. A healing! And I could come home, and it would be over."

Her hands fell limp in the dishwater. Her eyelashes swam in tears. Silently, the tears trickled down her face, her cheeks, and her chin.

I leaned toward her and kissed her. "I don't know what else to do."

She turned away from me, walked to the kitchen table, sat down, and wept more. "And what am I supposed to do?" she gestured toward the porch where the children were still playing. "Pray and worry every night, wondering where you are? Come home to this house alone?" she waved a hand toward the dining and living rooms. "Run the farm on the side? Teach Ham and Ginny to suffer in silence? While you fulfill some dream? Tommy! Oh, Tom!" she rose and placed her arms about my neck. "If that's what you want, I understand. But please don't go! Don't do it, Tommy! We need you here."

"I know!" I held her against my chest, as my tears intermingled with hers.

A year passed, then I drove to Bristol, took a physical, and a month later began basic training at Ft. Benning. I was selected for OCS and remained at Benning for the duration of the course. All the family attended the commissioning. Two months afterwards, I was flying into Tan Son Knut.

It was spring, 1968. The Tet Offensive had begun earlier and was still rattling everyone's nerves. The battle for Khe Sanh raged to the north. I was assigned to a mechanized infantry company, the Delta Company, part of a large battalion, of the 8th Brigade of a newly reorganized division that had not seen action since the Civil War.

We consisted of three platoons of infantry soldiers, plus one mortar platoon. Our 81 millimeters came mounted on tracks, or armored personnel carriers. We left them behind when fighting in jungle or sloshing through rice paddies and across dikes.

Our commanding officer was a Captain Luther Taylor, of St. Matthews, South Carolina. He spoke with intensity and enthusiasm. His lowcountry drawl mesmerized all of us. He came across as gung-ho, dedicated, focused, but humorous when humor was required.

"Well, Lieutenant Edmon's," he drawled, "just call me Lootha if you wish, but aroun' the men, Capt'un will do."

In fact, the entire Company called him "Capt'un Lootha." He loved it. His hallmark lay in treating everyone with equal respect. This was his second tour of duty, and his goal was to succeed in every mission, while sustaining as few casualties as possible. "Edmon's, do as I say, an' you and your men will survive. But the mission comes first."

"I understand."

"I doubt that you do, but you will once you come un-duh fire. I never order the men in until I'm sure of everything. Specialize in being invisible."

I commanded his 1st Platoon. He kept me in reserve for the first two engagements. They consisted of night ambushes. I was to his rear in both instances. But during the second deployment, the enemy approached behind his lines and ran smack dab into me. He had prepared me for what to do. We had set out grenade traps, with flares to go off. I had not yet learned to relax or make myself immune to the swarms of mosquitoes that buzzed around my neck and ears. Nor was I acclimated to the humid, stifling nights, punctuated by sudden brief downpours that drenched my shirt and flack jacket—though I was buried to my neck under an oily poncho. It had grown black as the devil's ass, if the devil has an ass. The night air grew still, the jungle uneasily quiet. My platoon sergeant, Sergeant Ellis, hunkered in the silence beside me, nudged my elbow and pointed toward the sound of water running off a palm frond. Something or someone had to have touched it. Just then, the night burst into a pinkish-red glow. The flash and pop of grenades exposed a squad of VC on the edge of our perimeter. Figures darted in and out of the flare's light. Small arms and automatic weapons fire flashed across the glowing space. Red tracers lit up the jungle. Suddenly, all became quiet. A dying VC's gurgling cough bubbled up from the smoke in the acrid darkness. I could smell feces, human guts, and blood. I lay there another minute or so before moving. My radio operator crawled to me. "It's the Captain," he whispered. "Dawn's comin' soon." He handed me the phone. "Red-Tail, you read me?" Taylor asked. "Yes, sir," I answered. "What's happened?" "Dead VC here!" I reported. "Afraid to stir yet." "Well, move on!" he ordered. "Fall back my way. If they've got mortars, they know where you are. Quick! I've got a man posted to guide you in. He'll click twice." "Yes, sir." As dawn came, we returned to the ambush sight. We had killed three VC. Blood trails disappeared into the dense growth around it. We followed them. We found two more bodies and a wounded boy. "Must have been their guide," the Captain groaned. "Shit! Dammit and shit!"

I soon lost count of other recons, night ambushes, and road clearing details. The saddest and most frightening assignments consisted in sweeps into villages suspected of harboring VC. It was dirty, dangerous, sleepless, and exhausting work. We were often out up to two weeks, once even three. Hungry and filthy, we approached villages with pulse-pounding apprehension. After encircling a village, we'd post squads at its entrance and exit to seal off any runners who might slip away to warn comrades or VC. We hated to shoot civilians, but if they saw us coming across their dikes and one of them ran to warn others, we shot them. We didn't have a choice.

The odor! I vomited the first time we entered such a village. A pervasive, musky body odor, accompanied by the smell of pig dung, water buffalo stench, and village garbage swept over me. "Capt'un Lootha" smiled, offered me his sweaty bandana, and poured a canteen of his chlorinated water over my head and neck. "Some things a man nev-uh gets used to," he drawled. "Pukin' is good for the soul, Lieutenant!"

I wiped my mouth and tired to avoid my platoon's smiles.

"Lieutenant, I still puke myself, sometimes," Sergeant Ellis comforted me. "I have scars on my throat from pukin'," he laughed.

Our easier assignments—though no less dangerous—consisted in road clearing operations, preparing helicopter landing sites, and providing perimeter security around firebases. Captain Taylor loved to call in artillery to clear landing sites. We'd crouch far back from the co-ordinates and listen as the howitzer shells came humming in.

In August we received orders to search and destroy a large encampment, thought to consist of an NVA regiment. It lay deep in jungle and mountainous terrain, but within range of nearby firebase units. The Captain assembled our platoon leaders and unfolded his map.

"Here!" he pointed to the site. "Recon flights affirm it's what we're af-tuh, all right. Should be a big one!" he grimaced. "Can't take our tracks in. Don't really relish this one. We'll land here and come up this river," he ran his finger along the map, "then slip around the village. Edmon's, your platoon will circle in from here," he thumped the coated chart.

"Yes, sir!"

Skimming over the treetops in our choppers, and zipping across rice paddies along the way, filled my stomach with a queasy, sickening turbulence. Julie's letters, along with Mom's, had been my primary source of comfort to date. I untucked one from my shirt pocket and reread Julie's latest admonitions.

> *Are you eating properly? Are you bathing enough? The children cry for you every night. I worry all the time. Albert died. So has Miles. Charles is our mainstay now. Your Uncle Everett has leased his house and farm to a doctor in Richmond. He has finally declined to seek another term in office. Thank God! He barley escaped death last week in a shoot-out near Damascus. He was shot in his wrist, but the bullet didn't sever any bones. He should recover.*
>
> *Please, darling, be careful! I age just passing the mirror. Little Ham spends half his days looking up at that portrait of the Captain in the hallway. Thank heavens he'll be in kindergarten this fall.*
>
> *Oh, do be careful! I pray for you every night. "Bring him home, safely, God," I pray. I am crying now. I love you with all my heart, with all my soul, with every stalk of hay in the horse barn. Yes, even old Mac and Nimble neigh for you. Come home! Come to us, darling! I will never forgive you if you get hurt, or killed. At least your great-grandfather came back alive.*
>
> *The children send their love.*
> *I cover this letter with kisses.*
> *Your Julie.*

"We're almost over the landing zone," the Captain's voice mumbled over the radio.

I could see the flares directing us in. They had been ignited by a Special Forces recon group. Down dropped the choppers. Out we piled, squad by squad. "Thomp, thomp, thump!" whirled the big blades. Their skids never touched the ground. Up and off the Hueys climbed, one after the other. The sound of their blades churned the acids in my stomach as they whined away.

We spread out in columns along the river's bank and moved toward our objective. Two hours later we came out above the village. We checked coordinates once again. The Captain gathered our staff and reiterated our positions. He assigned units to cover each end of the village's trails. We slipped quietly to an overlook to peer down at the village. It was huge! Far larger than we had anticipated.

"Damn!" drawled Lootha. "Are we at the right place?"

"Yes, sir," our artillery officer confirmed. He had been flown in earlier with his forward observers. "That's it!"

"Must be fifty, sixty huts or more! Look at those stockpiles of ammunition!"

"It's a big one all right!" the artillery captain emphasized.

"OK! Get in position," Luther directed. He looked at his watch. "In forty minutes, I'm going to call in the big stuff. No point in risking casualties. I'll radio each of you when it's time to move in."

It took my platoon thirty-five minutes to slip into place. Thick jungle foliage and vines concealed us above a series of dry, rancid, terraced paddies. I could see directly into the encampment, its thatched central hut, and other bamboo houses. Armed guards stood outside the large hut. A squad of local VC guerrillas appeared to be refilling sacks with grain or ammunition. Where were their surveillance people? Had we truly caught them this off guard? I checked my watch. Time for the bombardment! I signaled to my squad leaders to keep every man down. "No one! I mean no one!" the Captain had ordered, "mus' stand or move! No one, I repeat!"

Within seconds, the zing and whine of artillery shells came arcing over and down into the encampment. Thunderous explosions, disguised in carnival colors and hideous sheets of flame, soared skyward. On and on, the rounds fell. The acrid reek of gunpowder, of thatch, singed hair and flesh, rose in thick clouds of smoke, enough to satiate the goriest gods of war.

"I love such pow-uh!" the Captain had once confided. "I can call in all the hounds of hell, if I want. Why jeopardize the men, when smokey can do the work?"

For thirty, or forty minutes—I lost count—the guns poured in their reeling rounds of death. Then the gunships came swooping in, low and fast, the rattle of their strafing filling the jungle with muffled thumps. Pink flare puffs drifted from the edge of the jungle, where the second platoon had taken position. "Cease fire! Cease fire!" came Luther's voice across the radio. "Man down. Man down! End of mission! End of mission!" his voice choked with emotion. He was screaming at the helicopter pilots, but I could hear him over my operator's own receiver, as both of the Captain's radios were on. The big birds banked and rolled away. An eerie silence fell upon the valley below.

"Sir, for you!" my radioman handed me the phone.

"Red-Tail! That you?"

"Roger!"

"I've killed my own men! I've killed my own!" groaned the Captain. "I told them to keep their heads down. When the smoke clears, come in. We'll be at center of the camp."

"Yes, sir!"

We didn't bother with any body count. The scorched huts and ground, animal and human remains, were history. Nothing was left. Nothing to count! I glanced about at the smoldering debris, teeth, jawbones, entrails, and parts of vaporized bodies, along with dented and shattered cooking pots. "Shit!" I muttered. "Precious God, shit!" I thought of home, of Quilly Hall, of Abingdon, the Knobs, my father, and of my great-grandfather. "Shit, Sergeant!" I repeated. "Forgive me, Sarge, but shit!"

"Man, this is a big victory! These fuckers are out to kill us! Buck up, sir! This could have been our ass! You stay here a little longer and you'll appreciate these fuckers dead! They've got guns, man. Guns!"

"You're right! There're no innocents in war. How many of our own are hurt?"

"Don't know yet, but none in our platoon."

Back at base camp, a chaplain, a Major Holmes, came around to console the Captain. It turned out that only one man had died from friendly fire. Two were critically wounded. But that was small comfort to Luther. I was in his bunker complex when the chaplain dropped by.

"May I come in?" he asked. He was tall, composed, dressed in rumbled camouflage; his shiny cross was heavily polished. He removed his cap.

"I'll leave," I said, standing up and saluting the Major.

"No, don't!" Luther objected. "Please stay."

I sat back down.

The major extended his hand, first to Luther, then to me. "I know you must feel bad," he said to Luther. "We put him in the morgue and he'll go home tomorrow."

Luther listened, as he clasped his hands together, his eyes cast down at his feet.

"Captain! The Colonel tells me you're his number one commander. You did what had to be done. Sergeant Knoles tells me the man stood up and ran back when the gunships flew over. He disobeyed orders. Let that comfort you." He paused and pulled a small, black leather New Testament from his right chest pocket. "May I read from the Psalms? Remember, many of them were written by a warrior, himself. He even sent one man knowingly to death."

"Yeah! But that wasn't the same," stated Taylor.

"Who's to say? Death in battle is nonetheless death." The man turned to the back of his New Testament, creased down several pages. "Psalm 116. '*I love the Lord, because he has heard my voice and my supplications. The snares of death encompassed me; I suffered distress and anguish. . . . The Lord protects the simple. When I was brought low, he saved me. Precious in the sight of the Lord is the death of his saints. What shall I return unto the Lord? I will lift up the cup of salvation and call on his name.*' May we pray?"

Neither of us said anything. But we bowed our heads respectfully.

"Eternal Father, our guardian and judge of all, comfort your servant, Captain Taylor, with your right hand of justice and compassion. Lift his heart to your presence and fill him with strength and hope. Restore unto him the joy of thy salvation, and ennoble him with courage and peace. Through the holy wounds of your own dear Son, Amen."

Not all our missions proved fraught with anxiety all the time. Sometimes, when on recon patrols in pacified areas, we'd pause to enjoy an afternoon or evening. The jungle was unique to plants I had never imagined existed. One afternoon, following the usual monsoon down-pour around two o'clock—you could set your watch by them—we passed a huge bright red flowering plant, with petals that measured two-to-three feet across. Its yellow-speckled, red blossoms drooped to the ground. They were "raffleshias," I later learned. A variety of wild vegetation grew everywhere, from giant plants with pitchfork-like roots, to dense man-groves along the rivers, to exotic flowers of lavender and eerie shades of purple and pink. Ghoulish air plants dripped water from limbs overhead; huge, fifteen-foot high buttress roots supported trees; carnivorous flow-ers, with serrated petals that clamped tight on any insect that lighted on them, grew in abundance, as well as tiny flora swollen with fly larvae, lice, worms, and spiders clinging to them. The jungle made the naturalist in me giddy with excitement. Plus, the birds! On peaceful days, when you could listen to the rain forest without fear, they sounded like tinkling glass in the distance, their calls reverberating across the canopy. And the call of the gibbons! Sending their deep spooky hoots right through you! Of course, the Vietnamese ate all of these! Birds! Reptiles! Monkeys! I passed a shop in Danang that specialized in bottled snakes. Scores of milky bottles, filled with coiled, pickled snakes, in translucent yellow light, lined the merchant's shelves. He smiled at me when I grimaced. Great God of Creation!

Sometimes when we returned from a week out on patrol, you could see the troop trucks around the camp, filled with waving girls. The Captain would call in advance to make sure they'd be on hand, especially after arduous and grueling patrols. Nothing rallied the men like these girls.

"Have you ever fucked one?" Sergeant Ellis asked with a sly grin. "Some pussy! Let me tell you!" he smiled.

I wanted to. My groin ached. The girls were voluptuous to behold, with luscious red lips and gentle swells and cinnamon-yellow shiny thighs, visible beneath their split skirts.

"Precious Jesus!" Sergeant Ellis whistled as our chopper chugged to a stop. "You want one, Lieutenant?"

Of course! But I refrained. Not that I was any better or virtuous. "Shit! Shit!" That had become my rote mantra! It covered about everything. "Jesus God, shit!" If I couldn't have said "shit," I think I would have burst. "Fuck!" was its lingual cousin.

The one assignment I feared most involved tunnels. Ellis and a Corporal Tony Cirello, a second-generation Italian, relished the work. "Shit!" Cirello smiled, pointing to an entrance. "Let Zippo soften the hole. Ain't never seen his flamethrower miss a trick. Besides, I ain't 'fraid of VC."

Tunnels weren't necessarily all bad. If we were lucky, we would find maps, or charts with ambush locations, mine placements, and punji pits indicated in pencil point. "Damn! Now that I am scared of," Cirello once winced, as he and Ellis filled in a hole that bristled with seven cruel sharpened sticks.

On one particular afternoon, as we stumbled toward a ridge, a sniper opened up on us with a burst of fire. We dropped to the ground as the jungle grew deathly silent. Ellis, who was crawling in front of me, spotted fresh mud near a swath of dense growth. After poking around with a stick, he found an entrance. Without hesitation, he flopped in a grenade.

"Cover!" he shouted, as we hugged the leaves. Suddenly, another hole opened, and a VC sprayed us with AK 47 fire. Cirello returned fire, slitting the man's throat open—from ear to ear—with a magazine of M-16 bursts. We raced to the hole, firing on it as we ran, and peered in. Two more VC lay under the corpse of the first man.

"Now that's gratitude for you," Ellis stated.

Luther came jogging up. "Spread out! Keep low! No telling how many sons-of-bitches there might be!"

Yes. *Where's the son-of-a-bitch hiding?* I thought of Uncle Everett. I kept my head low and pressed on.

Within twenty minutes, we uncovered three more openings. Zippo came up to soak them with his flamethrower. The hot "swoosh" of his gun licked deep into each hole. After the smoke cleared, Cirello and a Vietnamese interpreter climbed in, each in a different hole. They returned in no time.

"Bodies! Bodies!" Cirello waved with his hands. "Jesus, God! Scores of bodies! It's a morgue." A visible series of tremors seized his back and shoulders. "Jesus! A morgue. I tell you, a morgue!"

Once the monsoon season swept in, we were miserable all the time. Everyday, we donned ponchos from noon-to-three, depending on how long the rains lasted. The swells came in opaque sheets. Sometimes the rain fell straight down, drowning out our voices and drenching our trousers and boots. Danger lurked everywhere, and some of our fiercest firefights occurred in these downpours. One time we suddenly came upon the enemy—a whole platoon of North Vietnamese—in such a storm. They had advanced within twenty yards of us before we realized what was happening. Luckily, Zippo was on my right. He immediately sprayed the closest men with his roiling, liquid plumes of death. "Whooosh!" the orange tongue of his pipe roared, as the enemy's grizzly silhouettes lit up the jungle with terrifying flames. The fire literally enveloped them. The odor of burning flesh engulfed us, amid the choking clouds of sizzling smoke. All Hell broke loose after that, as we raked the blazing scene with M-16 and BAR fire. We came off with two wounded. After the rain subsided, we counted eighteen singed and fried corpses. We searched them for any valuable maps or recon information, but little remained other than pools of blood, smoldering guts, and charged bones. As I stared down at the carnage, someone administered a coup-de-grace to a bleeding soldier. He had attempted to crawl off; his fingers clutched a grenade. His wallet contained a picture of two children and a thatched house beside a shoulder-high, red stucco wall. "Son-of-a-bitch!" Sergeant Ellis muttered, as he nudged his body with the barrel of his M-16.

And so the days and months passed. Captain Taylor grew restless and seemed a bit depressed. It came time for both of us to be rotated, but somehow Headquarters misfiled our papers, and our redeployments were delayed.

"Five more weeks, Edmon's," Luther drawled, "then, this lowcountry bas-tud's headin' home! Good ole St. Matthews! Capital of gar-duns of roses! Big tall rows of 'em every spring! Of every ku-luh! Red, yellow, rose, pink, white! You've got to come and see them, once you get home!"

"Just may," I smiled. "But our Knobs, I wager, are every bit as magnificent as your gardens!"

"'Knobs?' And what are 'Knobs?' Are they anything like these hills and jungles?" he stated with a sweep of his hand. "No thank ya! Had enough mud and mountains for a long time to come! Just want my roses, laid-back lazy afternoons, and Jim Beam at night."

On our last patrol under Luther's command—two weeks before his tour elapsed—our unit received orders to set up ambushes inside the Cambodian border. Of course, we weren't supposed to be there "officially," but there we were! All our maps indicated that our mission ran parallel with a section of the Ho Chi Minh Trail. The CO, a colonel, of the base camp assured us that the landing site had already been prepared and was being guarded by Special Forces. "We're going to strike them where it hurts!" he boasted.

After being airlifted in, we straight-legged it to our positions and set up our light mortars. Night soon descended. We could see the dim lights of trucks snaking their way slowly through the dark jungle, as the Trail wended its way down a pass. What we couldn't see involved the mortars that they had mounted on flatbeds. Only recon flights later confirmed their presence. It was a trap that the enemy had laid for us. As the faint drone of the trucks grew louder, we prepared for action. "Fire!" Luther's command crackled over the operator's phone. Fire we did! Up went the mortars, thumping with muffled explosions into the ridge. The heavy platoon company opened with its .50 calibers and grenade launchers. The night erupted with zipping tracers and deadly flames. Soon in-coming rounds began to burst behind us, then in front of us. They were bracketing us. Mud, leaves, and splitters splattered our backs. "Pull back!" came

Luther's order. "Keep firing but fall back!" He radioed in for air support. Two F-105s found us within minutes and began dropping their tumbling canisters of crackling napalm into the canopy over the Trail. Roaring plumes of brilliant mauve illuminated the solemn night. Convulsions of convoluted clouds rose in the darkness. But the enemy's shells continued to burst around us. With deadly accuracy, the Vietnamese were pummeling us in the darkness. "Out of here! Back to the landing zone!" Luther ordered. Suddenly Sergeant Ellis clutched his left leg, moaned, and fell. I ordered two men to drag him out. When we reached the landing zone, our lungs ached with exhaustion. The Chinooks' blades swirled and spun, ready for takeoff. Only Luther wasn't there. The colonel, who had landed in his own Huey, squatted silhouetted against the screen of eerie flares. "Where's Taylor?" he shouted. "Edmonds, get these men on board. Dammit, where is he?"

"I'll go look for him!" I volunteered.

"Like hell!" the colonel barked. "This mission's aborted!"

"Get these men on board," I called to a corporal. "I'm going out."

"No you aren't!" the colonel snapped. He seized me by my shirt and threw me down. "You're in command! Get your ass up and get these men out of here! That's an order! Now!"

I struggled to my feet. With the help of others, I evacuated Luther's company—platoon by platoon. The colonel ordered a flight of carrier bombers to stave off the enemy. Once they arrived, they dropped their loads about seventy yards or less from us. I watched as the jungle rolled orange with flames. A sickening feeling rose in my throat; my stomach broiled with fire. *Thou preparest a table before me in the presence of mine enemies. My cup runneth over.* Jesus, God! Just then Luther's radio operators appeared on the perimeter. I could see them in the dim light of the flares' sputtering glow. They cradled Luther between them. His helmet had fallen off, and his head sagged on his chest. He lost consciousness as we lifted him into the last big chopper. As we thumped away into the darkness, I could see the tracers coming up at us. I held Luther's hands in my own. "Please don't die! Please! Please!" I whispered. "Medic! Medic!" I shouted. I ripped open Luther's shirt to find his wound. My hands came up bloody with his guts! A huge shard of shrapnel glistened from a hole in his chest. He died, with my hands still clutching a coil of his entrails.

Toward the end of the monsoon season, I was transferred to the huge army air base outside Saigon at Long Binh. On September 3, 1969, I boarded a returning jet to the States and arrived at Ft. Benning on the 6th. Ten hours later, I rented a car and within eight hours more was in Julie's arms.

"Oh, Darling, darling!" she hugged me. "You're really home! You're really here!" She held my face in her hands and kissed my eyes and lips and mouth. "Darling! Darling!" Tears shimmered in her eyelashes and trickled down her face and lips and onto her fingertips. "You're home! You're really home! Don't ever leave me again! Never, ever, again! O Tom! Never again!"

The remainder of my military service was completed as a staff officer with a local reserve unit in Bristol. Three years later, I resigned my commission, hung up my uniform, and placed a photo of myself in jungle fatigues alongside my father's on the mantle. I had fulfilled my duty—to myself and to my country. My heart felt heavy, as the war ground on. But I was at peace, strangely, though perhaps aloof, if not even shy and afraid to relate my experiences. No wonder Great-Grandfather Howard whiled away so many hours, just strolling the Knobs. Now it would be my turn to resume the family mission. But I did so only after taking Julie and the children to South Carolina to visit Luther's grave and the Edisto Gardens. The latter were awash in row after row of roses, of every "ku-luh" imaginable, as Luther had put it.

CHAPTER TWENTY-EIGHT

I HAVE COME INTO the Knobs today, as I so often do, to try to make
sense of life. Retirement has been kind to me. Julie and I live alone;
our children are grown. Ham has his law practice in Roanoke, and Ginny
is married with three boys and lives with her husband, a physician, in
Atlanta. Sometimes when we visit her, I drive in by way of Chattanooga
and the Chickamauga battlefield. I always stop and follow the markers up
Snodgrass Hill. Julie waits patiently for me in the car.

When my mother died in 1989, Uncle Everett came to live with us.
He was sixty-eight, in frail health, and dying of emphysema. His knees
weren't strong enough for him to do more than sit on the porch and rock,
or take to the swing, if he felt up to it. His own farm was still under lease,
this time to a consortium of hunters, who raised quail and a few sheep.
They allowed me to hunt with them, but I had to pay to rent a dog.

In her will, Mom deeded the house in town to Uncle Everett, who in
turn was to deed it to me. Its old barn had collapsed and garden area had
returned to weeds. The bramble along the railroad had grown into the
cedars, many of which had died and loomed reddish-brown against the
gravel of the tracks.

Uncle Everett slept in Pearl's old room, although he favored the library and on cold days would wrap himself in a quilt and doze off with a
book in his lap. His sheriff's revolver and badge hung from a peg beside
the only window that looked out toward the Knobs. His breathing came
with painful difficulty. A large green oxygen tank, with stainless steel
knobs and plastic tubes, occupied a narrow space just behind his chair. I
had to keep moving it back, away from the stove, for fear the tank would
explode and sear him to death with its flames.

Sadly, death was in the air. It was on the wing. Julie, he, and I—all
three of us—knew it was a matter of time. We had moved my old bed
from upstairs down to the library.

"Uncle Everett, what do you miss doing most?" I asked him late one autumn evening. "Maybe I could arrange something for you, for us. Some place you'd like to visit, or go, or do?"

His lungs struggled for air. His breathing came with loud inhalations and weak exhaled sounds. He looked up at me from his chair. "Nothing!" he gasped in a reedy whisper. "It was a good life. Once is enough."

"I still remember our forays into the Knobs, the strawberry patches on your farm, the experiences we had when you were sheriff."

"Yes. Those were somethin'!" his eyes gleamed, as he fought for breath. "How your mother scolded my ass! You never knew the whole of it."

"I guess not!"

"I was lucky, Mr. Biggety! We were both lucky. That's all."

"Do you think I'll ever find Great-Grandfather Howard's stone? Or is it just a myth?"

"Can't say! Don't know what I believe anymore." He tugged at the quilt and looked up into my eyes. "Best go to bed," he held out a hand for me to assist him.

"Yes, sir! I guess I feel the same way."

By winter, his health had deteriorated; his breathing rasped with labored gasps.

"Tommy, he's not going to make it much longer. What do you think? What should we do?" Julie asked.

We were seated in the living room, in front of Grandmother's old fireplace and the mantle with my father's photo on it and mine beside his.

"I can't commit him to a home somewhere. We're all he's got! You and me and Quilly Hall, we're it! He's got no place else to go."

"But he'll die here, gasping for breath. Shouldn't we at least have him hospitalized? At least for a week or so?"

"I don't know. I want him here. I want to be with him when he dies. He and Marion are the only fathers I had. I can't abandon him now. I never felt so proud in all my life as when he'd tousle my hair when I was a boy. The sun rose and set on him, even during the time when Marion was my step-dad. He and Mom always had chemistry. You could see it in their eyes; hear it in their voices. She should have married him long ago. He once said that my father got to her first. He was gentler and not so impulsive. But I think Mom really loved him the most. I can't turn him over to someone else. Never. Maybe I need him more than he needs me. Am I right or wrong?"

"Probably a little of both. But, that settles it. He stays."

Toward late January, he asked me to find his cherry box—the one I had wanted to peek into that night at his house.

"Where is it? Where did you put it?"

"Upstairs bedroom. You'll find it under the bed."

"Yes, sir!"

"There are memories in it I want to relive, to sort through." He waved me away with a feeble hand.

I found his box and brought it down.

"Thanks!" he coughed, clutching it against his chest. "Now leave me alone. Go away!" he said, with a faint growl and dim sparkle in his eyes.

I left the room, but not first without glancing back over my shoulder. Night had fallen outside. The shades were drawn. The iron stove's red glow played softly against his white hair and weathered cheeks. He had never lost his ruddy complexion, though his hands trembled as he unlatched the box.

"Get on!" he called hoarsely. "Just go on."

I closed the door and stared at Quilly. I started to sit on the couch beside her, but even she seemed aloof and withdrawn. The old Captain stared straight ahead. If he had anything to say, he wasn't about to divulge it.

Toward morning, Julie and I heard a heavy sound, loud enough to wake us up.

"Tommy! Get up! It's your Uncle Everett. It's come from his room."

"I know. It sounds like his canister fell over."

I hurried to the library, drew open the door, and turned on the light switch. Uncle Everett lay face down, "face fo-mus," as Earl used to say. His quilt had caught in the rung of his chair. He had struck his head against the stove. I could see the bruise, the deep cut over his right temple. His mouth gaped open, revealing his teeth, which were stained with a smear of blood. He appeared lifeless. Mementoes from his box lay scattered on the floor. Two, small, letter-sized envelopes caught my eye.

Just then Julie came into the room.

"He's dead, isn't he?"

"Yes. He's gone to be with Mom and Grandmother. With Rachel and all the Edmonds and Lorrans!"

"Don't talk like that! He was your uncle! Special." She shook her head and bent down to cover his body with the quilt. "He seems so small now. Look at this! His treasures! So few! I wonder what he really thought about? Look, a knife, rabbit's foot, a chain, and this ring! It's a diamond. Look! And these pitiful letters! Only two." Tears welled up and burned red in her eyes. "He was such a man! No one would have dared cross him. Not as long as he was sheriff. Dead! It isn't fair to end this way!"

Fair? I thought of all the great adventures he and I had shared. Of the horseback rides, the fairground races, hog killing time, shooting dogs when they ran the sheep, his swagger, smile, and hands. Fair? "I don't know," I mumbled. I looked down at his quilt-covered body. "I loved him, Julie. Like a father! Like a big brother!"

I stooped over and picked up the envelopes. Each contained a letter. Neither appeared especially long. I unfolded the first and noted the date: February 8, 1937.

"What does it say?" asked Julie. "Can you tell who it's from?"

"My mother! It's only three sentences long."

Julie leaned against me and looked around my shoulder. "Your mother!" She saw the date. "When were you born?"

"That autumn! In 1937. Why?"

"Read the sentences."

I had.

Everett, for God's sake! I'm pregnant. What are we to do?

"That's all it says!" moaned Julie. "Was he your father? Is that what it means? That he's your real father?" Her lips had parted, and I could see her pink tongue, white teeth, and big eyes. "Tommy! He's your father! Your real father! That's what it means."

I opened the second envelope and slipped out its letter, or rather, its note. It contained no date.

I'm going to marry Hamilton. I don't know what else to do. We've been engaged too long. God, how I love you! Your Shaula!

"What the hell!" I wondered aloud. "What did my mother mean?" I held the letter up, as if I expected some genie to appear and solve the riddle. I stared at Julie, not knowing what to believe.

Julie put her arms around me and kissed my face and cheeks. Tears had begun to trickle down my nose, my lips, and chin. "Tommy! Uncle Everett's your father. And the man on the mantle, is your uncle!" She wiped the tears off my face with her thumbs. She stooped down and retrieved the ring. "Whose was this? It must be a full carat!" She turned it gently with her fingers; its facets sparkled in the morning light.

"Probably Aunt Rachel's. He loved her, too. They were more alike than he and Mom. She's buried in Wytheville."

Two days later, we laid him to rest in the cemetery in town, beside Mom, my grandmother, and all the other Edmonds. A cold wind blew with numbing gusts through the graveyard and flapped the green awning that protected us. Its frayed edges slapped hard against the canopy's metal poles. White flecks of fine snow flurried about us; we snuggled together to keep warm. After the service, Julie and I remained by the grave, until the last shovel of sod thumped into the hole. Our son and daughter and grandchildren sought refuge in their cars.

I stood there, holding onto Julie's hand, not certain what to think or believe. He was my uncle, I kept thinking. Yet my heart knew better. "He was your father," it whispered. "Here lies your father." I turned and kissed Julie and walked back with her slowly to our car.

CHAPTER TWENTY-NINE

ON THE NIGHT OF the 18th of February 2002, a cigarette, flung from a speeding car, fueled a fire opposite the house that raged, within minutes, out of control. Somehow, it spared the orchard, the barn, and Albert and Jessie's old place, but bramble crackled in its path as it raced its way up the hillsides. Wind drove it steadily passed the orchard and into the woods. Its crackling sheets of yellowish red licked the rocks below the lookout, circled the ledge, and raced on into the Knobs. It occurred at dusk and lit up the skyline for miles. A parallel ridge roared next with fire—an apocalypse of epic dimension.

I called the Forest Service's hotline and left a message, then hurried toward the barn. A new horse, Apples, had replaced old Mac. I quickly saddled her, along with a second horse, and with its reins in hand, galloped off toward Henry's. He and Pearl were standing on their porch's stoop, watching the blaze.

"One hell-of-a far! Ain't it? How fur back you think it'll burn?"

"Don't know, but Joe Paul, Charles's grandson, is stayin' in Uncle Jim's cabin. Can you ride back with me?"

"I ain't so young, Mr. Edmonds."

"Mr. Tom! Henry's right close at seventy-four! You're worse than Mr. Everett!" Pearl protested. "An' you ain't so young yer-self."

"Sorry, Pearl! But I need his company. We don't have much time."

"Well, if Charles's boy's got a lick of sense, he'll save hisself in the river," Pearl theorized.

"Let me fetch my coat, Mr. Tom. I'll be right with you."

Soon, Henry and I were bouncing along on Apples and Sugar, as they trotted up the lane toward Uncle Jim's. The fire had yet to cross the road, but hot embers glowed in the night overhead. They fell in hissing flakes into the damp woods and sodden leaves. The horses neighed and galloped faster, all on their own free will. A Forest Service chopper lumbered loudly somewhere above us. We could hear it but couldn't see it in the glowing clouds. Its presence meant they'd soon have their men on the ground. The fire continued to burn parallel with us, but mainly to the east and along the high crests. Once we topped the last ridge, we could hear the river and see Uncle Jim's house. We galloped past the graveyard and reined in beside the cabin. Joe Paul had come out onto the porch. He carried a kerosene lamp and held it up in our faces when we approached.

"Come with us!" I called. "You can ride behind me or Henry."

"No need to!" he spat a stream of tobacco juice on the ground. "I was just before saddlin' my own mare to high tail it out of here!"

"Well, come on! The fire's not reached the lane yet. Once it hits the river, who knows which way it will turn."

We waited while Joe Paul led his own horse out of the barn. He mounted it without a saddle. His only clothes consisted of long underwear and overalls. His brogans flopped loosely on his sockless feet.

"I'm followin' you!" he called. "First let me run in for my gun, and Daddy's pocket watch."

"Ain't no time for sentimentals," Henry warned. "Come on!"

The youth dismounted and disappeared into the house. He reappeared, cradling his father's long-barreled, 12-gauge shotgun. A shiny railroad watch's chain gleamed from his bib-overalls pouch.

I glanced at Great-Grandfather Howard's grave marker as we rode passed. Would it survive? Or crack and crumble? Hot flames had crept closer to the road and were beginning to burn into the dry grass. Soon, they would cross the lane and enkindle the dead honeysuckle vines and briars along the embankment. The horses balked and reared, but Apples kept prancing forward, as I nudged her flanks with my heels. Along the ridgeline, sheets of fire leapt into the night. They wobbled red and orange as trees ignited in their path. Hemlock and pine exploded, one after the other, as the heat raced toward them and consumed them in its appalling wall of blaze. As hot ashes and embers fell about us, we galloped down the road until at last we came into the lane beside the meadows. The redolence of turpentine and scorched bark surrounded us. We rode through it as if in a fog. Stifling smoke obscured everything; still, we could see car lights and men in yellow fire gear preparing to enter the woods. We dropped Henry off at his cabin. Pearl had come out to watch him dismount. He handed me his horse's reins "Don't you get no foolish notions," Pearl admonished me. "You hear, Mr. Tom?"

"Yes, Pearl. Thanks for loaning me your good man." We waved good-bye and rode on.

"Joe Paul, what's your wish? You're welcome to stay with Julie and me."

"Much obliged, Mr. Tom, but I'd rather wait here, in the meadow, and ride back at dawn."

"At least stay on our porch. We'll have hot breakfast and coffee for you. This fire's likely to burn all night."

"I reckon that's so. But if'n you don't mind, I'll stay at the barn."

"Good enough!"

For the next five hours, Julie and I watched the horrific fire from our porch. Toward 1:00 a.m., we collapsed into bed, but neither of us could sleep. I dozed off toward daybreak. When I awoke, Joe Paul was gone. He had already headed back into the Knobs. As I walked out on the front porch, fire crews were beginning to return. Heavy clouds of black smoke hovered over the scorched ground and blackened hills above the orchard.

Julie, with Pearl's help, had set up a coffee stand in the road. They were serving coffee and ham biscuits to the firefighters. Ashes and gray soot covered the men's coats, caps, and gear.

"Well, we done it!" one of the men said, as I walked out to learn the report. "All stared from some son-of-bitch's cigarette. Right out there," he pointed near the orchard. "You're a lucky man, Mr. Tom. Your old cabin back there was spared. And so was the barn and sheds."

"What about the graveyard? Was it damaged?"

"No, sir! Not that I recollect! The fire stopped just shy of the river and sputtered out as it turned back. It uncovered some graves, though, by the river. Burnt off a pile of undergrowth, exposing two skulls and some bones in a pit, along with some rusted wire. It was weird. Wasn't nothin' else left. Whatta ya know? Relations of yours?"

"Can't say. I'm surprised."

"Well, no need to fret, sir! Me and Rodney here," he gestured toward another man, "covered 'em up again. But you ought to mark it sometime. We left big poles in the ground, in case you do."

"Thank you! You can't know how appreciative I am. I've always thought there might be graves there. Such a peaceful spot!"

"It was our privilege!"

Precious God! Precious Earl! I rubbed my face with my hands.

As February gave way to March, and soaking rains bathed the area, I rode back through the Knobs to inspect the damage. All the good lumber, north of the lane, had been consumed. Only charged skeletal trunks of blackened trees stood silhouetted against the muddy slopes. Gone were the lofty poplars, the towering pines and graceful hemlocks. I roved over the ridges and crests and down into the naked coves. Even the green rhododendron and laurel bushes had been scorched. I turned Apples about and guided her toward the lane.

I rode down to Uncle Jim's old house. Joe Paul was sweeping off the porch.

"Warn't so bad, I reckon," he greeted me. "Might just make the best tobacco and corn crop we've ever had! This soil loves potash! Cinders make fine humus! But your poor woods ain't so pretty no more, are they?"

"You're a man after my own heart," I said. I turned in the saddle and glanced toward the hills behind the barn and cemetery. "At least, I've got those."

"Yes, sir! It's a plumb Garden of Eden, ain't it? Just ain't much of it left, no more."

"Take care!" I replied.

I guided Apples passed the barn and back up the lane toward the graveyard. As I sat in the saddle, I swept my eyes across the markers, bringing them to rest on Great-Grandfather Howard's grave. "Old friend, how I wish I had known you. I feel I do. If you're listening, help me find your stone! Your rock! I know you can't do that! It's just a thought. But, how I wish you could!"

With the coming of April, I returned to the Knobs. Spring was on the move. Wherever the sunlight poured though, jack in the pulpits, mayapples, and varieties of white and variegated trillium filled the burnt-over clearings and crowded the forest paths. The blackened ridges had burst into new life. Ferns had returned, as well as vines and tufts of grass. Pine seeds beneath the litter had germinated, and green slender seedlings had poked through the ash layers into full view. Juncos had returned, along with towhees, buntings, and wood thrushes. I could hear their melodic calls and songs in the grass. The woods were renewing themselves. Mother Nature had not forgotten her own.

I led Apples up a steep slope, near the campsite where Uncle Everett and I had spent the night where the cat had attacked us. All was new and vibrant. It was all so green against the black trunks and stark limbs of the dead trees. I guided Apples over the ridge and down a rocky ravine, then up another. If I had ever come this way before, I couldn't recall it. A strange feeling came over me. I felt Uncle Everett's presence—my father's presence—as Apples plodded along. We ascended another ridge, veiled in thin fog (caused from the warmth of the ground and the cool air on the ridge). I wished Marion or Earl could have been with me.

I stopped and glanced about. A precipice loomed ahead. Fire had ravaged the laurel and rhododendron bushes along its lip, making the ground and gravelly soil unsteady. Apples turned to her left as we set about to explore the ridge. As we rode into the mist, I could have sworn I saw a movement, a figure slip across the path and disappear into the shadows. It appeared to have been a man, with an old rifle slung across his shoulder. I rubbed my eyes. Probably a pileated woodpecker, or large owl swooping from limb to limb! I halted Apples, dismounted, and walked forward, cautiously, toward a glimmering patch of light. Like a glowing apparition, sparkles of sunlight danced between two stumps just in front of me. Silence pervaded the woods. A profound peacefulness came over me. A column of yellow butterflies rose and dissolved in the light. As I stepped closer toward the stumps, I stumbled over a hard object. I fell flat on my face, forehead, and hands, and bruised my right knee as I collapsed. A hot pain shot all the way down my leg and into my arch. My head ached as well. As I struggled to rise, I realized I had fallen over a huge stone, a large oblong rock, half-buried in soggy ashes and young ferns. I pushed myself up and stared down at the rock's rough surface. The fire had burnt its lichens to a crisp and had deposited a fine layer of white ash on its face. My heart thumped with a sudden beat. I was staring at words, a line of grooves, chiseled smartly and smoothly into the stone. I wiped off the ash. My temples pulsed with excitement. My God! There it was: "Roll me over and you'll find a treasure." The rock's grain sparkled with granite. I ran my hand across the words and my fingers into their grooves. I jumped up and searched for a stick, a large limb, or anything to pry up the stone. Everything lay charred. I returned to the rock and began pulling on it with my hands. Nothing happened. I couldn't budge it an inch. I reached out for Apples' bridle and plundered through the saddlebags for a rope, a cord, for anything that might work. Nothing resourceful appeared in either bag. I would have to find Joe Paul to help me. I stared up at the sky. Darkness would soon set in. Better hurry, I thought.

Joe Paul was in his barn, repairing tobacco baskets. "What's up?" he drawled. "You look like you've seen a ghost! You all right, Mr. Tom? You ain't sick, are ya?"

"No! I've found my great-grandfather's rock! The one he wrote on years ago. Can you help me roll it over? It's supposed to have a treasure under it."

"Mr. Tom! Even I've heard of that old yarn. It's just a story. You sure you're all right? Ain't that a bump on your head? It's bleedin'!"

"Yes, I'm fine! Get mounted and help me. It's getting dark and I don't want to lose it again."

"Yes, sir!"

By the time we returned, dusk had drawn its veiled mantle across the foggy ridge. We passed the campsite and followed the path that Apples and I had made into the ferns.

"It was right here!" I pointed to the ground. "Right around in here. Between two stumps!"

"Yes, sir! I'm lookin'," said Joe Paul.

I stopped and dismounted. "It was right here! I swear it was. It was big and long," I gestured, holding my hands about seven feet apart. "Huge, heavy! So help me God! I'm not making this up."

"I believe you, sir!" He studied my face with a twinge of uncertainty in his eyes. "Sometimes the fog plays tricks on a man, sir! I onced shot at a deer up here. I could o' swore it was a deer. I seen it drop right to the ground. Warn't nothin' but a hemlock bough. I cut it clean off! In one shot!"

"This was a rock, I tell you. I know a rock when I see one!"

"Yes, sir! But it's too dark to find anything here! Maybe in tomorrow's light, it'll be clearer. I'll be at the barn. I'll come back with you, if you want me to."

I stood there in the silence, in the cold chilling dampness. I knew it was there! It had to be! Right there! Or was it along the ridge, farther? Or over there? I felt confused, disoriented, embarrassed. I know it saw it. I know I ran my fingers across it and read the words: "Roll me over and you'll find a treasure." Precious God! Was I loosing my mind?

"You'll find it, Mr. Tom. Ain't no need to get upset. It cain't of just jumped up and run off on its own. It'll be here tomorrow. I'll come back and help you." He stared at me with bewilderment. "Mr. Edmonds, I believe it's time to go home. To start back. This fog's gettin' thick. Ain't no place to be in the dark."

I stared at the young man. He seemed so puzzled, so genuinely compliant and worried. "You're right," I sighed. "I'd best get home. Maybe tomorrow I'll locate it again." I tried to smile. I shook his hand. "I'll let you know when I find it. I'll mark the spot for sure. Thank you for helping."

"My pleasure, Mr. Tom! Give Miss Julie my regards."

I remounted Apples and rode behind Joe Paul to the top of the ridge and across others and down the slopes back to the lane. The moon had created a bright halo in the thin clouds that scudded silently overhead. I paused to marvel at the luminous wonder and listen to the night sounds.

"Good night! Mr. Tom," Joe Paul waved from his saddle, as he headed home in the translucent glow.

I watched him ride up the lane, until the mist swallowed him.

"Good night, to you, too, Mr. Joe!" I whispered as I turned Apples homeward and let the reins bounce loosely on her mane. From somewhere in the night, a whippoorwill began its call. On and on, it repeated itself, with a haunting perseveration of the wild! An owl responded. And from deep in the Knobs, I thought I heard the earth cough. As I passed Jessie and Albert's old place, the mist began to clear. The moon's glow filled their yard with magical sparkles of glittering dew. Dim stars twinkled faintly overhead. I looked out toward Quilly Hall. A shooting star plummeted in a brilliant flash of dazzling white, then sputtered and died in the moon's sheen. Over my shoulder I could see the dark silhouette of the ridge above the orchard. I turned in the saddle and gazed back at the Knobs. "*Sic jurat transcendere montes*," I could imagine Grandmother reciting. Yes! I would forever be crossing them, for the rest of my life. I guided Apples toward the barn, slipped off her saddle, watered her and brushed her down. I fed her several ears of corn, patted her rump, and closed the barn door.

For a long while I stood in the moonlight. I glanced up past the orchard, then walked slowly toward the house.

I know that was his rock. I know it was. O God above, I know it was!

The End